TESS WOODS

Beautiful
Messy
Love

HarperCollins*Publishers*

HarperCollins*Publishers*

First published in Australia in 2017
This edition published in 2018
by HarperCollins*Publishers* Australia Pty Limited
ABN 36 009 913 517
harpercollins.com.au

Copyright © Tess Woods 2017

The right of Tess Woods to be identified as the author of this work has been
asserted by her in accordance with the *Copyright Amendment (Moral Rights) Act
2000.*

HarperCollins*Publishers*
Level 13, 201 Elizabeth Street, Sydney NSW 2000 Australia
Unit D1, 63 Apollo Drive Rosedale, Auckland 0632
A 53, Sector 57, Noida, UP, India
1 London Bridge Road, London SE1 9GF United Kingdom
2 Bloor Street East, 20th floor, Toronto, Ontario M4W 1A8, Canada
195 Broadway, New York NY 10007, USA

A catalogue record of this book is available from the National Library of Australia

ISBN: 978 1 4607 5646 1 (paperback)

Cover design by Hazel Lam, HarperCollins Design Studio
Cover image by Irene Lamprakou / Trevillion Images
Author photograph by Heidi Lauri
Typeset in Bembo Std by Kirby Jones.
Printed and bound by CPI Group (UK) Ltd, Croydon, CR0 4YY

For Daniella Hassett – the brains behind the operation.

And always for Paul, Tommy and Lara –
ento kolokom hayati, *you are my life.*

A beautiful thing is never perfect
– Egyptian proverb

PART ONE

THE FIRST WEEK
OF MARCH

LILY – SATURDAY

It's funny what you remember about the biggest moments in your life. Lamb Korma. When Ben made the announcement that ended our relationship, I swallowed an unchewed mouthful of fatty Lamb Korma that lodged itself in my chest. I couldn't figure out if the pain was from the Korma or if it was because Ben had just told me that he was moving to rural Kenya to build mud-brick schools for the next two years.

And whenever I thought about Ben after that, the first thing that came to mind was fatty brown Lamb Korma.

I'd gone out for dinner that evening confident that Ben was about to ask me if I wanted to move in with him. For the last year I'd dropped hint after hint, which he never seemed to take. But his text message, two nights before, made me hopeful that the time had come.

Lil, I booked us a table for Friday at Madras Palace at 8. I've got something important to ask you! My shout ☺

He'd never, ever booked a restaurant before. We were both at uni, me studying medicine, while he was an architecture student. There wasn't any money for restaurants – Nando's in front of *Game of Thrones* was a treat for us. And then, when he came to pick me up, he produced flowers that had been hiding in the back seat. Red roses no less!

I'd been with Ben for almost four years. We were as serious as you could be without living together, so of course I assumed that moving in together was where we were headed.

'This is it, Lil!' He had an unhinged look about him. 'This is the direction I needed. You know how unsettled I've been this past year? Well, I've got a real purpose now!'

As it turned out, moving in with me was the last thing on his mind. Instead, thanks to his mum dragging him to church the previous Sunday, where he was roused by the inspiring homily of a visiting pastor, my boyfriend was now a missionary-cum-mud-brick-school-builder who had booked a one-way ticket to Nairobi, deferred uni, given notice to his landlord and signed up for a six-week intensive language course in Swahili, all in the four days before he bothered telling me about any of it.

And what did I do as I listened to him plot a new life that didn't include me? I just sat there, a fixed smile on my face like the village idiot, as he flapped a brochure in front of me.

When he stopped to take a breath, I ventured thinly, 'Um, Ben, what about us?'

He reached across the table and touched my cheek with sweaty fingers. 'Lil, I love you, but this, this is something I can't pass up. It feels like I've waited my whole life for an experience like this …'

While he continued to babble words that were lost in the fog inside my head, I went over what I thought he'd just said to make sure I'd got it right. Was he actually *breaking up with me*? He wasn't asking me to join him on this mercy mission and he wasn't reassuring me that two years would fly past before we knew it and then he'd be home again.

I looked Ben in the eyes. His eager nod and hopeful smile confirmed that I was right. It was only nineteen hours ago that he'd been feverishly shouting my name before he orgasmed and now he was dumping me?

My idiotic smile vanished and I gasped, accidentally swallowing the lump of curried meat, which I swore settled next to my heart and burned hotly for the months to come.

I picked up a pappadum and threw it at his face. It didn't quite have the impact I was after – floating lazily over the table, only just touching his nose and landing softly onto his plate – but nonetheless it made my feelings clear.

He had the gall to look shocked.

'I'm leaving.' I blinked hard.

'Oh, Lil, don't be like that. This will be great, I know it will – for both of us. It'll give us a chance to grow, you know, as individuals.'

'Grow? As *individuals*? Grow apart, you mean?' I stood up with my shoulders back, in an attempt to salvage any dignity I had left after throwing a pappadum. 'If this is what you want, fine. But don't expect me to be happy that you've ended our relationship on a whim.' I threw my bag over my shoulder and headed for the door.

'Hey, wait, Lil! I'll drive you.'

'I'll find my own way home,' I snapped, not turning to look at him.

'But, Lil, I didn't even get a chance to ask you the question yet!' he called out over the tinkling Indian music. 'Lil? Can Wally please come live at yours while I'm away?'

That was the important question I'd been anticipating? Whether I'd take in his *cat*? The same cat that hissed and spat whenever I went over there?

I spun on my heel to face him, noticing that our break-up was unfolding in front of the Madras Palace dining public. I spoke nice and loudly to make sure the spectators could hear me. 'You and your ugly hairless cat can go fuck yourselves, Ben.' I pushed against the restaurant door and ran out onto the footpath, tears dripping down the front of my Korma-stained dress.

'Excuse me, miss?' A waiter called out across the car park. 'You forgot your roses!' He jogged towards me.

'Oh, thank you. That was kind of you.' I gave him a grateful smile and then rammed the cursed roses into the first street bin I passed.

I didn't have money for a bus because Ben had said it was his shout, so I started the walk home, two suburbs away, along brightly lit streets, with the humid air sticking to my bare legs.

After a block, I took off the single set of heels I owned and carried them in one hand, while I wiped a steady stream of snot and tears with the other.

I went over all the clues I'd missed. Like how Ben hadn't actually joined in last night when I'd talked about our future children and who they might look like. And how he hadn't come over on Tuesday and Wednesday nights, offering a different excuse both times, when he must've been skulking off to Swahili lessons.

Two and a half hours after leaving the restaurant, at a quarter to midnight, I unlocked my front door and limped inside. The stinging blisters on the balls of my feet were nothing compared to the way my heart was hurting.

* * *

So I lost Ben to a visiting Kenyan pastor. Three years ago my mum took off to Africa with Médecins Sans Frontières after a Kenyan man knocked on her door looking for donations. Even though she moved back to Western Australia, she didn't come home to Perth, or to me.

Why were Kenyans intent on taking away those I loved?

* * *

I wasn't proud of the fact that I continued to sleep with Ben after Madras Palace night. It was impossible to see him and not sleep with him, and it was equally impossible to stop seeing him, even though I tried. I honestly tried. I ignored his text messages and deleted his voicemails without listening to them.

Then I saw him at a party and all it took was for him to tell me how much he missed me and there I was in bed with him again. The next morning I hated myself for being so weak and I kicked him out. Then we bumped into each other again. This pattern continued until the day he left.

Even as he was boarding his flight, I still held out hope that he'd change his mind. That he'd turn around and see how badly I was hurting and that he'd want to take that hurt away. He did turn around, but only to give me a big cheerful wave before he disappeared from my world.

And now, seven months later, here I was, still pining for him and holding onto his African-postmarked letters in which he sounded altogether far too happy. I hated Korma and I hated Kenya and I hated being alone.

Today I was tormenting myself about a woman called Karan. What kind of a name was Karan anyway? What was wrong with Karen? What made her so special that it was

Kar*an*? Ben had mentioned her in his past three letters. He hadn't admitted in so many words that they were an item, but I could read between the lines. Guys didn't call girls 'amazing' and 'inspirational' unless they were shagging them.

I received the latest Karan instalment in yesterday's mail. Which led to me slamming down a block of fruit and nut chocolate last night.

I decided I was going to ask him straight out what the deal with Kar*an* was in my next letter. I couldn't keep guessing. If he'd fallen for this woman whose parents couldn't spell, I had to know for sure so I could finally try to get my life together and make a real effort to forget about him. But I'd then have to wait at least a month for his reply, because he was off in some far-flung village where he couldn't text, email, Skype, or do anything that would give me sleep during that time.

I found one of the few vacant stools in the café of the hospital I was working at, sat down and threw my backpack onto the stool next to it. I pulled out Ben's letter from the backpack, spread it out on the table and wrapped my hand around my friend Arielle's cappuccino to give it extra insulation until she arrived.

I'd made Arielle read, dissect and discuss every one of his letters. I was sure she was well and truly over finding out about the goings on in rural Kenya, but she was too good a friend to refuse me.

'I would have bet my last dollar that you two would end up married, you know? I was sure he was the one for you, Lilz. He had me fooled. Anyway, he doesn't deserve you. You need someone who loves the way you love, who feels the way you feel,' she'd said the last time I showed her one of his letters.

She was right, I did want to be loved by someone wholly and unequivocally. I just wished that someone was Ben.

I took a sip of coffee and squeezed my eyes shut. Coffee this bad needed sugar. I couldn't be bothered going back up to the counter to get it, though.

It was noisy here. Sitting in the middle of a long table, I could have listened in on any one of the three conversations going on around me. But working as an admin assistant at the hospital through summer taught me I was better off not listening.

My clinical rotations were starting here on Monday so, instead of working, I'd be on medical rounds. Longer hours, no pay. And it would mean that instead of hiding in an office behind a computer, I'd be confronted by people dying.

I looked around and noticed that the girl sitting diagonally opposite me in the café was someone I saw at the hospital most days. She'd given her long dark hair a radical cut. It was very Ruby Rose now – all spiky and short but with a long fringe that fell over her face. She looked as though she was a million miles away, picking the seeds off her salad roll.

An old man shuffled past and knocked the back of her head with his lunch tray, hard enough to push her forward. She winced, touched her head and turned but he ignored her and kept walking.

Then she looked at me with huge caramel eyes peeping out from underneath long black lashes. If eyes really were the window to the soul, then this girl's soul was shattered to pieces. Those eyes were haunted.

'Ouch, are you okay?' I asked her.

'Oh yes, thank you. It did not hurt very much.' She had a low husky voice that was almost drowned out by the background chatter in the café, but I detected an accent. She rolled her 'r's.

She squinted at my name badge and then nodded quickly several times. 'You have a beautiful name, *Li-ly*.'

Her smile was pretty but it didn't take away from that haunted face.

'Thank you.' I smiled back at her. *What happened to make you so sad? Why are you always alone when I see you? Who are you visiting here? Do you need a friend?* 'And what's your name?'

'My name is Anna.' She reached out to shake my hand.

'Oh, Anna? Hi! I was expecting something exotic. Sorry, that was presumptuous of me, hey?'

'Not so presumptuous, no. My real name is Anwar, so you are right. But I prefer Anna.'

'Don't you like Anwar?'

'It is not that I do not like it. It is that it is a man's name. I prefer Anna.'

'Oh right, a man's name – as in Anwar Sadat?'

Her eyebrows shot up. 'Yes, precisely. You have heard of Anwar el-Sadat?'

'I studied modern history at school. So, were you actually named after him?'

'Partly. But mostly because the name held a special meaning for my mother.' She didn't elaborate and picked more seeds off the roll.

'Oh? What special meaning?' I prompted her. God only knew why. She clearly had issues with the name. Why couldn't I just shut up?

'It means "full of light".' She hesitated then added, 'And my family name, Hayati, means "my life".'

'Full of light – my life, now that's a special name. Makes plain old Lily, after a flower, seem dull doesn't it? If my name had a special meaning like yours it would probably be "she who can't shut up"! Ha!' I snorted, wondering why exactly it was so impossible for me to just shut my huge mouth.

'I think Lily is beautiful. It suits you. But for me, I prefer Anna,' said the girl whose eyes belied the meaning of her name.

Arielle turned up then with a handful of 'Excuse me's as she stumbled between the tables like a drunk. She was hauling three over-filled plastic bags that hit people in the head or shoulder as she squeezed past them. Nobody seemed to mind.

'Forty per cent off sale at Evolution – I'm dead broke now though, hey? Ha ha!' she announced to the café in general.

The people sitting around all smiled. But that's the way it had always been with Arielle. People looked at her and smiled. Even before she had bright pink hair.

'Heya!' She kissed my cheek and plonked herself down. Her face was flushed. 'Hi!' She beamed at Anna. 'Love your hair! Totally gorgeous. Makes me want to cut mine like that. Oh, yummo, cappuccino! Thanks, Lilz.' She threw her head back and gulped some down. 'Hey, I just heard Nick being interviewed for the game. You going?'

'Yep. Mum and Ross are here too. We're all going together.'

I'd only ever missed a handful of my brother's home games, ever since he played junior football as a four-year-old. The difference being that these days I shared the spectator stands with a minimum of thirty-thousand people chanting his name.

I made a mental note to send Nick a text before the match started. It was the first game of the season, plus it was his comeback game after last year's stress fractures. He'd be nervous for sure this morning.

'What are you up today?' I asked Arielle.

'Gregory the Gorgeous is coming over this arvo and he's cooking me dinner. I know what I'll be having for dessert.' She rubbed her hands together, grinning.

I tried to keep a straight face. Gregory the Gorgeous was anything but gorgeous and the idea of her 'dessert' made my stomach turn. Rather than hear more details about that, I slid Ben's letter under her nose.

'Ugh, no. What's he done this time?' she asked loudly enough to make other people gawk.

I pointed to the word Karan all six times it appeared.

'Arsehole!' she barked.

She picked up the letter, holding it close to her face, while I sipped the awful sugarless coffee.

A guy walked up and pulled out the stool directly opposite mine. Really, the person who designed these ridiculous narrow tables had no concept of personal space. When he sat, he was close enough for me to see the three concentric circles of ever darkening blue around his pupils. Wow. And his aftershave smelled good, really good. When had I ever noticed aftershave before?

He held my stare for an extended second. Seriously, wow.

'Hi,' I said, because it was weird to be this close to someone's face and not say anything.

He raised his eyebrows.

Then we both looked down before locking eyes again. He took a deep breath and glanced from side to side, obviously feeling uncomfortable.

'Feel free to go sit somewhere else,' I blurted out before I realised how bad that sounded.

He stared at me, scratching at the stubble along his jawline.

'I mean, I know we're cramped here so it's kind of weird for you to stay sitting this close.' I bit my lip. That sounded even worse! 'What I mean is, you can move and I won't be offended. If you want to move. But you don't have to move if you don't want to. It's not like I want you to. I just thought *you* might want to. You know?'

He kept his eyes fixed on me.

I lowered mine and they rested on his biceps bulging under his T-shirt.

Arielle glanced up from Ben's letter to say, 'Ignore my friend. She goes a bit stupid around hot guys.'

I felt myself go a nice shade of fuchsia.

He gave a low chuckle. Did this man not speak?

Arielle went back to reading the letter, and grumbling 'arsehole' a few more times.

The guy slurped his coffee and pulled a face.

'I know, the coffee's gross.' I pointed at my cup and wrinkled my nose in a show of solidarity to try and redeem myself.

He nodded. 'I asked for a flat white with one. This is a bad white with none.' His voice was deep and scratchy. And he had smoker's breath. I should've been turned off. But I wasn't. Not even a little bit.

'Yeah, mine's the same. It's awful.' I inhaled and resisted the urge to cough. 'And there's no sugar on the tables but I didn't want to go back and ask for it.'

'Hmm.' He pushed his chair back and stood up to full height, which from where I sat looked over six foot. He walked with purposeful swagger towards the counter. I kept my eyes firmly on the back of his jeans, then lost sight of him briefly as he disappeared in the queue. But he was back, right in front of me, a minute later. Wordlessly, he picked up my hand and pressed a packet of sugar into it. The touch of his warm calloused fingers sent an electric shock through me.

The voice, the breath, the aftershave, the arms, the eyes. My palms sweated a little.

Then Arielle handed me back Ben's letter. And it hit me that Ben had established a whole new exciting life with someone else while in my own miserable existence, a stranger giving me a packet of sugar was the most romantic thing that had happened in seven months. Out of nowhere, I found myself crying.

'Oh no. What's the matter? Did I do something to upset you?' His eyes were wide.

'No, no, it's not you.' I waved my hand in front of my face, willing away the tears. 'It's my ex-boyfriend. He moved to Africa and he met this girl and they're being all humanitarian together and here I am still obsessing over his stupid letters. And I've been so lonely that you touching my hand was the most special thing to happen to me for ages. Meanwhile Ben's living it up in Kenya, shagging K-K-Karaaaaan!' I wailed for the listening pleasure of the entire café.

Arielle put an arm around me.

'Is that a letter from him there?' The guy pointed to Ben's letter with his chin as he ripped open a packet of sugar and stirred it into his coffee.

'Uh-huh.' I nodded, wiping my nose with the back of my hand. It left a long wet smear up my forearm.

'Rip it up and forget him.' He gave his dark hair a quick comb through with his fingers. 'He's moved on. Why aren't you doing the same, instead of getting yourself worked up over that shit?'

I nodded again, feeling pathetic, not to mention mortified as people on either side of us had now put down their coffees to openly stare at me and listen in.

He swallowed a mouthful of coffee and looked right into my eyes. 'The humanitarian's a dick. It's his loss.'

Neither of us blinked and, with our faces almost touching,

for a second I could swear he was going to kiss me. All the noise in the café faded away and the roaring silence between us was all I could hear.

Then he stood up, turned and left. No goodbye. Nothing.

I gaped at his back until he disappeared through the doors.

'He was yummy.' Arielle sighed. 'See his blue eyes? They were something else. He looked like Paul Walker, didn't he? You know, that guy from *The Fast and the Furious* who died? The one with the eyes?'

Her words washed over me. I took the humanitarian dick's letter and tore it to pieces.

But as soon as I got home, I rummaged through my backpack for the torn paper and spent twenty frantic minutes trying to stick it back together.

Then Mum and Ross turned up after a morning on the beach, bringing me to my senses. I gathered up the sticky- and unsticky-taped bits in both hands, pushed my foot down on the kitchen bin pedal and watched them fall in like snowflakes. Blue Eyes was right, I didn't need that shit.

* * *

The distraction of Nick's first game of the season was just the thing to take my mind off Karan, who I had now renamed Karan the Talking Horse, because it comforted me to imagine her having an abnormally elongated head.

Ross drove us to the ground, all of us draped in the Rangers' red, white and green. Nick played an absolute blinder and, by three-quarter time, my voice was just about gone.

It wasn't until well into the last quarter with the Rangers comfortably in front that I noticed Nick running at half his normal speed in a chase along the wing. The camera closed in on his face as the ball went out of bounds. He was grimacing.

I nudged Mum in the ribs. 'There's something wrong with Nick.'

'What do you mean?' She kept her eyes on the big screen.

'He slowed down suddenly. He could easily have got to that ball but he let it bounce out of bounds. And I saw his face just then – he looked like he was in pain.'

'He just looks exhausted to me. He was probably squinting at the bright sunshine,' she replied.

No, he wasn't squinting at the sun. He was in pain.

'Ross can I have a go?' I held my hand out for his binoculars.

With Nick magnified by the lenses I followed his every movement.

'He's favouring his right leg, guys. He's limping.'

'Is he? Show me,' Mum said, but I ignored her and hung onto the binoculars.

Nick ran through the centre of the ground. When he moved back towards the wing I saw him wince again – every time his left foot hit the ground.

My stomach sank.

'Lily's right, he's definitely bringing his weight down more on the right leg. Can I have a closer look, please, Lily?' Ross leaned over Mum, who was sitting between us and reached for the binoculars.

'Oh dear, I can see it now,' Mum said softly. She paused before adding, 'Are you thinking what I'm thinking?'

'Yep,' I sighed. 'Some of the stuff he was doing only six weeks after the stress fractures was insane. Why would they do that, Ross? Would you get your patients doing high-level exercises six weeks after stress fractures?'

'I guess it would depend on the MRI results.' Ross shrugged. 'If the MRI was clear, then yeah, I can understand. Being as important as he is to the team, they'd be keen to get him back to form as soon as possible.'

'That's the thing, they never did an MRI. He had clear bone scans but that was it.'

'No MRI?' Ross raised his eyebrows. 'Did I know about that?'

'I don't know,' I replied. 'But I think his bones would have been re-absorbing the cells faster than his body could produce them, the way they were pushing his rehab so early. I don't think they were fully healed. And now look, he's gone and done it again. He'll be devastated.'

'Don't jump to conclusions, Lil. Maybe it's nothing more than a cramp or some muscle tightness. It *is* his first game back, after all,' said Mum, ever the optimist – or the queen of denial – I couldn't decide which.

'Good point, Mel,' Ross agreed.

I watched the way Nick lagged behind the rest of the team coming off the ground, the way he broke into a jog but three strides later was walking again. And I watched his face. 'That's not muscle tightness. He's using the same gait, with left foot eversion, that he used last time this happened. The stress fractures are back aren't they, Ross?'

* * *

Twice on the drive home I tried to call Nick from the back seat of Ross's Land Cruiser, but he didn't answer. And he didn't reply to my text.

***

I said goodbye to Mum and Ross soon afterwards. They were going out for drinks then spending the night at a friend's apartment in town before heading off tomorrow for the twenty-five-hour drive to Derby, where Ross was the only orthopaedic surgeon for two hundred kilometres in either direction, and Mum used her GP skills as a home-birth doctor.

I was sorry to see them go, especially Mum. They'd only been here a week. I sometimes resented her decision to live so far away from Nick and me, but I suppose they needed her more up there than I did here.

'It was good to see you, sweetheart,' Mum said through the car window when I went to kiss her goodbye. 'Good luck starting uni on Monday. And remember what we said – try and make up for your lack of pre-reading tonight and tomorrow, love.'

'Don't remind me, Mum. I'm trying to pretend it isn't happening.'

'Lil, I understand. Oncology round is just about the hardest one after Neuro. But if you stay on top of the study, you won't struggle too much.'

'Mmm, okay.' I pushed back a cuticle until it hurt.

'You'll be fine, I'm sure you will be.' She rested her hand on my cheek. 'Only two more years and you're there. Just think, you've already done four years – and done them well. You're getting closer and closer to making that dream come true.'

Whose dream? Mine or hers?

Mum checked her watch. 'We need to make a move on. Chin up, Lily – everyone hates the start of the school year.'

I stood on the driveway and watched them disappear down

the road. Then I walked back inside the empty house, which to all intents and purposes was mine while Mum and Ross lived in Derby. I didn't have to be alone, there was a house-warming I could go to. But I couldn't bear the idea of spending yet another Saturday night out pretending I was happy when I had a bin full of torn-up bits of Ben's letter. I didn't even understand why I kept writing to him when all that happened each time he replied was that I fell to pieces again.

No, that was a lie, I did know why. I said yes to that because I said yes to everything. I was Yes Lily – the nickname Dad gave me because I was the agreeable child, forever eager to please. The one who made up for Nick's pig-headedness. And I always, always lived up to my name. So of course I said yes to staying in contact with the person who broke my heart.

In bed that night, when I couldn't sleep, I fell back on my old self-destructive pattern of bringing to mind memories of Ben and me. This time I remembered us spooning on a lazy Sunday morning. But that memory disappeared after only a few seconds and was replaced by something new that made me blush, even though I was alone. It was of Blue Eyes in the café, and he was staring at me. And my tummy did crazy flip-flops with arousal.

Well, well, this was a surprise. I liked that I was turned on by a man who wasn't Ben. I liked that a lot.

I hoped others like Blue Eyes would come along and I wouldn't spend the rest of my life obsessing about Ben.

But what if others like him didn't come along and I ended up a lonely old lady whose only companion was a hissing hairless cat like Wally?

I shook that thought away and conjured up Blue Eyes again until I fell asleep.

ANNA – SATURDAY

I knew that when I fell asleep the smoke would fill my lungs. I knew that I would wake up with the taste of ash on my tongue. But it never frightened me to dream of the fire, it comforted me, because it brought me Noor.

Mama was asleep beside me. Her face hidden by her matted hair so that I could not see her expression. Was she dreaming of the fire? She had not cried out yet so I could only hope she dreamed of nothing, that her thoughts had faded to white and that these few hours of sleep brought her peace. Still, it was only two in the morning, there were four hours left for her to scream before the alarm woke her so she could be at Ricky's bedside again.

Even sleeping, Mama looked fragile. I loved that word! Fragile *sounded* fragile. Tomorrow I would write a poem for Mama and name it 'Fragile'. Tomorrow being today, of course. It tired me to think that. I knew I should switch the lamp off and lie down. But it was as hot as the hottest of summer nights, even though it was the first day of autumn. I had been praying for a drop in temperature to come with the changing season and hoped Allah would answer my prayers soon.

The quick cold shower I had to wash out the chlorine

from my hair had cooled me when I'd stood under it but I was sweating again now. I needed only another hundred and eighteen dollars, which I would have after one and a half more shifts at Black Salt, and then I would have enough money to replace the broken air conditioner.

My good uncle, Ahmo Fariz, did not know the air conditioner was broken because he rarely came into our room. He would have bought us a new one if he knew, but he had been too kind to us already, letting us live here at no expense. And anyway, very soon, after my next pay, with a new air conditioner in place, I would surely feel less tired during the day and hopefully it would also give me more energy in the pool.

My half-hour swim today depleted me even though I swam only three kilometres instead of the usual four. Was it the heat or the lack of sleep or both causing me to be so slow?

At least my hair was not making me hotter tonight. Cutting it was the wisest thing I had done in a long time. And I liked it short, it suited me. I did think I should go to the hairdresser soon and have a professional fix it up, but I was still proud of my haircut. The feeling of fresh air on the back of my neck today was heavenly and I was particularly fond of the fringe that I had left long enough to tuck behind my ear.

Mama liked it too, I think. She did not say anything but she smiled, and then she even laughed a tiny laugh when she felt the bits on top, hard from the gel, tickle her palm.

But Tante Rosa hated it. She yelled at me in English – so that the milkman could also enjoy her insults – that I looked like a Lebanese, and that now everyone would think I was a Lebanese and that I would bring shame to the family, and that all our patrons would stop coming to Masri's – my uncle's restaurant – leaving us destitute.

I laughed, 'Tante Rosa, do you mean that I look like a lesbian? Do you think it is the style of my hair that will make people think that? Do you truly think it is that simple?'

Tante Rosa replied in Arabic now that the milkman had left, 'The only thing that is simple is you! Your poor mother, Allah have pity on her. At least I can say to people, "What can I do about her cutting her own hair so it looks like a toilet brush? She is not my daughter!" But poor Leila has no such excuse to save her from the shame you bring.'

Ah, what to do about Tante Rosa? I reminded myself that if it were not for Tante Rosa giving up her big bedroom for Mama and me and moving into the tiny bedroom in the house we shared behind the restaurant, then we would have had nowhere to stay. But, still, it was hard to ignore Tante Rosa's tongue at times.

And today had been one of those times. It started with a lipstick.

I was passing the hospital pharmacy this morning and saw a tray of brightly coloured cosmetics for sale. I remembered how Mama used to love wearing pretty colours on her lips and leaving a kiss mark in the shape of her lips on our foreheads before she went out to the important State dinners that she used to attend. And I had the thought that a new lipstick might bring her some happiness, no matter how temporary. So I went in and chose one for her.

When I gave it to Mama she did smile, but for one short moment only. 'I have no use for this, *habibti*. Who would I wear lipstick for?'

'Wear it just for you, Mama, and for me and Ricky, so we can see how beautiful you look.'

But she dropped her head and said, 'Give it to your Tante Rosa, *habibti*. My days of lipstick are over.'

'As you wish, Mama.'

So I gave Tante Rosa the lipstick, which happened to have the magical name of Sugar Plum. It reminded me of the enchanted princess in 'The Nutcracker', a story I had enjoyed as a child.

'Tante Rosa, perhaps your prince will be waiting tonight, disguised as a restaurant patron instead of a nutcracker!' I took her hand to give her a twirl.

But she shooed me away and growled at me, 'The only thing cracked in this restaurant is you!' as she dropped the lipstick into her apron pocket.

I suspected that perhaps she was cranky on account of Ahmo Fariz's comment. 'You are wasting your money, Anna *ya habibti*,' he had said, 'buying lipstick to draw attention to the lips of a woman who does not bleach her bushy black moustache.'

That was not the kindest thing for Ahmo Fariz to say about his sister, in my opinion.

I retold Mama the story of the nutcracker, who was really a prince, when we were in the bathroom getting ready for bed, and she smiled at all the parts where I changed the name of the Sugar Plum Princess to Princess Leila. I promised Mama I would take her to the ballet one day to see the real nutcracker.

'But I have already seen "The Nutcracker",' Mama said with a faraway smile. 'Queen Rania was my guest when the Russian ballet performed it in Cairo.'

'Well, one day you shall see it again with Queen Anna.' I gave her a deep curtsey, pulling out the sides of my pyjama pants as I would a fancy dress.

The laugh that escaped from Mama was hollow.

I promised myself that one day I would make this happen. One day, I would have saved enough money that I could take

Mama to the ballet, and she could wear something beautiful and be out among people and feel alive again. What I would not give to see her enjoy herself once more?

I checked the time again. I would now only have five hours sleep.

I rolled onto my left and slowly, slowly opened the bedside table drawer, careful not to disturb Mama. I pulled out the worn journal from underneath a tissue box and smiled at the photo of my beautiful sister and me in our shared stroller as two-year-olds on a sunny Alexandria morning. Flipping the book over, I pressed my lips to Noor's forehead in another photo, this one of her at sixteen standing outside La Glace – our favourite gelato shop at the beach closest to us. She had lemon gelato on the corner of her mouth and her head thrown back in laughter.

Pulling the lid of a pen off with my teeth, I settled in to write in the hope that a letter to Noor, a letter which would never be posted, like all the other letters in this journal, would make my eyelids grow heavy and then maybe I would fall asleep in spite of the heat.

Darling Noor,

You will be pleased to hear that Ricky continues to grow stronger every day. He was up for long periods this afternoon, watching Tom and Jerry and laughing and laughing. Oh how his laughter melted my heart! Mama tells me that he ate both lunch and dinner with no vomiting, just like yesterday. One of the nurses removed the drip this afternoon, which left angry red marks on the skin of his forearm and made him cry a little (which made me cry a little on the bus after I left).

I hope and pray that tomorrow sees Ricky improve even more, the way the doctors promised he would after all these transfusions.

Twelve transfusions! Now that he is eating again, Mama said we shall ask Tante Rosa to prepare him hot falafel in pita bread and baklava drowning in rosewater to take to him tomorrow.

Before I left the hospital, I read another two chapters of The Folk of the Faraway Tree *to Ricky. Tomorrow he shall discover what happens to the children in the Land of Dame Slap. And the best thing of all was that when I kissed him goodbye, his forehead did not taste as sour, of poison. A good sign, yes? Yes, I think it is.*

What else can I tell you about today? Ah, well, at Ahmo Fariz's restaurant this evening we had a large group of forty, celebrating the fiftieth birthday of a surprised lady by the name of Laura. I have told you before, of the Australian custom of the surprise parties, where everybody hides and then they all jump and shout 'surprise' which usually terrifies the poor surprised person.

Tonight, it was the lady Laura's turn to be surprised. I think she was indeed shocked because as she walked into Masri's, through the kitchen, she was deep in a loud argument with her husband and she called him a 'lazy git' twice in the same sentence for parking at the back of the restaurant instead of the front.

The lazy git did not seem too happy that he had organised his wife a party and in return she had called him names in front of us. In the end, it seemed the evening was pleasant for all, with many presents opened and glasses of pink champagne drunk, and Ahmo Fariz improved the lazy git's mood when he served him his first beer 'on the house'.

There was something else that happened today. Something quite funny and quite beautiful when I was at the hospital visiting Ricky. There is a girl I have seen around, I think she may work here. She has golden ringlets that fall down to her waist. And while I ate my lunch at the table, I saw her fall in love. Noor, I saw it with my own eyes! She does not know she is in love, of course, and neither did the man, Toby, realise that he fell in love too.

I know Toby from the oncology ward. I have mentioned him to you before. He is the tall one with the worried face who visits someone in another room. Perhaps his mother? I do not know. For the last two weeks he has been coming and going alone, often arriving as I leave. We mostly wave or say hello in passing.

I am happy for Toby that he fell in love, even if he is not yet aware of it. Lily and Toby have given me hope that maybe someday I will also fall in love when I am not expecting it and that I will also be loved in return.

Do you think this is a possibility for me, Noor? Or am I too damaged?

I will try and get some sleep now my darling. I know you are nearby and ready to come to me and I welcome you.

Goodbye, my beloved sister,

A x

I switched off the lamp and lay the pillow flat. Mama stirred and I kissed her lightly on the cheek. I did not look forward to the nightmare that awaited me. But I knew that just before I woke, when the smoke had taken over every pore in my lungs and I could not stand it any longer, I would see Noor, floating up, up, up above me and smiling in her serene way. And then I would be comforted. I did not fear the fire that engulfed my dreams every night. How could I, when it was the only way that I could be with her?

TOBY – SATURDAY

I threw the still half-full coffee cup into the first bin I passed in the corridor on the way back to Jen's room. As soon as I pushed open the heavy frosted-glass door, the scent of the dying slammed into me the way it did every time I walked into this ward.

Her door was slightly ajar, how I'd left it. I walked in, treading as lightly on my feet as I could.

'Tobes.' Jen's voice was croaky.

Shit, she was awake. I never wanted her to wake up to an empty room.

I strode to her bedside and picked up her icy hand. 'Hey, how long have you been up? I just went to get a coffee.'

'S'okay. Just woke up.' Her breaths were shallow. 'What were you thinking about?'

'What do you mean?'

'You were miles away.'

'Really? I wasn't thinking about anything important. Just about how a girl in the café had a public meltdown about her ex.'

She took a shaky breath. 'Was she pretty? I bet she was by that gaga look on your face.'

I shrugged. 'Oh, you know, average looking.'

Jen snorted. 'Bullshit. Describe her to me.'

'Why would I do that?' I laughed.

She gave me her all-knowing look. 'I'm curious about who turned you on.'

'You're so full of it.'

'Just describe her, would you?' she insisted.

'Okay, fine.' I sighed. 'She had this curly blonde hair. It was really long, like Rapunzel-long, and she was tallish, I think.'

'What colour were her eyes?'

'God, Jen, I don't know!'

'Don't lie to a dying woman.'

'What makes you think I'm lying?'

'Because you're doing that thing with your mouth. It's bunched up to the left.'

I laughed. 'Okay, they were kind of like … bluey-greeny, almost aqua.'

'Nice,' Jen murmured. 'How old is she?'

'How should I know? I didn't make her fill in a questionnaire, you know.'

'Like our age or younger?'

'Younger.'

'Illegal-to-screw young?' She smiled.

'No! Not that young. God, what's wrong with you today?'

She winced as she tried to sit herself a little higher. This was the most alert I'd seen her in days and the most words she'd spoken in sequence for longer than that.

'Did you get her number? If there's an ex, she's single.'

'No, you lunatic, I didn't get her number.'

'Why not? She's single, you're single.'

My heart snapped as I took in her white lips and the transparent skin hanging loose over her sunken cheeks. I pressed a kiss on the back of her hand. 'Jen, don't.'

'Don't what?'

'Don't say I'm single.'

She looked away. 'I wish you were.'

'Hey,' I leaned my head close to hers and whispered. 'Stop that.'

She rested her head back on the pillow. 'Love you, Tobes,' she slurred.

She was asleep in seconds, the smile faded on her face.

'Love you more,' I whispered back to my somehow, even now after everything, still beautiful wife.

I sat back in the chair and watched her. She whistled softly through her nose. At least she was in less pain today. That was the one thing they managed to get right. The morphine was doing its job.

But the morphine, her saviour, was also her killer. The doctors had told us that there was no way she could take these doses and survive more than a fortnight. They'd said that six days ago. And since then they'd upped the levels twice.

But I couldn't think about that so I reached for the remote control and flicked on the television to mute my thoughts. I had the volume on so low I strained my ears listening to the sports update – a preview of the afternoon's match. They were replaying footage of Nick Harding out on the ground last night, at the week's final training session. Yes, he confirmed to the sports reporter, he was fit to play.

'Yes!' I whispered.

The news moved onto tennis and I yawned. I jolted upright when I heard Marcia say my name.

I stood up and gave my mother-in-law a weak hug. She clung onto me longer and tighter than I felt comfortable with.

'I'm glad to have your company this afternoon, love,' she said. 'You can help me with my Sudoku.'

Excellent.

I squeezed my hand into my front jeans pocket and pulled out my keys. 'I might go grab something for lunch up the street, Marcia. Give you some time alone with Jen. I'll be back in an hour or so.'

'Oh, yes, of course, go and enjoy yourself.' Her narrowed eyes and the way she spat the words out left me in no doubt that Marcia most definitely did *not* want me to enjoy myself over lunch. Like there was any chance I could, anyway.

She sat in the same chair I'd just been snoozing on and took out her knitting. She'd aged another five years in the last week. It shocked me the way the grief had ravaged her. Her hands looked as if they belonged to an eighty-year-old, not a woman in her early fifties, and over the last year she'd stopped colouring her hair so it was mostly white now instead of brown.

I walked over to Jen's bed and planted a kiss on her forehead. She stirred and opened her eyes, squinting at me.

'Your mum's here. I'm going to get something to eat and come back, okay?' I stroked the damp hair off her face.

She smiled and nodded.

'Hello, my princess,' Marcia whispered, appearing at Jen's bedside. 'Less pain now is there, my darling?'

'Mmm, so much better.' Jen turned her head back to me. 'Tobes?'

'Yeah?'

'Today's Saturday, right?'

'Yeah.'

'Doesn't the footy start today?'

'Yeah.'

'Why aren't you going?' she slurred.

'Uh, because I'm here … with you.'

'No, no,' she protested. 'It's the first game. You have to go. I want you to.'

'No, I don't care about going to the footy. I'd much rather be here.'

She chuckled hoarsely. 'Your mouth's bunched up again. Please go.'

I gave her a long questioning look and she squeezed my hand.

'Go!' she nodded.

I imagined myself at Subiaco watching the Rangers rather than sitting there doing Sudoku with my mother-in-law while Jen slept.

'Okay, if you're sure, I'll go.' I turned to Marcia. 'But I'll have my phone on me. So if anything changes or Jen needs me, please call me, Marcia, and I'll come straight back.'

Marcia's face was pinched. She gave me a sharp nod, avoiding eye contact. My shoulders slumped under the weight of her judgement.

'Can't miss Harding's comeback game.' Jen smiled. 'And Tobes?'

'Yeah?'

'I'm fanging for lemon pie. Bring me some after the game.'

Ever since I'd known her, Jen had always been 'fanging' for something or other.

She hit me weakly on my stomach with the back of her right hand, which didn't have a drip attached to it. 'I'm serious.'

'Sweetie, I'll bring you some lemon pie tomorrow,' Marcia cooed.

But Jen shook her head. 'I want it tonight. And I want *him* to make it.'

Luke walked into the room, looking unsure of himself. Poor kid, he was only nineteen. He shouldn't be living this nightmare with his sister.

I nodded. 'All right, I'll bring back some pie for you tonight.'

'Lemon,' she coughed.

'Lemon,' I confirmed.

'But don't buy it. Bake it.'

'What? Bake it?' My voice came out in a squeak. 'Jen, I don't have a clue how to bake a pie.' I looked to Marcia for help.

'Now, Jenny, come on, darling, that's a lot to ask of dear Toby,' Marcia scolded.

Jen held out a shaky hand out for Luke to hold as he squatted beside her head. 'Hey, Lukester. Bake me a lemon pie, Tobes,' she scowled at me. 'I mean it.'

Then she had a coughing fit that only ended when she spat a giant glob of blood-stained mucus into a tissue that Marcia held under her chin.

I left with a heavy heart, wondering if it was a big mistake to go to the football. I hoped I didn't end up regretting it.

I'd almost reached the car when I got a call from John.

'It's gone twelve and I haven't heard from you. Are you coming to the game or not, you big girl?' He sounded congested. 'Or can I give your ticket to Ren?'

'Are you still pissed?' I laughed. 'You sound it.'

'Mate, I feel like shit. I'm not drinking again, ever, I swear.'

'Too bad,' I said, 'seeing as though I'm up for a pint at the footy. I'm on my way home now.'

'Excellent!' His voice lost its thickness. 'First game of the season, *maaate!*'

I got home to find John lying down, resting on his forearms on the lounge room floor, with sections of the paper spread far and wide across the room. He slurped on his spoon as he shovelled in mouthfuls of Nutri-Grain. His wavy brown hair was in messy clumps, his stubble was well past the point of being trendy, the whole room reeked of Bourbon and a large portion of his arse crack was showing over the top of his Mr Happy boxers. My brother.

He looked up and grinned at me, scratching his head with the back of the spoon. I sat down next to him and we discussed the Rangers' line-up and what we would do better if we were coaching instead of Craig Mears.

John sent Renee a text message to say she couldn't have my ticket, and when she replied asking if he wanted to meet up for dinner after the game, he deleted her message.

'Best way to get out of anything you don't want to do, mate,' he said with a wink. 'Sooo sorry, babe, I never got that text message. That bloody mobile network must be playing up again.' He hauled himself up off the floor and hit me between the shoulder blades with three hard slaps. 'Listen and learn, mate. Learn from the master.'

I rolled my eyes. 'Like I'd take relationship advice from you! Poor Renee.'

We got changed into our Rangers jerseys and John chanted the team song as I drove us to the station with hope in my heart that our team would show more dash in their first game of the season than the way they did towards the end of last year's.

We had a stiff moment on the train when he asked about Jen and I tried to make it sound less awful than it was. Being the shallow bastard that my brother was, the awkwardness didn't last long and he moved straight onto whether the Rangers would score a win for Big Bruce in his two hundred and fiftieth game.

Over the next two hours, I kept imagining that I saw Jen in the crowd. I hated the way my mind messed with me.

Since we were kids she and I had shared a love of footy. We spent countless days playing kick to kick at the park at the end of our street. And then, when we were in our last year of high school, after a Rangers' night match that we watched at her house when her parents were away, we slept with each other for the first time. She even walked down the aisle to the Rangers' team song.

Going to Rangers' games had never felt the same since she stopped coming with me, which was a long time before the cancer got to her.

I felt the sun beat down on my face, listened to the roar of the crowd, and my eyes watered because it wasn't fair that she'd never experience these things again.

The football was epic. Surrounded by thirty-one thousand others, we celebrated a convincing win against the Cats. Joel Coombs and Nick Harding both starred, and the captain, Big Bruce Everett, was carried off the oval at the end of the game on his teammates' shoulders, while we joined the crowd in a standing ovation.

We hit the nearest pub straight after the victory, flaunting our scarves, but I had to leave after one drink to shop for the lemon pie ingredients.

'Stuff that, mate!' John screwed up his nose when I told him why I had to go. 'Drive past Black Salt on the way to the hospital later. There's at least a third of a lemon pie that Chef made fresh yesterday sitting in the cake fridge.'

'Do you know how stupid you sound calling Wayne "Chef"? You run a coffee shop with six employees, not a bloody Michelin star restaurant.'

'Hey.' He pointed at me. 'It's the impression that counts. If I say "Chef", it takes the whole establishment up a notch. It's called creative marketing, mate. Give things a fancy name and they become instantly more desirable.'

'Is that right, *Gianni*?' I snorted.

'That name's scored me a shitload more girls than John ever did.' He smirked. 'And who would you want making your coffee? John Watts, born and bred in the Western suburbs of Perth, or *Gianni Tavello from Roma*?'

His attempt at an Italian accent made me cringe.

'Like the saying goes, Tobes, if you can't dazzle them with your brilliance, baffle them with your bullshit!'

'All right, well, I'm going to leave the bullshit to you, mate, because I promised Jen a homemade pie, and that's what I'm going to give her. I'm leaving now. You coming or not?'

He didn't answer. He was focused on a blonde woman in a skin-tight white mini-dress. There wasn't much of her left to the imagination.

'Think I'll stay on,' John said dismissively, not taking his eyes off her. 'I've seen something I might like to eat for dinner.' He pulled out his phone and took a burst of photos of her from behind. 'Topping up the wank bank for later.' He winked at me.

'Ugh, are you kidding me? You can't do that. Delete them.'

'What's your problem, Constable Watts?' John laughed. 'It's just a bit of fun.'

'It's not funny, it's actually illegal, you fuckwit. Delete the photos, John.'

I watched as he deleted them and then I left. Why the hell Renee put up with him, I'd never understand.

I sat squished between two other blokes on the packed train home, googled 'best lemon pie recipe' and took a screen shot of the ingredients list. Eleven eggs. *Eleven eggs?*

As the train rattled along, I remembered how yesterday after work I'd sat and stared at Jen while she slept. Her knuckles, elbows and collarbones were poking up against her paper-thin skin. We'd laughed about it a few weeks ago, how she'd fought a lifelong battle with the scales – was the sort of girl to get excited if she ever caught a tummy bug and dropped a kilo or two – and now she'd ended up thinner than in her wildest dreams.

'You were always beautiful. I don't know why you were so worried about your weight. Your body was gorgeous, perfect,' I'd told her that day but she'd looked away.

'Don't, Tobes. Don't say nice things to me.'

'Why not? It's the truth.'

'Because it just proves to me that I never deserved you. And it makes me feel like shit.'

'I never wanted anyone else, so it's not a matter of who deserved who.' I insisted.

She blinked back tears. 'Thank you for being here, after everything. Nobody else would still be here.'

I picked up her hand and kissed the back of it. 'There's nowhere else I'd be.'

The train screeched to a stop at my station. I couldn't remember any of the journey. As soon as I stepped out of the carriage, I smoked two cigarettes in a row and considered a third.

I got in the car and drove straight to the shops to buy a pie tin, hoping it would be the right size. I found a shop assistant and asked him to help me hunt down ingredients I'd never used before. Armed with two bags of groceries and forty-six dollars poorer, I went home to bake for the first time in my life.

I didn't get far. I gave myself thumb cramps trying to mix the flour and butter with my fingertips until it was supposed to *resemble fine breadcrumbs.* That alone took fifteen minutes. I smacked an icepack between my hands, cursing Jen and her stupid cravings while I read the next instruction.

Leaving a 3 cm overhang, blind bake pastry for ten minutes after it has been rested for at least half an hour in a disc. Then return to oven and bake without weights for a further ten minutes.

What the fuck?

I rang Mum. 'What does blind baking mean?' I read out loud the recipe I'd printed off, adding notes in the margins as she explained the bits I didn't understand.

'Why don't I come over and help?' Mum offered.

'Thanks, Mum, but she really wants me to bake it myself so that's what I want to do.'

'Well, how about I come over and talk you through it but you do all the baking yourself?'

'That would be perfect, thanks.'

She was at my door ten minutes later. She pulled up a bar stool and, holding the printed-off recipe sheet in one hand and a glass of wine in the other, she talked me through the pie. I found myself with an all-new respect for anyone who'd ever baked a pie and actually stepped back into a kitchen again to bake another one.

At eight o'clock, with a perfect lemon pie tucked up in an esky, I walked gallantly into Jen's room. It was clear she'd gone downhill during the day. She made small whimpering noises and wriggled around on the bed. She gave her mother a long hug goodbye and Marcia walked out fast, keeping her head down.

I shook the chills off my spine and fixed a smile on my face. 'I have one whole lemon pie for you here, Jennifer. Made from fucking scratch.'

'No way!' she whispered. 'You made it?'

With flair, I pulled out the pie that Mum had placed on a copper platter to make it look fancy. I spread out a small chequered tablecloth over the trolley next to her bed (again thanks to Mum), sliced a small piece of pie, and fed it to Jen with a silver spoon. She had a tiny mouthful and chewed it slowly. I watched her. Then she started to cry.

And despite every promise I'd made myself never to do it in front of her, I cried too. I continued to feed her until there were only a few crumbs left on the plate, then I hopped up into bed next to her, being careful not to hurt her or pull on any of the tubes. She rested her head in the crook of my arm and fell asleep quickly. I stayed awake and repeated every prayer I could remember from my childhood.

NICK – SUNDAY

I draped a heavy arm over my grainy eyes as the sunshine broke through a gap in the blinds right onto my face. Why did sunrise have to be so damned early? It was just rude. It was Sunday, for Christ's sake. People needed to sleep.

I smacked my lips together, tasting last night's Jack, and turned to face the other side of the bed. It was empty, the sheet was pulled halfway down in a neat diagonal and the indentation from her head was still on the pillow. I listened for any sounds of Bridget in the house. She might have been the type to settle in with a coffee watching Netflix while she waited for me to wake up or, worse, be in the kitchen making breakfast. But all I heard was the distant hum of a lawnmower, my dog, Bluey, and the Alsatian a few doors down barking in a duet, and the sound of traffic off the main road.

At least I didn't have to take her out for breakfast, my tried and tested way of getting girls out of my house without hurting their feelings. Taking them out for breakfast was usually enough for them not to run to the papers. I hated those breakfasts, with their awkward daylight small talk and the exchanging of phone numbers and the fake promises to meet up for dinner during the week. But they were a necessary evil.

Thankfully Bridget seemed to have accepted our night together for what it was and left without expecting a romance to spring from it. Hang on, it was Bridget, wasn't it? Bridie? Could've been Bridie. Hopefully she didn't steal anything.

Shit, did she take any photos of me before she left? Would I be all over social media again today? Would I have Craig ranting at me, about how I was letting the whole team down *again* and how I was failing in my duty as a role model? My head pounded into the back of my eyeballs.

I reached for my phone and squinted at the bright screen while my heart raced at the thought of what I might find. Nothing. Thank God. I'd dodged another bullet.

I dropped my head back down on the sweat-soaked pillow and stared at the lock screen image on the phone. It was of Dad and me, standing back to back on the sand, holding our surfboards out in front of us. I was about sixteen when Mum took that shot of us on the Gold Coast. I stared at the screen until it blacked out.

'No more, Dad, I promise.'

I had half woken up just after 2 am feeling dead inside as I watched the girl sleeping, her long legs entwined in mine. I'd wished in that sleepy moment in bed that we meant something to each other. I wanted to wake her up and apologise for what had happened between us. But I didn't. And now she was gone.

I'd met her for the first time a few hours before when she slid up behind me on the dance floor and wrapped her arms around my waist by way of introduction, before dropping one hand down and stroking my penis through my jeans in time with the music.

She'd never know that I watched her sleeping and wondered

what it was that possessed her to come home with a complete stranger, and what made me do the same thing?

It had never felt good afterwards. But it felt particularly shit today. I didn't want to be that guy anymore. I hated that guy.

I swung my legs out of bed, scrounging around for boxer shorts. I was through with this shit. Sunday was technically the first day of the week. New week, new attitude. No drinking, not even one drop, until the end of the season, or maybe ever. My teammates didn't touch alcohol for the entire season. They all took the responsibility of being in peak physical condition seriously. It was time for me to do the same.

I swallowed against the scratchy dryness of my throat and something inside me knew with full conviction that last night would never happen again. I'd finally had enough.

I'd had enough of having to watch my back for cameras whenever I was up to no good, enough of feeling seedy, of trying to piece together the movements of the night before, of possessive drunk boyfriends imagining something where there was nothing and looking for a fight; enough of feeling like an arsehole. I'd had enough of the whole deal. But most of all I'd had enough of not having any respect for myself or for those girls I ended up with.

Dad was the most respectful person I ever knew. He treated Mum like a queen. And look at what I did – I was worried that a girl whose name I didn't know had robbed me. How the hell had I turned out like this?

I found my boxer shorts turned inside out in a ball on top of my jeans, which were also inside out from my hurry to get out of them and into the girl last night. I slid my legs into the shorts and stood up.

Uh-oh. There was a sharp twinge in my left foot. I took another step, hoping I'd imagined it. I hadn't. The searing pain shot up my fifth toe towards the ankle. I put my head in my hands.

Not again. Please, God, not again.

I gulped down the dread along with two Nurofen, and kept the bulk of my body weight on my right foot while I hobbled through the house to the back door. I fiddled with the stiff lock and let Bluey in. He galloped past me, just about bowling me over, and raced mad laps all over the living room. Only once he'd sniffed out every corner was he satisfied that all was as he had left it the night before and he came to greet me. He bent his head down and licked the top of my bare left foot.

'How can you tell it's sore, mate?' I ruffled the top of his head. 'Clever boy you are, hey? You hungry, Blue? Come on, food time.'

Hearing the f-word, Bluey stopped his inspection of my injured foot and bounced around on his front paws. I left him scoffing dry biscuits on the back deck and made my way back to the bathroom to wash Bridget/Bridie and the remnants of last night off me. My foot throbbed under the hot water and I felt my career slipping away.

Don't panic – you don't know it's that.

But I did know, deep down I knew. I'd felt it for the first time with five minutes to go in the last quarter. It had started as a niggle but as I ran from one end of the ground to the other, it worsened until I was limping by the end of the match. Not so anyone would notice. Anyone except Lily that was. Nothing escaped Lily. I ignored her calls and texts yesterday because I couldn't face the barrage of questions I knew she'd throw at me.

I didn't tell anyone in the club rooms about it after the game. I didn't want to dampen the atmosphere of our first win of the season or the collective relief in the team that I'd seen out the whole game. Anyway, I reasoned, it could have been nothing more than lack of match practice.

It got worse in the evening, so I went into denial by getting blind drunk in full view of the entire coaching and management staff. Thanks to the alcohol, I didn't feel a thing last night. But this morning I knew.

When I was dried and dressed, had sunk a Red Bull, and felt strong enough to handle the sound of my own voice down the phone – as well as hers – I rang Mum's mobile.

Ross answered. I stiffened, even though it was him that I was really after. I told him about the foot and he said they'd come straight over. As far as orthopaedic surgeons went, there weren't many around more experienced than Ross. I trusted his judgement.

I limped back outside and patted Bluey's back. 'Sorry, mate, can't walk you. My foot's buggered. We'll see if Mum will take you for a walk, hey?'

Bluey bounded over to where I kept his lead and looked expectantly over his shoulder at me. Instead, I found his sodden tennis ball half buried in the grass. I pulled up a bar stool from the veranda and spent the next fifteen minutes throwing the ball around the small garden while Bluey sprinted to fetch it until he was panting.

With Bluey forgetting he'd missed his walk and happily snoring on the couch, I hopped around and did a quick tidy up of the house before Mum and Ross arrived. Not that it did much good, the place was a disgrace. I really did have to get a new cleaning lady. Sharon mysteriously disappeared late last year, along with a stack of hundred dollar notes I had in the top desk drawer. So it had been roughly five months since the floors were mopped or the shower had been scrubbed. It didn't bother me but it would bother Mum and she'd bother me.

The doorbell rang just over an hour after I spoke to Ross. It still unsettled me to see Mum with him. I wished it didn't. Ross was a genuinely good guy, he adored Mum and he was always friendly with Lily and me, never overstepping the mark. But he wasn't Dad, and every time I saw him, no matter how nice he was, it reminded me that it should be Dad by Mum's side.

After Mum's predictable 'Nick, your house is revolting. Have you no shame?' speech, I showed them the offending foot. Mum sat close by, watching, as Ross did the assessment while I lay back on bent elbows. He was silent as he prodded and twisted my foot with his large cold hands. I gasped sharply and cursed when he hit the spot.

He stroked his chin when he was done. 'Nick, I'm really not sure. Given your lack of pain through the pre-season and the fact those last lot of bone scans were clear, it could just be that you overdid it yesterday and it's only a bit of inflammation that will settle down. But it might be that the stress fractures have come back, mate. I wouldn't rule it out without an MRI.' He avoided my eyes when he said that.

I groaned loudly.

Ross turned to Mum. 'Mel, let's order an MRI, to be safe.'

Mum reached into her handbag and pulled out a referral pad that she handed to Ross.

They didn't stay long after that. We'd already said our goodbyes after dinner on Friday night before the match. They'd been living up north for a year now. They met in Kenya, Mum and Ross, when they were both volunteer doctors there, and then Mum followed him home to the outback. I wouldn't see them again until the finals. If we made it that far into the season. If I made it that far.

I shook Ross's hand at the front door.

'Catch you for finals, Nick.' He patted my back. 'I've got a good feeling about the Rangers holding up that cup this year with you leading the charge, mate. I can picture it clearly.'

I mustered up a smile. He tried hard, Ross.

It was only when they'd left that I realised I'd forgotten to ask Mum if she'd walk Bluey.

I sat on the couch with my leg up and called Craig.

'Nick, what's up? Tell me you didn't get into trouble when I left last night,' he groaned. 'We're going to need another serious chat about drinking during the season after what I saw of you yesterday.'

He sounded fed up. It was little wonder. He'd spent much of last year in damage control while I wreaked havoc all over Perth. It was only his second year coaching me but already he was exhausted.

'I know, I'm sorry. I promise no more drinking. Honestly. But, Craig, I'm ringing because my foot's bad,' I said heavily. 'It hurts to walk. A lot.'

He sighed. 'Shit.'

'Ross White, my mum's partner who's an orthopaedic surgeon, came over and checked it out this morning. He's written me up an MRI referral.'

'And? What does he think?' I could hear the tension in his voice.

'He said it's hard to say – it might just be inflammation. He's not ruling out stress fractures though.'

There was a long silence.

'All right, Nick, I'll call Aaron and get him to line up that scan for first thing in the morning. Stay off it all day, all right?'

Five minutes later, Aaron, the team's head doctor, called to say I had an appointment at nine tomorrow morning. MRIs normally had a three-day wait list.

As the pain became more and more intense, a knot formed in the pit of my gut. I couldn't afford to have stress fractures again this early in my career. It spelled disaster. And now I'd run out of painkillers too.

I drove to a local pharmacy where I was tempted to park the Range Rover in the disabled spot directly outside, but then I imagined the impact on the club if a photo of that appeared in tomorrow's paper. And today was the day I stopped being an arsehole, so parking in a disabled bay wasn't the way to go. I drove around the corner and parked in a regular spot.

'Oh, cool, Nick Harding! Look, Dad, Nick Harding!'

'Is too! Well spotted, Joshy! Onya Harding!'

I smiled, gave them a double thumbs up and limped into the pharmacy.

I walked in self-consciously, the way I did everywhere, knowing my every move was more than likely being watched. Luckily, it seemed empty, except for the voices in the dispensary.

As I passed by the birth control section on my way through, I had a quick flashback. Pretty sure that was the last condom in the box I'd frantically grabbed last night. I reached out for a pack but stopped myself. No condoms in the house meant no more Bridgets. And no more Bridgets meant no more hating myself after Bridget-type nights when I ignored Bridget-type text messages.

I left the condoms where they were, bought some over-the-counter anti-inflammatories and went into the coffee place next door for the first time since it had changed hands and been renamed Black Salt.

It was packed in there. Shit. This place used to always be empty. I was super careful to hide the limp.

People were sprawled out on black oversized beanbags and lounging around on red vinyl sofas. Two preschool-aged boys were attempting to climb a giant Buddha water feature in the corner. Couples swung on indoor garden swings and on hammocks tied to wooden beams. A group of teenage girls were writing their names on the blackboard-painted walls with coloured chalk dangling from twine. There wasn't a single table to be seen, just wine barrels painted with motivational phrases dotted around the place between the sofas.

Great, just what Fremantle needed – another overpriced hipster café.

'Yeah! Haaaarding,' a guy around my age drawled from a beanbag. 'Yer a bloody legend, mate!'

'Good to have you back, Harding,' his mate chimed in. 'We missed you, mate.'

I smiled, gave them the regulation double thumbs up and walked extra, extra carefully to the queue at the counter, biting down on my lip as I put my full weight through the foot. Lots of sets of eyes were on me. I wished the windows to this place weren't tinted – if I'd known how busy it was I never would have come in.

When it was my turn to order, I leaned on the counter and forced a smile at the girl who hurried back from pinning the last order to the kitchen alcove.

'Hello and a warm Sunday session welcome, sir, to Black Salt café. You're in luck because our amazing Best of Brunch food mood boards have landed. Our all day brunch is now served up straight on the chopping boards and it's fresher than ever!' Her huge caramel-coloured eyes peeked at me from a long fringe that fell over her face. The rest of her dark hair was super short and in punk style spikes. Even though she was tall and broad-shouldered, there was something in her eager-to-please expression that made her appear vulnerable, fragile almost. She was beautiful. Really beautiful. 'Have you a preference, sir, for which Best of Brunch food mood board you would like to sample? I can very highly recommend the Feeling Frisky Best of Brunch food mood board, because the glazed chorizo and the chilli lime squid on the Feeling Frisky Best of Brunch food mood board is a very good brunch combination, hokay?'

Did she just call me sir?

'Uh, actually I just wanted a take-away coffee, thanks.'

'Oh yes, of course, sir. I should have asked you that first, yes? Please let me explain to you the Craving a Coffee menu, hokay?' She took a deep breath and launched into another spiel. 'There is the Banging Brazilian Blend—'

'I'd just like a large flat white with one, if that's okay.'

'Of course, yes, sir. Gianni our barista will fix that for you personally, sir, hokay?' She smiled again.

'Excellent.' I smiled back at her. 'I'm just going to sit on the swing in the corner there while I wait, if that's all right.' I desperately needed to get off my foot.

'Oh, you will not be sitting with your friends in the "Chillax Zone"?' She pointed to the football fans who had called out to me when I walked in.

'Oh, no, um, no we're not friends.' I paused. 'I don't actually know those people.'

She frowned. 'Hokay. Very well, sir.'

I sat and swayed on the zebra-striped swing, not taking my eyes off her while she served the next few customers. She jutted her bottom lip out and blew air up her face making her fringe fly. She wiped sweat off her brow but the whole time her smile stayed genuine and warm with each person in line.

She wasn't my type, not by a long shot. My type was very much the Bridget type – the flirty, wouldn't say no to anything, wouldn't be out of place on the cover of *Maxim*, the longer the (preferably blonde) hair and the tighter the clothes, the better. Long painted nails, extra high high-heels – that type.

She looked over to where I was. I smiled at her. She stopped talking for a second and smiled back at me. Our eyes stayed locked. Whoa. I gulped and she blushed a deep red. She looked back at the customer she was serving, tucking rogue strands of fringe behind her ear and she started talking to them again, shifting her weight from one foot to the other. Could she sense me watching her?

A couple of minutes later, another girl walked up behind her and tickled her on the waist. She turned and laughed and untied her apron, pulling it up over her head and hiding it behind the counter.

At the same time, my ticket number was called out by Gianni, who looked more Australian than Vegemite. I was about to heave myself out of the swing when I saw her motion at me to stay sitting and she walked up to the coffee bar to grab the cardboard cup.

She walked towards me, looking at the ground. She had a loose black T-shirt on that hung halfway down her thighs with the words 'It's LeviOsa not LeviosAR' emblazoned across the chest. Her green zig-zag striped leggings were tucked into bright purple Doc Martin boots. I hadn't noticed it when she was serving me, but she had a good twenty leather bracelets stacked up high on both forearms.

Attitude hair, attitude clothes. Hmm, interesting.

'Your coffee, sir.' She said self-consciously, handing over the cup.

'Hey, thanks.' I took it from her hands and our fingers touched for a quick second. Whoa – again. Seriously, what was with that? I swallowed and said, 'That was really kind of you to bring over my coffee. You didn't have to do that.'

'But you have a sore leg, so of course.'

'How can you tell? I thought I was doing a good job hiding that.'

'No, not such a good job, sir.' She smiled, tugging at the bottom of her T-shirt. 'Is it very bad, the pain when you walk?'

'Nah, it's all right.'

She gave a little laugh. 'Australians always say, "It is all right" when it is not all right.'

I laughed too. 'Yeah, we do, don't we? So where are you from?'

'I am from Alexandria, in Egypt.'

I liked the sound of her husky voice. A very sexy voice.

'Oh? You're the first real-life Egyptian I've ever met. Have you been in Australia long?'

'A little more than a year since I came here, sir.' Her eyes had a distant look about them. They looked almost haunted.

'You don't need to call me sir, I'm just Nick.' I reached out my hand and she gave it a weak shake. Wishing I didn't have to, I let her soft hand go after a few seconds. 'So, what's your name?'

'My name is Anna, sir.' she nodded.

I laughed again. 'Not sir, just Nick. Okay? You really don't have to call me sir. My name's Nick Harding. Well, it's Nicholas Harding, but I prefer Nick.'

I waited but there was not a hint of recognition from her. Oh, that was great. Beyond great.

'It is a pleasure to meet you, Nick. Nice weather we are having, yes?' She smiled with her whole face and nodded at me quickly a few times.

My heart skipped a beat. 'It *is* a nice day.' I let my eyes rest on hers and she looked at her boots.

Gianni was watching us from behind the bar. He looked kind of pissed off.

'Hey, is it okay that you're here talking to me? Will you get in trouble with him?' I indicated with my chin in Gianni's direction.

'No, no,' she said dismissively.

'He keeps looking over, though. Is he your boyfriend? I don't want any trouble.'

She broke into a low husky laugh and looked over her shoulder at him, giving him a shoo-away sign with her hand.

'Gianni, my boyfriend? Not if he was the last man left on the Earth!'

'Is he really that bad? You'd rather let humankind die out as a species than repopulate with him?'

'Definitely. But he is a very nice boss, even though he is a terrible boyfriend to poor Renee.'

'Why does he look annoyed with us, though? Is it because you're talking to me rather than working?' I threw Gianni a warning look but it didn't stop him staring.

She shooed him away with her hand again, in a more pronounced way this time, and he finally looked away. 'My shift is finished. Ashlee has taken over for the afternoon.' She pointed at the girl behind the counter who was also staring at us. 'Gianni is not annoyed at us, rather he is annoyed that we are too far away for him to hear what we are saying. He is the kind of person who has to know everything.'

So she'd come over to chat instead of running for the door, like anyone else would have, after finishing a shift in a busy café on a Sunday morning.

'If you've finished your shift, do you want a seat then?' I patted the swing.

'It is hokay, I am happy to stand. So what is wrong with your leg?'

'Hurt it running. I'm having a scan to find out what's wrong with it tomorrow.' That was the truth after all. 'What does that writing on your T-shirt mean? What's a Leviosar?' I asked, dragging out the 'o' sound.

Her jaw dropped. 'Nick, this is one of the most famous quotes from *Harry Potter and the Philosopher's Stone*. You do not recognise this quote?'

I shook my head. 'I haven't read any Harry Potter books, haven't seen any Harry Potter movies either.'

'But, the story of Harry Potter is the most wonderful story ever told so I am afraid you are missing out greatly by not reading it, sir, not sir, Nick.' She looked genuinely worried about me not having read it.

'That's a big call – the most wonderful story ever told. I might have to download it then. I'm stuck at home with this stupid foot anyway. That's as good an excuse as any to read the most wonderful story ever told.'

'No, you do not need to download it. Wait.'

She raced off to the back of the café and disappeared through the plastic swing door. A few moments later she reappeared holding a book in her hand.

She gave it to me with a flourish. 'You can borrow it.'

'Thanks.' I inspected the tattered copy of *The Philosopher's Stone*. 'So if I read this, I'll understand what your T-shirt says?'

'You will indeed. And if you enjoy it, I have the whole series here that you can borrow.' She pulled her shoulders back proudly.

I leaned back in the swing and had a swig of coffee. My body relaxed as the heat spread inside me. 'That's really sweet of you to offer. Thanks, Anna. Great coffee too.' I raised the cup. 'Just what I needed to pick me up today – a hit of good strong coffee.'

She laughed. 'Of course Gianni makes a very good coffee indeed. But Nick, this is a flat white – it is not a strong coffee. If you want a real coffee, then you must try Turkish coffee. It is the only way to have coffee when, as you say, you need something strong.'

'Is that a kind of espresso? I don't do espresso. That's not coffee, that's toxic tar.'

She put her hands on her hips. 'Espresso is not coffee? It is the *only* coffee. In Egypt, everyone will kill themselves with laughing if they see milk in coffee, and in such a big cup as this.' She pointed at my cup. 'But, you know, Turkish coffee is not just any espresso. It is pure velvet, Nick. If you truly want to drink coffee in the proper fashion, you must most definitely try a Turkish coffee. It is so thick, almost like a syrup. A velvet syrup.'

I pulled a face. 'Ugh, coffee syrup? I'm sorry, Anna, I'll read your book but I won't drink your coffee.'

'Very well, suit yourself. You can keep drinking this pretend coffee and telling yourself it is strong.' Her rolled 'r's made me smile. That accent was so damn sexy. Maybe she was my type.

She looked at her watch. 'I must be leaving now. It was very nice to meet you, Nick.'

I cleared my throat. 'Um, can I ask for your number, Anna?'

'Why?' She gave me a confused look.

'So I can call you and tell you what I think of the book. So we can perhaps go out together some time?'

Why was I so nervous?

She flicked her fringe back and looked up at the ceiling before making eye contact again. 'That is a very kind offer. Thank you, Nick, but no.'

I was taken aback. 'Oh, okay. Can I ask why not?'

'Because I am not a girl who gives her telephone number to somebody she does not know. A book? Yes. My telephone number? No.'

I felt the heat creep into my cheeks. 'Okay, so no phone number, but could I take you out for dinner tonight? Just dinner?'

She gave me a long look and then took a big breath in and out. 'I am working tonight.'

'But you just finished working.'

'I am not working here, of course. I am working at the restaurant that belongs to my Uncle Fariz.' She twisted one of the leather straps around her wrist.

'Oh, I see. Which restaurant?' I tried to make the question sound light, innocent.

'Masri's. It is Egyptian food, very wonderful food.' Her smile returned.

I spread my arms out. 'My favourite!'

She laughed that low husky laugh again.

A family walked into the café then. They stopped talking when they saw me. The father pulled out his phone and I sensed a photo session coming on.

'All right, Anna.' I pushed off on my hands and stood up. 'I'll let you go and I'd best be going too. But I'll come back and give you my verdict on Harry Potter, okay?'

'Hokay. I shall look forward to this ... very much. Bye, Nick, have a nice day.' She tucked more strands of fringe behind her ear.

Our eyes locked together once again and neither of us smiled this time. I got a deep longing way down low. I looked away before I embarrassed myself.

'Bye, Anna.'

The family walked up with their expectant Rangers fan smiles on. I smiled back at them, gave a double thumbs up to each of the three gobsmacked kids and left quickly, hurting my foot even more in my rush to get out.

As I hobbled to the car the sky was a brilliant cloudless blue and the whole streetscape looked shiny. What a magnificent day it was!

I sent a group text to Joel and Bruce once I was in the driver's seat:

I know it's short notice but are you guys up for dinner out tonight? I've got a hankering for Egyptian food.

LILY – SUNDAY

When I woke up in the morning – actually it was gone one in the afternoon – the first thing I did was mentally work out what the time would be in Kenya. I imagined Ben and Karan huddled up in bed. With the taste of Korma in my mouth and a pen in my hand, I sat out on the back patio and replied to Ben's letter.

Ben,

I couldn't help but notice the number of times you mentioned Karan in your letter. I'm glad you've found somebody to warm your sleeping bag, which I hope is infested with the larvae of a thousand fleas.

Being a holier-than-thou churchy type, I hope Karan is the kind of girl who will tease you with hand jobs but no actual sex because she's saving herself for marriage. And I hope that, being desperate to 'go all the way', you do rush into marrying her (long horse face aside, I'm sure she's a stunner) and that on your wedding night you undress your blushing bride to find that she has a small but noticeable penis.

Lily.

P.S. Never write to me again.

I read the letter over, had a split second where I thought about sending it, and then I screwed it up and started again.

Dear Ben,

Hi, thanks for the letter. Sounds like you're doing a great job teaching the village kids to play soccer – awesome! And the food you described from those underground ovens sounds delicious.

Thing is, Ben, whenever I get one of your letters I kind of fall to pieces all over again because I miss you. I miss the sound of your voice and I miss the smell of your shampoo. On Friday nights I stay home alone and watch The Block *by myself instead of with you, and we're not eating Cherry Ripes and you're not saying how they make those renovations look shit easy but really there's no way they did it all themselves and they have a heap of helpers off camera.*

I miss how you'd come over and do your assignments while I crammed for anatomy exams.

And I miss how whenever I cried about Dad, you'd hold me and make it go away.

I promise, I'm not telling you all this to be manipulative. I just need you to know that your letters hurt me. I know that's not your intention but it's what happens.

So Ben, that's why I don't want you to write to me anymore. I want us to make a clean break and I want to say goodbye for good in this letter. But before I go, I want to thank you for four great years together. You'll always be the one I loved first.

Take care Ben.

Lil x

P.S. Please don't write back.

I read the letter over and cried enough tears to fill a bath.

I spent the rest of the day under a pile of textbooks, studying oncology for the clinical round starting tomorrow. In the afternoon, I took a break to cook a lasagne. I kept a couple of serves for myself and then divided the rest into plastic containers and froze them for Nick.

The smell of garlic and red wine relaxed me and I lost myself in the kitchen. I took my time washing up, daydreaming as I played with the warm soap bubbles in the sink, squishing them between my palms.

Then I warmed myself up a serving and realised, after thinking it tasted particularly meaty and having a dig around with the fork, that I had forgotten to put any actual lasagne in the lasagne.

After the lasagne-less lasagne, it was back to studying oncology which had to be the most desperately depressing way to spend the evening. At eight o'clock I gave up, admitting to myself that I couldn't commit to memory all the different kinds of cell slides or learn a whole unit in one day when I should've been studying for weeks leading up to tomorrow. Tomorrow – when I'd have to plaster a smile on my face and start another difficult year of study towards a career I didn't want.

The worst thing about it was that nobody ever forced me to choose this path. It was all me. I was the mess of a human being who never made her own decisions. Mum and Dad thought I should study medicine – I studied medicine. Mum suggested it would be lovely to honour Dad's name by becoming an anaesthetist – I decided to become an anaesthetist. It was easier being Yes Lily than Lily Who Had to Think for Herself.

I flicked on Netflix, grabbed a tube of Pringles and the rest of the bottle of red wine that I used in the no-lasagne lasagne. Pouring a glass, I settled in to numb myself with season one of the *Gilmore Girls*.

Anna – Sunday

Mama was fitful again tonight. The screaming, oh, the screaming! I laid her head on my lap and hummed her favourite song, 'La Vie en Rose', until she was soothed. But I failed to soothe myself. My hands still trembled long after I had settled her back to sleep. I was thankful that Mama did not have the presence of mind to question why my voice was so shaky while I hummed.

It was a long day for Mama at the hospital. Perhaps this was why her dreams terrified her so greatly tonight. She had spent too many hours surrounded by looming death on the oncology ward.

It was a long day for me too. The shift at Black Salt began with a brief but exceptionally loud argument between Gianni and Renee. Renee, who was sitting in the back room watching television as she often does on a Sunday, stormed over to the coffee bar and screamed at Gianni while she waved his phone about in the air. There was a photo message that had just come through on his phone, which he had left in the back room on the table right beside Renee. (If I was Gianni and I did the things that Gianni does, then I would have made certain that my phone did not leave my sight to keep my secrets safe!) The photo that had upset Renee was one that a naked woman took of herself. It was such a clear photo in fact that I could see just how naked this woman was even though I stood some feet away at the counter.

Gianni looked far less shocked and embarrassed than he should have looked, in my opinion, for a person who was sent a naked photo of a woman who was not his girlfriend.

'Hold your tits,' Gianni yelled back at Renee, pushing the phone away from his face. 'I never even asked for that, it's not my fault she sent it.'

'How does this skank even have your phone number in the first place?' Renee shrieked.

The entire café fell silent.

'It's on my business card, it's on the webpage. My number's everywhere, all right? I've got no idea who she is, I swear.' Gianni threw his hands in the air. 'Can we do this later, Ren? I don't have time for this paranoid shit of yours now.'

And even though it was clear to me that Gianni was lying, it was not clear to Renee. She apologised to Gianni and retreated quietly to the back room again. Poor Renee.

The rest of the morning at Black Salt passed uneventfully until a man by the name of Nick Harding came in to order a flat white with one. We had a brief conversation that I enjoyed and, although I found myself attracted to and intrigued by this stranger, it may not have been a particularly eventful thing that we met today had he not come to see me at Masri's tonight.

He came to Masri's just to see me!

I was balancing a bowl of hummus in one hand, a bowl of *tabbouleh* in the other and with a plate of *warak enab* resting on my forearm, when he walked in with two other men who were almost as tall and as broad as he was.

And there was Ahmo Fariz, madly shaking Nick's hand while he himself stood there shaking with his whole body. I could not understand why Ahmo Fariz behaved in this most excitable way. He ushered Nick and the other men to table eighteen, right in the centre of the restaurant and he tucked the 'reserved' sign from the table into his shirt pocket.

There were many eyes on Nick and his friends, and much whispering and pointing coming from the other patrons, and I thought to myself, either Nick or one of his friends is famous.

'Anwar!' Tante Rosa bellowed from the kitchen and I hurried back in there where she had the *kobeba* and *pasticcio* ready for table three.

When I walked back out again, I looked to the table where Nick and his friends were seated and he was looking straight back at me. When our eyes met he smiled a very small smile, I think one that was intended just for me to notice and in that moment it was as if I was falling out of a plane without a parachute.

Nick kept his eyes on me, smiling that smile, until I had to look away because it was all just too wonderful. But when I looked back again a few moments later, he was still watching me and still smiling.

I returned to the kitchen where Ahmo Fariz cried at Tante Rosa, 'Three of them! Three of them here! Here in *my* restaurant!'

'Stop acting like a donkey and settle down,' Tante Rosa sniffed. 'And speak in Arabic. We are Egyptians. Egyptians speak Arabic.' It annoyed Tante Rosa greatly when her brother spoke to her in English – she often said that he did this only to show off about how much better at English he was than her. Perhaps if she spoke more English, she too would improve.

Ahmo Fariz ignored her demand and repeated in English while he danced around the kitchen, 'Here in my restaurant! What a joyous occasion!'

'You are a fifty-nine-year-old man and look at you, swooning and clutching your heart like a lovesick little girl!' Tante Rosa gave the back of Ahmo Fariz's head a loud slap.

'We're the Western Rangers. We'll show you how it's done. We give every game our all, till the Premiership is won!' Ahmo Fariz chanted in his deep booming voice that echoed off the kitchen walls as he clapped his hands in front of Tante Rosa's sour face and swung his hips from side to side.

'Your uncle has lost his mind,' Tante Rosa grunted at me. 'All because there are three stupid footballers sitting out there without a brain between them. The way he is acting, you would think the Queen of Sheba has come visiting to request his hand in marriage for her daughter the princess!'

I finally understood why Ahmo Fariz was jumping around the kitchen on his toes as though the floor was made of hot stones, and why he had given Nick and his friends such a warm greeting, and why the customers at Black Salt this morning and now the patrons here were interested in Nick.

He was an Australian rules football player for the Western Rangers.

Ahmo Fariz was as devoted to the Rangers as any person could be. For six months last year, every weekend he sat on the couch wearing his Rangers scarf and he cheered and hooted and flew into the air shouting, 'Goal!' and 'Ball!'

I myself tried once or twice to watch the football with him but I found it much too confusing. Also I was frustrated by the way the game stopped and started every minute or two. It did not have the flow of real football (which they call soccer here).

I grabbed Ahmo Fariz's arm. 'Ahmo Fariz, I met Nick Harding today – he came into Black Salt. I told him I worked here and how great the food was.'

Ahmo Fariz scooped me into his arms with a crushing hug. 'Nick Harding is the best AFL player of this generation. He is a god, Anna, a god! Harding is Hercules, the golden-haired son of Zeus! And you, *habibti*, you already know you are the light of my life and now you have brought not only Nick Harding, but Big Bruce Everett and Joel Coombs into my restaurant and their presence has made tonight the greatest night Masri's has ever seen!

'More, *ya Rosa, ya ghelsa,* more than this beggar's amount on the plate. What are these prison rations you serve? These men are our honoured guests, add at least six more falafel!'

And with that, darling Ahmo Fariz carried three plates overflowing with our best selection of food to the table where I was certain Nick and his friends had not even ordered yet.

The restaurant was so busy that I did not have a chance to speak with Nick all evening. But whenever I stole a glance at him he had his eyes on me. His friends also watched me as I worked.

I found it difficult to concentrate on my duties and three times Tante Rosa reprimanded me for making foolish mistakes. Each time I kissed her cheek, apologised and told her she was too beautiful for one's eyes to behold. Which might be true if she did something about her bushy moustache.

Never before had so many photographs been taken in Masri's. Nick and his friends were patient and gracious with all the people seeking photographs and then even more patient when Ahmo Fariz had many, many photographs of himself taken with his special footballer guests.

Although most tables eventually emptied, the table where Nick sat did not. The three of them ordered four rounds of coffee (not Turkish coffees mind, just weak flat whites) one after the other, after the other, until they were the only people left sitting. And still Tante Rosa did not let me near their table. She ordered me to start washing the dishes! I felt like shaking her so hard it would make her teeth rattle.

At eleven-thirty, Nick and his friends finally came up to the counter to pay. But Ahmo Fariz, the generous soul, did not take a single cent from them. Through the gap in the kitchen door I could see Ahmo Fariz bouncing up and down on his toes again.

A warmth spread through my chest when Nick said, 'Fariz, mate, that was the best meal I can remember in a long, long time. Thank you for your amazing hospitality, we'll definitely be back.'

'You must come on a Saturday night!' Ahmo Fariz exclaimed. 'That is when Shamia comes, the best belly-dancer in all of Australia. She is from Beirut – where the most beautiful women come from. Very beautiful, very nice hips. And when she dances, ah, her titties, boom, boom, boom – up and down like this. Mwah!' Ahmo Fariz shook his hands in front of his chest and then bunched his fingers together and kissed his fingertips.

Nick and his friends laughed loudly at this.

'Could I please have a quick word with Anna, if you don't mind, Fariz?' Nick asked Ahmo Fariz when the laughing quietened.

'Anwar is too busy to come out and waste time with these oversized cretins,' hollered Tante Rosa in Arabic from the kitchen before Ahmo Fariz could even reply to Nick. 'She has her hands in the sink! Tell them to leave so you can get in here too and help us with this mountain of dishes. Enough now of your arse-kissing!'

'Come, ya Anna,' Ahmo Fariz called. 'I will take your place in the kitchen, come and speak to your friend.'

'So you are a very famous footballer?' I approached the counter slowly where Nick stood with his friends behind him.

'Well, I'm a footballer.' He nodded, running his fingers through his blond hair which fell in waves that almost touched his shoulders.

'And I just heard you say you enjoyed the food. I am very pleased. But you did not try our coffee.' I smiled.

'No.' He laughed as he pulled at the rolled-up sleeves of the white shirt that he wore loose over jeans. 'But maybe I'll come back another night to try one, hey?'

'Okay, yes, that is good. I shall look forward to your next visit, Nick.'

The silence that followed tempted me to say I was needed back in the kitchen. But for some reason the words did not come out. I stood, unable to utter a single sound as my brain flooded with thoughts about his lovely hair and his handsome face, his warm smile and his muscly arms, and his big and masculine hands – none of which I could say out loud.

Nick scratched his jawline. 'If I asked for your phone number again, Anna, would you let me have it now?'

I played with the buttons on the EFTPOS machine and did not answer. Because yes, of course, *yes*, I wanted very much for him to call me but what would I say if he did call? I did not want to be a mute on the telephone as well as in person.

'All I want is to get to know you better.' There was pleading in his voice.

'Why?'

'Because I like you.'

'Nick, you are a famous footballer. And you are charming and handsome. I imagine you would have many women interested in you. So why would you waste your time asking for *my* telephone number?'

'You think I'm charming and handsome, do you?' He tilted his head towards me.

'You did not answer my question.' I looked down, feeling myself blush.

'Are you serious, Anna? I actually have to tell you why I like you?'

I lifted my eyes to meet his. 'I am interested to know why me, yes.'

'Um, all right … well … you seem like a good person with a big heart and I like that. You're sweet and I can tell that you're smart. And,' he paused, 'and you're beautiful, of course.' He inspected his hands while he spoke. 'I'd like to take you out to get to know you more. What do you think? Would that be okay?' He asked with an earnest expression.

Tante Rosa, who had followed me out of the kitchen and stood less than three feet away, pretending to count the money in the till, yelled at Nick in English, 'No! Is no okay. I knows you. You no is Muslim! My eyes sees you with the womens. You is no good match for mine nice virgin Anwar. You no get no number for no telephone. You go to your houses please now and leaves Anwar alone.'

I could have stuck my head in the bread furnace and not been any redder in the face!

Nick's friends snorted with laughter but Nick kept a serious look on his face. 'I can assure you that I only have good intentions with Anna, um, Anwar. I would treat her with the greatest respect.'

'Anwar has honour.' Rosa crossed her arms across her chest so they sat up almost as high as her face. 'My eyes sees you in *Woman's Day* – you has no honour, no even no clothes!'

Nick lowered his eyes and his jaw muscles contracted. His friends leaned on each other and cried with laughter.

Tante Rosa pointed her finger at them. 'You and you! You shut up your mouse!'

This made them laugh even harder.

I gave Tante Rosa my back. 'Nick, I am very flattered you would like to ask for my phone number but I am simply too busy to spend time with you.'

He looked hurt but I continued, 'For instance, I am working at Black Salt tomorrow morning, and even though my lovely Tante Rosa is generous in giving me the evening off work here at Masri's, I am still too busy to see you because I will be enjoying a swim in the indoor fifty-metre pool at Challenge Stadium. I will be in lane eight, wearing a red swimsuit between 5.30 and 7 pm. So thank you very much for asking for my phone number, Nick, but I am afraid I must refuse because as you can see I am too busy.'

'No problems, that's fair enough.' He nodded. 'Thank you all for your hospitality. We had a great night.' And he turned to leave with his friends.

As he walked away, he winked a wink so discreet, that at first I thought I had imagined it, but then he smiled his slight smile and I knew that I had not.

No sooner had they left the restaurant, than the door was pushed open again and Nick marched purposefully back to the counter.

'Why coming you again, please? Why?' Tante Rosa shook her finger at Nick but he did not respond to or even look at her.

Instead, he leaned over the counter and whispered in my ear, 'Please do me a favour and don't google me tonight, Anna. See you tomorrow.'

His hot breath on my neck as he spoke sent shivers all the way down to my legs.

As soon as Nick left, Tante Rosa shouted at me that I was a fool if I thought anything would come of this and that he would break my foolish heart the second he tired of me. I ignored her loud pleas to Allah to burn down the house of Nick's mother's mother.

'Let me tell you the three words, Anwar, that will be your fate as surely as the sun will rise in the east in the morning. Three words if you let this sinning man into your heart. *Hamel. Weh. Wahida.*' She held up one finger at a time as she enunciated each word. 'This will be your future, Anwar, hear my words and be warned. Pregnant. And. Alone.'

I did not respond to her as I hummed while I mopped the floor under the bench. I kept my head down because I could not make my smile disappear.

I was even smiling now as I lifted Mama's head off my thighs and pulled out my journal. Remembering Nick had finally settled down my trembling after Mama's screaming.

Looking at the journal I had in my hands now, I whispered to Noor's photo '*Ya rohi ana. Shufti, ya Noor? Aho! Shufti?*' I hoped she had seen. I hoped she had seen *everything* that happened. I would never know either way.

I flipped open the journal to where the ribbon was left from last night and started writing on the next fresh page.

Habibti *Noor,*

Do you remember Mama telling us the story about the day that Tante Rosa invited her back to her home when they were sixteen and that when she met Baba there for the first time, it felt to her as if she had spent her entire life missing him?

I know now what she meant.

The person I have been missing is Nick. Nicholas Harding, but he prefers Nick.

His eyes, Noor, it was his eyes. They held deep-blue oceans of pain in them. He had a happy smile but his eyes were filled with pain. And I recognised that in him, as though I was holding up a mirror to myself.

I have been worrying about why I never once had that yearning feeling in nineteen years. I thought that maybe the tragedy of our family was so great the grief swallowed up the part of me that was capable of such desire. But it was there all along, I had just not met the person to make me feel it yet. Until today.

I am so very grateful for this new distraction that has come into my life. Instead of sitting here as I do every night, consumed with worries about Mama and Ricky, and with sadness at the past, I now have something new and exciting to think about that lightens my heart instead of weighing it down.

I wish you were here so we could sit together and I could tell you every wonderful detail but I know you are here in my heart, my sweet one.

With all my love,

A x

I put the journal away and resisted the urge, with my phone right there within arm's reach, to search for Nick's name. For him to have run back into Masri's the way he did, it meant he must have been terribly worried about what I might find out about him online. I knew these were stories or pictures I did not wish to see. So why go searching for them only to upset myself?

Instead, I reached for my phone and responded to the two emails I found there from the organisation I volunteered with. Then, seeing it was past three in the morning, I lay myself down next to Mama and waited for Noor to come and be with me in my dreams. In my nightmares.

LILY – MONDAY

I slept in. I mean really slept in. The *Gilmore Girls* binge-watching session and what ended up being three-quarters of a bottle of wine left over from my cooking (when I didn't usually drink) fried my brain enough for me to think I'd set the alarm when I hadn't.

I woke up at nine and was out the door and driving to the hospital at four past nine with a pounding headache and a gurgling stomach.

Because there was a God and he was indeed great, peak-hour traffic had mostly passed and I arrived at the hospital only ten minutes late for the start of the ward round at ten. But now God wanted to play funny buggers and not one street parking spot remained. I couldn't afford to pay for the carpark so the tantalising vacant bays inside the gates remained out of bounds for me.

For a fleeting moment, I considered parking in the clearway, but I'd had my car towed a month ago for a similar offence (parked in a drive-way – I was especially late that day), and Nick would give me hell if he had to fork out for it to be released from the impoundment lot again. So I drove Dad's old BMW around the same blocks over and over and by the time I ran into the hospital, I was now twenty minutes late.

Throwing on my lab coat in the lift, I rubbed my index finger across my front teeth and threw two chewies into my mouth. I raced onto the ward towards the group of students at the opposite end of the corridor and tried to slink in among them so the supervisor wouldn't notice. Problem was, none of them were fifth year med students. This was not my group.

I'd come to the endoscopy unit where I'd worked over summer on level four. I was supposed to be on the Harry Perkins ward, one level down. I bolted back along the ward in the direction of the stairs. But just as I was sprinting past the lift, the doors opened so I thought that would be quicker and hopped in.

It was not quicker. The lift went past level three and straight down to ground where two orderlies were waiting to wheel in a patient's bed. Then it stopped at levels one *and* two. *Fuck*.

I finally arrived where I was supposed to be and saw my group were standing in a huddle, listening to the supervisor. Again, I tried to sidle in unnoticed, but sidling in unnoticed was only possible if the supervisor was not staring balefully at you.

'Hi,' I panted. 'Sorry, parking problems.'

Silence. Everyone stared.

Then the supervisor exhaled with a whistle through his nose and peered at me from underneath bushy grey eyebrows. He was short but huge. One of his shirt buttons had popped open and his hairy stomach bulged through the gap.

'Are you sure it wasn't all that time spent fixing your hair that made you late, Medusa?'

I was pretty sure he wasn't comparing me to the goddess in a good way.

'The first five rooms we do each morning on this round are

the hospice beds.' His voice was spectacularly squeaky, as if he'd downed a bowl of helium instead of cereal for breakfast. He stopped to wipe his clammy face with a big white handkerchief.

Ew, that was *a lot* of sweat.

He continued, 'You know what a hospice bed is, don't you, Daryl Hannah?'

Daryl who? Wasn't that a boy's name? But I nodded.

As though I'd shaken my head, he continued, 'A hospice is where people come to die. The people in these rooms are never going home. Most of them have had chemotherapy. Most of them have lost their hair. So could you please show a little more respect and compassion and turn up on time tomorrow, with your lovely long ringlets tied back so you are not reminding the people in there that although they may have only moments left to live, you're growing hair to your feet?' At the word 'feet' he just about squealed.

I gulped, accidentally swallowing the gum.

'Young lady, do you care to share your name with us, seeing as you're the only one here who hasn't bothered with a name badge?' He used his handkerchief to wipe down the top of his shiny scalp.

'Lily Harding,' I said to the floor.

'Excuse me? Could you speak in a voice human ears can register, please?

I cleared my throat. 'Lily Harding.'

'Harding? Adam's girl?'

I swallowed the lump in my throat at the mention of Dad. 'Yes.'

'Ah, there you go, then! Great, great man, Adam was. Top anaesthetist. Top bloke too. I heard he had a daughter coming through. Excellent, excellent. Very sorry about your loss, Miss

Harding.' He didn't sound annoyed anymore. He looked at me with the 'sympathy face.' I'd come to recognise from people who knew Dad.

Then he continued addressing the others, back to his mean Helium Man voice again. 'So remember, you are fifth-year medical students. You're not doctors. You're not even *close* to being doctors. In these five rooms, more than any other, patients don't need to feel like guinea pigs being watched by the likes of you lot, so you will be as inconspicuous as possible. Later in the morning, we'll leave the hospice and continue with the rest of the oncology round. I'll decide then if any of you are to have a more active role there, but here you stand back, watch, listen, learn and shut up. Understood?' His eyes darted around the group.

We all nodded in unison and followed him into the first room. It was hard not to gasp at the living corpse in the bed. I was lucky, I'd never lost anyone I loved to cancer. This was the first time I'd been this physically close to someone dying of cancer. And its awfulness knocked the wind out of me. It had literally eaten chunks of this person's skin away from underneath their chin down to their throat, revealing a yellowed jelly layer of tissue. I couldn't tell if it was a male or female until Helium Man said, 'Hello, Gloria.'

I looked at my shoes so Gloria and Helium Man couldn't see me cry.

Twelve weeks of this for someone like me who fell to pieces at everything. I was so screwed.

We went into three more rooms, seeing almost the same thing – skeletal, hairless bodies gasping for air in their sleep. In each room, the sight took my breath away. And in each room I learned next to nothing because I was focusing on my shoes the entire time and listening to my inner voice repeating, 'You don't belong here'.

But in the last room on the palliative ward, it was different.

Sitting up in bed was a woman who looked not much older than me. She was ghostly pale and stick thin but she was awake. She had a full head of chestnut hair in a short bob and she was alert, looking straight at us.

'Good morning, Jenny,' Helium Man said in the kind tone he used for his patients, not his students. 'How's it going today?'

She sucked air in shakily and it took her a while to say, 'Pain is so bad in my neck. I need more morphine.'

He nodded and checked her chart. 'Jenny, you're on an awful lot of morphine as it is. Are you sure you want it increased?'

She shut her eyes. 'Yes.'

When she opened them again, she looked at me and made a weird sound, like she wanted to laugh, but it came out like a moan. 'It's you.'

What? Who did she think I was? Was I expected to respond?

'Could you dose her up with more pain relief right now? She's really struggling, as you can see.' A male voice spoke from behind me.

I turned around and standing in the ensuite doorway was Blue Eyes from the café.

I felt myself blush, but he wasn't looking at me. He was staring hard at Helium Man. 'She's not getting enough relief, no matter how many times she hits that PCA. She needs more and she needs it now.'

'Certainly, Toby. I'll see that your wife is comfortable as quickly as is humanly possible,' Helium Man replied gently.

Excuse me? Did Helium Man just say 'your wife'? That was his *wife*? She was dying in a hospice and he was in the café downstairs two days ago practically coming onto me? I was dizzy with rage.

I crossed my arms over my chest and gave him my filthiest stare. He stared back at me with a look I couldn't read. We stayed like that while Helium Man played around with Jenny's drip.

Toby finally looked away and walked up to Jenny's bedside. He told her he'd be back in a few minutes, then he left with his eyes fixed on the door.

A couple of minutes later, Helium Man said, 'I've just written the order for more morphine for you, Jenny, and I've overridden the PCA so you'll have less pain in a matter of minutes.'

'Thanks.' She sighed. 'I want to talk to her. Alone.' She pointed a trembling finger straight at me.

What? Why?

Oh Christ, I needed to pee.

Helium Man gave me an odd look. 'You two know each other?'

'She's Toby's friend,' Jenny answered, not taking her eyes off me.

I froze. And I mean I actually froze. It was if I'd been dunked in ice all the way up to my neck.

Everyone followed Helium Man out and she beckoned me over. I walked in baby steps to her bedside.

'I'm so sorry you're in here.' I was embarrassed at how unsteady my voice was and how my eyes were welling up again.

'Tobes – he's a good guy.' She paused. 'I left him. Then I got sick.' She stopped and grimaced and she took a sharp breath in. When she exhaled, it was a loud wheeze.

'Are you okay, Jenny? Do you want me to call a nurse?'

She shook her finger 'no' while she coughed, then coughed more. When the coughing fit subsided she said, 'He took me back when I got sick.'

She put her hand out towards me palm side up and I placed mine on top. Her hand was so tiny and frail it felt as if I could break it just by holding it. It was also icy-cold.

'Toby,' she whispered, 'is a really good guy.'

'Jenny, I don't understand. Why are you telling me this?'

She laughed – a dying person's laugh, moany and wheezy. Chills raced down my spine.

'You're Rapunzel from the café with the bluey-green eyes.'

My belly did a tumble-turn. He called me Rapunzel?

'But ... I don't ... I don't get it. He's your *husband*.'

'No, I left.' She winced as she reached for the phone on her bedside table. 'Give me your number?' she panted handing me the phone.

Without thinking, I keyed my number in. She took her phone back and my own phone vibrated in my pocket seconds later.

'That's his number.' She rested her back on the pillows.

'Jenny, I don't know that I'm comfortable having your husband's ...' I started to say but she let out a howl that turned into a drawn-out sob.

Was she crying because of the pain? Because she was dying? Because of Toby? I had no idea how to comfort her.

'Ring him next week,' she whispered through her tears. 'Promise me.'

I nodded mutely.

'Say promise,' she urged.

'Promise,' I whispered back.

She closed her eyes. 'Good girl.' Then she moaned, clutching her neck, 'Ow, ow, oh God!'

I stroked her damp hair. The nurse walked in and gave me a perfunctory nod as she set about topping up the drip.

Jenny whimpered for a minute or two longer but then the panting settled right down and her eyes stayed closed. Her cheeks were wet so I pulled out a tissue from the box on the bedside table and wiped the tears away. She stayed as she was.

What did I do now? Was I supposed to leave her and catch up to my group? What if she woke up and nobody was here? I couldn't leave her.

Just like all other rooms in the palliative ward, this one looked more like an apartment than a hospital. I imagined the hours that husbands, wives, parents, children would have spent on the pull-out sofa beds, trying to catch a few hours of sleep with heavy hearts and anxious minds. I pictured family members taking turns making tea in the kitchenette in the corner, and finding comfort in a cup of tea poured into the colourful polka dot mugs while they stared at the painting of dolphins, wondering how they got caught up in the nightmare they were living.

Had Toby pulled those navy curtains closed at night and dimmed the downlights before kissing his wife goodnight? The wife who left him?

Eventually I heard footsteps coming into the room. Toby entered and stepped to the other side of the bed, and we looked at each other with Jenny lying between us.

My pulse sped up.

He tugged at his ear. 'I know what you're thinking, but you've got the wrong impression of me,' he said in a low voice. 'Jen and I, well, it's not what it looks like.'

'She told me.'

'Oh.'

He had dark circles under his eyes.

'You must be exhausted.'

He shrugged. 'Did they up the morphine yet?' He frowned at the drip.

'They did, yeah.'

'Okay. Good. That's good.' His drawn face relaxed a little.

Jenny half opened her eyes and breathed hard through her nose. 'Rapunzel and Toby sitting in a tree,' she slurred.

He rolled his eyes and smiled at me.

Oh. My. God. He was crazy hot.

'You're a shocker of the highest order, Jennifer,' he murmured to Jenny, chuckling softly.

She didn't answer, she was out to us again.

'I should go and catch up with my group,' I whispered. 'I didn't want her to be alone, but now that you're back ...'

'Thanks for staying with her, Rapunzel.' He stared at me again and it was like we were back in the café.

The butterflies inside me slammed into each other so hard I wondered if he could see my stomach moving.

I could feel his eyes on my back as I walked out. I went to the staff toilet and locked myself in a stall. Standing with my back against the door, I took long slow breaths with my eyes shut until my heart rate returned to normal. Then I pulled out my phone and stared at Toby's phone number.

I had a missed call from Arielle so I sent her a text:

Hey A! Missed call from you? What's up?

Nothing. Bored shitless – property law's even worse than
superannuation law. I want to be back on holidays. How's it
going there?

I'm locked in a toilet freaking myself out on the palliative care
unit.

Oh no! Want to ditch it and meet me at Stimulatte?

No, it's only my first day. I can't ditch. Later though? 5?

5 is good. See you then ☺

I threw cold water on my face, twisted my hair up into a bun,
and walked out of the bathroom in search of Helium Man and
my group.

NICK – MONDAY

Press. Crap. I threw my head back against the headrest and shut my eyes for a few seconds. There was a television crew on standby directly outside the radiology clinic less than fifty metres away from where I'd parked. How did they know? How did they *always* know?

Sometimes I really did wonder if my phone was tapped or if they had people watching me. I'd never said as much. I didn't want to come across as paranoid or obnoxious. But when they were already here waiting for me, when the only person who knew my appointment time was Aaron, I had to wonder.

They spotted me and the sports journalist jogged over, followed closely by the cameraman. I knew this reporter. He was a bigger arsehole than most of the others.

He made a circular motion with his index finger and the red light lit up on the camera as I got out of the car and walked around to the footpath. It was at least twenty degrees hotter outside than it was in the car and I started dripping sweat from my armpits right away.

'Morning, Nick.'

'Brad,' I replied through clenched teeth, pulling my sunglasses down off the top of my head.

'Hear you're booked in for an MRI this morning, Nick. Is it the same problem that had you miss the end of last season? Are the stress fractures back, Nick?'

He put the microphone close to my face, reaching up to do so because he was a good foot shorter than me. I kept my mouth shut and limped quickly in front of him. The foot was so sore today that I couldn't even fake it.

'Must be a big concern if you're having an MRI. Stress fractures would be enough to keep you out for the majority of the season wouldn't they, Nick? That's a fair limp you've got there.' He was right on my tail with his nasally voice ringing in my ears and the cameraman had run around in front of me and was now walking backwards, filming.

I pushed open the door to the clinic and immediately sent Craig a text message:

Just arrived for scan. Brad Marshall outside. Got footage of me limping.

Ignore it – don't stress. Good luck with the MRI.

I made myself known to the dumbstruck receptionist – Samantha, according to her name tag.

The other patients in the waiting room all stared at us as she ushered me into a private waiting room only to tell me that the radiologist had been held up and would be another half hour at least.

I sifted through the magazines but they were all women's ones and they were so outdated that an interview with Robin Williams was on one of the covers. I flicked through Facebook and Instagram on my phone and read the latest football news. Half an hour came and went with no sign of the radiologist.

Samantha came back in and batted her eyelashes. 'So sorry for the delay. Can I get you a coffee while you're waiting, Mr Harding?'

'No, I'm good, thanks.'

'Well, I'm right here if you need anything,' she purred. 'Anything at all.'

When she turned to go she tugged down on the tight red skirt that barely covered her butt and gave her hips a little wiggle, looking over her shoulder with a smile. But Samantha's skirt and her butt wiggling didn't hold my attention. All I could think about was Anna from when I saw her last night.

We'd only just been seated in her uncle's busy restaurant when Joel and Bruce figured out what my sudden hankering for Egyptian food was all about. They saw me stealing looks at Anna and they laughed.

'Egyptian food, hey, Harding?' Joel smirked. 'More like a piece of Egyptian arse!'

Bruce snorted, 'Come on, Nick, leave her alone, mate. Look at her – she's like twelve years old. She's only a baby lamb.'

'And the wolf is going in for the kill.' Joel rubbed his hands together.

I picked up a menu and busied myself reading it. Heat prickled the back of my neck.

'She's pretty for an Arab, though. I get it, mate. That kind of innocence on a hot body, yeah, I get it.' Joel nudged me with his elbow.

I put the laminated menu down and glared at him.

He raised his arms up in surrender. 'Don't worry, mate. She's all yours!'

'So, Nick,' Bruce grinned. 'Did you actually make it back to your place with that blonde slapper you were dry humping on the dance floor last night? Or did you just fuck in her the taxi so you didn't get your sheets dirty?'

They reached out to each other across the table for a high-five.

A group of semi-pissed men came over to our table to give us their take on the game.

Bruce and Joel settled down during the meal, still guffawing if they caught me looking at Anna. But the drive home was insufferable.

'Oh, *Niiick*,' Joel mimicked Anna, 'I will be in *rrred* swimsuit, hokay?'

Bruce, crying with laughter, joined in. 'No, no, you must *rrrememberrr* what my Aunty says, I am nice Muslim *virrrgin*, hokay? Oh, mate, to think I was going to say no to coming out tonight. That was totally worth having the missus crack the shits over! Best laugh I've had for ages.'

I waited until we were in my driveway and then I switched off the engine and turned to look at them both. 'You pricks talk about her like that again and I swear I'll kill the pair of you. Show some respect. And you can find your own way home, I'm not driving you.'

They both doubled over in their seats, bellowing with laughter. I left them in the car and stormed out.

'Hey, Nick,' Bruce called. 'Better have your excuses ready for Craig at training tomorrow, mate. I saw the look on his face when you were throwing back shots last night and, mate, you're fucked! When are you going to pull your head out of your arse and realise you can't drink during season?'

'Or is that the only way you can get the old boy up?' Joel said. 'Bit of Dutch courage needed with the ladies, mate?'

I slammed my front door hard.

I was angry because they were right. They were right about me needing to pull my head out of my arse and stop drinking during season, and they were right about me and Anna. She *was* just like a little lamb with her huge trusting caramel eyes, and I was indeed a wolf.

Of course, I wanted to have sex with her. And right this minute I wanted her more than I'd ever wanted anyone else. Her smile when she saw me walk into the restaurant gave me goose bumps. And every single time she looked at me from under her long fringe, it sent the adrenaline soaring through me.

But all I was hoping for, for now, was to be allowed into her life. There was a lot going on behind those beautiful eyes – secrets that I wanted to know.

My thoughts were interrupted by the arrival of the radiologist. He looked at me over the clipboard he was holding.

'Morning, Mr Harding,' he mumbled, straightening his glasses. 'Sorry for the delay. You don't mind if we take a quick selfie before we do the scan, do you?'

Was he serious?

'Ah, yeah, sure thing.'

He pulled out his phone and put an arm around me, resting his hand awkwardly on my shoulder. We both fake smiled.

'Thanks for that. I'll be a popular dad tonight.'

Finally the scan was done and I was relieved to find no press waiting on my way out of the clinic.

* * *

Three hours later, I was back in the club rooms to meet with Aaron. He wouldn't say anything over the phone.

The head physiotherapist, along with Craig and the head of conditioning were all waiting for me in Aaron's room.

Oh, God.

My shoulders slumped and my stomach sank. Leaning up against the examination bed was a pair of crutches.

Oh, God.

'Take a seat, mate.' Aaron blew out hard through flared nostrils and said the few words that would see me sidelined for months and could perhaps even end my career. 'Multiple metatarsal stress fractures.'

I felt myself sway, so I gripped the seat of the stool I was perched on with both hands and watched Aaron's mouth moving. I didn't hear another word and shut my eyes.

'Nick. Nick! You okay, mate?' Craig was standing in front me. 'You look like you're about to faint.'

'Yeah, I'm okay, just got a bit dizzy for a second there. Sorry, Aaron, can you run through that again?'

'I said it's time to go home, Nick, and rest it for ten weeks, mate,' Aaron repeated. 'We've laid out a rehab program for you between us – here's a copy for you too, Craig. So the plan is to get you doing non-weight-bearing sessions at the gym every day, followed by a hydrotherapy session. We'll reassess each week and up the program as we need to.'

I nodded again and he continued. 'I'll get one of the dieticians to give you a call and talk to you about getting back onto an off-season diet. You'll need to swallow a shitload of bone-building minerals too, but just check that they're not on the banned list first before you buy any. We'll order another MRI in five weeks to check progress, and then again in ten weeks, and hopefully your foot's as good as gold by then and we'll take it from there.'

'Ten weeks?' Craig squeaked. 'Isn't that overkill?'

Aaron shook his head. 'Under normal circumstances it'd be more like six to eight weeks. But this is Nick's second onset in six months. We have to be careful here. We can't risk getting him back out on the park too early. The fact that the fractures are already back suggests we may have rushed his rehab last year. So we have to avoid that this time.'

'By the time I'm back to match fitness, it'll be June or July. You're telling me half of my season's essentially over, right?' I asked Aaron the question I already knew the answer to.

'Sorry, Nick.'

Craig was massaging his temples. 'So you heard Aaron,' he said flatly. 'Turn up for the gym or pool every morning and physio in the arvo. Don't worry about showing up for team meetings until about week six or seven. Obviously forget training, just do the rehab. And like last year, on game days throw on a suit and sit in the box so you at least get a feel for the competition.' He sighed long and loud. 'Fucked if I know who to put on the wing. Dave was good replacing you but he's out with his knee. Maybe Chris?' He arched his eyebrows at me and I shrugged.

Chris was shit on the wing.

'We'll release a statement tonight at training with a live cross. You want to be there for that?' Aaron asked me.

I couldn't shake my head any faster.

I headed out into the car park on the new crutches. They dug into my ribs, and after only a few steps I could tell exactly where the blisters on my palms would be. I remembered how getting in and out of the car, let alone walking, was a nightmare.

I hated what my injury meant for the club. I felt bad for my teammates who were used to how I played and now needed to get accustomed to someone new. I felt accountable for every game where they'd get creamed on the wing. And I was embarrassed that the club was still required to pay me.

But most of all, I was devastated for myself. My life had no point when I didn't play.

I sped away from the car park with sweat dripping into my eyes, blurring my vision. The fractures were back. They were back. And they were even worse than last time.

I pulled the car over to the kerb a few blocks away, staggered out and vomited in the gutter.

Once I was back in the driver's seat, I hugged the steering wheel, blasted the air-con on, and breathed deep until the nausea settled. And then I rang the only person I wanted to talk to. I listened to the dial tone and prayed that she'd pick up. She did.

'*Fuuuuuck,*' Lily whispered down the phone when I told her the results. 'I had a bad feeling about that on Saturday.'

'I know,' I moaned. 'What am I going to do?'

'Hey, it's okay. It'll be all right. Listen, I've got some fresh lasagne that I made for you yesterday. Actually it's not really lasagne because I forgot to put the lasagne in it. I'll duck over tonight and bring it over okay?'

I smiled to myself. 'You forgot to put the lasagne in last time too.'

'Shut up, Nick. It tastes just fine without it.'

'There's no need for you to bring me food, Lil. I've already got a freezer full of your meals anyway. I only rang because I wanted to tell someone.'

'You know, I can always repeat this unit. I've got an arsehole of a supervisor; I hate the cancer ward so badly I can't even tell you. It's only lunch time and I don't even know how I'm going to get through the rest of the first day, let alone the whole twelve weeks. So I don't mind chucking this round. What about if I move in while you're stuck on crutches?' she said. 'I could help you with cooking and stuff and I could walk Bluey. Honestly, you'd be doing me a favour,'

'Thanks anyway, but I don't want you doing that. No way. I'm a big boy you know. I can look after myself.'

If Lily didn't pass this oncology unit, she wouldn't just have to repeat the unit, she'd have to repeat the whole year. I couldn't believe she was prepared to suffer through another year of study that she hated just to care for me. Well, actually, I could believe it – that was Lil, she'd do anything for me. I felt a huge surge of love for my little sister.

'I wish Mum would come home,' I thought out loud.

She sighed. 'You and me both. But I'm right here.'

'Thanks.' I swallowed. 'Lil, they've paid me three-quarters of a million dollars for the season. To do what? Plus after last year's crappy end of the season, losing all those games in a row, our membership numbers are down. So the club's pushing hard for a final's start this year to motivate people to sign up. We can't get to the finals unless I'm out there on the wing, it's that simple.'

'Don't do that. You can't put that kind of pressure on yourself. You're not responsible for the entire club. That's crazy.'

'I'm their highest paid footballer. Yes, I bloody well am responsible! I've got one and a half million dollars in endorsements for this season alone,' I moaned. 'Kids aren't going to nag their parents for footy boots·if I'm not seen running in them. Men aren't going to rush out and buy aftershave or underwear being modelled by some loser who keeps getting injured. The advertisers made it crystal clear, for products to sell, people have to want to be me. Every single campaign I'm in is based on kids wanting to be me, blokes wanting to be me, women wanting their partners to be me. Who the fuck's going to want to be me now?' It was hard to take a deep breath as the enormity of it hit me.

'Hey, hey, hey.' She used her gentlest voice. 'Stop talking as if your injury's deliberate. None of this is your fault. They'll make squillions off you later in the season and every season after that so don't even worry about that.'

It didn't matter what she said to try and make me feel better, the bottom line was that I was worthless unless I was out there playing.

***

Bluey whined through the back gate when I pulled into the drive.

I balanced on one crutch to pat him. He sniffed the crutches and whined pitifully. Was he smart enough to remember that these aluminium sticks meant no runs together for us?

'We're going to have find you a dog walker again, mate.' I scratched under his chin.

I defrosted some pasta from one of the dozen meals Lily had left here and flicked on the TV. I watched Saturday's taped game and picked apart my performance.

My phone rang at three o'clock. It was Craig. Channel Seven had requested that I be at the live cross as they broke my story. We were contracted to them so I had no choice but to be at the club by quarter to six.

***

There was nothing I hated more than live television. As they set up the bright lights and cameras in my face, I began to overheat. The girl who fixed my earplug in place wiped her hands on her skirt afterwards. My mouth was dry the whole time we were on air but most of the questions were directed at Craig and Aaron, who both gave away as little information as they could about my injury and prognosis without looking like we had something to hide.

Then I was asked if I was hopeful of coming back this season.

'You better believe it,' I answered with a smile and a double thumbs up.

I checked my watch, 6.35. Not a lot of time to get to Challenge Stadium before Anna left at seven. I pressed on the accelerator.

The closest parking spot was a hundred metres from the entrance. I checked my watch again – 6.50. No time for crutches. I jogged inside. Each time my foot landed on the bitumen it sent searing pain up my shin.

I hobbled into reception and smiled at the people hanging around there.

'On ya, Harding!'

'Love your work, Harding!'

'*Oh my God*! It's Nick Harding!'

'Hey, Harding, can I please get a selfie with you?'

One selfie turned into four.

I paid for a swim and took the ramp into the pool area. It wasn't just the humidity that was making my palms sweat. I hadn't felt this excited about a girl since my crush on Arielle in high school.

The pool was packed. There were dozens of swimmers going up and down each lane. I couldn't remember which lane she said she'd be in. Red bathers, look for red bathers. I couldn't see any. My heart sank as I walked further along the width of the pool.

But then I found her. In the farthest lane, I spotted her gorgeous olive skin in a bright red one-piece.

Unable to control what I knew must be an idiotic grin, I squatted down near the end of her lane, putting all my weight on the right with my sore foot out in front.

Her freestyle was flawless as she glided towards me. It looked completely effortless and with a beautiful steady rhythm. I was ridiculously turned on watching her bare legs kick through the water.

She saw me just as she approached the end and a smile escaped before she turned her face back into the water for the last couple of strokes. When she reached the wall, she rested her forearms up on the edge and with one hand she took off her goggles and shook out her hair.

'Hey.' I leaned my head down close to her so she could hear me above the noise. 'Sorry I'm so late.'

'I thought you decided not to come,' she panted.

'I was always going to come. But I had to do an interview at the last minute. Sorry.'

'Oh yes, of course, I see.' She wiped the dripping water from the tip of her nose and off her eyebrows.

'Do you want to grab a coffee, Anna?' I took a couple of slow breaths to settle my racing heart.

'Hokay.' She nodded several quick little nods and pulled herself out of the pool in one graceful motion so that we stood face to face. 'I am happy you came, Nick.' She beamed and walked past me to reach for a blue beach towel on a nearby plastic chair.

Somewhere in the distance people were calling my name but as I watched her wrap herself up in the towel and dry off her hair, I heard nothing. She was tight and toned and had curves in all the right places. I couldn't stop staring. I gave up altogether on trying to slow the heart rate down.

She looked around us and then at me. 'Does this happen everywhere you go? This shouting of your name and this cheering, and people taking photographs of you? It seems like everybody here is watching you.'

'Yeah, it's pretty normal. Not just for me though. It's like this for my friends too.'

'This is a hard way to live. Being well known brings too much pressure.'

'Mmm, yeah. You ready to go?' I was suddenly uncomfortable with everyone's eyes on us and felt the need to shield her.

'Of course I am not ready to go.' She laughed. 'I am dressed in only a towel! I will get changed into some proper clothing and you will wait here, hokay?'

I stared at her calves until she disappeared from my view into the change rooms.

While she was gone, I signed autographs for kids and posed for more selfies with teenagers. One girl in a teeny bikini, who wouldn't have even been sixteen-years-old yet, cocked her head to the side and with an inviting smile asked me if I'd like her number. I pretended I didn't hear her.

'Hi, Nick,' came a breathy voice from behind me.

I turned around to see a girl I didn't know. She was spray-tanned orange and wearing tiny gym shorts and a crop top that was way too small for the breasts that swamped it.

'Hi.' I looked away as another kid called out to me.

'It's me ... Monique.' She poked the tip of my shoulder with two fingers.

I turned my attention back to her. Monique? Who was Monique? 'Oh yeah, Monique. How's it going?'

'You don't have a clue who I am, do you? Do you, Nick?' she said with spite, loudly enough for people walking past to turn their heads.

'No, I do,' I lied, trying not to look at her orange boobs falling out of the bottom of her crop top.

'Bullshit you do. Well, you were bloody keen to know me at Pulse, even if you don't remember me now.' She spat, flicking her long bleached-blonde ponytail.

Shit. I sucked in the humid air. 'I'm sorry, Monique. If we met at Pulse I was most likely pissed, so that's why I'm a bit slow remembering. I know it's lame, sorry. It's good to see you again anyway.' I felt about a foot tall.

Anna appeared beside me. She smiled at Monique. 'Hello,' she said brightly.

Monique looked her up and down. 'Nice clothes.'

Anna was in a spotted yellow T-shirt tucked into striped overall shorts along with the same purple boots she had on yesterday. 'Thank you,' she said in a faltering voice.

Monique stared at her some more, rolling her tongue around inside her cheek. 'Don't go thinking you're anything special, sweetie. You're probably the last girl left in Perth he hasn't screwed yet. He's obviously gone through the pretty ones.'

Anna jerked her head back as if she'd been slapped.

Monique then turned back to me. 'You're scum, Nick Harding – and everyone knows it. I can't believe you don't remember me. Thought I gave you the deepest best blowjob you ever had. Your words, Nick, your words.'

My voice cracked, 'There's no need for that.' I looked at Anna who was studying her black-painted fingernails.

'I am ready to leave now, thank you, Nick,' Anna said in a barely audible voice.

I put a protective arm around Anna's shoulders as we walked out.

'Have fun with your woggy dyke, Nick!' Monique called after us and I felt Anna stiffen.

I ignored the other people who called my name and shouted congratulations for Saturday's win. The bile was thick in my mouth.

As soon as we were away from the stadium, out far enough in the car park that nobody could hear us, I stopped and turned Anna by the shoulders to face me.

'I'm sorry! I'm so sorry that happened. I had no idea who that girl was. I honestly can't even remember meeting her.' I held my forehead. 'And those horrible things she said to you, they had nothing to do with you. She was just trying to rile me.'

Anna's bright smile from before was gone. She looked at me steadily and spoke in a quiet measured voice without breaking eye contact. 'I will tell you truthfully what I am thinking, Nick. I am thinking that I am not a girl who wants to be forgotten. And I am not a girl who will sleep with you just because you are a famous footballer. I am a girl who wants something real and meaningful.' She swallowed. 'I understand that we are coming from very different cultures and walks of life, the two of us. But when you came to my uncle's restaurant, I was happy. That is what I know for certain – that seeing you made me happy when I had not felt much happiness lately. And I felt the same way again seeing you here tonight. I do not know if in a day or in a week or in a year we will realise that we are not suited to each other, but at the moment I feel a pull towards you that I cannot explain.' She took a long breath before continuing. 'However, I am only willing to get to know you if you have a genuine interest in me – not if your intention is to sleep with me and then forget about me. I am not prepared to be a scorned girl like the one we just met.' She rubbed her arms and shivered.

Who was this girl? What had she done to me? All that mattered was what she thought of me. And I had no freaking idea why that was so important. But it was.

'I'm being completely honest, Anna, when I say that more than anything in the world, I want to get to know you and hopefully come to mean something to you. And I could *never* forget you. Even if you walked away now, I'll never forget you.'

She nodded. 'Am I a fool, Nick? Am I a fool to still be standing here talking to you after what happened in there? There is also the knowledge that my aunty recognised you from being in magazines with other women. And you asked me not to google you – that cannot be good. If you are somebody who has hurt other girls, will you make a fool of me too?'

'No. I promise you, no.'

'Why? How is this different?'

I took a deep breath. 'I admit that I have been with a lot of girls. I'm not proud of it. I'm actually ashamed of myself for it. I know it sounds crazy, but it feels like I was meant to meet you when I did and that I was meant to start fresh – with you. Yesterday, I desperately wanted to bring meaning to my life because it had been toxic for a long time and I couldn't remember the last time I was genuinely happy. So I made a promise to myself to become a better person. And then, only a few hours later, I met you. I don't know what else to say except that since I met you I feel like a different man to the one I was before. And whatever it is that's going on here between us is special to me.'

She bit her lip and looked away. 'Yesterday? That was when you wanted a fresh start? Only yesterday? So the day before yesterday?'

I looked at the ground.

'Oh,' she said in a small voice.

'The day before yesterday is what I'm leaving behind. I'm sorry I have a past to be ashamed of, and I'm sorry that my past goes right up until two days ago. Look, you can go home and google me if you want. You'll find images of me possibly drunk and with different girls. I can't make that stuff go away. But it's over now, I swear it is.' I clasped my hands behind my head and waited for her answer.

She looked long and hard at me. 'I believe you.'

She believed me?

I couldn't do anything to break that trust, to break that innocent heart. It struck me again how fragile she was.

'I'm so relieved to hear that.' I dropped my arms from behind my head and felt the tension leave my shoulders. 'You know, you come across as such a strong person but there's also something fragile about you. I barely know you, but I have this overwhelming need to look after you, to protect you.'

'Hmm, "fragile" is my favourite word, Nick. Such a beautiful word "fragile". I wrote a poem I called "Fragile" only this morning.'

'Did you really?'

'I did indeed. But you are mistaken. I am not fragile and I do not need looking after. Believe me, I know how to look after myself.' Her eyes had a hardened look when she said that.

'I can believe that. How old are you, by the way?'

'Nineteen.'

I raised my eyebrows. 'Really? I thought you were older.'

'For someone with so much experience with women, you have not yet learned that you are supposed to tell a woman she looks younger not older than her age?' She smiled for the first time since we'd walked out of the pool. 'Maybe there are still some things left that I can teach you.'

I wanted to know all that lay beneath the surface of this nineteen-year-old woman-child who had a favourite word and a sexy husky laugh and who wasn't afraid to lay down the law to a man she'd only just met.

'Did you drive here?' I asked.

'No, I came by bus.'

'Do you want to come in my car then to go get that coffee?'

'Oh. Ah, no thank you, Nick. You see, when you said 'grab a coffee', I thought you meant here in the pool coffee shop. I did not realise that you wanted to go somewhere different. My mother will be worried if I am much later than expected. So I will catch a bus home now and perhaps we can meet again another day?'

My heart sank. 'Can't you ring your mother and say you'll be late? We've hardly had a chance to talk. I don't know anything about you yet.'

'Why such a hurry? We have tomorrow and the day after and the day after that.'

'Well, let me drive you home then.'

'Hokay, Nick, thank you. That is a kind offer.'

'Your English is amazing considering you only left Egypt a year ago.'

'Yes that would be amazing if it was the case but I have been speaking English my whole life. I was educated in English schools. But I am trying to improve. My uncle tells me I still sound too formal and foreign.'

'No, you sound perfect. I really like your accent … It's sexy.'

'Is that so?' Her eyes twinkled. 'Well, I really like your accent too.'

'Do you think it's sexy though?' I grinned.

She laughed but didn't answer.

My gaze dropped from her lips to her neck and to the line of her cleavage, peeking out just a fraction. I desperately wished I could kiss all those parts. The tension was playing havoc inside my shorts.

I walked her to my car and opened the door for her before getting in the driver's side.

'Your foot is very bad, isn't it Nick? I can see you are in pain. Did you have the scan?' She asked once we were both in the car.

'I did, yeah. It's broken,' I admitted with a heavy sigh. 'I've got stress fractures in the bones, which means lots of small breaks.'

She rested her hand on my forearm. My skin under her touch felt red hot.

'Oh, no! So you cannot play football?'

'Not for the next two and a half to three months at least. I'm not even supposed to be walking on it.' Saying the words out loud depressed me.

'Then why are you walking on it? You should be following orders.'

'I was running late for you. I left the crutches here in the backseat so I could get in there faster.'

'Nick, this is not just any broken foot. This foot belongs to Nicholas Harding from the Western Rangers.'

I chuckled. 'I like it when you say my full name. It's sexy hearing you say it like that, like I'm in trouble.'

She clicked her tongue. 'This is sexy, that is sexy. Is everything sexy to you?'

'Yeah, with you, yeah.'

She blushed under the look I gave her. 'Listen to me, Nicholas Harding.' She cocked an eyebrow. 'This is an important foot. I do not want to be responsible for making the foot of my uncle's favourite footballer worse. You walked on it when you are not supposed to just for me – that is quite foolish but also very sweet.'

'Sweet?' I shot her a sideways look. 'You're not supposed to think I'm sweet. I'm dangerous and mysterious.'

'Ha! Not so much. So, tell me, you cannot play football but can you still work?'

'That *is* my work. None of the Rangers have other jobs – playing in the AFL is a full-time job.'

'Ah, I see. So what happens now?'

'I'll have a lot of free time, that's what.' I sighed. 'I have to go to the gym and do hydrotherapy. I'll go to some meetings, do a bit of charity work. That's about it.'

'Why do you look so worried? Is it that terrible?'

I turned in my seat to fully face her and told her the long story of how the same thing happened last year. 'Basically I'm worried that because the fractures came back in my very first match after rehab, it might mean these bones in my foot are particularly weak. So the fear is it might happen again after this rehab. If it did, I'm pretty sure that would be the end of my career. I don't think any club would sign me after that.'

'I understand. I hope this is the last time you have this injury. But now what will you do for an income while you are injured?'

So I told her about how my contract worked and about my guilt at letting everyone down. I talked to her about my dreams for this season being over and how I didn't have much going for me apart from playing.

She listened without interruption. When I stopped, she stayed silent and looked out her window. After a while she asked, 'It is not just your foot that is broken, is it? The way you speak, even something about the way you look, is like someone who has a broken heart. Am I right?'

My heart tugged in my chest. 'You are. It's funny though because I thought the same thing about you.'

'Yes, well you are right. My heart is broken.' She blew air up her fringe and stared out the windscreen. 'Is it time you drive me back to my house now, Nick?' It was more a statement than a question.

'Sure.'

I turned the key in the ignition and the car came to life. Anna was still staring out the windscreen, deep in thought.

Oh crap, she was obviously upset remembering whoever it was that had given her that broken heart.

'You okay, Anna?'

She turned to face me. 'Yes, yes, I am hokay. So this hydrotherapy rehabilitation – this is swimming, yes?'

'Yep, it's exercise in water. Swimming's part of it. Why?'

'Would you like to join me for a swim here tomorrow?'

I broke into a huge grin. 'Hell, yeah, I'll come swimming with you!'

'Good! I thought perhaps if we swim together then it would be not so lonely for you to do the rehabilitation.'

'You're literally the sweetest person ever. And then could I take you out for a meal somewhere after the swim tomorrow?'

'No, the only time I will have free is when I come for the swim late in the afternoon. I am busy all day aside from that.'

'Surely you stop to eat though?'

She shook her head. 'I will eat lunch on the bus to the hospital after my morning shift at Black Salt, and I will eat dinner in the kitchen at Masri's just before we open for the evening.'

'Hospital? What hospital?' I switched off the ignition.

She looked down into her lap. 'My family care for a little boy. His name is Ricky. He had leukaemia but he is healing now. He has had the last of the blood transfusions so he should be coming home this week.' She paused. 'I hope so anyway. And then we will just need to take him back for regular blood transfusions and he will be hokay. This is what the doctors say.'

'That sounds intense. Great that he's doing better, though. I can't believe how packed your day is, working two jobs and going to the hospital. Is that a normal day for you?'

She nodded.

'So you're not a student then? I don't know why but I assumed you were a student when I saw you at Black Salt.'

'I am not a student at the moment but I will be in July.' Her eyes lit up. 'Next semester I start at Curtin University School of Law.'

'Law? I'm impressed!'

'Well, do not be too impressed until I pass.' She laughed.

'So why are you starting in July instead of now? I thought university started this week.'

'It did, yes.' She sighed. 'It was more complicated than you can imagine to get accepted even with the recognition for my International Baccalaureate. A long and frustrating process that began last July and was only settled last month. By then the places for law for this semester were taken and I got into the next semester under special consideration.'

'Ugh, what a pain. So, will you be going full-time?'

'No, no. I need to work. And I must help look after Ricky. So if I do the first year part-time over two years, God willing by then Ricky will be in remission. And my mother ...' She stopped and bit her lip. 'My mother will be better by then too, and perhaps be able to get a job herself, so then I could increase to full-time studies.'

'Is your mum sick?'

She considered this before answering, 'In a way, yes.'

Hmm. I decided to leave my questions about that for later. 'Will you still work both jobs while you study next semester? Surely not?'

'I will keep both jobs, yes.'

'Really?'

'Yes, helping at Masri's is the least I can do for my Uncle Fariz. And I also need a job that pays, so I cannot give up my work at Black Salt.'

She worked in her uncle's restaurant for free? 'Your uncle doesn't pay you to work for him? That's terrible!'

'Oh no, Nick, my Uncle Fariz is the most wonderful, wonderful man! He has given us a home, he buys everything for us and he pays all the bills. He even pays for everything for Ricky – all the medical bills, the lawyer bills to keep him in Australia. Helping in the restaurant some nights is nothing compared to what he does for us.'

'Hang on, is Ricky a refugee?'

'Soon he will be. For now he is still an asylum seeker, but his paperwork is almost complete. He is being sponsored by my uncle and aunty, even though my mother and I are his carers. We are not allowed to be his sponsors.'

'Is that because you're refugees too?' I held my breath.

She blinked and nodded, and instinctively I reached for her hand.

'Do you want to talk about it?'

She took a big breath. 'Yes, I would like talk about it with you. But not tonight. It is not my entire family who survived, you see, and it is not an easy story for me to tell.'

'Your dad?' I ventured.

Her eyes met mine. 'Yes.'

I gulped. 'My dad passed away too.'

'So you understand then, Nick.' She exhaled.

I nodded, not trusting myself to answer. We sat in silence and I stroked the back of her hand with my thumb.

'I seriously can't believe how much you do already and that you're about to take on a law degree as well,' I said after a while.

She let out a tiny chuckle. 'I have not told you about Asylum Assist yet.'

'Don't tell me you have a third job.'

She laughed. 'I volunteer for Asylum Assist every Friday afternoon for three hours in the office in the city.'

'Any wonder you don't have time to stop and eat during the day! So what is Asylum Assist exactly? What do you do there?'

'We are a group who advocate for children in detention on

Bluff Island. I help coordinate the applications and I help with translating English documents into Arabic and vice versa.'

'Don't you get overwhelmed? That's really full on.'

'Of course, I get overwhelmed … all the time. But every day that I am fortunate enough to spend in this peaceful and free country, there are children growing up in offshore prisons. I must do what I can to help. I deserved asylum no more than any of those children who were denied it. I was raised to fight for what I believe in and I believe in this. So I will not give up until those children are all given asylum.' She spoke with a fiery passion.

'Is that why you're studying law?'

'Precisely. The more knowledge I have, the more powerful my voice will be.'

I made a mental note to look up Asylum Assist when I got home, and to look up Bluff Island Detention Centre, and to basically look up whatever I could to educate myself on these things that had never been important to me before.

'Seriously, though, do you ever get free time?' I asked.

'Swimming is the thing that is just for me.'

'I feel very privileged, then, that you invited me to join you, even though that's the only thing you do for yourself.'

She grinned.

'But what about a social life? You know – pubs, clubs, cinemas, going out for meals. When do you get to see your friends?'

'I do not have time for friends,' she said. 'I had friends in Alexandria, when my life was different. Here in Perth, I enjoy the company of the people I work with at Black Salt and at Asylum Assist. We text each other or chat on Facebook sometimes. But going out? Pubs and clubs? No. No time.'

I let this sink in. 'What about me? Will you have time for me?'

'For you, I will make time.'

I gave a little fist pump and she smiled.

'So tomorrow at five o'clock, you are free to come and swim with me, Nick?'

'I'll clear my busy schedule of lying on the couch to make sure I am. But can I take you out another night this week? Like on a real date?'

She was quiet for a bit. 'Thursday. Take me somewhere on Thursday.' She checked her watch and gasped. 'It is late, Nick! My mother, she will worry.'

I picked a strand of her wavy wet hair and tucked it behind her ear. She inhaled shakily and I smiled, encouraged by her reaction to my touch. But straightaway, her aunt's voice rang in my ear about how innocent she was, then Joel's voice joined in, reminding me that I was a wolf.

And I thought about how her aunt had her hair covered in a hijab. Even though Anna wasn't dressed how I thought Muslims dressed, she was still a Muslim girl, new to Australia, and had a whole different culture with different standards.

My life was – and as long as I played for the Rangers would remain – a three-ringed circus. I had no right to be dragging her into it.

'What is it, Nick? What is troubling you?'

'I was just thinking about how my life is really full-on, Anna. More than you can think. It's unfair to bring you into it. It would be like feeding you to the wolves. That girl who was mean to you back there? That would be the tip of the iceberg.'

'I can understand this, yes. But people like that girl do not concern me. As long as you treat me well, Nick, nothing else matters, hokay?'

'But what about you being Muslim?'

She belly-laughed. 'What about it?'

'Well, I don't know.'

How could I make myself not sound like a bigot? 'Don't you have rules about going out with non-Muslims?'

She was still laughing. 'If you follow the Koran to the letter, then, yes, there are such rules. Just like if you follow the Bible to the letter, then you should not be in a relationship with a Muslim, yes?'

'I suppose. I don't really know the rules in the Bible that well, to be honest. So are you, like, practising and stuff? I know I'm going to sound like a dickhead here, but, you know, your hair, the way you dress – I had a different idea about how Muslim women looked. I mean, it's not like I think you have to be totally covered head to toe or anything. But I didn't expect for a Muslim woman to have your kind of hairstyle or wear a top that shows a bit of ...' I came to a stop when she crossed her arms and gave me a pointed look.

'A bit of what, Nicholas Harding?'

I let my eyes drop to her cleavage. 'You know ...' I literally couldn't say the word. I was shocked at my own prudishness. And worse – I could feel myself blushing!

She reached into her bag and pulled out her phone.

'What are you doing?' I asked.

'Sending my mother a message that I will be late. I think I need to teach you some things about Muslim women before you drive me home.'

Once she read her mother's reply, she put the phone away and clasped her hands together.

'Nick, the world is full of Muslim women who wear the hijab and dress conservatively, of course. But there are just as many of us, maybe even more, who do not. There are Muslim women who are bikini models. It is just that they blend in with non-Muslims more so you do not notice them. Just like most men who practise Buddhism do not shave their heads and wear robes, but that is how Buddhists are imagined the world over, yes?'

'Right, okay. I'd never thought of it like that. So are you religious? Do you pray to Allah? Do you fast?'

She gave me a quizzical smile. 'Why are you so interested in my religion?'

'I don't know. Just trying to find my feet with it all, I guess. So … are you a practising Muslim?'

'I believe in Allah, yes. The same God you believe in. You are Christian, yes?'

I tilted my head from side to side. 'Er, kind of. I was raised Christian. Yeah, I guess I believe in God. I pray, you know, sometimes. Mostly when I want something.'

'Well, we are the same. We both believe in God and we both pray when we want something.'

'So do you fast? Do you eat bacon?'

'No and no. Have I passed the religion test yet, Nick?' She raised her eyebrows.

Now I really did feel like a dick. 'Sorry. It's just that this is all so new to me. I've never even met a Muslim person in real life before you.'

'You have most likely met hundreds of Muslims before me. It is just that you did not know it because they were in disguise as *regular people*.' She paused. 'I am, in fact, as much of a Christian as I am a Muslim.'

'Huh?'

'I have enjoyed seeing your reaction to me as a Muslim woman, but my mother is Christian.'

'Really? Why didn't you say?'

'If I had told you my mother was Christian, you would have automatically assumed that this must explain the way I am dressed. Am I right?'

'Yeah, for sure.'

She smiled. 'So I wanted you to understand that I can present in exactly the same way, whichever religion I follow.'

'Lesson learned,' I conceded. 'So do you identify as a Muslim or a Christian?'

'You have so many big questions of someone you have only just met, do you know that?'

'Sorry,' I chuckled. 'I didn't mean to grill you like this, I'm just fascinated, that's all.'

'If anyone was to ask me what religion I am, I would say Muslim. When I fill in forms, I write that I am Muslim. But my parents believed that each person should make their own choices in regards to faith, so I was never forced to follow the laws of the Koran. In my old home both Muslim and Christian feasts were observed. For example, my father would fast during Ramadan and my mother would fast during Lent. Presents were given out at Eid and Christmas. But neither religion was pushed on me. I have taken different ideals from both.'

'That's an unusual way to grow up.'

'Perhaps to you. But in Egypt, marriages between Muslims and Christians are common. Many children are raised this way.'

'I never knew that. That's actually really cool. So you follow some rules from each religion and kind of make up your own faith as a mix of the two, is that right?'

'No, not at all. I follow none of the rules from either religion. I refuse to be told by others in what way I have to connect with Allah. But I believe in Allah wholeheartedly. In my eyes, Allah cannot be a doctrine or made to fit into any text, you see. He is too big for that. Allah is everywhere and in everything.'

'But you said you don't eat bacon.' I frowned, completely confused. 'That's an Islamic rule, isn't it?'

'I do not eat bacon because I do not like the taste.'

'Ah.' I pulled a face. 'Well that makes me look like a real idiot. But hang on, you say "Allah" – isn't that Muslim too?'

'Allah is simply the Arabic translation for God.'

'Right, now I look like an even bigger idiot! But I'm still confused. If you don't follow the rules of the Koran, why do you call yourself Muslim?'

'In Egypt, because I was born to a Muslim father, I am considered Muslim.'

'Do you mind that?'

'No, not at all.' She shook her head. 'It makes me happy and proud. It is another way for me to honour my father, like taking his name. Also, Nick, you need to understand, the core of Islam is truly beautiful. It promotes peace and love and kindness. It is not the Islam broadcast by the media, the Islam that is smeared by oppressive and violent people.'

She sighed and then gave me a sideways look. 'So, after this very long philosophical discussion, have you found your feet with my Muslim identity?'

'Not really. Your aunt still scares the shit out of me with all her talk about honour!'

She burst out laughing again. 'Ah, yes, of course, you have good reason to be very afraid of Tante Rosa!'

'Tell me about it! But, Anna, there's something else I want to know and I promise this is the last question. Forget your aunt, just between you and me, are there any rules I need to stick to? I just want to make sure I respect your values.'

I chewed my lip, hoping she understood my meaning.

She took forever to answer.

'One rule.' She held up a finger. 'Do not treat me badly because then you will feel the wrath of an Egyptian woman! And if you are wondering what an Egyptian woman is capable of when she is scorned, just familiarise yourself with the stories of the pharaohs, hokay?' She nodded. 'But I know *exactly* what you are thinking about, Nick, when you ask about rules between us, and the answer to what you are thinking is no.'

My heart sank. I certainly didn't intend on sleeping with her right away, but God, a straight-out no?

But then she continued. 'Between you and me there are no rules you need to *stick to*, as you said. I do not like doctrines, remember? I make my own rules.' She smiled. 'But now, Nicholas Harding, it really is time for you to take me home, hokay?'

I was aching to kiss her. 'Hokay.' I ran my index finger along her jawline.

She pointed at me with a smile. 'I do not remember giving you the right to poke fun at my accent.'

'But off courrrse I would nawt do zat, hokay?'

'Stop that or I will poke fun at your funny way of walking. You will drive me home now and tomorrow we shall swim, yes?'

'Hokay, off courrrse, yass.'

She threw her head back and laughed.

TOBY – TUESDAY

I wasn't around when Jen died yesterday. Because she kicked me out. I left the hospital knowing I'd never see her again. I told myself that it was okay, that this was the way it should be – just her and her family together at the end. But it wasn't okay. I was her family too and her final act towards me was one of rejection – the past repeating itself until the bitter end.

Her last ever word to me was 'out'.

When she'd woken up yesterday, after a solid sleep where I'd eventually fallen asleep beside her in that narrow hospital bed, I knew it would be her final day. Her colour had changed overnight from yellow to a scary shade of grey, a deathly shade. And as soon as her eyes opened, she was in agony, whimpering and unable to speak more than a few words at a time. She kept crying my name and there was nothing I could do to comfort her.

I raged at the nurses to turn up her morphine but they said we had to wait for medical rounds with her specialist – and the medical rounds were still hours away. In the meantime they put cold compresses on the back of her neck and on her forehead, which did fuck all to help her. It killed me to watch her in that much pain. It killed me.

Marcia, Pete and Luke arrived together just after seven and I went home to quickly shower and change before heading straight back to the hospital. Soon after, the three of them left to meet with the hospital's chaplain. When Marcia stood up, her legs gave way. Pete and Luke helped her walk out, holding an arm each.

Not long after that, Jen's specialist walked in with a bunch of university students trailing warily behind him. I asked him to turn up the morphine and he said he was already onto it.

I was taken aback to see that the Rapunzel girl from the café was one of the students. And she was watching me. I could tell she was judging me when she heard the specialist say that Jen was my wife. It was obvious that I was into her in the café and then she saw that my wife was dying. Of course she judged me. Who wouldn't?

And even though I didn't know the girl at all, it mattered to me that she was judging me. I wanted her to know the truth. When she looked at me, my guard fell, and I walked out fast before crying like a baby at the unfairness of everything.

When I finally got my shit together, I went back up to Jen's room where I was stunned to find the girl was still there, by herself at Jen's bedside. She held Jen's hand in one of hers and stroked her hair with the other as she hummed softly to Jen who had her eyes closed. I swallowed the lump in my throat. With her long golden curls, her gentle expression, and that sweet music she made, she was just like an angel watching over Jen. A real life angel.

When she saw me, she didn't have the judgemental look from before.

Jen opened her eyes and it was clear the medicine had taken hold. 'Rapunzel and Toby sitting in a tree,' she drawled.

Even on her death bed, spaced out on drugs, she was still trying to set me up with girls. Did she honestly believe that if I met someone else, I'd be okay without her? How deluded she was.

But my heart did skip a beat (and I hated myself for it) when the girl's beautiful bluey-green eyes locked on mine. I was relieved when she left.

Jen was awake on and off over the next half an hour, but the morphine did its job quickly. When she opened her eyes after that, they rolled backwards so I could only see the whites, and what she slurred I couldn't understand.

I knew I should have used the time to say goodbye to her but I just couldn't. Instead, I pulled out my phone and looked through all the photos of the two of us. I talked to her about all the places we'd been and all the things we'd done when those shots were taken.

When I came to the end of the camera roll, I sat with her freezing hand in both of mine. 'Jen, this is the last time we'll be together, just you and me. I know you're listening, so I want you to know you're the best thing that ever happened to me. All of my favourite memories have you in them. Listen, I know you never stopped beating yourself up about what happened, so I need you to know that I forgive you. I forgave you a long time ago.' I kissed her fingers. 'And I'm grateful for this time that we had together again.' My lips began to tremble. 'Beautiful girl, I love you. I hope wherever you go, that there's every food you fang for and footy every day and that you're surrounded by children. See you later, my sweetheart.' It was impossible to hold myself together when I kissed her unresponsive lips.

Her family walked in with the parish priest. I wished she

was awake to see. She would have laughed so hard at a priest by her bedside. Jen was the poster child for atheism.

'Do you want to stay while we do her last rites, Toby?' the priest asked in a sombre voice.

And for the first time in over an hour, Jen spoke. 'No!' she moaned with her eyes closed. 'No, no!'

'Sweetness, what is it?' Pete bent over her. 'What's wrong?'

She slurred something indecipherable and slipped out of it again.

The priest set up his stuff on her trolley and she called out. 'Tobes ... out.'

My heart stopped.

'No!' she cried. 'Tobes ... out ... out!'

'You want Toby to leave, Jenny?' Pete stroked her hair, and gave me a shrug with a confused look on his face.

'Out!' she wailed, her eyes still closed, and then her head flopped forwards so her chin rested in her breastbone. 'Tobes,' she mumbled, as Pete lifted her head and rested it back up against the pillow. 'Out.'

Luke started crying in soft sobs. Marcia drew him close to her.

'Stay,' Pete mouthed to me as the priest opened the Bible and took two steps towards Jen. 'She's asleep. She won't know. Stay.'

But I couldn't stay. She wanted me out. I couldn't deny her that final request. So I took one last look at her and left.

I drove home in a haze and sat at the dining table, chain-smoking for the rest of the day.

I got a call from Pete just after John forced me to eat the pasta he'd brought home from Black Salt for dinner.

'She's in heaven, mate,' Pete whispered before hanging up.

John came out of the bathroom, stark naked.

'She gone?'

'She's gone,' I sobbed.

Several minutes later he said, 'She died on a Monday, just like she wanted, eh?'

'I was born on a Monday, I want to die on a Monday.' Jen had announced more than once. 'That would make it neat,' she said. 'Everyone hates Mondays. When does anything exciting ever happen on a Monday anyway? You may as well die on one.'

'Can you go get some pants on, please, mate?' I sniffed, wiping the last of my tears away.

He came back out again, dressed in his boxer shorts. He cracked open two stubbies. We took a couch each and drank in the dark.

'So did it just happen in her sleep?' he asked.

'Don't know.'

His phone screen lit up the room with a text message and he responded. His phone pinged several times over the next ten minutes and I nursed my beer, grateful for the silence.

He eventually put his phone away.

'Renee?' I asked.

He snorted. 'Nah, mate.'

'I should've guessed.' I sighed.

'Want to see some pics? There's this chick who's been coming into Black Salt lately who just sent me her nudes. She's hot, Tobes. Want me to AirDrop them to you?' He pulled out his phone again.

'Really, really no.'

'Suit yourself,' said the man in a committed relationship with Renee for the past fourteen months.

I downed the rest of the beer and went to bed.

* * *

I found out in the morning, in a series of texts from Luke, what happened in the end with Jen. Apparently it was peaceful. She opened her eyes just a fraction for a couple of seconds about two hours after I left, and she smiled before going back to sleep. A few minutes later, she took two big gasps of air, one after the other. And then she stopped breathing.

The funeral was this afternoon. Marcia and Pete had the funeral directors, who were close family friends, on standby and organised days ago. Jen's gravesite was ready and waiting, so as soon as her body was released and the paperwork was handed over by the hospital, they came to collect her.

We stood around a hole in the ground with a civil celebrant less than twenty-four hours after she died, in accordance with her wishes – 'Don't let me hang around in a morgue with dead people, being dead!' It was a quick funeral. 'Make it short, just like my fucking life. No church service, just bury me and be done with it.' No eulogies. 'No thanks, no pathetic stories about what an inspiration I was, yuck!' And there were only six people there. 'No hangers on, just you guys and Nan and Pop.'

Throughout the short service, I felt nothing, heard nothing, saw nothing. It wasn't until the coffin was lowered that I noticed I'd been standing on my own far away from her family, who were all huddled together.

I walked over to Jen's grandparents who were seated next to her grave on camp chairs, and squatted down to give them my condolences. Their faces had the look of people who knew how wrong it was that they had outlived their only granddaughter.

Marcia buried her head in my shirt and sobbed until the shirt was soaking. Still, I felt nothing. Pete and Luke returned my wordless hugs with flaccid arms.

I walked back to the ute and the radio came on when I turned on the ignition. Christina Perri's haunting voice floated out of the speakers. 'A Thousand Years'. Our bridal dance.

I stayed parked at the cemetery until I was expected at Mum and Dad's for dinner. John was already there. The clang of the cutlery and crockery was the only noise throughout the meal.

My parents had become instant friends with Jen's when they moved in as next door neighbours twenty-seven years ago. I knew it had been a tough day for my family too, being close to Jen for most of her life and then not being at her funeral. I was glad when dinner was over and I could finally go home.

John said he'd be staying at Renee's overnight. He would've dreaded being around for a repeat crying performance from me so his sudden desire to 'check in on the old girl' didn't surprise me.

Back home I paced around the lounge room, not knowing what to do with myself. I smoked some more. How could I wake up tomorrow, go to work, and carry on with life as normal when a few hours ago I'd thrown a fistful of dirt and a blue iris over my wife's coffin as it lay six feet down? How was anything ever going to be okay again?

My phone rang.

I didn't recognise the number displayed. Random condolence caller or prospective client? I answered it only to have one less call to return in the morning.

'Watts Building. Toby speaking.'

There was silence on the other end. And then a faltering female voice. 'Um, hi, Toby. It's Lily here. I'm, um, I'm the student doctor from the hospital. Um, you know the one yesterday, who Jenny—'

'I know who you are,' I swallowed hard. 'How'd you get my number?'

'Um, Jenny gave it to me. I didn't ask for it,' she added quickly. 'I didn't want it. I mean, it's not that I didn't want it, it's just that she gave it to me without me asking for it. It was Jenny who made me ring you. No, I mean I wanted to ring you anyway – she didn't actually make me. Oh Jesus.'

I said nothing.

'Toby, I'm so sorry she died.'

'Thank you.' I got stuck on the words and had to clear my throat.

'Yesterday Jenny made me promise to ring you next week, and I said yes, but deep down I thought I probably wouldn't ever have the guts to. But when I was back at the hospital this morning and found out she'd died, I really, really wanted to ring you. Not because she asked me to, but because *I* wanted to. I hope it's okay that I have.'

'It's okay.' I walked into my bedroom, sat on the edge of the bed and placed my head in my hands.

'When's the funeral? I thought I might come along if you didn't mind.'

'Today. It was today.'

'Oh.' She was silent for a bit. 'Are you okay?'

Just like yesterday in Jen's room, she made me cry again. As if I hadn't cried enough already, I was crying on the phone to a girl I didn't know.

'Toby, are you alone?'

'Yeah.' I choked.

'Do you want me to come over?'

I didn't even need to think about it. 'Yeah.'

'I'm glad. I really wanted to see you. What's your address?'

I wiped my tears roughly and told her how to find me.

'Scarborough, great. I'm close by in City Beach. I'll be there soon.'

I hung up and stared at the phone in my hand. 'What the fuck have you done, Jen?'

My doorbell rang half an hour later. I opened the door to find her standing there, holding two take-away coffees and with a questioning expression in her bluey-green eyes.

'Flat white with one?' She held one cup out. 'I made sure it's got sugar in it.'

I took it from her. 'Thanks. Come in.'

She brushed past me – close enough that I felt her body heat – and she followed me into the lounge room. She stood in the middle of the room, looking around at the prints on the walls.

'This is just stunning.' She took a step closer to the photo of a Cable Beach sunset. 'Who took this?'

'I did.'

'Did you take all of these?' She waved her arm at the walls.

'I did, yeah.'

'Serious? But you said Watts Building on the phone.'

'I'm a building supervisor.' I kicked at the carpet with the point of my sneaker.

'So you're not a photographer?' She frowned.

'Nope. Just a builder.'

'Oh. Do you sell your photos on the side?'

I blew my cheeks out. 'Nope.'

'So, these are just for you? You don't make any money out of them?'

'Pretty much, yeah.'

'That's not right, Toby.' Her eyes zoned in on mine. 'That's not right.'

Boom. She'd got me right in the weak spot.

She walked up to another print. It was a dawn shot at Sunshine Beach in Noosa.

'This is my favourite. It's the most perfect beach photo I think I've ever seen.' She stood there staring at it.

It was my favourite too.

'Do you want to sit down? Lily, isn't it?' I cleared my throat again. I wished my words would stop getting stuck in there.

She perched herself on the edge of the couch, watching me while she took sips of her coffee.

I sat hugging my knees on the carpet facing her. 'I'm glad you came. I've been thinking about you.'

'Me too, a lot,' she said softly. 'Thinking about you, I mean, not myself. God! What the hell is it with you? I can't string two words together without sounding like an idiot whenever I'm around you.' She looked away, blushing.

'I feel strange around you too.' My heart sped up. Then I remembered why she was here and I hated myself for noticing that she was bare chested under that low-cut dress. I hated myself for wanting to touch her curls. I hated myself for wanting so badly to take her to bed.

'Toby, I'm sorry about Jenny.' She slid down off the couch and sat on the floor, facing me. 'She told me briefly what happened. You must have loved her an awful lot to get back together when she was sick.'

'We never really got back together.' I scratched my head. 'I looked after her, but it wasn't really a marriage anymore.'

She blew on her coffee and kept her eyes fixed on me.

I tugged on my shoelaces. 'She was still in love with the prick who walked out on her when she got sick. The one she left me for.'

She put the coffee down and inched forward, closer to me. She rested both her hands on my knees. I felt their warmth, even through my jeans.

'That's an incredibly kind thing you did.'

Bloody hell, the hot tears burned my eyelids again. I turned away from her and when I turned back again her eyes were brimming with tears too. She was revealing herself to me in those eyes. And what I saw was pain. Whether it was from the boyfriend who left her or pain from something else, I couldn't tell. But it was there and it was real. And all I wanted was to take away her pain and mine.

I got up onto my knees and leaned closer to her, cupping one hand around her neck.

'Don't be sad,' I whispered.

She leaned forward and kissed away the tears that had escaped from me before her mouth found mine. We kissed long and slow.

I slid my hand down off the back of her neck and onto her shoulder, dropping the strap of her dress down her arm. Then I slid off the other strap and kissed the hollow of her neck.

She shivered. 'Toby, are you sure you want to do this?'

I could barely speak with arousal. 'More than anything. What about you? Are you sure *you* want to do this?'

'More than anything.'

Our kissing got more desperate.

She stood up and let her dress fall to the floor. She was left wearing only on a pair of tiny pink cotton knickers. She reached down and pulled them off her legs.

I was awestruck. She was like a mermaid, a goddess. Her hair partly hid her breasts and her willowy curves had me hypnotised.

I held my hand out.

She took it and I pulled her gently down onto the carpet. I rolled on top of her and kissed her everywhere, tasting her salty tears mixed in with her sweet almond skin. I kissed along her collarbones, and then her nipples, and her belly, her hips, between her legs. She let out long low moans and her fingers played with my hair while my tongue found its way inside her.

'I want you,' she whispered between gasps.

I stood up and threw off my T-shirt and jeans. She helped me pull off my underwear and she reached across to her purse. I slipped on the protection she handed me.

And then I loved her in a way I'd never loved anyone before.

She melted me with her kisses, and her touch, and her bluey-green eyes, and when she cried my name out loud with her orgasm, I came too.

I rolled onto my back afterwards and stared at the ceiling. I sensed Jen's presence as if she was standing directly over me, making me feel exposed and ashamed.

Lily turned to face me, biting her bottom lip. 'What just happened?'

I stroked her still wet cheek with my thumb. 'I don't really know.'

'I don't have casual sex,' she said in a rush. 'I don't want you to think that's why I came over. But this meant something to me. It meant more to me than you could—'

'Shhh.' I placed my finger on her lips. 'I don't do casual either.' I stretched out my arm for her to come in closer.

I was an arsehole for what I'd just done only hours after burying Jen. A complete and utter arsehole. But I didn't regret it. Lily was worth the shame, worth the self-hatred. Because she was the first woman who'd ever made love to me and actually meant it. Somebody finally meant it.

ANNA – TUESDAY

'Look!' Tante Rosa yelled. 'Look at what you have done! The shame you have brought us! How can I ever show my face again?'

I sprang upright in bed and my sleepy mind took a second or two to understand that Tante Rosa was standing over me, waving a newspaper under my nose. Why was she in my room and why was she yelling? What terrible news was there?

Tante Rosa threw the newspaper onto the bed. I rubbed my eyes and squinted at the front-page headline. 'Injured Harding Falls for 'Fast Lane' Mystery Brunette.' Underneath was a short article that did not say much at all except that Nick Harding was seen at Challenge Stadium with an unknown woman yesterday evening whom he watched swim in the fast lane of the indoor pool, and that afterwards they remained in his parked car for close to half an hour before leaving together.

There were also six photographs of Nick and me at Challenge – one of me in the water talking with Nick who was squatting down at the end of the lane, two of me drying myself, one of us walking out, one of us facing each other in the car park and the last photograph was of me getting into Nick's car.

Tante Rosa's face was a deep-purple colour, as though she had forgotten to breathe.

'Tante Rosa,' I began but I could think of no words to follow.

'Well?' Tante Rosa screamed. 'Hurry up and explain this! Or did the footballer take your tongue as well as your honour? Speak up, child!'

The paper shook in my hands.

Ahmo Fariz came running. 'What is it? What happened?' he called out. When he reached the doorway he rested his hands on his knees and panted. (There was a lot of Ahmo Fariz for his feet to carry when he ran.) 'What is all this noise about, Rosa?' He wheezed between the words.

Tante Rosa snatched the paper from my hands, rolled it up and hit Ahmo Fariz over the head with it. 'Are you happy now?' she yelled at him. 'Are you happy, you stupid old goat, that you encouraged our niece to be photographed like a prostitute for the world to mock us! Allah, we will never have another customer walk through Masri's doors again now that this filth, this filth …' she burst into tears.

Ahmo Fariz gave me a confused look before he took the paper from Tante Rosa and examined the front page.

While he did so, Tante Rosa threw herself onto the carpet near the foot of my bed and began praying. On her knees she went, touching the floor with her forehead and then coming up again throwing her arms in the air, many times over, reciting passages from the Koran.

I sat unmoving and unspeaking. All I could think was *I need you here, Mama*. Mama would have known what to do, what to say, to calm Tante Rosa. She had a kind of magic over

Tante Rosa that always settled her. But Mama had already left for the hospital.

'You are facing the wrong way,' Ahmo Fariz snapped in Arabic. 'Listen to you reciting verses you do not understand and facing south – at your age, how do you still not know in which direction to pray? Get up, *yalla emshi ya* Rosa. Let me speak with my niece. Alone.'

Tante Rosa ignored Ahmo Fariz's order to leave and wailed her prayers even louder. But as she did so, she shuffled herself around on the floor to face west.

Ahmo Fariz looked at me with unblinking eyes and did not use the soft tone of voice that he usually reserved for me. 'What is this about? Explain this to me.'

I pushed down the panic rising inside. My voice was shaky and my words tumbled out. 'Nick came to see me when I was swimming yesterday. We talked in his car and then he drove me home. Ahmo Fariz, nothing happened, all we are doing is getting to know each other.'

Ahmo Fariz nodded slowly and looked at the photographs in the paper again. 'Is this a romance between you? Already?'

'For now, it is a friendship.'

He frowned a deep frown. 'Did he disrespect you in the car?'

I shook my head quickly. 'No, no the opposite, Ahmo. I swear to you, he was very respectful.'

Ahmo Fariz rubbed his face all over with his hands. 'I cannot see what you can have in common with this man. I love you as if you were my own child and it upsets me to see photographs like this of you alone with him in a parked car at night. You are a young and naive girl and a man like this does not share your values – our values. My brother is not here to protect you, Allah rest his soul. So it is my duty to see that you are kept safe. You are only a child. I do not want to see you hurt.'

'See her hurt?' Tante Rosa flew up off the floor midway through a prayer, waving her arms at Ahmo Fariz. '*See her hurt*? What is this, a soap opera? What about her honour? Her reputation? The name of our family? Allah help us, "See her hurt," he says! One brother is dead and now the other has lost his mind! Allah, you have robbed me of two brothers, not one!'

And then there was more wailing from her.

'*Ekhrasi, ya* Rosa. Shut up,' Ahmo Fariz said in a quiet voice without even looking at her.

'Ahmo Fariz.' I climbed out of bed and stood in front of him. 'How can you think of me as naive? As only a child? Do you forget the horrors I have lived through? Do you forget that I have been responsible for my mother since the day of the fire? Do you forget that I am now raising a child myself? I may be young in years, but my soul is that of an old woman's. I am many things, Ahmo Fariz, but I am neither a child nor naive.'

Ahmo Fariz's eyes watered. 'It breaks my heart to hear you speak like this and to know how greatly you have suffered. You are right, *habibti*, you carry the scars of an adult not a child. But I cannot watch this man add to those scars and stand by like a statue, doing nothing to prevent it.'

'Ahmo Fariz, you could not prevent any of the things that caused me pain. Please do not prevent the one thing that might make me happy.'

He sighed and threw his hands in the air. 'What if he hurts you, Anna? What if he humiliates you? Or betrays you? Allah, what if he *rapes* you? How will I forgive myself then? You are putting me in a very difficult position.'

'But what if Nick does none of those things? What if all he does is bring me joy? How would you forgive yourself if you denied me that?'

Tante Rosa bent over, clutching at her heart. 'Allah, I think I am having a heart attack! My heart, it is stopping. Aye! The pain ... Fariz ... help me! *Ya Rab*!'

Ahmo Fariz placed his hand in the small of Tante Rosa's back, pushed her out of the room and closed the door.

Rosa yelled from the other side of the door. 'Mark my words, this will end in catastrophe for us all! We have invited the devil across our threshold and our children's children will bear this curse that has begun. Fariz! Are you listening to me?'

'What children's children do you speak of?' Ahmo Fariz called over his shoulder. 'We are almost geriatrics, the pair of us, with no spouses, let alone children. If you are having heart trouble, go and chew a QuickEze. At least it will keep your mouth occupied for a minute or two, so I can hear myself think.'

He turned back to me and lowered his voice. 'Anna, he has been seen with many women. He is not respectful of them. This is not a respectable person you are dealing with.'

'He wants to change his ways, Ahmo Fariz. He promised me.'

He rolled his eyes. 'Well, of course this is what he will say to fool you! Men like him know how to fool women.'

'Naive women, maybe,' I countered. 'But we have established that I am not naive. He has promised to treat me well and I believe him. I can tell he is a good man, Ahmo Fariz. I beg of you now to trust in my judgement. For the first time since I left Egypt, I am happy.' The unshed tears stung my eyes. 'I am *happy*.'

Fariz shook his head and sighed. '*Habibti*, you have to understand that my instinct is to protect you from this man. If you wish to see him again, make sure it is with others, never alone. Perhaps his friends from the Rangers can act as your chaperones. If it was my choice, I would not let him near you again.'

'Ahmo Fariz, you know I respect you the way I respect a father. But this is not your choice.'

'You are a stubborn girl, Anna. I know what is best for you.'

'I am a woman, Ahmo Fariz. I am a woman who makes her own decisions.'

We stood in silence.

He rubbed his hands over his face.

'Your father was the most progressive man I knew. So in honouring my beloved brother, I will not stand in your way.'

I kissed his hand. 'Good. Thank you, Ahmo. Now, tell me, is what Tante Rosa says true? Do you think people will stop coming to the restaurant because of the photographs?'

He rolled his eyes again. 'What I wish is that I knew these photographs would be taken. Had I known, I would have insisted you wear the black T-shirt with the Masri's logo. Nick Harding is the most popular footballer in all of Perth. It would triple our business to be associated with him, not harm it!'

I hugged Ahmo Fariz with all my strength and he left to go and calm down Tante Rosa who was still shouting at him to call an ambulance for her heart attack.

When I was alone in the bedroom, I checked my phone. I had two messages from Nick and one from Gianni.

Gianni's message was displayed first:

Nick Harding? You little dark horse. Here I was thinking you
were all sugar and spice and you go and bag Nick Harding.
Impressive work, Miss Hayati – very impressive. I've taught
you well.

I laughed out loud and then looked at Nick's first message,
which made my heart beat like I had just finished a race:

You were my first thought when I woke up. You and your red
bathers, that is. I miss you already. Can't wait to see you at the
pool today x

And then his next message:

Oh no! Have you seen The West? I'm so sorry. I should have
known better and protected you from that. Has your family
seen it? Text me as soon as you can.

I replied to Nick first, of course:

I am thinking about you too. Do not worry about the
photographs in the newspaper. All is well with my family. I am
rushing for work now. See you at the pool! (I am looking forward
to racing you in the water!) x

He replied immediately:

Phew! Been so stressed about it. Race me, hey? You do
remember who you're racing right? You think you can handle
me?

When I read this message, there was a deep tickle down low in my stomach. I finally knew now what Noor meant when she used to describe feelings like this about her many meetings with Patrick Doha, from downstairs. Back then I would block my ears so I did not have to hear it, but now I was desperate to share my feelings with her.

It was because of those deep tickles low in my stomach that I typed a message back to Nick that I hoped would give him tickles like that too.

Handle you? Oh I can handle you, Nicholas Harding x

I bit my lip while I waited for his reply.

You can handle me all you like. Off to take a shower now. A cold one!

After this, I replied to Gianni's message:

I will have you know that Nick Harding is not somebody I 'bagged'. Please show a little more respect.

I laughed to myself when I hit 'send'. Gianni's response made me laugh more:

Listen to your mate Gianni. Don't be one of those chicks who saves herself for someone 'special'. This is Nick Harding we're talking about, it doesn't get more special than that!

I responded:

I will never delete this text message so that I can use it
against you in a sexual harassment case. I sincerely hope
that you never do anything to turn me against you.

Gianni replied:

Hurry up and get to work, Hayati. I'll dock your pay every
second you're late.

* * *

I expected to find Gianni in a jovial mood when I arrived at
Black Salt after the joking ways in our texts, but I was surprised
to find him untalkative. And as the café grew quieter later in
the morning, he stayed bent over his mobile phone instead of
sharing details of his latest conquests with Chef Wayne.

I approached him at the end of my shift. 'Gianni, is
something the matter? You seem sad.'

'I'm all right.' He smiled, but behind the smile he was
hiding something.

'No, you are far from all right. What is it?'

He took a few moments to answer. 'My sister-in-law died
last night. She had cancer.'

I never even knew that Gianni had a brother let alone a
sister-in-law. He had never once mentioned his family at work.
I had in fact wondered if he was estranged from them.

'I am so sorry to hear this.' I put my hand on his arm. 'That
is such sad news, Gianni.'

He did not reply.

'I have an idea. You could ring Joe and ask if he is free to
cover for you for the rest of the day,' I suggested. 'He came
looking for work last week, remember?'

'That's actually a really good idea.'

So he rang his friend Joe and then he left, which meant that I stayed back an extra forty-five minutes to make the coffees until Joe arrived and took my place.

Gianni's news sent ice rushing through my veins. I prayed a silent prayer for Ricky. *Please Ya Rab, keep the cancer away.*

After work, I used the front entrance at home to avoid Tante Rosa. When I walked into my room, I could not believe it, the air was cool on my skin! I looked up to the corner where the old air conditioner used to be and saw a new air conditioner there in its place.

I rushed out to find Ahmo Fariz, barely able to contain myself. 'Ahmo Fariz, what is this new air conditioner in the bedroom?'

'I have no idea where it came from, *habibti*,' he said. 'But when I came into your room this morning, I noticed how hot it was in there. So I checked the unit and found it to be broken. I told myself I must remember to fix it, but before I had a chance to do anything, kapoof!' He clapped his hands together, 'A brand new air conditioner appeared in its place.'

There could never exist a kinder man than this! Apart from Baba, of course. So now I had one thousand three hundred and seventy dollars in savings and no air conditioner to buy. I was rich! I could spend some money on clothes for Mama and myself. Ricky could have new Matchbox cars and Lego, and I would buy Ahmo Fariz something wonderful too. Perhaps a new season Rangers jersey. Nick could sign it for him! I had to give some thought to what kind of present I could buy Tante Rosa that would not make her curse me.

As soon as I had changed and packed a swimming bag, I went directly to the hospital.

I walked into Ricky's room to find him watching *Toy Story 3* on Ahmo Fariz's iPad for what must have been the hundredth time. He ignored my hugs and kisses.

The smell of Mama's oatmeal shampoo filled the air. She had showered herself without me having to remind her! She was also sitting up, alert, rather than curled up small on a chair and staring into nothing, which she often did when she was watching Ricky for me. I slipped out of my shoes and climbed onto the couch next to Mama, snuggling myself against her warmth. I did not mention to her that I was late because Gianni's sister-in-law died. But of course I had to tell her about Nick.

'Mama, I have some news to share. I met somebody.'

She pulled her head away from me. 'A man?'

'A man, yes.'

'Well then, tell me, where did you meet him?'

'I met him on Sunday at Black Salt. Then he came to Masri's and yesterday he met me at the pool.'

The sound of Mama's laughter filled the room and my heart with happiness. It had been many weeks since I last heard her laugh like that.

'What is he like, this man who is following my daughter everywhere? Is he someone deserving of you, *habibti*?'

'I think so.'

'And what does he do? Does he work? Is he a student?'

'He plays football for Fariz's Western Rangers.'

Mama's eyebrows shot up and I continued quickly. 'He has the kindest eyes and I can tell that he has a good heart.'

'Mmm. Is he handsome, this man with the kind eyes?'

'He is.'

Mama looked at me sideways. 'He must be very handsome for your face to turn this pink at the mention of his handsomeness.'

'Oh Mama, I barely know him at all but I have been thinking about him all day. Am I foolish to be thinking so much about someone I barely know?'

'Anna, *habibti*.' Mama smiled. 'Sometimes being foolish is the best thing to be. In nineteen years, this is the first time you have spoken to me of a man with a sparkle in your beautiful eyes. You are young – be young! And if you think he has a good heart, I would bet on my life that he indeed has a good heart. How old is he?'

'He is twenty-three.'

'Oh. Do you have a photograph of him?'

I did a Google image search in his name on my phone. I kept my eyes strictly focused on the photographs suitable to share with Mama rather than some of the other photographs that were calling for my attention. I clicked on one of Nick dressed in a dark suit, looking very handsome indeed.

She squinted at the photograph, 'Aye, Nick Harding! Really? You like *Nick Harding*?'

My eyes almost fell out of my head. 'You know him, Mama?'

She laughed. '*Habibti*, we have been living with Fariz for a year. Of course I know who Nick Harding is.'

'Why is it that I have never heard of him, then?'

Mama sighed. 'Because, my sweet girl, you work day and night like a slave, you worry about me, you worry about Ricky, every spare minute you have is for Asylum Assist. When would you ever have the time to sit and listen to the names Fariz does or does not shout at the television?' Mama dropped her gaze to the floor. 'I will never forgive myself for this life I gave you. I'm sorry, *ya rohi*, for everything I've done, and continue to do to you.' Her voice was heavy.

'Mama, please, you know it upsets me to hear you speak like this. Now tell me something important instead of this silly talk. What is your impression of Nick?'

She took my phone from me and scrolled through more photographs of him, frowning as she did so.

'Mama, say something. You are killing me with your silence.'

'Very well. My impression is that this is a handsome, confident man who has had a great deal more experience than you, and that worries me. But, at the same time … your father was the same when I met him, and a better man I could not have found.' She touched my cheek. 'You are wiser at your age than I am even now at mine. And I know you are smart enough to know what starting up a relationship with a man in the public eye will mean for your privacy. So if you are prepared to overlook his reputation, and the fact that you will be under great scrutiny by the media, then who am I to stand in your way?'

'But, Mama, what if the media puts you under scrutiny again too?' I had given no thought until that very second about protecting Mama.

'There is nothing they can do to me now that they have not done already. It is only you I worry about.'

'Thank you, Mama.' I hugged her hard.

'So will I get a chance to meet him myself?'

'Thursday. He is taking me out on Thursday,' I announced with pride. 'So you will meet him then.'

'Just do one thing for me, *habibti*. Keep this news just between you and me for now and let me be the one to tell Rosa. She needs this news of you being chased around by a footballer with this kind of reputation broken to her gently.'

'I am afraid it is too late for that, Mama. Somebody took pictures of us at Challenge last night and it was on the front page of today's paper. We had to get a locum doctor to come to the house this morning because Tante Rosa was convinced she was about to die of a heart attack.'

Mama laughed so loudly that Ricky turned and frowned at her even with his ear plugs in.

'Allah have mercy on us all.' Mama wiped her eyes.

'She thinks I am the biggest fool in the world, Mama.'

'Let me tell you something important – it is better to be a fool who experiences happiness than a genius who misses out.'

'Mama, why is Tante Rosa so angry with me all the time? I can do nothing to please her.'

'She sees you as a mirror of herself. You look very much like her when she was your age, and sometimes, when you speak, you sound just like she used to as well. I think perhaps you remind her too much that her own life did not turn out as she hoped.'

'Neither did your life or mine, though, Mama.'

'Anna, show me one person whose life turned out as they planned and I will show you a liar.'

I stayed at the hospital for an hour after that, but of course when I stood up to leave, this was the exact minute that the *Toy Story* movie finished and Ricky begged me to play Guess Who with him. When I beat him he sulked, so we played a second and then a third game until he finally won.

On the bus to the pool, I received a text message from Nick:

After today's front-page news, maybe it's not such a good idea to meet at Challenge? Do you want meet somewhere

more discreet? It doesn't worry me but I just don't want you
to get into any trouble if more photos are leaked of us there.

I replied:

That is very thoughtful, thank you, but I do not need
protecting from photographers. I would very much like to
keep to our plan of meeting at Challenge because there is the
fifty-metre pool there where I am looking forward to beating
you in a race, remember?

Nick wasn't at Challenge when I arrived, so I found a seat near
the lanes and to fill in time, I took my journal, which came
everywhere with me, out of my backpack.

My dear Noor,

*If I tried to tell you in words how happy I am right now in
this moment, I would fail, so it is a lucky thing that you always
know what is in my heart anyway.*

*On the bus trip here I decided that I will let myself be a
fool, just like Mama said. And I do hope she is right and that I
start to feel young soon. Because you and I both know after all
that has happened, I have forgotten what it means to be young.*

*I hope that Nick will help me forget how old and battered
my soul is. I also hope he kisses me today. I cannot stop thinking
about what it would be like to kiss him!*

Oh, he just messaged me. He has arrived!

*See you in my dreams tonight, my sweet love. Goodbye for
now.*

A x.

NICK – TUESDAY

I'm in the car park. Text me when you get here ☺

I hit send and reached for my cap, which I pulled low over my eyes. I'd never successfully gone unnoticed with a cap in the past. People always recognised me from my size alone. Not to mention that I was on crutches, so if there was any doubt that it was me hiding under the cap, the crutches would take care of that. Why was I even bothering with the stupid cap?

For her. I was bothering for her. She was in my head this morning before my eyes were fully open. And even though my bed was empty, I felt less alone than I had for years.

I sent her a message as soon as I woke up, excited that I could – grateful she'd agreed to give me her phone number. Even after our long talk in the car last night, I was still worried she'd keep her number from me but she cheerfully typed it into my phone when I asked again.

Minutes after sending her that first message today, I checked Facebook. Joel had sent me a link to the *West Australian* page. I ignored Bluey's yelps for attention as I zoomed in on each photo.

How could I have been so careless with her? I messaged her immediately. After an agonising wait she replied, and miraculously she didn't seem fazed by it at all.

So I'd found a girl who wasn't worried about media attention but wasn't out to get it either. It couldn't get more perfect than that.

* * *

If today was a normal day, I would've joined in with everyone early this morning for a recovery session on the coast. Then I would have driven out with one of the rookies to a primary school for an Auskick fundraiser that had been scheduled in since last year. But instead they sent Joel to the school to play kick-to-kick and lecture kids about bullying, while I met up with one of the team physios who started me on the boring non-weight-bearing gym program.

Then it was straight into the hydrotherapy pool for forty-five minutes of laps, just like a little old lady after a hip replacement. The only difference being that I did it in deep water with a vest and was expected to jog not walk. When I got out, I was so dizzy from the humidity I reached for the wall, worried I was about to pass out.

I walked out of the club rooms to the stands and watched the team training together for a few minutes – new season, all pumped, all fit, all united with a clear goal. The boundary fence may as well have been sky high and it wouldn't have been any more of a barrier between us.

Back home, I drove Bluey down to the local dog beach. I'd forgotten how hard managing crutches in sand was until they sank in deep with my first step. I sat myself down as close as

I could get to the sea but where the sand was still dry. Bluey bounded after the stick that I threw at least fifty times – jowls flapping, ears back, in his nirvana.

'All right, enough. Go play!' I ordered him when my shoulder ached. 'Off you go.' I pointed at the ocean and he took off.

I leant back on my forearms and watched him make an idiot of himself in the shallows. He was joined a few minutes later by a white fluff ball about a quarter of his size. The fluff ball had a pink bow between its ears and yapped at Bluey as he sniffed its butt.

I looked to see who the dog belonged to and saw a girl jogging along the water's edge coming up from the south. The fluff ball's yapping turned more desperate as Bluey tried unsuccessfully to hump her. She was too light on her feet for him. But she kept hanging around, running up close enough to give him a taste and then bounding off as soon as he tried to get her in his grip.

'Fifi! Fifi! No! Shoosh!' The girl slowed her jog down to a walk. 'Fifi! Come!'

Fifi didn't come. Fifi, I thought, was having way too much fun teasing poor Bluey with her pink backside.

'Hi there!' The girl panted, pulling out her ear plugs.

'Hey,' I said. 'Cute dog.'

'Argh.' She laughed, looking at the dogs. 'She's so naughty. Fifi! Come I said!'

Fifi still didn't come.

'Mind if I sit for a minute while they play?' she said, as she plonked herself down on the sand next to me, wrapping the earplug wire around her phone.

The wind blew my hair in front of my face, so I lifted off my sunnies and used them as a headband.

'Oh my God! You're Nick Harding!' Her eyes widened.

I pulled my sunnies back down. 'Hi.'

'I'm Tanya.' She smiled. 'It's sooo cool to bump into you like this. Oh look, your crutches, how sad.'

'Ah well, shit happens.'

'So I guess you can't even train or anything?'

'Not for a while, nope.'

'Aw, you poor thing. I feel so sorry for you.'

The seasoned warning bell in my head sounded. Her tone. I knew that tone. Just as I was beginning to wind down and relax out here at the beach too. I tensed up between the shoulder blades.

'So what are you going to do with yourself for the rest of the day, Nick? I bet you're bored,' Tanya purred.

'No, nope, it's all good.'

'Still, it's kind of lonely, isn't it, just hanging around at the beach, *alone*?' She flicked her blonde ponytail and pulled down her fitted running singlet, wriggling a little. 'Are you lonely, Nick?'

My eyes, drawn to the movement, noticed her breasts. They looked good. I took in more of her. Toned body, pretty hair, pretty face, really pretty smile.

She bent her long legs up and her running shorts gaped. Because she was facing me, this gave me a perfect view of her butt cheeks. There were no knickers showing. I let myself imagine her in the G-string she must've been wearing – or better still, nothing at all.

'Nope, I'm not lonely at all,' I replied, unsmiling. 'How far are you running today?'

I had no interest in how long her run was. But I needed to distract myself with a question, any question. I peeled my eyes away from her tight butt and watched the ongoing game of cat and mouse between our dogs instead.

'Short run for me today, six k's.'

'That's impressive for a sand run.' I kept looking out to sea.

Tanya shuffled herself forward right in front of me, so that she was now between me and the water.

'Not as impressive as what Nick Harding does.' She gave my leg a nudge with her elbow. 'Hey, have you made any plans for lunch? I was thinking of grabbing some sushi. Want to join me? You're welcome to bring your dog round to mine if you like. I'm just up the road here and we've got the best Japanese takeaway at the end of the street.' She smiled her pretty smile.

I nodded. 'Thanks, but I can't.'

'Are you sure?' She tilted her head down and looked at me over the top of her sunglasses. 'We could have a fun afternoon. Just saying.' She cocked her eyebrow up and slipped her hand around the back of my calf. Her fingernails tickled my skin.

I clenched my jaw, angry at my stupid body for betraying me with its arousal. No better than Pavlov's fucking dogs, I was.

I pushed myself up off the ground. 'Sorry, I really can't. I'd better get going.'

I didn't make eye contact with her but could imagine her offended look as I bent down for the crutches. 'Nice to meet you and everything,' I mumbled before whistling for Bluey. 'Blue! Come on!'

Tanya brushed the sand off her legs as she stood up too, bending right down in front of me.

I looked away.

She shook out her ponytail. 'You wouldn't regret it, Nick. Nobody regrets coming to back to mine.'

Another erection threatened.

'I've got a girlfriend so I actually would regret it.'

'Oh, I didn't know. Well that's fair enough then.'

Bluey bolted over, saving me from the uncomfortable silence that followed. He stuck his nose right into Tanya's crotch before I sharply pulled him away and clipped his lead on. 'See you later.'

'See you,' she replied without much enthusiasm. 'Fifi! Come!'

I started the hard trek up the sand back to the car. When I looked back down at the beach. Tanya was chasing the fluff ball, still calling, 'Fifi! Come!'

Fifi didn't come.

Back home, I made myself a toasted sandwich and picked up *Harry Potter and the Philosopher's Stone*. There was an inscription in pink pen with big girly hand writing on the inside cover –

This book belongs to Noor. You can borrow it, but only while you're in Australia. This does NOT mean it is yours to keep. I hope I have made that VERY clear!

I added 'So who's Noor?' to the growing list of questions I had for Anna.

I rolled my eyes at the blurb but starting reading anyway, just so I could tell her I had. What I would have preferred was to pick up the new James Patterson book that was sitting right there waiting to be read. But when I looked up from the pages for the first time, over two hours had passed and it was time to go to the pool. Any wonder she raved about it! If it wasn't her who I was heading off to meet, I would have been annoyed to have to stop reading until the book was done.

I threw a towel over my shoulder, tucked my wallet and phone into my board shorts pockets and wore my goggles like a bracelet. I couldn't wipe the smile off my face as I drove barefoot to the stadium.

* * *

Hmm, it was now twenty minutes since we'd agreed to meet and half an hour since I messaged her. Should I message her again?

My phone vibrated:

I am here! Come inside I am waiting – lane 8 ☺

I grabbed the crutches and got in there as fast as I could. I paid for a two-month pool pass and wondered if that was too cocky. Would she still be wanting to meet up with me then?

I expected people to stop me for photos when I went into the pool area, but nobody paid me any attention. It was quieter than yesterday – just a few mums with toddlers in the kiddie pool and the odd person doing laps, as well as an oldies water exercise class. All the schoolkids weren't here yet. Excellent.

She was sitting at the end of the lane with her feet dangling in the water and those sexy red bathers on again. Her goggles sat high up on her head and when she saw me she waved with her hand tucked in close to her chest. I didn't regret getting the two-month pass.

I waved back and rested my crutches on the floor behind her. The second my cap was off I tensed up, waiting to hear my surname being shouted. But it didn't happen and I relaxed. I emptied the contents of my pockets – wallet, keys and phone, tucked them into the cap and then crossed my arms over my stomach and peeled off my T-shirt.

I walked over to the lockers and when I came back, Anna's eyes were glued to my abs.

'Hi Anna.'

She didn't answer. She kept staring.

I smiled and pulled my goggles down so they hung around my neck. I eased myself off the edge until I was standing chest-deep in the warm water in the lane beside hers. I did a quick look around for onlookers with phones. There weren't any.

Anna stood up and executed a perfect dive, emerging out of the water with a grin.

'Nice dive.' I said, raising my eyebrows. 'Where'd you learn to dive like that?'

'Oh, at school. Now let's race.' She gave me a huge smile.

'So you're serious then? You actually want to race me?' I asked, amused. 'I've done an Ironman challenge, you know. I'm a qualified surf lifesaver. I'm an *elite sportsman*. And in case you hadn't noticed, I'm also six foot six. You *sure* you want to race me?'

She nodded, grinning.

'What do I get if I win?' I leaned my face in close to hers.

'What would you like your prize to be, Nicholas Harding?'

I chuckled. 'I want you to come home with me after this.'

She looked away and laughed. 'I am working. What else?'

'I get to kiss you.' I stroked her cheek with my knuckles. The feel of her skin on mine gave me a rush.

She tilted her head to the side. 'Deal.'

'Where?'

'What do you mean where?' She looked alarmed.

'Where can we go so I can kiss you if you won't come to

my house after the race?' I found her thigh under the water and ran my fingers along it, keeping my eyes locked on hers.

She inhaled sharply. I explored the smooth skin on the outside of her leg for a few seconds before she placed her hand firmly over mine.

'It does not matter where you want to go for this kiss, Nick, because I am going to win. There will be no kissing prize today.'

'Is that right? So what do you want if you win?' I was trying hard to control my breathlessness. It was ridiculous how turned on I was just from touching her leg for a few seconds.

'When I win, my prize will be that you let me make you a Turkish coffee, and you drink it all up.' She laughed and pulled down her goggles. 'Eight laps. Freestyle. You ready?'

'Eight laps? That's four hundred metres. Why so long?'

'Endurance, Nick. You *are* an elite athlete, are you not? Show me what you can do. Your height is too big an advantage for one or two laps. I need more laps because then I can tire you out.'

'You think you can tire me out? That's cute,' I snorted, putting my goggles on too. 'All right, on the count of three?'

We both pushed off and I led from the get-go. Towards the end of the first lap, I was surprised to find her just over a body length behind me and, by the end of the second lap, I was more surprised to find her still there. I took it up a notch for laps three and four, but so did she and she closed in on me. I went even harder but still I couldn't shake her off. It had been a long time since I'd had to swim this hard but no way was I losing to her, so I put more into each kick. She stayed on my tail and no matter how fast I went, I couldn't put more distance between us.

For the last hundred metres I sprinted, giving it everything I had – taking huge gulps of air, kicking fiercely and ploughing through the water with my arms. My throat burned, my legs felt like jelly and my shoulders were screaming in pain. My hand slapped the wall a split second after hers at the finish.

I pulled off my goggles and gasped for air. 'What the hell was that?' I shook my head at her, laughing. 'Explain yourself, woman!'

'You should find out who you are competing against before laying bets.' She smiled, getting the words out a few at a time in between deep breaths. 'I was national champion for two years running in Egypt, and world champion in the four hundred, and the fifteen hundred free when I was sixteen. Oh, and for seven weeks I held the world record in the four hundred free.'

'*What*?' My eyes were just about hanging out of their sockets. 'A world champion? How could you not have told me that last night?'

She shrugged. 'Perhaps if you did not spend so much time obsessing over whether I ate bacon or not I might have had more time to tell you.' She stretched her shoulders. 'Excuse me, professional surf lifesaver, Ironman, *elite sportsman*, huge six-foot-six man. I am going to continue with some slow laps now. Do you think you can keep up?' She pushed off from the wall while I hung off the ropes, watching her go with my jaw hanging wide open.

My mind raced while I swam. When we stopped for a break after four more laps, I asked her, 'So do you still compete?'

'No, not since we arrived in Australia.'

'Why not?'

She wiped the water from her face and answered slowly. 'It was impossible to focus. I had no sleep, I had no energy. I was grieving. And I blamed my swimming for why my mother and I were in Australia in the first place.'

'What do you mean by that?'

'She was with me for a competition, one of the lead-ups to the World Championships. Either my mother or father always accompanied me to international meets.' She paused. 'Do you really want to know all of this now, Nick – here in the pool?'

'Of course I want to hear it. I don't care where we are. But would you rather tell me later?'

'No.' She sighed. 'Now that I have started I want to finish. I just do not want to make you uncomfortable with heavy news such as this.'

I reached for her hand. 'I'm not uncomfortable. Tell me the rest.'

'I will swim a lap and come back,' she said.

'I'll come with you.'

When we reached the end again, we rested with our backs against the wall.

'My mother is Leila Hayati.'

'You're looking at me like I should know who that is.'

'You don't?'

I wracked my brain and came up blank. 'No.'

'Well, a little over a year ago her name made headlines here. That is why I assumed you would have heard of her, of us.'

'What kind of headlines?'

She gulped. 'My mother was the leader of the Egyptians for Peace Democratic Party.'

'Like a *major* political party?'

She cleared her throat. 'Yes. She was going to run for president in the next elections and she was the favourite to win. She was popular with the majority of Egyptians – Muslims,

Christians, Jews. Everyone loved her. She had tolerant policies and she promised to restore our country to its former glory, the way it was before it was corrupted by politics and radicalism.'

'Okay.' I worked at keeping a poker face. *Running for president?* 'And?'

'There was another party called the Islamic Alliance. They had been opposed to my mother for years because of what they considered to be her blasphemous ways. They did not like that a *woman*, especially one who was a Christian, had this much influence over the people. They felt threatened, I think, that she had such progressive views, and they hated her for not converting to Islam.' She spoke staring straight in front of her. 'My parents were worried about our family being targeted by supporters of the Islamic Alliance. So we had bodyguards twenty-four hours a day.'

I swallowed the dread that was building up as I listened.

'When I started coming up through the ranks of swimming, the Islamic Alliance took offence to my swimsuits. I was not wearing a burkini, you see. They held a press conference to denounce my parents. They believed that the daughter of a highly positioned Muslim academic – my father was the Dean of Alexandria University – should be showing more modesty. They also made a big issue of the fact that I didn't wear a hijab.'

She blew air up to her wet fringe. 'Of course my parents believed that the decision to wear a hijab or a burkini was a personal one to be made by each individual woman, not a sanctioned law to be enforced without question on all women. So they ignored the protestations of the Islamic Alliance and I continued to compete wearing a regular swimsuit.' Her eyes were locked on mine now as she wound and unwound her goggles around her wrist. 'The week before we left for

Australia, a video was sent to Channel 5, which is Alexandria's big news television station. It was a short clip of a jihadist calling for the immediate resignation of my mother and my withdrawal from the Egyptian swimming team unless I wore a burkini. He said that if we did not listen to his warning, there would be consequences.'

'Oh no.' I gulped.

'My mother called a press conference that same day and said, "Of course we will not let terrorists scare us, nor will we let them threaten the very freedom that makes Egypt the jewel of the Middle East."' Her voice wobbled. 'And the next week, we came to Australia for me to compete. My mother was defiant to the end. She knew we would be filmed at the airport so she had me wear my hair out, and even though she usually held hers back she wore it out too.'

The skin on her wrist had turned an angry shade of red where she'd been twisting her goggle strap.

'And then what happened?'

'They set off a bomb in my father's car.'

As soon as the words were out she broke down.

'Jesus,' I whispered.

She hung her head and said through tears, 'One of our bodyguards, Hamdy, who my father loved like a brother, was wearing the device.'

I ducked under the rope and into her lane and took her in my arms. She silently sobbed into my chest.

A teenager seated a few feet away from us had a red recording light on the phone she was pointing at us.

I called out. 'Oi! Cut it out!'

The lifeguard was already jogging over.

'That girl filmed us,' I told him, pointing.

He gave me a thumbs up and started talking with the girl.

I rubbed Anna's back. She was pulling herself together now. 'Let's go, Anna. Let's get you out of here.'

I walked her to the door of the female change rooms and then hobbled back to my crutches and dried myself off. It was well over thirty degrees in here, the humidity had fogged up all the windows but still I was shivering.

The pool was just starting to fill up now that school was out. I signed autographs without thinking and ignored the kids who called out to me. I refused all requests for selfies with a shake of my head.

A mum told her son, 'Don't worry, mate, he's a stuck-up prick, that Harding.'

Anna took so long in the change room that I began to worry she wasn't okay in there. But when she came out her eyes were dry and she looked fresher.

'Forgive me for keeping you waiting. I needed to sit and collect my thoughts.'

I drew her close to me and we walked out in silence.

I drove us a few blocks up the road and parked in a quiet street. 'I don't know what to say. I mean, I can think of a hundred things but none seem right.'

'I realised as I was getting dressed that I did not finish answering your question from before about why I do not compete anymore.'

'Oh? What's the answer?'

'The answer is I could compete again if I wanted to, if I was prepared to. In fact, I was invited by Swimming Australia to train at the AIS as soon as we were granted permanent residency.'

'Why didn't you do that?'

'Guilt.'

'But how in the world could you possibly blame yourself? These are sick terrorists who did that. It's not your fault.'

'My swimming career destroyed my family, Nick. And not only that, my mother might have been elected and brought much-needed change to our country, but instead she was exiled. If it was not for me none of it would have happened. How can I ever compete again after all that? The least I can do now is to continue the work my mother started. I cannot save Egypt, but I found a situation as desperate as ours in the Middle East right here in Australia.'

'Asylum seekers right?'

'Yes. Children spending years in detention is just as big a tragedy. My dream is no longer about breaking records and winning medals that I do not deserve after what I did.'

'But you didn't *do* anything wrong, Anna!'

'Yes I did.' She sighed. 'I did.'

'Well, just so you know, I'm in awe of you. And I think I'm actually more in awe of you right now than I've ever been of anyone I can remember.'

She smiled sadly. 'There is nothing to be in awe of. I have done nothing special.'

'Pfft,' I scoffed. 'So, back to what happened – you and your mum were here in Perth and what? You never went home? You've been here since?'

'Yes. My mother was well known and on very good terms with some people in the Australian government. She had met with the Prime Minister and Foreign Minister more than once. We were granted permanent protection visas immediately when the second video was made the day after the fire.'

'The fire? What fire?'

'The explosion – the fire,' she clarified.

'Oh, sorry.' I felt like a moron. 'What second video?'

'The same group released a second video with footage of the bomb. A jihadist appeared in front of the camera and claimed responsibility. He then said that if my mother or I returned to Egypt, they would kill me and make her watch. And that they would tape my beheading for the rest of the world to *enjoy* as well. He was smiling into the camera as he said it. If you google "Hayati terrorist video" you'll see it.' She swallowed.

'Oh my God.' I felt sick. 'Please tell me you haven't watched it again since that first time.'

'Nick, I think I've viewed it perhaps a thousand times.' She looked at her lap.

'Oh, no.'

'You see now why we made headlines here a year ago?' she said. 'All of this happened the evening before I was due to compete. Of course I did not race.'

'I can't believe I missed all of that. The whole thing doesn't even bring back the foggiest memory. Head up my own arse as usual.'

She smiled. 'I like this saying. I have heard Gianni also say it. It is very funny.' She checked her watch. 'Nick, I have to get to work. Can you please drive me home? I have had enough of talking about this now.'

'Of course, but if you want to talk about it again later on, I'm all ears, okay?'

'Thank you. Let us change the subject. How was your morning?'

I told her about taking Bluey down to the beach, leaving out the part about the girl whose name I'd already forgotten. By the time we arrived back at Fremantle she was laughing and cheerful and the awful things she told me about her past seemed far from her mind again.

'I must go inside,' she said after we'd been parked out the back of the restaurant for a couple of minutes.

'You work for your family. What are they going to do, sack you? Stay with me a bit longer.'

She chuckled. 'We have been together two hours. Is it still not enough?'

'Just a few more minutes.'

'Very well.'

'Hey, I started reading *Harry Potter*!' I announced, remembering.

'Oh!' She clapped her hands together. 'And you like it?'

'I do. I like it a lot.'

She laughed her husky laugh. 'I am so happy you like it.'

Her laughter faded after a few seconds. We fell into silence. There was a look in her eye, a signal I immediately recognised.

I took a shaky breath in. 'Anna, I know I lost the bet, but would it be okay with you if we kissed anyway? Or is it too soon?' I gulped. 'If you want to get to know each other more first, and it feels too soon for you, I understand.' It was the first time I'd ever asked a girl permission to kiss her in such a formal way.

'I want to kiss so very much.' She smiled the sexiest smile in the whole wide world.

So I held her wet hair in one hand and cupped her face with the other and I touched her lips with mine. She kissed me back, but it was barely more than a graze of our lips. She was trembling.

I pulled away. 'You're so nervous. Have you kissed before?'

She blushed. 'No, never. Is it that obvious? Am I no good at it?'

'Not at all. I don't want to rush you, that's all.'

'I am not feeling rushed. I am just nervous.'

'Don't be.' I stroked her cheek with my thumb. 'You're so beautiful.'

She smiled. 'As are you.'

I leaned in and kissed her again. We kissed each other with closed mouths for a minute or two and then I gently probed open her lips with my tongue and found hers. She relaxed into the kiss and our tongues tentatively explored each other's. Her innocence and her sincerity and her warmth were all there in her mouth.

And because I wanted to be sure that she was enjoying it and that she was comfortable, and because I'd fallen for her so hard, I kissed her with more care and with more emotion than I'd ever kissed another girl.

It was my first kiss as much as it was hers. 'I could kiss you for hours,' I murmured when we came up for air.

'Mmmm,' she replied through half-closed eyes.

I'd always be turned on by the smell of chlorine from now on because it would remind me of the moment I discovered how good it tasted on her.

My need for more physical contact with her hurt, it actually hurt down there. But I kept my hands cupped on her face to stop myself taking it any further.

She seemed to sense my urgency and she pulled away. 'Okay, now I am very late and my Aunt Rosa will skewer me like a shish kebab.'

I ran my index finger along the neckline of the white lace dress she was wearing over spotted black and yellow leggings and her signature purple Docs.

'I like how you dress.'

She snorted. '*Nobody* likes how I dress!'

'Well, I do. It's cute. And it's sexy. I like that you don't dress like anyone else I know.'

'That is very nice of you to say, Nick. I liked that white shirt you wore to Masri's, and I liked how you looked in your swimsuit.'

I dropped my finger a bit further and it made contact with the very top of her breast, which made my stomach dive. 'You know I wasn't listening to a word of that, don't you?' I said, transfixed by her soft cool skin.

'Nick!' She flicked my hand away with a laugh. 'Okay, I am leaving now.'

'Why?' I groaned.

'Because of work. I have to work! The restaurant opens in five minutes. I should have been there an hour ago.'

'Can I see you tomorrow then?'

'Yes.' She smiled with a few of her quick little nods. 'Five o'clock again?'

'Okay, but what about a quick coffee back at my house after the swim. What do you say?' I held my breath.

'If I agree to come and spend half an hour or so with you at your house, are we of the understanding that kissing is where it stops, Nick?'

'Can I touch that bit of your breast again at my house?' I grinned.

'No.'

'Okay. Can I touch it if you've got clothes covering it?'

'Nick.' She raised her eyebrows. 'Kissing you in a car when I have known you for less than three days is quite enough to make me question myself and my morals. If I come to your house you will keep your hands to yourself. Yes?'

'Yes. Okay, yes.'

'I am hoping that tomorrow we are told Ricky can come home. So I might be in an extra special good mood. Or if the test results from yesterday are not so good, then I may be in a sour mood.'

'They'll be good,' I said with fake assurance. *Please, God, make the results good.* 'Do I get to meet Ricky when he comes home?'

'Of course.' She beamed. 'And my mother wants to meet you too. I hope you will meet them both on Thursday when you come and pick me up for our dinner date.'

'Your mum?' I widened my eyes. 'She'll nail me! She was going to be a president. Oh God, I'm screwed, aren't I?'

She shook her head. 'That woman is no longer my mother. My mother is a shell now, Nick, a shell.' She had that faraway haunted look again.

I wanted her smile back.

'Where have all your hokays gone? I miss them. Here yesterday, gone today. What happened?'

'Hayatis are quick learners.' She grinned.

'I want the hokays back, though,' I protested. 'I love those hokays.'

'That will teach you to poke fun.' She chuckled. 'So tomorrow, Nicholas Harding, you will tell me more about your career with the Western Rangers, because I know very little about football and I need to be educated, yes?'

'Yeah, I can tell you about the Rangers if you want, but you'll be bored to tears.' I felt a stab of betrayal towards my team and wished I could take the words back. I cleared my throat. 'Hey, can I come inside with you? Weren't you going to make me drink a Turkish coffee with that bet?'

'Perhaps we should give my Aunt Rosa some more time to adjust to you being my boyfriend before you come back to Masri's, so that she does not poison your coffee,' she said with a wry smile.

'Boyfriend? Who said I'm your boyfriend?'

She tapped my thigh. 'I said.'

'That's a bit presumptuous of you, Anna. I'm not even sure I like you in that way yet,' I murmured, before pulling her in for one last kiss that I dragged out for as long as I could.

'*Ana bahebak*, Nick,' she whispered when she finally broke away.

'What did you say? Anna *what* Nick?'

'*Bahebak*. It means Anna says goodbye to Nick.' She smiled her gorgeous smile again. '*Ana bahebak*, Nick.'

'Hang on a minute.' I dug for my phone and pulled it out of my pocket. 'Give me that smile again.'

She didn't do what other girls had done whenever I'd asked them to pose for a photo. She didn't protest that she looked ugly or grumble that she didn't have makeup on. She didn't make me wait while she checked her hair or pulled out a lip gloss. She smiled. She just looked at me and smiled and she let me freeze it forever. She didn't even ask to see the photo.

I watched her jog towards the back door of the restaurant.

My girlfriend. My first girlfriend.

'She was worth the wait, wasn't she, Dad?' I said out loud as I swapped the photo of him and me on my lock screen with the one I just took of her.

I wasn't going to do anything to mess this up. No way.

LILY – WEDNESDAY

I opened my eyes to the realisation I'd pulled an Arielle. I was in bed with a man I had shagged two and a half times (technically speaking, the last time didn't involve actual shagging) a few days after meeting him.

But I didn't have a single regret.

He slept soundly next to me, his warm calloused hand tucked in between my legs. I didn't want to wake him but I desperately needed to pee. So I slowly, slowly slid backwards until his hand fell away. He let out a muffled groan and stayed asleep. I stood at the foot of the bed and watched him.

My heart was leaping. It was actually leaping around in my chest. I put my hand over my bare chest in disbelief. I'd had a racing heart but I'd never experienced *that* before.

It took me a second to figure out there was no ensuite as I looked around the room, and that's when I saw the framed photo of him with Jenny on their wedding day above his chest of drawers.

I came crashing down fast.

That special smile he had for me was right there in the photo. That piercing stare I thought signified the intensity of his feelings towards me? That was how he was looking at her.

There was another framed photo of the two of them together, they were no older than about sixteen with their arms around each other in the surf. They couldn't have seemed more in love.

I may have found someone who rocked my world in the man sleeping right there, but the man sleeping right there had just lost someone who rocked his. I squeezed my eyes shut. *Lily, you idiot! What did you expect?*

I took long slow breaths to prevent the anxiety attack I felt curling itself into a fist around my heart, just before it started delivering the punches. I practised the skills the psychologist taught me for dealing with my anxiety after Dad died. I breathed in for the count of four, and out for seven, until the dread passed, and then I tiptoed naked through the house looking for the toilet.

While I peed I thought about what I was going to do. *I can't stay here. I have to leave this house, and I have to make sure that I never see him again.*

I jumped when the toilet door was pushed wide open in one big swing and a guy I'd never met took a step in with his hands on his fly.

'*Holy fuck!*' he roared when he saw me.

I screamed a scream worthy of a horror movie.

'*Who are you?*' His eyes went wide with terror.

'*Tobyyy! Help!*' I screeched in a voice I didn't even recognise as mine. '*Get out! Get ouuut!*'

The guy quickly pulled the door shut, a look of horror still on his face, and I leaned back against the wall, hyperventilating.

Then I heard Toby shout, 'What the hell are you doing here?'

And the guy shouted back, 'I live here, you fuckwit!'

Oh dear God, it couldn't get any worse. I locked the door.

'Bit late for that, Blondie!' the housemate yelled at me through the door when the lock clicked shut. And then he said in a quieter voice, that wasn't quiet enough for me not to overhear, 'I came home to check in on you before work. I was making sure my brother was all right the morning after he *buried his wife*. I didn't expect you'd be out on the pull on the day of the goddamn funeral.'

Nope, I was wrong. It could get worse. It wasn't just a housemate, it was his brother.

'It wasn't like that,' Toby said in an even quieter voice that I was straining to hear. 'She's special. She isn't just a random girl I picked up. She came over to help me last night.'

'Ha! Yeah, yeah, of course that's what it is. Sit and counsel you, did she? And then just happens to still be here the next morning, naked?' His sarcasm cut through me. 'And to think you judge me about Renee – what a hypocrite you are.'

Toby's voice took on a dangerous tone. 'This is *nothing* like what you do to Renee. She's important to me, all right?'

My heart leapt and leapt.

'You're right,' his brother replied. 'This *is* nothing like me and Renee. You know why? Because I didn't go on for two years about how I'd lost the love of my life only to get her back again and then fuck some blonde the day of her funeral.' He snorted. 'If that chick in there's so special and important, why have you never mentioned her before? Hey? You're just using her to fuck the grief away. Don't pretend it's anything more.'

'Get out,' Toby growled. 'Just get out.'

'With fucking pleasure. And make sure the blonde's gone when I get home.'

I clasped my hand over my mouth and burst into silent tears.

Toby knocked on the door. 'Lily?'

'Go away!' I sobbed.

'Lily, he's gone.' His tone was warm, gentle. 'It's all right to come out now. It's only me out here.'

I cried harder.

'Lily.' His voice sounded closer, like he might be leaning his head on the door. 'Please don't pay attention to John. He's nothing but a dickhead who misunderstood what happened here last night.'

'No, he didn't,' I sniffed. 'He was spot on.'

'Lily.' He gave the door another gentle knock. 'Can you please come out?'

'No.'

'Look, last night was, well, it was perfect. It was exactly what I wanted, needed. I don't regret it. And John? He doesn't know shit about what happened between us.'

'He just saw my naked bits!' I wailed.

He chuckled. 'I'm going to kill the bastard for seeing those bits. I love those bits.'

He said love! 'Toby? Were you just fucking the grief away last night?'

'No. Not even close. Last night meant, it meant … more than anything.'

More than anything. My belly tumble-turned remembering when he said that the night before. 'Toby?'

'Yeah?'

'I know I don't know you properly, or at all, but last night I swear I felt like I was falling in love with you.'

Silence.

Oh Jesus! Why did I say that?

Could I escape through that small window high above the cistern? No, it had a heavy grille on it. I'd just have to spend the rest of my life in this man's toilet.

But then he said, 'I felt like I was falling in love with you too.'

'How can you be falling in love with me, you lunatic?' I shouted in hysterical tears. 'You don't even know me!'

He acted as though this was really funny.

'It's not funny. This is hopeless,' I moaned. 'Your wife died two days ago. It's just hopeless.'

'It's not the best timing, but ...' he cleared his throat, '... you reached out to me on the worst night of my life when I needed it the most. What happened between us was, I don't know, when I was with you it felt almost like it was ...'

'Like it was meant to be?' I suggested.

'Yeah, like it was fate.'

'That's how I felt too.' I sighed. 'I'm so ashamed, though. It feels wrong. It *is* wrong. Everyone will judge me.'

'Nobody needs to know. Just you and me.'

'And John.'

He chuckled. 'And him. Are you planning on ever opening the door?'

I unlocked the door. He gently nudged it open.

His eyes roamed up and down my body. 'Good morning, Rapunzel,' he murmured, pulling me into his arms.

Then he kissed me. In the toilet.

His soft kisses and the feel of his stubble on my chin made the butterflies in my tummy start dancing and the frogs in my heart start their game of leap again.

He held my face in both his hands. 'Can I make you some toast and a coffee?'

I nodded dreamily. 'That sounds perfect.'

Then I stopped nodding and froze. It was Wednesday. It wasn't the weekend. I felt the blood drain from my body.

'What time is it?'

He flicked his wrist and checked his watch. 'Five past nine.'

'Oh my God, I'm fucked! I'm so fucked! I'm the fuckedest I've ever been!'

Helium Man had put me on ward duty. And it had started five minutes ago. In Subiaco. And here I was in a toilet in Scarborough – a twenty-minute drive away.

I got dressed in seconds. I hadn't worn a bra here. Crap!

As I bolted out the front door, I made plans with Toby to catch up later in the day. He followed me out onto the driveway. I gave him one last manic kiss, before I sped off with the taste of his smoky breath in my mouth. I scrambled blindly around in my bag with my free hand until I found some gum.

Adam Harding's daughter or not, Helium Man was going to skin me alive.

Yesterday I felt like I did okay. I didn't cry in any rooms (I cried plenty in the toilets but managed to keep my shit together on rounds). Plus, I didn't get told off. Great – I'd had one day of staying out of trouble and here I was about to be slammed again.

For the trip into Subiaco, I barely thought about Toby because I needed all my focus on keeping the other drivers and myself alive while I drove like I was in a Formula One race.

I ran out of the lift onto the oncology ward at nine thirty-seven.

Everyone was standing around the reception area, looking bored. There was no Helium Man, though. I asked one of the students what the story was and he shrugged. Nobody knew where Helium Man was. *Oh, I love you, Lord Jesus. I love you! I am absolutely, definitely going to church this Sunday … Maybe.*

Then I realised that we were standing opposite the room Jenny had been in. And the elation was replaced with doubt. I slept with her husband only a few hours after he buried her. I sent her an apology as I looked into her empty room with the stripped bed.

Despite what Toby had said about fate, he would surely realise today that his brother was right – that all he was looking for was a way to dull his pain and that I was conveniently there to do just that. Then he'd be figuring out ways to diplomatically get rid of me, because he was a good guy. I'd probably caused him all kinds of anxiety and guilt today.

Helium Man appeared and I forced myself to push the mess with Toby out of my head. I needed to bring my A-game today.

Helium Man apologised to the group, saying he'd been delayed due to unforeseen circumstances. Everyone nodded as if this was a completely acceptable excuse needing no further elaboration and I made a mental note to use 'unforeseen circumstances' should I need it in the future.

Then he saw me and he froze. I froze too.

'Decided to thrill us by coming in fancy dress for ward duty, did you, Miss Harding?' He sneered, taking in my summer dress peeping out from the lab coat, rather than black uniform pants. At least I had proper shoes on – only because I'd left them in the car yesterday.

'Um, no, Dr Leslie. Just unforeseen circumstances, Dr Leslie.' I was literally trembling.

He furrowed his massive sticky-out eyebrows and nodded in understanding. Wow, this line was good. Why had I never used it before?

'And I see you've brought back *the hair*?' he squealed.

I gulped. 'Yes, Dr Leslie. Not on purpose though, Dr Leslie. I meant to have it held back like I did yesterday. It's just those unforeseen circumstances.' I screwed up my face to show him how annoyed I was too.

'Shall we proceed then, Miss Harding?'

I smiled as if I would love nothing more than to have this group of people watching me try to hold it together around really sick cancer patients, and led the way.

We met with the nurse in charge who gave us a brief handover and then we all filed into the first room with shaky-legged, shaky-voiced me leading the charge.

The room had an underweight little boy in there, called Ricky.

I'd missed the ward round in Ricky's room on Monday because I was with Jenny in her room. So when the others went home on Monday, I'd gone to Helium Man's office to find out about the little boy. He was leaning against his desk, dictating notes into a dictaphone when I knocked on his open door. 'Yes?' he huffed. 'What can I do for you?'

'Ah, excuse me, Dr Leslie.' I took a tentative step inside his office. 'I was just, ah, I was wondering if it would be okay if it wasn't too much trouble if—'

'Get to the point, Miss Harding.'

Behind him on the wall was a massive poster of Todd McKenney's face, the judge from *Dancing with the Stars*. Why was there a framed photo of Todd McKenney in Helium Man's office? Since when were there even posters of Todd McKenney's face in existence?

'Miss Harding!' He clicked his fingers in front of my face. 'Are you still with us?'

'Sorry, yes, Dr Leslie. I just, it's just that I noticed that poster of Todd McKenney. Are you a *Dancing with the Stars* fan? Or do you know him or something?'

'Miss Harding.'

'Mmm?'

'Please get to the point of why you interrupted my dictation.' His voice hit new heights in squeakiness.

I guessed the mention of Todd McKenney could do that to a person.

'I was just curious, I mean, why Todd Mc—'

'Miss Harding!'

I swallowed. 'Yes, sorry, Dr Leslie. I missed a room on the round this morning and then this afternoon I saw that there was a child in there so I just came to ask about him.'

He turned his chair to face the desk, giving me his back, pulled out a file and began writing.

I coughed. 'Um, so, Dr Leslie, I was wondering why that little boy was here.'

'He has cancer, Miss Harding. You're at a specialist cancer hospital.' He continued writing notes.

I turned to leave. Maybe one of the nurses could give me the lowdown on the little boy who gave me a big gap-toothed smile when I had a peek in his room today. When I reached the door, I spun around. 'Dr Leslie, I really want to know more about the boy.'

He sighed. 'Sit down.'

I sat.

He sharpened a pencil. 'Ricky Abadi is a six-year-old Nigerian asylum seeker whose parents drowned when the boat from Indonesia capsized.' He sharpened another pencil.

'Oh God. How did he survive then?'

'He was strapped into one of the few lifejackets on board. Twenty-nine survivors. One hundred eighty-six passengers.'

'That's just horrendous. I can't believe he survived in open sea, even with a life jacket.'

'An Australian Navy ship was about to intercept the boat anyway. They were able to quickly rescue the few who didn't immediately drown. He would have had a few minutes in the water at most.'

'So was he brought to Perth as a refugee? Who looks after him?'

'No, Miss Harding. He isn't a refugee. He was taken to off-shore detention.'

'Oh my God. He wasn't granted asylum?'

I imagined the little boy in a detention centre after losing his parents.

'No.'

'So was it the cancer that had him brought to Perth?'

'Exactly.' Helium Man tipped the sharpenings of three pencils into the bin. 'On Bluff Island, he became sick. Very sick. So he was transferred and admitted to hospital. He was diagnosed with a rare and aggressive form of cancer – juvenile myelomonocytic leukemia. Look up JMML when you go home.' He swivelled around so I was forced to look at the back of his head again. 'If that's all, Miss Harding, I have important work to get back to. I'm a very busy man, you know.'

No, that wasn't all! 'I don't understand why he's here and not at the children's hospital. I mean where's the money coming from? And, well, he's a little kid in an adult hospital. Shouldn't he be at PMH on the oncology ward there? Who's looking after him? Is he in a foster home or anything?'

He grunted again. 'You really are quite the sticky-nose. If you have to know, he's here because the family looking after him specifically requested I be in charge of his care. I was involved in running clinical trials for JMML a few years back. And the money is from a local Egyptian restaurant owner sponsoring him. He was living with the family after he was discharged from hospital. But a recent blood test showed his white cell count wasn't good, so he's been back for another round of chemo and radiation.'

'Oh no! Is it bad?' I gasped.

'He has metastatic cancer, Miss Harding. It's not exactly good.' He paused for bit. 'It could be worse. It hasn't reached his organs. Yet.'

'Do you think it will?' I bit my lip.

'The short answer is I don't know. His cell count's back to normal range and we've got it down to less than ten per cent of his cells affected, so he's in the clear for now. He'll be discharged this week all things being equal.'

'He doesn't have to go back to Bluff Island does he?'

'No, no – he won't be sent back. I believe the paperwork is almost complete for his permanent asylum so he'll stay with the Egyptian family.' He sighed. 'Are we quite done now?'

'Yes, thank you very much, Dr Leslie.' I stood up to leave but then sat again. 'Dr Leslie?'

'Yes?'

'With the clinical trials you did with JMML, were any of the drugs successful?'

He looked me in the eyes and shook his head.

'And what's the longest anyone survived after it metastasised?'

He looked up at the poster of Todd McKenney for a bit and then back at me. 'In my limited experience, not long. Not long at all.' He must've seen the expression on my face because he added, 'I have a feeling, though, that the Abadi kid might outlast the others.'

'Oh? What makes you say that?'

He shrugged. 'Hunch.'

I nodded. 'Well, thanks again. I'll leave you to it.'

'You're not suited to this job.' He rubbed his hands up and down the front of his legs.

I gulped. 'I know.' I knew that better than anyone.

He cleared his throat. 'I mean being an oncologist. Don't consider it when you finish up next year.'

'I won't.' It was hard to reply without my voice breaking.

It was the first time any supervisor, lecturer, tutor, anyone, really, had ever been less than complimentary. He was the first person to see exactly what I knew to be true – I didn't belong here.

'See yourself out and close the door behind you.' He flipped open his Mac. 'And for Christ's sake don't cry on round tomorrow or I'll start deducting marks from your final grade.'

And that was how I finished the day on Monday.

***

Yesterday during ward round, Ricky was sitting on a middle-aged woman's lap. She'd held him tight the entire time, as if trying to shield him from us. He didn't look frightened, but still she'd cradled his bald head close to her chest. She'd seemed reluctant to release her grip on the little boy when Helium Man asked to examine him.

Helium Man moved a stethoscope over Ricky's chest, checked his fingernails and pulled down his lower eyelids.

'All good, buddy,' Helium Man said when he was done. Why didn't he squeak at patients? Why did he save his squeaking for us?

He looked at the woman and spoke quickly, 'Seems good. We'll run a blood test today and assuming he stays well, we're still on track for discharge this week.'

Did she understand him? Her expression didn't change.

The woman rattled me, but I couldn't pinpoint exactly what it was that made me feel uneasy around her. At first glimpse, she had the appearance of a regular person – plain blue jeans, plain white shirt, brown hair pulled back in a standard ponytail, no makeup on, no jewellery apart from a nondescript wrist watch, nothing to make her seem anything other than ordinary. But she wasn't a regular person. The way she sat dead straight, her shins crossed and her ankles locked together – completely still and poised, and the way she held her head tilted slightly up and to the left so that she looked down her nose at everyone was not what regular people were like. She was completely intimidating before she had even said a word.

After a long pause, she nodded once and with a tight smile answered, 'Thank you, Miles.'

Miles? She was the first person to use Helium Man's first name. Even the senior medical staff called him Dr Leslie. Literally all of them. This woman was the only person on the ward, maybe in the world, who didn't seem in awe of Helium Man. Who seemed superior to him somehow.

'I'll be back later in the day.' Helium Man bent down and patted Ricky's shoulder. 'Next room, students.'

'I'd like a word, Miles,' the woman said as we were just about out the door.

She had a strange accent. When she first spoke I thought it was American, but it wasn't quite American.

'Of course,' Helium Man gulped.

He was totally intimidated by her! What was the story here?

The woman gave Ricky's bottom a light tap and he hopped off her knee. She straightened her shirt and walked out ahead of us with long confident strides, her shoulders back.

Out in the corridor, she stood face to face with Helium Man and crossed her arms. 'Miles, your refusal yesterday to give me a specific prognosis in relation to Ricky's odds of survival is infuriating. It is impossible to believe that you have no statistics, or figures, zero. How can this be?' She didn't wait for an answer. 'I understand it is not the most common type of leukaemia, but it is not so rare that there would be no record-keeping of the numbers of survivors and years of survival after a recurrence. I could look on the internet but we both know not to believe what we read online. So give me the facts please, Miles.'

He opened his mouth to speak but she didn't give him time to get a word in before she uncrossed her arms and pointed a finger at him.

'And even if you don't have exact statistics, at the very least you could indulge my family's need to know what to expect in the coming years by revealing what *you* personally predict his prognosis to be. The only reason my brother-in-law has spent his savings to have Ricky transferred was because we were told *you* were the leading expert on JMML. Surely you must have some opinion on the matter, one way or another? As the expert?'

She was taller than Helium Man so, like me, she would have had a good view of the sweat beads shining all over his scalp.

'I have a rule not to guess survival periods in my patients.' He pulled out his handkerchief and wiped his forehead. 'If it was a ninety-nine per cent chance of survival, the one patient I told that to would undoubtedly end up being the one in a hundred who didn't survive. In this job, I've learnt that statistics mean nothing. But if you're so insistent on statistics, then against my better judgement, I'll tell you this – going by what I've seen clinically, which matches what you'll find in the research should you choose to look it up yourself, and despite your denials, I'm sure a woman of your calibre has already done her research and wouldn't rely solely on my say so …' the clipboard shook in his hands '… is that kids who've had their levels get this high a second time by such a young age rarely reach adolescence. Having said that, if anyone's going to do it, Ricky will, and I have every faith in him.'

'I see,' the woman took a big breath. 'Thank you, Miles. That's all I need to know.'

She walked back into the room with her chin up.

Helium Man took a minute to compose himself. He looked at us one by one. 'Does anyone remember the former Egyptian politician Leila Hayati?'

'The one whose family was blown to bits by ISIS?' asked one of the boys standing behind me.

'Not the most respectful way to phrase it and it wasn't ISIS, but yes, that's the one,' he replied, with a tilt of his head towards Ricky's room. 'You just met her.'

My jaw fell open. I had watched that footage at least ten times in disbelief the day it appeared on my newsfeed last year. I remembered how I couldn't look away from that horrible, horrible video.

'That was Leila Hayati?' I gasped.

Helium Man met my eyes and nodded.

Well, any wonder I thought there was something intimidating about her! And then the penny dropped. Anna/Anwar Hayati, the girl with the caramel eyes from the hospital café was *the* Anwar Hayati, the Egyptian world champion swimmer and Leila Hayati's daughter.

The one whose sister I would never forget when she became an instant celebrity through her awful death. Noor.

* * *

I was still rattled by Leila from yesterday and she was there in Ricky's room again today, but this time Anna was with her. Anna was reading to Ricky while Leila watched on – still sitting up as straight as a rod, her hair tightly held back, and a tight fixed smile on her face.

Ricky was laughing while Anna read. She used funny voices for the different characters.

I remembered with embarrassment how I had behaved in the café, carrying on like a banshee, crying into my coffee about Ben. Maybe Anna wouldn't remember me. *Please God, make her not remember me.*

I straightened my spine, pulled my shoulders back, plastered a big smile on my face, and walked in with as much fake confidence as I could pull off when all I wanted to do was hide.

'Good morning, Mr Ricky,' I said brightly.

Anna turned at the sound of my voice and when we made eye contact, a smile exploded onto her face. I returned the smile and relaxed a little.

'Hello, Lily!' she exclaimed. 'So you are a medical student? How wonderful!'

'Hi, Anna. Great to see you. Hello there, Mrs Hayati.'

Leila didn't reply. Instead she got up from the couch where she was sitting and positioned herself on the bed between me and Ricky.

I turned to Ricky, feeling my underarms dampen under Leila's stare.

He was wearing Shrek pyjamas that seemed two sizes too big. I bent down to him. 'And tomorrow I'm makin' waffles!' I put on my best Donkey voice, which wasn't anything close to Donkey's voice.

Ricky didn't laugh. Hmm.

'You know Donkey, right?' I asked him.

'Yes I know what donkeys are.' He looked at me like I was an idiot.

'No, Donkey. From *Shrek*. The one on your pyjamas.'

He lifted up his arm and looked at his sleeve. 'Oh! No. I haven't seen *Shrek*.'

I awkwardly explained who Donkey was and who Shrek was and how they met. But then I heard Helium Man whistle through his nose and Leila was looking less amused by the second. 'Anyway, he's all happy that Shrek's letting him stay with him and be buddies so he wants to make him breakfast and that's when he says, "and tomorrow I'm makin' waffles",' I said in one breath. 'So to sum up, good movie. Highly recommend. Anyway, how are you today, Ricky?'

'Oh Lily, he is so strong and healthy today!' Anna answered for him. 'For breakfast, he ate a whole bowl of muesli *and* an apple! And he has been wide, wide awake all morning.' She looked past me at Helium Man. 'Can he come home, Dr Leslie? Please, can he come home?' She nodded her head up and down really fast and looked between him and me with pleading eyes.

Leila sat still, poker-faced.

'Yes. You can go home, Ricky. We'll arrange everything here so that you can go home tomorrow,' Helium Man answered.

Ricky jumped into Anna's lap and she bear-hugged him, whispering excitedly in his ear.

Leila and Helium Man looked at each other. She gave him a curt smile.

'Mrs Hayati,' he said, 'I'll just write you up the scripts that he'll need once the current lot have run out.' While he was writing, he snapped, 'Students wait outside.' And without looking up, he added in a low voice intended just for my ears, 'Less snivelling from you in the next room, please.'

'Yes, Dr Leslie.'

As I turned to leave, Anna flew off the bed towards me. She took a hold of my forearm and said in a hushed voice, 'I hope you have been thinking less about the man who wrote you that letter.' Her perfume was sweet and floral. It suited her. She was nothing like her mother. Nothing.

I swallowed and whispered back, 'I have, thanks Anna.' I placed my hand over hers and gave it a squeeze.

Out in the corridor we walked past Jenny's empty room again. The bed was now dressed in crisp white sheets. Ready for the next person to die in. It was as if Jenny never existed.

Next, I had to assess a mother of four children under the age of twelve. Her breast cancer was incurable but she was having intensive chemo in a last ditch effort. I ignored my thudding heart as she lifted off the gauze that covered her breast. She asked if there was anything that could be done about her terrible itchiness.

'Could adding an antihistamine to her medicines help?' I ventured.

'Yes, antihistamine could help, certainly. Which one?' Helium Man replied.

'Zyrtec?' I suggested as I took a good look at the area around her mastectomy for signs of infection.

'Why not something like Zandos?' He frowned at me over the top of his glasses. 'Wouldn't Mrs Brooks's relief be much quicker with that?'

'I want the Zandos. I want the quick one,' she announced.

'Shall I write up the script for Zandos, then?' prompted Helium Man.

I looked up from the clipboard and shook my head in confusion. Was he serious? I distinctly remembered being taught this last year in pharmacology. There was no way I could let him do that. I cleared my throat. 'Um, Dr Leslie, I thought that Zandos could cause serious heart complications when combined with the tamoxifen in Mrs Brooks's chemotherapy.'

'I don't want the Zandos anymore. I want the one you said.' Mrs Brooks nodded at me.

'Indeed. 10 milligrams Zyrtec please,' he said to the nurse who wrote it down.

As we walked out of her room I felt a hand on my shoulder.

'Good work,' Helium Man said shortly before brushing past me.

***

The afternoon was a series of tutorials run by a registrar. I was shocked when I checked my watch, thinking surely it was time to go home, only to see I'd been there for just an hour. There were still two to go.

At the end of the day, Helium Man gathered everyone around

and said that if he caught anyone crying again, it would be an instant fail for misconduct. When he said 'anyone', he meant me.

'Crying is reserved for patients and their loved ones. Composure is for doctors. If you can't be composed you shouldn't be a doctor. If you can't be professional around people who are experiencing difficulties, go and serve ice cream at Cold Rock and you'll be around happy people all day.'

Working at Cold Rock seemed like the best job ever right now.

When everyone left, he held up his hand to indicate for me to stay.

'I gave you nine out of ten for today, Miss Harding.'

'I'm sorry, Dr Leslie,' I mumbled. Wait! What? 'Nine out of ten?'

He smiled, and it was the first smile I'd seen from him. I didn't know Helium Man *could* smile. 'Yes, nine out of ten. I took off one mark for the crying, you're lucky it wasn't more. But your professionalism and pharmacological knowledge when Mrs Brooks asked you to examine her herniated breast was very impressive. That was quite a confronting sight and you remained composed even when I tried to trip you up.'

'I can't believe you thought I was professional.' I blinked away new tears.

'Hmm, yes, well that's said without taking the crying into account. Which is precisely why I don't want to encourage you into an oncology career. Judging by the tears I've seen you shed over the last three days – Oh for the love of God, Miss Harding, *really*! Crying again?'

He waited while I pulled myself together.

'Now, you've gone and made me lose track of what was I saying.' He sighed.

'You were saying how I shouldn't go into oncology,' I reminded him.

'Oh yes, stay away from cancer. You're not cut out for it. But after the last three days observing you, I already know you'll make a fine doctor. Adam would be very proud. I'm stunned, to be frank, at how good you actually are when you present yourself so poorly. But I guess it's the old "don't judge a book by its cover" thing. Keep up the good work.'

Helium Man was nice! Who knew?

'And make sure you study over the next twelve weeks, because all of these weekly validations will mean nothing unless you pass the exam. And if you turn up looking like you did today, even if it's only one more time, I'll be giving you an instant fail for misconduct. Have you got that, Miss Harding?'

'Yes, Dr Leslie.'

On reflection, maybe he wasn't that nice after all.

***

I checked my phone in the lift on the way down to the ground floor, with the same sick feeling I got whenever I had to check exam results. I was positive there would be a text from Toby saying he'd made a mistake and didn't want to see me anymore. There wasn't. So I sent him a message.

Just leaving the hospital now. See you soon?

Would he reply telling me not to go? That he regretted everything?

Great. See you soon!

Okay then.

As I walked out of the automatic sliding doors, the daylight blinded me. I fumbled for my sunnies but they weren't in my bag. I remembered I'd thrown them on the passenger seat in my rush to get the lab coat on when I arrived late. I screwed up my nose, squinting, and walked out onto the street where I'd parked.

But my car wasn't there. I looked up the sign that said it was a Tow Away Zone from 3 pm – 6 pm and I texted Toby to say it would be more like an hour before I could get there – 'unforeseen circumstances'.

Then with my tail between my legs, I rang Nick and asked him if he could drive me to the impound and to make sure he brought his wallet.

It wasn't that I didn't see the sign when I parked there in the morning, it was just that I was utterly incapable of learning from my mistakes.

***

While we were driving to the impound, Nick was unnaturally quiet, rather than being a prick like usual. He was obviously gutted about his fractured foot. I was sad for him too. What was he going to do with himself being stuck on crutches for so long? I offered to have him over for dinner tomorrow night and cook him fajitas. I knew he loved them, and it was also an easy meal to whip up after a day on the ward.

'You don't have to cook,' he replied flatly. 'Just park where you're supposed to from now on.'

'I promise I will, but I'd like to cook for you anyway. Think of it as a "Thank-you for paying to get my car out of the impound", "Sorry I got my car towed again" and "It's crap news about your foot" dinner.'

He mumbled, 'Can I bring someone with me?'

My eyes couldn't have been any wider. 'Someone? Like a *girl*? You want to bring *a girl* to dinner at my place?'

He nodded, clenching his jaw, and a red streak splashed across his cheekbone.

I squealed and he gave me his filthiest look.

I slapped his arm. 'You never bring anyone to my place. You must be serious about her! Do I know her? Who is it, Nick? Tell me! Tell me now!'

He shook his head. 'Forget it, I'm not bringing her. You're a bloody embarrassment. I don't know what I was thinking.'

'I'm sorry, please bring her. I really want to meet her.'

'If I do bring her, you better promise to be normal while she's there,' he grumbled. 'On second thoughts, no, don't be normal. Your normal isn't normal. Be like any other sister, who isn't you. Be like that.'

'Okay I promise to not be myself! But promise to bring her, okay?'

'Okay.'

We were silent for a while before I announced, 'Nick, you'd never guess who's at the hospital these days. We're not supposed to talk about it but there's that spouse clause where you can talk to your partner and I don't have a spouse so you'll do. That former Egyptian political leader Leila Hayati is there every day visiting a little boy who—' I stopped mid-sentence. 'Why have you got that stupid smile on your face, Nick? Did you hear what I just told you? I met that famous politician Leila Hayati. You know that car bombing video? And I met her daughter too, the one who was the swimming champion.'

'Yeah, yeah, I know who she is.' He nodded, sucking on his cheeks in a pathetic effort to stop smiling.

'So why are you smiling? It's a tragedy.'

'It's just cool that you met her, that's all – you know, big politician like her.'

I rolled my eyes. 'God you can be such a douche.'

I wanted to lay into him more. But he was about to pay to have my car released so I held back.

* * *

I gave Nick a bone-crushing hug when, for the second time in five weeks, he swiped his credit card to the value of $485 so I could have the luxury of a car again. Then he drove off to go dream about his new girlfriend, who he refused to tell me anything about, even her name, no matter how much I begged. He got me my car back, but he was still a world-class douche.

I was grateful that I could finally go see Toby. The vision of Jenny giving me his number came into my head but my desire for Toby was far stronger than any guilt I felt about her.

Before I took off, my phone beeped with a text from Arielle:

Nick, Nick, Nick, you naughty boy – even crutches can't keep your big brother down, eh?

There was an attached link underneath that I opened and its contents made my jaw drop. There were a heap of photos next to an article from yesterday's *West Online* of Nick with a girl. Oh my God! *Anna? How?* Where would those two have even crossed paths? I stared harder. It was definitely Anna. If I had to pick the one girl in the world that would never be with my brother, I would have picked Anna.

I texted Arielle back:

> I know her! It's the girl who was sitting opposite us in the café on Saturday whose hair you liked. And get this – her mother's Leila Hayati, the former opposition leader of Egypt. She's that swimming champion, Anwar Hayati whose twin was killed by the suicide bomber. Remember that story?

> OMG, it is too! Oh, the poor girl. What's she like?

> She's absolutely lovely! Way too good for Nick.

> Sweetie, everyone's too good for Nick!

This was too exciting to keep to myself! I forwarded the link straight to Mum and added:

> Mum! Look!! It's all true. Nick has an actual real-life girlfriend! And I know her, she's GORGEOUS! She's Leila Hayati's daughter. That's Anwar Hayati he's fallen for, the champion Egyptian swimmer! Can you believe it?

> I can't believe my eyes! Thanks for sharing it with me. How's the oncology round going?

I didn't reply to that. My phone beeped with another text from Arielle:

Hey want to come over? I broke up with Gregory but I met
this cute engineering student today in student services.

You're unbelievable. You don't waste time do you A? ☺ I can't
come today sorry. I have something on.

I knew what she'd say next. She'd say what could I possibly
have on? She knew I was a loser who sat at home and did
nothing.

Oh FFS, what could you possibly have on? You'll be doing
nothing but being a sad arse loser on the couch watching
Netflix.

I wasn't ready to tell her about Toby yet, but I couldn't lie to
her either. I decided the best approach was 'truthful but vague'.

I'm seeing someone this afternoon.

I wasn't kept waiting long:

It's Paul Walker's doppelganger from the café, isn't it? The
one with the dying wife.

I stared bug-eyed at my phone. How did she know?

How did you know?

Please. Give me some credit. You fucked him, didn't you?
You totally fucked him.

Don't judge me. I know you're judging me.

I knew you would as soon as you said the wife gave you his
number. I'm not judging you, but you can't keep seeing him.
His wife is dying. It's not allowed.

She died. So technically he's not married any more and he's
not at the hospital anymore either so it doesn't count as a
doctor/patient thing if that's what you're getting at.

Fuck, this is worse than I thought. You've literally lost your
mind. I'm calling you.

I turned off my phone.

* * *

Toby was sitting on a wooden bench on his front verandah
when I pulled up in the drive. He was wearing blue jeans but
no shirt. Jesus Christ, that body. He was barefoot with his legs
crossed, sunglasses on, and smiling a slow sexy smile that sent a
thrill rising inside me. All I could think about was ripping those
jeans off him.

I climbed out of the car and he stood up, sauntered over
and stopped a few feet away from me, his hands in his pockets.

'I was sure you wouldn't show up,' he said. 'All day I kept
thinking you'd regret last night and not want to get involved
with a guy whose wife just died.' I was about to reply but he
kept talking, raking his fingers through his hair. 'I can't stop
thinking about you. What the hell does that say about me?'

'Maybe I'm just a way for you to avoid thinking about her because it's too painful for you,' I said softly.

'No.' He stared straight into my eyes. 'You're more than just a distraction.'

He took my hand in his, planting a soft kiss on it and stroking my palm with his fingers. 'This is the worst situation ever.'

'It is,' I agreed. 'I don't know how we can make this work. It's too messy.'

'I don't know either, but I know that I really want to try.' His eyes had gone hazy. 'Do you want to try?'

'More than anything,' I said looking at his mouth.

He took a step closer to me, resting his lower hand on my back. And he covered me with desperate kisses. His erection against my groin was rock hard.

'That feels so good,' he whispered as I sucked his earlobe. 'I need to get inside you.'

I had to stop myself throwing my clothes off there and then in his driveway. 'Yes please,' I panted.

He lifted me up and I wrapped my legs around his waist. He carried me along the drive, up the step onto the porch, through the open front door, all the way to his bedroom and back to his bed.

While I sat on top of him, feeling him move deep inside me, he promised me that he would make it work, he promised me that he would make me happy.

And I let myself believe him.

TOBY – WEDNESDAY

'Here it is.' I squatted down next to the wire cage protecting a patch of dirt.

Lily crouched next to me. I was reluctant for us to get dressed and leave the bedroom but now that we were here, at her insistence, I was glad we'd come.

Neither of us said anything for a few minutes.

Under the cage was a copper plaque that read '960548 Jennifer Rose Strachan'. No dates, no epitaph, not even a sealed patch of grass. Just a number and her name and then her, somewhere beneath the dirt, surrounded by a cage. Just like a prisoner. Which, in the end, she was.

'They let the earth here settle before they lay fresh grass and put in the permanent plaque. It'll look nicer then,' I explained to Lily, but really I was just saying it to make myself feel better.

'Uh-huh, yeah. I know.'

And then we fell silent again.

How was it possible that Jen was under the dirt? Cold, stiff, decomposing already perhaps. Were there ants crawling inside her clothes? At what stage did the maggots come?

Lily sat right up close to me, with her arm around my knees. After a while, she knelt up and pushed the bouquet of daisies that she'd picked from my front garden and tied together with twine through the cage. She managed to get it in but she cut her finger.

'What was she like?' She sucked on the finger.

I blew the air out of my mouth. How could I do Jen justice without making her sound like a saint?

'She was funny,' I began, pulling at the neck of my T-shirt. 'Funny without even trying to be. She had a mouth on her though. If I was ever feeling a bit full of myself she'd bring me back to earth real quick.'

Lily smiled. 'What else?'

'She loved dancing. When we were younger, she'd stay out dancing till closing time at clubs. She was a kindergarten teacher and she was great at it. She was shattered when she got sick and couldn't work anymore. All she wanted was kids of her own. Things turned ugly between us when she found out she couldn't have them.'

'Why couldn't she have them? Because of the chemo?'

'No, no. Way before that.' I took a deep breath. 'She wanted to start trying for kids as soon as we were married but after a year she still wasn't pregnant. So we went and got tested and it turned out that the shape of her uterus meant she could never become pregnant naturally. Even if we did IVF she wouldn't be able to carry a baby to term.'

'Oh, no. The poor thing … So you said things turned ugly? Why?'

'It was why we broke up. Jen kind of turned on me – she became cold, resentful. She told me later she didn't know how to handle the guilt. She blamed herself, saw it as a failure on her part.'

'How did you feel? Did you blame her?'

'God, no. Of course not. I mean, I was disappointed but I certainly didn't blame her.'

'I can understand how she blamed herself. Obviously it wasn't her fault and there was nothing she could do about it,' Lily said. 'But it would be hard not to. I'd probably be the same.'

'Yeah, well, it changed her. It changed who she was. And then she met some guy at the gym and they started sleeping together. He didn't want kids. She left just before our fourth wedding anniversary but it had been going on for ages by then, over a year at least.'

'You never suspected a thing?'

I took a while to answer. 'No, I knew. But I never asked her about it. That way I could pretend it wasn't happening. But then one night she told me she loved him, packed her bags and didn't speak to me for the next two years.'

'That's just *awful*,' Lily gasped. 'And you took her back even after that?'

I sniffed. 'Yeah. Two years later she got brain cancer. She began chemo pretty much straight away. Apparently she got out of bed one morning after the second round of chemo and a big clump of her hair stayed on the pillow. She said he freaked right out. Totally lost his shit. They had a fight and she left the house, spent the night at her parents'. When she went home the next morning all his stuff was gone. No note, nothing. He vanished into thin air – left his job, changed phone numbers. Just vanished. So, she moved back home. Our parents live next door to each other and—'

'Your parents live next door to each other?'

'Yeah, since we were three years old. Anyway, I decided after she'd been there for a month or so to finally go and see her. And when I saw how sick she was and how her mum was with her – her mum was just ... ugh ... totally suffocating her – I couldn't leave her there. So she moved back in with me.'

There was a pause, then she asked, 'Were you still in love with her?'

'I don't know. Maybe.' I gulped. 'I just knew I couldn't let her live like that.'

'But you never slept with her when she moved back in, right?'

'Um ... no ... we did sleep together a bit.'

'That's not the impression you gave me last night.' Her tone stayed even but she flicked her fingernails against each other.

'You probably won't believe me but I think it was more an outlet for our grief than anything. It was nothing like it used to be back before she left. I mean, she was sick for a start, so it was all pretty tame. And there was so much water under the bridge, the passion had died.'

'You'll never get over her,' Lily said quietly.

'Yes, I will,' I argued. 'We would never have gotten back together if she wasn't sick.'

'I mean get over her death,' she corrected me. 'There'll come a day when it sinks in, and you can get a better handle on it, just don't expect it to happen soon, that's all. But I'm telling you, Toby, you'll never get over it.'

The lights came on around us.

I hesitated before taking out a packet of cigarettes. 'Um, do you mind?' I hoped against hope she didn't mind. I really, really needed a smoke.

'No, light away.'

We were the only people in that section of the cemetery. It was silent except for our voices and the sound of the wind and the crickets. That was why we both jumped when my phone rang. It was a noise to wake the dead.

'My mother-in-law,' I told her before I answered. 'Hi, Marcia.'

'Hello, Toby. Just checking in, sweetheart. How are you today?' Her voice was weird. Too cheerful.

I felt queasy. Ever since Jen moved back in, Marcia acted as though we had never separated and that we were a normal happily married couple. She ignored us when we tried to set her straight.

Now that Jen was gone, I wished Marcia would let me go too. She'd already messaged me today, twice, asking me to go see if there were any souvenirs I wanted to keep from Jen's room. I ignored her texts because, fuck, Jen had only just died. Why was her room already being cleaned out? And I still had enough of her stuff at my place anyway.

'Sorry I haven't replied to the texts, Marcia, I've been flat out at work today.'

'Well, are you still at work now?' Her voice switched to clipped, accusing.

'No, um, actually, I'm at the cemetery.'

'Oh, Toby, poor, poor Toby.' She flipped again to cooing. 'We're all so terribly worried about you. Why don't you come for dinner tonight? I know Luke is *desperate* to see you and Pete would appreciate your company. In fact he's standing right here and he insists that you come.'

'Marcia, it's too late for dinner.'

'We haven't eaten, we were waiting for you. Please come, Toby. Please.'

God, why was she begging? I hated the begging. Lily was busying herself pulling blades of grass.

'All right, Marcia.' I closed my eyes and massaged my forehead. 'I'll be there soon.'

I hung up and told Lily about Marcia and her delusions. 'Sorry,' I reached for her hand. 'I feel like I should go.'

'Do you want to come over to my place afterwards?'

'Yeah, I'd really like that. I'll go there now and get it out of the way.'

'Come for a walk first?'

We walked along the lit paths. I thought we were just walking for walking's sake until she stopped and knelt next to a ghost gum tree.

I bent down to read the plaque she was cleaning with the bottom of her dress and it was then that I understood where the pain in her bluey-green eyes came from. And it had nothing to do with her ex-boyfriend.

In ever loving memory of Adam Harding
13/12/1960–30/01/2011
Beloved father of Nicholas and Lily.
Devoted husband to Melissa.
Peace of the quiet earth to you.

Lily's eyes were shiny. She looked at the ground and stroked the grass. 'Dad, this is Toby.'

I sat next to Adam Harding's resting place. Marcia could wait.

'We had this massive party for my mum's fortieth.' She wiped her tears with her forearm. 'And he asked me to dance with him. We were on the yacht, he named it after me you know, *Sweet Lily*. And when we were dancing … I wish I could remember what song it was, I've spent years trying to remember but I can't. Anyway, when we were dancing, he leaned in close and said, "You're my princess, my angel. Never forget how deeply I love you. Even when we're not together, remember that I'll always be with you." The next morning he had a brain haemorrhage and drowned. And if you knew my dad,' she let out a small sob, 'you would know he *never* said stuff like that and you would swear he knew he was about to die.' She paused. 'I've never told anyone that story.'

'Come here.' I took her into my arms and held her while she wept.

Some time later she said, 'We better go. Jenny's family are waiting for you.'

She climbed into my car. 'You know, this time yesterday I was still tossing up whether to call you or not.'

***

I drove slowly to Marcia and Pete's, after dropping Lily off at my house where her car was still parked. She put her address into my phone and I left her with the promise I'd be at her house in less than a couple of hours. I had no intention of staying with Jen's family a minute longer than I had to.

They lived close enough to my house that even with the slowest driving I could get away with, I still got there too quickly.

Pete opened the door after a few loud knocks. He was still in the same clothes he wore to the funeral yesterday.

His bloodshot eyes widened in surprise when he saw me. 'Toby, hello, mate. What brings you?'

Bloody hell, Marcia, you liar.

'Marcia rang and asked me over for dinner, but seriously,

I don't have to stay. Happy to go and leave you guys alone, really.'

Pete shook his head and ushered me in.

Marcia came into the entrance hall. She had full makeup on but it was smeared, and her hair was half falling out of its bun. She was also still in yesterday's clothes and she wore a vacant fixed smile. She looked terrifying.

She wobbled towards me with her arms out and crushed me in a bear hug. 'Oh Toby, what a lovely surprise. It's so *good* of you to drop in on us like this. Why don't you join us for dinner?' She batted eyelashes that were clumped with mascara, in a failed attempt at winking. She reeked of alcohol.

'Um, yeah, all right, thanks.'

Pete stared straight past me.

'I've made a simply delightful mushroom risotto. I know how much you *love* my risotto. Don't you, Toby dear? Always saying, "Why don't you make your fabulous risotto, Mum?" Aren't you, darling?' She staggered into the kitchen on skinny heels that click-clacked on the floor.

I couldn't think of a single time that I'd ever had risotto here and I'd never ever called Marcia 'Mum'.

Pete followed us, his head hanging low, but then he turned into the hallway and disappeared into a bedroom. There was a burning smell coming from the kitchen. I stood at the bench, leaning my palms on the same cold marble where I was served frothy milkshakes as a three-year-old, and I watched Marcia. She hummed while she went hell for leather stirring the risotto. The metal on metal of the spoon against the saucepan made a creepy accompaniment to her humming.

It felt icy in my chest and I couldn't come up with a single thing to say.

I stared at the family portrait taken sixteen years ago on the opposite wall. Jen was fourteen back then. She had hilarious white-blonde tips she'd done herself and her trademark all-knowing grin. I'd fallen deeply in love with her around that time and I used to spend many frustrated hours cursing myself for being too gutless to tell her.

I needed a smoke.

Marcia's humming got higher pitched. Why couldn't Pete or Luke come out and save me?

Marcia giggled and muttered to herself and occasionally spat words at the pot on the stove in language that turned the air so blue, I was surprised she'd ever heard those words, let alone knew how to use them.

She stumbled past me to the pantry, pulled out a three-quarters empty bottle of wine and slammed two glasses onto the bench.

'Let's have a little drink before dinner, shall we, Toby?' she slurred.

As she poured, the bottle shook in her hand. Most of it missed the glasses and sploshed over the bench. She knocked back one glass and immediately backed it up by draining the second one.

How deep was the hurt she was trying so hard to numb? She drove Jen crazy with her erratic controlling ways. But crazy or not, Marcia was still her mum. Who could feel more pain than a mother? I knew the right thing to do was support her through this, for Jen's sake. Jen would be devastated seeing Marcia acting this ugly. But as much as I hated myself for it, I just couldn't be the one to care for Marcia – it couldn't be my job. I had to leave.

'Dinner, everyone,' Marcia called out in a shrill voice after fifteen more torturous minutes of silence.

Nobody came out.

The smell of burnt rice was overpowering.

'Peter, Jenny, Luke, *dinner!*' she screeched, slapping the bench with both hands.

Luke skulked into the kitchen, earplugs in, wearing only boxer shorts. He stared at the bowl of dried-up risotto and walked out again without taking any. Pete didn't appear at all.

I took a shaky breath in. 'Um, Marcia, the risotto looks lovely, but I'm actually really full. I should've told you on the phone but I had a bit of an early dinner before you rang. So I might just head home, if that's all right.' I buried my hands deep into my jeans pockets.

She narrowed her eyes and hissed the words more than spoke them, waving the metal spoon near my face. 'Now you listen to me, Toby Watts. We're still your family. I'm not going to abandon you now. You're still my son and I'm not giving up on you.'

'See you soon, Marcia.' I almost jogged to their front door.

'*Dinnnerrr!*' I heard her holler as I raced down the driveway to the ute.

I realised when I got in the car that I'd been holding my breath.

As I was pulling out of Pete and Marcia's drive, John pulled into Mum and Dad's and waved, so I steered my car beside his and we both wound the windows down.

'You leaving?' John asked.

'Yeah. Marcia's blind.'

'Mmm, been drinking since last night apparently. Mum says she's on a shitload of sedatives too. Mum's about to take dinner round there.'

'Fuck. Good luck with that, Mum.'

'Has that chick you banged come out of the dunny yet?' He guffawed.

My whole face burned. 'I already told you. She isn't just some chick I banged. Her name's Lily.'

'Yeah, whatever,' he snorted.

'I'm going home.' I took my foot off the brake. 'And you better not tell Mum and Dad about Lily.'

He flicked me the bird and I drove off.

Lily didn't deserve to be a joke to him. Once they all got to know her, it would be better. They'd understand how special she was. But I couldn't see myself introducing her to my family any time soon. Even though I'd been telling myself all day that Jen was the one who orchestrated it between me and Lily, and even though Jen and I split up years ago, it didn't mean that it wasn't too soon to be with Lily. It was way, way too soon, no matter what kind of logic I tried to apply to it.

***

I stopped caring about it being too soon when I tapped my fingers against the front screen door and heard Lily running towards me. She swung the door wide open and threw herself into my arms. She smelled shower fresh.

'I missed you.' She murmured between long kisses. She'd already undone my fly and had her hand inside my jeans. 'More than anything.'

'It was awful, Lily.' It was hard to talk when I was this aroused. 'Not going back there again.' I breathed fast while she licked the hollow of my neck.

She pulled me inside and slid her dress down off her shoulders.

'Jesus Christ.' I brushed my hair back with both hands and took in the sight of her.

She had no underwear on.

She sank down to her knees.

'Oh, Lily,' I moaned. I already knew from last night just how good things were about to get. 'Oh, fuck,' I exhaled.

***

At two o'clock in the morning, we were still up.

Her chest rising and falling against mine as she took long sleepy breaths, soothed me. She was leaning back against me and the sweat from her lower back and my stomach stuck our skin together. I couldn't remember it ever being this hot in March.

'I wish I didn't have to go to work tomorrow, Lily.'

'Why? Don't you like your job?'

'Nope.'

'What, like not *at all*?

'Nope.'

'So why are you a builder then, Toby?'

'I don't remember a time when I wasn't going to be a builder. My granddad started the company. Dad took over and then there was John and me. Since we were five or six, Dad put hard hats on us and took us out to sites. It was a given that we'd take over the family business.'

'When did you realise it wasn't what you wanted to do?'

'I think I was about twelve, thirteen.'

'Wow.' She laced her fingers through mine. 'That long, huh?'

With my free hand, I played with one of her curls. 'Yeah, that long. I remember a teacher going on about a still-life painting I did. It was of apples in a bowl. It was the first time I consciously thought, *I want to be an artist*. Soon after that I got my first SLR camera and discovered I liked photography even more than art, but yeah, it was too late by then.'

'But why? Why was it too late?'

I released the curl and found a new one to twirl.

'Because I was old enough then to know how much it meant to my dad that we carry on the family business. He was always telling everyone how his sons would one day pass Watts Building onto their sons just like his father did before him.'

'But didn't he pick up on how into the photography you were?'

'He did,' I sighed. 'But I don't think he ever considered I'd want to do it for a living. He thought of it more as a hobby. I never made it clear to him that it was more than that. I didn't want to disappoint him. The shittiest part is that John never became a builder. Dad had built a café in Freo, and when the old tenants moved out, John took over. He's made it a massive success.'

'What? Are you serious?' She turned herself around so we were face to face, our hot skin peeled off each other. I took a sharp breath in with her breasts so close to my face.

'Why are you stuck in building but John got to do whatever he wants?'

Her body, slick with sweat, made me struggle to keep my mind on the conversation. 'I was already in my first year at university by then. John was smart enough, brave enough, whatever, to speak out and say what he wanted. It's not Dad's or John's fault that he got out of it and I didn't, it's mine. I'm the one who chose to be silent.'

'Toby, you need to say all of this to your dad.'

'It's too late now.'

'You're thirty, not sixty! It's not too late at all. You have to tell him.'

'Nope.' I bent my head forward and teased her nipple with my tongue.

I didn't like the turn this conversation was taking and needed to put an end to it. 'Enough talking.' I cupped her breast, taking it into my mouth and sucking on it deeply.

'This conversation isn't over,' she slurred, shutting her eyes. 'Oh my God, I love how you do that. I love that a lot.'

I gently pushed her backwards and when I was back inside her, I was whole again.

ANNA – WEDNESDAY

Today Mama disappeared again into the black fog, the same fog that had swallowed her before. I was heartbroken each time the darkness stole her away, but today, for the first time, I was angry. Ricky was coming home tomorrow. So why *now*? Why had she succumbed to the darkness? Why alarm and upset us this way when we could all have been rejoicing instead?

I was also angry that I had failed to pick up on the signs that she was falling again. I had gone instead to meet Nick with a heart as light and free as a butterfly and no hint of what was to come later in the day.

But then tonight, when I was cleaning up in Masri's after we had closed for the evening, Ahmo Fariz called my name in an urgent voice. I dropped the mop and ran out of the kitchen to find him kneeling by Mama's and my bed. He was doing his best to comfort Mama with soothing words, but when she became like that there were no words that helped.

'My baby, my baby, I'm sorry I betrayed you. I'm sorry they killed you because of me. Allah, why did you spare me? Why did you spare me?' Mama wailed as she lay curled up on her side rocking herself, clutching a photograph of Noor to her chest.

Ahmo Fariz stood up, his knees creaking. 'Do you think we should call the doctor? Or take her back to the hospital?' he whispered.

'Let me watch her tonight and we shall decide tomorrow. You go now, Ahmo Fariz. It is late and you are tired. Leave me with her.'

'Are you certain? I can stay as long as you need.'

I could see the fatigue in his eyes and the way his shoulders drooped.

'Yes, I am certain. Go and get some sleep. Mama will be fine and so will I.'

'Call out if you need me, *habibti*.' He kissed the top of my head. 'Perhaps sleep with your bedroom door open and I will leave mine open too.'

When Ahmo Fariz left, I checked inside the top vanity drawer in the ensuite. I found what I expected to find. There they were – eight more tablets than there should have been in the packet. It was only because I had been so preoccupied with Nick that I did not prevent this from happening. I grunted at my reflection in the mirror, 'Look what happened because you lost concentration!'

I knew Mama's patterns. I should have realised yesterday at the hospital that she had stopped taking the medicine. Every time, it was the same. Mama would secretly stop taking the medicine that controlled the depression. And for a short time she would be back to being my old mama again, the one who talked and listened and laughed. But afterwards she always, always disappeared into the black fog.

I understood why she hated the medicine. Truly I did. I understood when she complained that it made her brain feel numb and small and that it left her without anything valuable to say. I understood when she told me that the medicine deadened the pain in her heart so effectively that it actually stopped her feeling anything at all, as if she had a hollow tin chest.

But none of that was as terrible as the state of her now. Mama had no idea how bad she became when she stopped taking the tablets. I wished she could see herself like this. How much she scared me.

'*Yalla*, *ya* Mama. Up you come.' I hooked my arms under her armpits and helped her to sit up.

Mama sobbed against my chest. 'Anwar, why do you make me live against my will? Why won't you please, *please* just let me die so I may finally have some rest from this pain and you may finally have a rest from the burden of me? I am no good to you. I provide you with nothing but more grief. Let me go and then you will be free.'

Whenever Mama spoke like that, it was as if she took a knife and stabbed me deep in the soul, so sharp was the pain I felt. When Mama wished she were dead, part of me wished she were dead too. Because she was right, nobody should have to live with the pain that she had to. But I was selfish, and even though she craved the peace that death would bring, I refused to stop fighting to keep her alive.

I could not imagine a life without my Mama in it. So she had no choice. No matter how much she resented it, she had to keep living for me. And to keep living, she had to take the tablets every day. Making sure she took them was my job.

I reached for the glass of water I had put on the bedside table and I pushed out two of the tablets. 'Swallow, Mama. You will feel better soon. *Yalla*, swallow. Well done.'

'I'm sorry, *habibti*, I'm so sorry I ruined our lives.'

I wiped her nose with a tissue. 'My life is far from ruined. And one day you will feel the same about yours. Sleep now, Mama. Tomorrow is a new day. *Allah ho'akbar, ya* Mama – God is great. *Yalla*, sleep.'

I helped Mama lie back down, took off her slippers and covered her with the sheet. I climbed into bed next to her and stroked her knotted hair. Her rapid breathing slowed down and her eyelids stayed closed.

'I'm sorry,' she mumbled one last time before she fell asleep.

'I am the one who should be sorry, *ya* Mama,' I whispered. 'I am the one who did the ruining.'

Tante Rosa knocked on the door. She looked long and hard at Mama. Then she looked at me. 'Allah is punishing you for sneaking around with that footballer. He is punishing you by making your mother unwell.'

It was a gift she had, Tante Rosa – the way that she always managed to say exactly the worst possible thing at the worst possible moment. A true gift.

I had told Nick about my troubles with Tante Rosa earlier today. It was almost as if she'd heard my complaints to him and wanted revenge, because she was waiting for me when he drove me home later.

She stood by the door, and as I came out of the car, she began screaming across the car park. 'Do not come crying to me when you end up alone, Anwar. No man will ever touch you after you have given your innocence to this non-believer and he has soiled you. Rest assured this *Nick Harding* will spit you out like an olive pip the minute he has had enough of you! You are a foolish dreamer, Anwar. Do not think I did not see you kissing him in full view of the whole world in his car just now. Listen to your Tante Rosa and wake up before it is too late and you are ruined. It will not just be your poor mother who is insane but you as well.'

The sound of Tante Rosa's screaming annoyed me but her words had no effect on me. Instead of trying to convince her it was not this way with Nick, I walked straight past her and began the evening's peeling, grating, slicing, and lemon squeezing. All night, although we worked side by side, I said not a single word to her, nor she to me.

Knowing that Ricky would be coming home, and after the wonderful afternoon I spent with Nick, I thought today could not be a more perfect day, so I was determined not to let Tante Rosa ruin it.

In the end though, how could it be a perfect day when Mama wished for death over life with me?

Mama slept peacefully now and, *inshallah*, by morning the medicine would have worked its magic once again. I had to remember to give her another tablet the minute she woke up. This was what her doctor recommended we do the last time it happened.

I'd felt sleepy before I even finished cleaning the kitchen tonight, and I had very much been looking forward to my bed. Now I could not be more awake. My mind galloped away with frightening memories of the last time Mama tried to end her life – on her birthday last year.

I shut my eyes tight and made myself think of something wonderful.

The wonderful thing I chose to think about was Bluey. When we arrived at Nick's house after our swim this afternoon, I heard loud barking from the back garden and my heart jumped for joy. I had not held a dog in my arms for over a year, since leaving Lucky behind in Alexandria. When Nick opened the gate and Bluey came bouncing towards me, I dropped to my knees and he jumped over me while I covered his head in kisses.

Nick laughed, 'The mutt's getting more action from you than I ever have! Aren't you, Bluey? Lucky boy.'

Bluey rolled onto his back and I scratched his stomach just like I used to scratch Lucky's. 'Who is walking him while you are on the crutches, Nick?'

'Ah, nobody yet. I still need to organise a dog walker.'

So of course I offered to be Bluey's dog walker. I had been excited about our first walk together tomorrow morning but now I sent Nick a text message saying:

My mother is unwell this evening. I am very sorry to cancel the first morning walk with Bluey, but I need to be with her tomorrow morning when she wakes up. So I will not be able to come to your house. By tomorrow evening I expect she will be better and I hope to still have our first date night xx

He did not reply, he must have gone to bed, but at least he would see the message in the morning.

Ahmo Fariz was collecting Ricky from the hospital in the morning and *inshallah* by the time they arrived home, the tablets would have started to affect Mama so that Ricky could have the special homecoming he deserved. I had prepared all the streamers and balloons and the 'Welcome Home' sign and Tante Rosa had baked *kunafa* so everything was ready.

By tomorrow night, Mama would have taken her medicine and be more settled. I could then have a special night with Nick. I shocked myself with the thoughts I had about him today. So many thoughts!

While Mama lay peacefully asleep beside me, I went over the words she spoke to Noor and me when we turned sixteen.

On that chilly December evening in Alexandria, she sat us down in her bedroom with steaming cups of hot chocolate and said, 'Sex is just that. It's sex – nothing more, nothing less. Our culture is obsessed with it and even more obsessed with making laws about who can have it, when they can have it, with whom they can have it and in what way they can have it. But, Noor, Anwar, listen carefully, both of you. The most important thing of all is that it is *always* your right to say no.'

She took a long sip of coffee from her glass and continued. 'Respect yourselves. Only have sex if you feel ready, not because you feel pressured. You are letting another person share your body – your precious, sacred body – so make sure that this person is deserving of that.'

Mama spoke with passion. 'If you share your body with everyone, then it is special to no one. So take your time and be very sure.' Mama pointed a finger at each of us and continued. 'Do not make decisions about sex when you are in a man's arms. Believe me that decisions made then are never wise decisions. But remember this – it is not sex when you are unmarried that will ruin you, like we have all been led to believe. Sex with the wrong person is what can ruin you. Falling in love with someone who is bad for you and having sex with him – *that* is what can ruin you.'

The only blessing in Noor's death was that the Mama who was passionate and intelligent and who often gave us important lessons to help us through life was the only Mama she knew.

I took out my journal.

Habibti *Noor,*

Let me tell you some wonderful things because I need to do that tonight to stop myself from breaking.

I will tell you wonderful things about Nick!

First there is his smell. I have spent a considerable amount of time with my nose close to Nick's neck and his aftershave fills me with desire.

And then there is his deep, deep voice. You know how people have always been amused at my husky voice? I can only imagine how funny a conversation between the pair of us must sound with my husky voice and his very deep one.

And do you know that he frowns whenever I speak? I asked him why he does this, because I was worried that he did not like the things I was saying. But he replied that it is because he is worried he will miss something. He said it is at times difficult for him to keep up when I speak so quickly with my accent and he wants to be sure he misses nothing.

And then there are his tattoos. My boyfriend has tattoos! Never in my wildest dreams did I imagine this could ever be possible nor did I imagine just how much I would love them.

He has two dark-blue tattoos, one enormous tattoo of angel wings spread right across his shoulders and another smaller one going up along the inside of his right forearm that has the words Semper Superne Nitens.

When I asked him what these tattoos meant to him, he told me that the one on his arm is Latin for 'always striving upwards'. He said it is there to remind him to aim higher. And the wings, they are angel's wings to symbolise that his father is always with him or as Nick said, 'that my dad has my back'.

Noor, this gave me an idea. Perhaps one day I shall have a tattoo drawn on my skin, too, to honour you and Baba. But

I do not want wings and I do not want it on my back. I would like a tattoo somewhere that I can always see it, perhaps on my wrist would be a good place. And I think I would like to symbolise you and Baba with an Ankh to represent our eternal bond. Yes! One day soon this is what I shall do.

I love you my darling sister and I am ever so grateful for our eternal bond,

A x

I tucked the journal back in its place and I took Noor's photo that was now face down next to Mama and placed it back on the dresser next to Baba and Mama's wedding photo. I pressed my fingers to my lips, kissed them and touched Baba's cheek in the photo. It comforted me to know that Nick shared with me the unique pain of losing a father.

In Nick's house this afternoon we spoke together about our fathers and how much we admired them, what good men they were.

Nick said to me, 'The night before my dad died, we'd just arrived home from celebrating my mum's birthday with a huge party on Dad's boat. He came into my bedroom and stood behind me with both his hands on my shoulders and said, "I can't tell you how proud I am of you and how happy it makes me to see the man you've grown into. Feel my hands here, on your shoulders? That's where I'll always be, Nick, right here behind you. I'll always have your back. I love you more than you'll ever know."'

'Oh, Nick, these are beautiful words to be told before losing a parent. It makes your tattoo even more meaningful. I cannot believe he said these things to you the night before he died. That is incredible. I do not remember the last words my father spoke to me.'

'He never spoke like that normally. I'm convinced he knew he was about to die,' Nick said with a heavy voice.

'But you said he drowned in the ocean. How could he have known that?'

'He drowned because he had a brain haemorrhage while he was out in the surf. He was a doctor, he would've recognised the signs. I went on a research rampage after he died and found out everything I could about aneurysms. They don't just happen without warning. Dad would have had gradually worsening headaches, like really severe headaches, not regular ones. And he would have had dizziness, confusion, nausea in the days before it happened. He would've known something was very wrong.' He gulped.

'To have a son like you, he must have been a wonderful man.'

'He was ten times the man I am that's for sure. What hurts is that he never knew I got signed by the Rangers. It was Dad's dream for me, ever since I first put my hands on a footy. But in the end he never knew.'

'He knows Nick. You can be sure of that.'

'It's good to talk to you about this,' he said. 'It helps.'

'And speaking of my father to you helps me too,' I replied. 'I do not think it is through luck that you came into Black Salt on Sunday. I think you and I are two people who were destined to find each other.'

'I think you're right,' he agreed. 'The only person I've ever been this open with is my sister, and today I've told you things that I've never even told her.'

'You have a sister?'

'I do, yeah.' He had a funny expression when he said that.

'How old is she?'

'Lily's twenty-two.'

'Why are you smiling strangely like that, Nick?'

'I'm not.'

'You are not now but you were a second ago. Anyway, I love this name, Lily. In fact, it is my new favourite name. I know a Lily who is a student doctor. She is an angel. And what does she do, your sister Lily?'

He chuckled. 'She's a student doctor, but she's no angel, she's a complete nutter. You and her will get along just fine.'

'What is a nutter?'

'A crazy person.'

'Are you saying I am also a nutter then, Nicholas Harding, because I will get along *just fine* with another nutter?' I gave him a questioning look.

'No, but you dress the part,' he laughed pointing at the flared velvet dress I bought for four dollars at Vinnies last year.

'But you love how I dress. This is what you said only yesterday!'

'I do, I do.' He grinned. 'I love this purple puffy dress. It's the prettiest purple puffy dress ever,' he murmured as he leaned closer to me on the couch.

I looked into Nick's eyes while he played with my fringe and it was then that I made a discovery that caused me to jump up onto my knees on the couch. 'Nick, does your sister have blonde ringlets down to her waist?'

His funny expression returned. 'Yes, I believe she does.'

'And is she a student doctor at a cancer hospital?'

He laughed. 'Yes, I believe she is.'

'I know her!'

'I know you do.'

'How? How do you know?' My voice was much louder than usual.

He sat himself up higher. 'Okay, just before I came to meet you at the pool today, I picked her up from the hospital. On the drive she told me about meeting you and your mum.'

'Ha!' I clapped my hands. 'This is the most wonderful thing! Did you tell her about me?'

He coughed. 'Kind of. I told her there was *someone* but I didn't say who.'

'Why not? Are you ashamed of me?'

'Hardly.' He kissed the tip of my nose. 'No the reason I didn't tell her and why I wasn't going to tell you was because she invited me and 'the *someone*' I'd told her about to her place for dinner tomorrow night. So I thought it would be fun for both of you to have a surprise then.'

'That is very bad behaviour, Nicholas Harding,' I pointed my finger at him. 'Very sneaky and very bad.'

'Bad behaviour is the best kind of fun, though.' He kissed me as he rolled the hem of my dress between his fingers before sliding his hand under it to gently caress my inner thigh. 'See, bad behaviour really is the best kind of fun,' he whispered in my ear. 'You're so sexy.'

Oh how hard it was to stop him when he touched me this way! His hand, so close to my underwear was driving me to distraction. I wanted to guide that hand inside my underwear instead of asking him to stop. But I did ask him to stop.

'Nick,' was all I needed to say and he withdrew his hand from under my dress and rested it on my hip.

After we kissed for longer I said to him, 'So, you didn't tell your sister about me, but meanwhile I have been telling my twin sister every detail about you.'

He frowned. 'Hang on, you've got a twin sister?'

'I had one, yes. An identical twin. Now I have a guardian angel. Her name is Noor. I write to her in a journal and every day this week I have been telling her about you.'

'What happened to her?'

I took a minute to answer. 'The day that Hamdy strapped a bomb to his chest, Noor was in the back seat of the car.'

'Oh, God,' he whispered. 'I thought it was just your dad who died in that attack.'

'No, it was Noor, too. So you see, Nick, every time my mother looks at me, looking back at her is Noor. I am a constant reminder to Mama of all that she lost. This is why I wear "nutter" clothes,' I explained. 'I choose clothes that are as different as possible from the way my sister dressed. And then last week I had the idea to cut my hair in a style as different as possible to the way Noor styled her hair. These are things I can change. But unfortunately there is nothing I can do to change my face.' The tears escaped while I spoke. 'Mama is stuck looking at this face of mine.'

'I'm glad you can't do anything to change your face,' he murmured, stroking my cheek with his thumb. 'It's the most beautiful face in the world.'

And he kissed me again. He kissed me until I stopped crying and all I could think about was him, not Noor, not Baba, not Mama, just him.

We kissed so much today that I ended up with a rash around my mouth from his stubble. Another word I learned this afternoon – stubble. I was a big admirer of stubble! I especially enjoyed feeling stubble around my neck and as far down as my collarbones. It excited me just imagining how the feel of stubble would be on my breasts and elsewhere on my body.

One day I would find out. One day but not yet. I did not want to rush into sex with Nick, not because I was afraid of sex but because I was afraid of sex *with Nick* on account of Mama's words those years ago about falling in love with the wrong person and giving them the power to ruin you. I was one hundred per cent certain that I was already very much in love with Nick and I knew without doubt that having sex would only cause me to love him more deeply. What if he was the wrong person and I lost him? What would I do then?

I had the evidence before me of what losing love had done to my mama. And a fate like Mama's was not a fate I wanted for myself. So I would wait until I was certain that I would not lose Nick and only then would I have sex with him. Then and not a moment before.

NICK – THURSDAY

It had been only five days since I played and my fitness and motivation were already slipping away. Here I was deep-water running, lap after boring lap, for the third consecutive Groundhog Day.

Bruce, Joel and a few of the others had stopped by to have a chat when I was in the gym this morning. Craig came in and invited me to sit in on their martial arts class with the Australian national karate champion.

They were trying to keep me included, but the thing was, I didn't want to be. I'd feel even more isolated as the only person not taking part than I felt here in the water. If I knew it would only be a week or two that I'd be out of the loop, instead of nearly three months, I might have felt differently about it.

If it wasn't for Anna, I would've been beyond miserable by now. Having her in my head was the only thing that got me through these endless laps up and down the pool. I was completely, one hundred per cent obsessed with that woman.

When I wasn't with her, I was counting the hours until I was. And when I was with her I couldn't get enough of her. Every time she sent me a text message, I got a hard-on. Every. Single. Time. It was like I was fifteen again.

Being the first guy she'd kissed was more special to me than I would ever have thought. But it came at a price — she refused to get naked, and if my hands wandered, she put a stop to it. It was just kissing and more kissing. When it did finally happen between us it was going to go off for sure.

'Shit!' I almost lost my balance when Craig stepped in front of me as I hopped out of the hydrotherapy room on the crutches. 'Sorry, Craig. Didn't see you there, mate.'

'Yeah, you were a million miles away.' He crossed his arms and blocked my way. 'Where do you think you're going?'

His tone and expression sent a burning drip down into my stomach.

'Home. I've just done my hour in the pool.'

'I was watching you, Nick, slow as a snail. Get back in the water. I want another twenty minutes of laps. Run like you mean it this time.' He didn't blink.

I hung my head. 'Okay.'

Craig had never once had me repeat a drill before. He had to with some of the others. Never with me.

'And I heard you ditched gym after half an hour yesterday. It's only week one of rehab. You can't be this slack in week one when you've got nine to go.' He turned to leave. 'On second thoughts make it forty minutes, not twenty. And make them count,' he called over his shoulder.

When the door shut, I was alone in my glass cell again.

I ripped the towel off my waist and flicked it down hard on the floor, strapped the weighted vest back on my chest and set the timer on my watch for sixty minutes, not forty. I ran so hard that by the time I got out, much of the floor area around the pool was drenched.

'That's more like it, Harding!' Craig shouted from the corner of the gym on my way out.

Pretending not to hear him, I pushed the door open and left.

* * *

It was Anna's mother who answered when I knocked on the door of the house at the back of the restaurant.

I'd spent a couple of hours last night reading about her online, and by the end I was stunned that I'd never known who she was before.

Leila Hayati was a powerhouse – a force. I watched video after video of her passionate speeches about the decline of Egypt and how her party planned to revive the country.

She looked the same in all her photos, whether she was shaking hands with Pope Francis in the Vatican or sharing a private joke with the Queen. She was always dressed in dark-coloured pant suits with barely any makeup and her hair pulled back in a ponytail.

And even though I knew I shouldn't, and I felt horrible for doing it, after resisting for two days, I just had to watch the clip of Anna's dad and sister walking down a sunny street in Alexandria along with their bodyguard to a waiting limousine. Anna's identical twin, Noor, was exactly that in the video – identical to Anna, just with longer hair. Which is why I choked down vomit when she spotted the camera and stared straight into it with a quizzical squint, before the driver opened the back door for her. She climbed into the car two or three seconds before it erupted in a giant ball of explosive fire.

I tasted blood and realised I'd bitten a hole into my cheek as I listened to the bearded militant arsehole whose face flashed on screen after footage of the bomb cut out. Just as Anna had told me, the subtitles read that Anna would be beheaded while Leila was made to watch, and that the execution footage would be released to the public if either of them ever returned to Egypt. Then the picture changed to a menacing static bringing to an end the two and a half minutes of evil I'd just witnessed.

I sat there unmoving, staring at the blank screen of my Mac for close to an hour afterwards.

* * *

As Leila stood before me at the front door now, it was hard to reconcile her with the woman I'd seen online. If it wasn't for her long dark ponytail, she would have been unrecognisable. Her cheeks were sunken and her eyes were too large for her face. The power suit was replaced with jeans and a plain black T-shirt that hung off her shoulders.

She held out a bony hand. I was surprised to find she had a firm, almost too firm, handshake.

When she smiled at me her white lips cracked, but the smile didn't reach her sad puffy eyes, with their black bags underneath.

'Hello, Nick, I'm Anna's mother, Leila. Welcome.' Her accent was mild and the ease with which the words rolled off her tongue showed that English was obviously second nature to her, unlike the concerted effort Anna made when she spoke.

I cleared my throat. 'Hello, Mrs Hayati. It's great to meet you.'

'Call me Leila. I've heard good things about you from Anna.' She indicated with her arm for me to come in. 'She's nearly ready.'

I stared at her pointy elbows as she walked ahead of me.

'You can wait here.' She pointed to a small lounge area and disappeared through a doorway, calling out Anna's name. Her voice cracked and she coughed before trying again.

I didn't even notice the bald little boy, tucked up in a beanbag in the corner behind a couch, covered to his neck in a brown blanket, until he coughed.

My breath caught. I waved to him from where I stood. 'Are you Ricky, mate?'

He nodded. 'Are you Nick?' he said with a huge smile that showed his missing front teeth.

I nodded. 'I am.'

'I barrack for the Rangers now,' he announced. 'I was Lions before, but not anymore.'

His dark skin was blotchy with itchy-looking rashes on his cheeks and forehead.

'Cool!' I dropped the crutches and hobbled over, lowering myself down until I was sitting next to him on the carpet. 'Lions, hey? What made you go for a Brisbane team?'

'To annoy Ahmo Fariz.' He grinned. 'But now I've changed to the Rangers, because yesterday Anna said I have to or else I had to stay in hospital and I wouldn't be allowed to come home.'

I laughed. 'You could be both, Lions and Rangers, and when we play each other you can't lose.'

He thought about this for a minute. 'Do you like *SpongeBob*?' He looked at me sideways and I felt like our new friendship depended on my answer.

'I've seen every *SpongeBob* episode ever made,' I answered truthfully.

'Yeah, I'll just go for the Rangers now,' he said solemnly.

These kids always got to me. I'd spent a heap of time in hospitals with them as part of club duties. But this one was special to Anna. Maybe she could bring him over on Saturday and we could watch the away match together.

'So what year are you in at school, Ricky?'

'I'm in Year One. But I only went for one week and then I got sick again. Anna said I can go back next week but Leila said it's too soon and I need to stay home.'

'So who'll win that argument do you think?'

He took a few seconds to consider his answer. 'Anna. Leila always forgets what she says.'

On cue, Leila walked in to the room, followed by Anna, who blushed a deep red when we made eye contact.

My eyes just about fell out of my head. A sparkly silver clip held her hair off her face. There were no spikes in it today, it was just soft. A short red-and-white dress showed off her gorgeous curves, and strappy heels drew my eyes to her toned legs. It was also the first time I'd seen her with makeup on.

She was beyond beautiful.

'Oh my God,' I breathed. 'You look ... stunning. *So* beautiful.'

She reached a hand up to fiddle with her hair clip.

I suddenly felt underdressed in my white T-shirt and denim shorts.

'You did not get dressed up, Nick.' She bit the corner of her lip. 'Should I change?'

'No, don't.' I stood up. 'You look too perfect to change.'

'Okay, if you think so, I will stay as I am.'

I really did miss her hokays.

She kissed Leila on the cheek, and bent down to give Ricky a cuddle, lingering near him. 'Are you sure you will be all right, *habibi*? Ahmo Fariz will take your beanbag to the kitchen and you can watch TV there.' She looked at Leila. 'Promise me, *ya* Mama, you will do nothing to alarm anyone while I am out? Yes? *Mesh keda?*'

'Yes, yes. *Aiwa keda, ya habibti.* Go, go! Have fun. Be young.' Leila shooed at her.

Anna turned to Ricky. 'Call me if you need me. Call me, you hear?'

He nodded.

'And is your phone charged and with the ringer on full volume?' Anna checked with him.

He held up his phone to show her.

I said my goodbyes and we left. It was another scorcher outside as the autumn heat wave raged on, but that wasn't why my palms were sweaty.

As soon as we were in the car, I turned to her. 'Are you sure you're still happy to come out? It's totally okay if you want to cancel. Lil won't mind. I feel bad stealing you away on Ricky's first night home.'

'Mama is much better tonight. And my uncle and aunty are wonderful with Ricky.' She patted her purse and smiled. 'I have my phone right here if he needs me.'

Yesterday, she'd told me how Ricky had come into her life through Asylum Assist.

'I visited him when he was transferred from off shore to the hospital, because being an orphaned child, he was under the care of Asylum Assist. His future was so uncertain. He broke my heart. And he was such a brave, sweet little boy too. I knew that Allah had meant for Ricky to come to us. He needed a mother and Mama needed a purpose. I took Mama with me to the hospital and she has been at his side since.'

'There's no chance that he could be taken away from you all now, is there? Made to go back to Bluff Island?'

'No, he will not be taken away.' She paused. 'Except if Allah takes him away.'

I squeezed her hand.

'Did you ever track down any of his remaining family?' I asked.

'No, there is no family.' She sighed. 'After his parents escaped, their entire village in Nigeria was massacred by the military because it was suspected they were hiding members of Boko Haram there. The *entire* village gone. The military did it as a warning to others. Can you believe it? So he has no relatives at all left – they either drowned or were killed.' Her voice cracked.

After I researched Leila last night I also looked up the town Anna said Ricky was from, Baga. I wished I hadn't. I'd never be able to get those images of the children's bloodied bodies stacked on top of each other out of my head. Having now met Ricky, the idea that it could have been him …

Anna broke into my thoughts. 'You do not need to look so worried, Nick. It took me a long time to get ready for our first date and I insist you take me out!'

'Okay, let's go, then.' I started the engine, then remembered what was on the back seat. 'Hey, I bought you these. To mark the occasion.' I reached for the long-stemmed red roses I'd stopped to buy on the way to her house.

'Oh! I have never been given flowers before. Thank you!' She buried her nose in the roses. 'They smell beautiful. You spoiled me.' She looked at me over the top of the bouquet.

'I wish I could take you back to my place now instead of Lil's.' I ran my finger along her bare collarbone. She rested her head on the headrest, giving me her sexiest look.

'Maybe we can go to your house after dinner for just a little while, Nicholas Harding. What do you think?'

'I think a little while is all I need.' I took her hand and kissed the tips of her fingers while I drove away from the restaurant. I was already turned on just imagining the kissing we'd do later.

***

We pulled up at Lily's and I parked behind an unfamiliar black ute.

The Rangers team song blared at us when I pressed the doorbell. I pointed out the 'Rangers Fans Only' doormat to Anna and rolled my eyes.

She laughed. 'So what? She is proud of her brother. You should be flattered.'

'She's as mortified about it as I am,' I replied. 'It's all my mum's doing.'

Lily swung the door wide open. Without looking at me, she threw her arms around Anna and her squeal was so piercing I winced. '*Anna!* Oh my God, I've been so excited waiting for you! Did you know I was Nick's sister?'

Anna's smile was the biggest I'd seen it. Her words tumbled out. 'Only after I last saw you. But of course I should have known immediately because you are so similar to each other!'

Then Lily turned to me and roared, 'You're a douche!'

A guy appeared in the doorway and draped his arm casually over Lily's shoulder, resting his fingers lightly on her breast. How was he that familiar with her already? I gave him the once over. He was too old for her – at least thirty. He had a cigarette lighter poking out the front pocket. I didn't like this guy.

He smiled at me in a way that I recognised – an overawed Rangers' fan smile – but he quickly collected himself and extended his hand. 'Hi, mate. I'm Toby. Toby Watts. How's it going?'

I gave him the firmest handshake I could and stifled a smile when he grimaced. 'G'day, I'm Nick.'

'Hey, there.' Toby turned his attention to Anna and gave her a warm smile. 'I know you!'

'Hello, Toby.' Anna smiled back. 'This is amazing – the two of you together!'

I cleared my throat. 'Ah, I'm kind of lost here. How do you two know each other? Actually how do *you two* know each other as well?' I nodded at Toby and Lily.

Toby looked at Lily. 'Ah, Lily and I met at the hospital café on the weekend.' He turned back to Anna. 'And Anna was sitting at our table when we met. But I'd seen Anna around before that.'

'You only met him on Saturday?' I gave Lily a look.

'You and I only met on Sunday,' Anna said.

I couldn't argue with that, so I ignored the comment.

'So you said you and Anna knew each other already? How?' I asked Toby.

'Um … from the oncology ward.' He shuffled his feet.

Anna gave me a quick warning glance and then she clapped her hands together. 'When I saw you both in the café, I knew in my heart it was fate that you met.'

Toby raised an eyebrow and murmured, 'See? Fate,' to Lily.

I saw the look that passed between them and I didn't like it.

'Come in, everyone!' Lily shouted way louder than necessary.

Anna turned to me just before we followed them inside. 'Be nice!' she whispered.

Lily tied on a bright orange apron and started frying thin strips of beef and chicken, red capsicum and onion in a large frypan.

Toby joined her and set about mashing an avocado. She said something in his ear and he grinned.

The hairs on the back of my neck rose.

'How's Ricky gone at home today?' Lily asked Anna.

'Very well. It is like he never left. Toby, I will not be at the hospital anymore,' she explained.

'Neither will I,' Toby said in a quiet voice. 'Jen passed away on Monday.'

'Oh no!' Anna put her hand over her mouth. 'I'm very sorry to hear this.'

Toby smiled with his lips together. He cast a quick glance at me and looked down. His jaw clenched while he continued to mash the avocado.

There was something fishy about that Jen.

'Was that a relative of yours, Toby? The one who was in hospital?' I crunched on a corn chip. It was hard to keep the accusation out of my tone.

'Actually she was my wife.'

The chip caught in my throat and I spluttered and coughed. Anna passed me a glass of water that I gratefully took.

Lily rested her palm on Toby's shoulder. 'Toby cared for Jenny right up until she passed away, even though they'd actually split up years before.'

Anna cooed at this.

'What?' It came out sharper than I planned.

'Jen moved back in with me, before she was admitted to palliative care.' He looked me right in the eye.

'That seems strange – living with your ex-wife.' I returned the stare. I didn't care if it pissed him off. This was my little sister's heart at stake.

'Not ex-wife.' He crossed his arms. 'Just wife. We were separated, not divorced.'

I could almost feel him daring me to challenge him.

Bloody oath I'd challenge him! What the fuck was he doing with my sister?

'Huh, well. Things have moved pretty fast for you two, considering ...' I trailed off.

He shrugged defiantly.

Lily put down the wooden spoon she'd been using and glared at me.

Nobody said anything for a while.

'We only met on Sunday.' Anna broke the silence.

'My wife didn't just die, though,' I replied, keeping my eyes locked on Toby's.

The room fell silent again.

I dropped the crutches, sat down and took two cleansing breaths like the team was taught to do by a sports psychologist last year. *Take two cleansing breaths and focus on one of the five senses.*

Smell. The whole room smelt of Lily's cooking.

Anna joined me at the dinner table and rested her hand on my thigh. She gave it a couple of sharp squeezes. The message was clear – *ease up.*

I brought to mind the line I used to get myself out of confrontations on the field whenever I felt myself losing my cool. *You're better than this. Cleansing breaths – focus on the smell of the food – you're better than this.*

'Is there anything you need me to do in the kitchen, Lily?' I asked when I'd found the calm I was looking for.

'No thanks, arsehole features, I think we're just about done.' She wiped her hands on her apron and gave me a long filthy look.

I mouthed, '*Wife!*' at her.

She flipped me the bird and Anna snorted.

Toby opened the fridge and passed me a beer, taking the top off the stubby for me before I had a chance to say, 'No, not during season.' Oh well, it wasn't like I needed to be off the stuff to be match-ready anymore, was it?

'So what happened?' He motioned towards the crutches as he pulled up the chair opposite mine.

'Stress fractures are back,' was all I managed to get out before Lily interrupted.

'I've had a good look at the scans you gave me yesterday. That fifth metatarsal's a bit dodge. One of the breaks is really close to the proximal diaphysis. Like, really, really close. The report says it's an undisplaced fracture of the shaft, but I'm suspect about that. It's only two millimetres away from the diaphysis at the most.'

Toby was hanging off her every word.

'Lil, speak English, please.' I rolled my eyes, but I was quietly proud. I liked it when she showed what a great doctor she'd be.

She leaned on her forearms at the kitchen bench. 'Basically, I'm wondering if that fifth metatarsal should have been fixated. I think there's a good chance it's an avulsion fracture.'

'What does this mean, Lily?' Anna frowned.

'I'm worried about the bone along his foot that connects to his little toe, Anna. It's broken right at the tip. Sometimes what happens when a bone breaks that close to a joint is that a bit of it pulls away so it can't heal on its own and it needs surgery.' Lily turned her attention back to me. 'I'm probably wrong. And you've had the Rangers' medical team examine it and they know a hell of a lot more than I do about it. But, I examined that scan three times, and each time I swear it looked more like an avulsion fracture to me. I'd feel more reassured if you asked the doctor to go over the scans once more. If he does and then he still thinks letting it heal conservatively is all it needs, I promise not to bring it up again.'

'Okay.' I nodded. If Lily Harding said take another look, then I'd make sure that Aaron would take another look. With all my injuries, big or small, she'd never once been wrong.

It was time to change the topic, though. This wasn't the sort of thing I wanted some guy I'd known for five minutes listening in on. 'So, what do you do for a living, Toby?'

'I'm a building supervisor. I work for my dad's company. Mostly residential stuff.'

Five years on and my gut still clenched at the word 'dad'. 'Good way to earn a crust?'

'Yeah, it's all right.' He said without any enthusiasm.

'It's not all right at all,' Lily called out as she pulled open the door of the oven and peeked inside. The room immediately filled with smoke. 'Oh no, burnt tacos! Crap!' She emptied the tray of tacos in the bin and opened another box. 'He's a wasted talent, you know.' She resumed the conversation. 'He's an amazing photographer. I'm trying to convince him to follow his dream, but he doesn't want to let down his dad. Isn't that right, Toby?'

Toby's lips turned white. Honestly, Lily's mouth needed to be taped shut.

'It's not really your place to tell him what he should do with his dad or his life, Lil.' I was surprised to find myself defending Toby.

He threw me a grateful look. 'I can't let my dad down. He needs me.' He stared hard at the guacamole.

'Dinner's served, lady and gentlemen,' Lily sang.

***

'Oh, Lily, look at this beautiful feast!' Anna exclaimed. The table was filled with food.

I was touched by Lily's efforts to make a special dinner after a long day of hospital rounds.

Most of the conversation round the table was Lily asking Anna a million questions about Ricky. And Toby asking me a million questions about the Rangers.

'I want to know how you two got together.' Lily pointed at us.

'I sort of stalked her until she agreed to go out with me.' I grinned at Anna.

'I got tired of saying no to him!' She laughed.

'Do you know you're the first girl he's introduced to me?' Lily announced to my horror.

Anna gave me a quizzical smile. 'No, I did not know that. I feel very special.'

She tickled the inside of my thigh just above my knee. It was innocent enough but the graze of her fingers on my skin was all I needed to get turned on.

'Thanks, Lil,' I said through clenched teeth. I gave Anna a

little shake of my head to stop what she was doing and placed my hand over hers. It wasn't kosher to allow myself to get turned on in Lily's presence.

Anna ignored me and kept wiggling her fingers on my thigh. 'Good things come to those who wait, yes, Nick?'

Her smile widened when we made eye contact. She inched her fingers slightly higher up. I gave her a sterner look and she winked at me. I was so hard now it hurt.

She knew what she was doing. I saw her glance down at my erection. She knew and she wasn't stopping.

'Well, I knew Arielle but you didn't introduce me to her, I introduced her to you,' Lily said, unaware of what was happening on our side of the table.

'Oh? Arielle?' Anna gave me a teasing smile. 'And who is this A-r-r- r-i-elle?'

Before I could answer, Lily blurted, 'She's my best friend. Out of all the girls in the world, Nick decided to fall hopelessly in love with her when he was seventeen and we were sixteen. Oh hey, you saw Arielle, Anna! You too, Toby. She was the friend I was sitting with at the hospital café on Saturday.'

Toby nodded. 'Yeah, I remember her.'

'The girl with the pink hair?' Anna asked.

Lily nodded. 'Yep.'

Anna turned to me with a sparkle in her eyes. 'You like pink hair?'

'No, yuck.' I pulled a face. 'She had blue hair back then.'

They all laughed.

'Anyway,' Lily continued, 'Arielle was Nick's first but they were only together for one week at the most before Arielle had enough of him. Only took him two years to get over her!'

'That's such crap!' I protested. But it was one hundred per cent true.

'Not crap at all,' Lily guffawed.

'Two years to get over her? Hmmm. That must have been a very good week. I think I am a little jealous of Arielle with the blue and pink hair.' While she spoke, Anna's fingers moved a little slower and a little higher. Jesus! I couldn't take it anymore. All I could think about was how good it would be if she slid them just that tiny bit further up my groin. As I thought about it, she did so and I had to disguise my moan with a cough.

Lily went on. 'Don't be jealous, Anna. He's got it way worse with you than he ever did with her, I can tell. And anyway, he and Arielle are like brother and sister now.'

I could barely hear what Lily was saying. Anna's fingers were turning my brain to mush.

'God, I thought I'd never hear the end of it when she dumped him,' Lily continued, oblivious. 'And since then, he's never mentioned another girl. So cheers to you, honey, for finally breaking the Arielle spell!' She reached across the table and clinked her glass of wine against Anna's.

Anna smiled at me and cocked an eyebrow up. It was getting dire. I had to get up before I orgasmed at my sister's dinner table. But as much as I willed myself to stand and end it, I couldn't. What Anna was doing to me was just too addictive. I simply didn't have the willpower to walk away from her.

'So are you working, Anna? Or studying?' Lily asked.

'I work at my uncle's Egyptian restaurant, Masri's in Fremantle, and I also work part-time at a café three blocks away from Masri's called Black Salt. I'll be studying law next—'

'Black Salt?' Toby interrupted. 'My brother John manages that place.'

'Gianni is your brother?' Anna laughed. 'Truly an amazing coincidence! But I must say, I do not think you are much like your brother from what I have seen of you, Toby.'

Toby almost spat out his beer. 'If I'm anything like John, shoot me now.'

'So is it John or Gianni?' Lily asked.

'Bit of both,' Toby replied.

'He sounds intriguing.' Lily stood up to clear away the plates, Toby followed her lead, and I finally got a reprieve from Anna's teasing hand as she helped clear up too.

I wished I could will her fingers back. My skin tingled where they had been.

'I'm just heading out for a smoke. Excuse me,' Toby announced, once he'd stacked the plates in the dishwasher. He slid open the back door leading out to the terraced garden.

I shot Lily a look that she pretended not to see.

'Have you told him you're an asthmatic?' I frowned at her.

'Not yet, no.'

'Yes Lily strikes again, huh?'

'Shut up, Nick,' she muttered.

I called out through the flyscreen door. 'Toby, did you know Lily's a severe asthmatic?'

Her face fell. '*Nick!*'

Toby froze with the cigarette dangling from his lips. He put it back inside the packet and walked into the kitchen. 'Lily? What the hell?'

'It's nothing. Nick's exaggerating. Don't worry about it, Toby. Smoke away.'

'She takes preventers every day,' I told him.

'I've been smoking right next to you for the last forty-eight hours. How could you not tell me?' His voice was strained.

She shrugged.

Toby scratched his stubble and, shaking his head, walked to the fridge and pulled out two more beers.

'I'll give you a heads up about my sister,' I said as he handed me one of the bottles. 'She'll never ever tell you something she thinks you don't want to hear.'

He nodded. 'Right, okay. Good to know.'

'Be careful with her, she's fragile.' I said in a low voice that only he could hear, while the girls talked to each other in the kitchen.

He stared off to the side then looked back at me. 'I'm not going to hurt her, Nick.'

'I hope not.' I took a large swig of beer.

We were silent until the girls came back to the table, Lily holding a platter of chocolate brownies and Anna behind her carrying bowls and a tub of ice cream.

Once dessert was done with, I fake yawned and asked Anna if she was ready to be taken home.

I was relieved to be saying goodbye.

* * *

'Nick, I wish you were there to see when they first met each other,' Anna said dreamily on the drive home. 'It was love at first sight, a truly amazing thing to witness.'

I sighed. 'But, his wife just died. She *just died*. How can you not see a huge giant problem with that?'

'The night before we met you were living a different life. You told me that you changed the day you met me – you felt it was destiny to meet me when you did. Maybe it is the same for Toby. You heard what Lily said, he and his wife had split up. Maybe the timing of her passing away was Lily and Toby's destiny.'

I shook my head. 'Any way you slice it, his relationship with Lily is wrong. It's not going to end well for Lily. I can feel it.'

'She is an adult, Nick. Trust her judgement. Now tell me, do you still want me to come to your house for a little while or are you too consumed planning your sister's life for her?'

'Pfft, who cares about Lily? She's an adult, I trust her judgement.' I grinned.

Forty-five minutes later, we were at my place. I hopped over to the couch and beckoned her to join me. She took off her heels and sat beside me with her legs tucked up underneath her. I pulled her legs out so that they rested over mine and she left them there.

'Very bad girl at dinner,' I said into her ear before I nibbled on it.

'What did I do that is so bad?' Her throaty giggle was my favourite sound in the whole world. 'Can a girl not rest her hand innocently on her boyfriend's leg?'

'There was nothing innocent about that,' I murmured, between kisses. 'And it wasn't exactly following your "no more than kissing" rule.'

'I decided maybe kissing, and a little bit more than kissing.' She showed me how little by holding her thumb and index finger a few centimetres apart. 'Am I allowed to change my mind, Nicholas Harding, or shall we go back to only kissing?'

'Depends what you have in mind. I mean, the hand under the table thingy tonight was all right I suppose. But I might not like other things. I'm very fussy, you know. I think you need to show me what you mean by a little more than kissing.' I said huskily.

'If you are so fussy, Nick, perhaps you should be the one who shows me. Bear in mind I said *a little bit* more than kissing, not a lot.'

'What about this?' I slid my hand under her dress and pressed my thumb over her knickers. I could feel her heat.

'Mmm,' she moaned softly. I changed my mind. Her giggle wasn't the best sound in the world – *that* was the best sound in the world. I moved my thumb the way I knew turned girls on the most – applying pressure, easing off and then pressing down again and I stroked her lightly between the thighs with my free fingers.

She held her breath and then gently moved my hand away, back up over her dress. She intertwined her fingers through mine. 'That was *not* a little, Nicholas Harding. That was the direct opposite of a little.' Her face was flushed.

'But you loved it,' I murmured in her ear.

'I did,' she breathed. 'But I am not ready yet to love things as much as I loved that. It is less than a week, Nick.' She touched my cheek. 'I do not even know how you feel about me yet. And the place you were just touching me is a very private place. I only want to share this part of myself with a man who truly loves me.'

That's when I told her that I loved her.

She slapped my shoulder and laughed. 'You love me? And you are sure that this is real love and not something else – like, hmmm, let me see, a way for me to let you put your hand inside my dress again?'

I looked right into her eyes and swallowed. 'I love you, Anna. No agenda. Hands under or over your dress, I just love you.' I was surprised by how emotional I felt saying it.

She leaned her forehead on mine. 'Truly?'

'Really and truly.'

'You love me?'

'I do.' I kissed the tip of her nose. 'Well … do you love me back?'

'Of course I do.'

'I want to hear you say it then.' I couldn't believe I was asking, but it was the first time I'd ever put those words out there and I needed them said back to me.

'You want to hear me say it?' Anna murmured, looking down at my lips before she gave me a long deep kiss. Then she whispered in my ear. *'Ana bahebak, ya* Nick.'

I pulled my head back to look at her properly. 'Doesn't that mean goodbye? You told me that meant goodbye.'

She shook her head. 'The difference between us, is that I could not wait five whole days before I told you I loved you.'

I covered her face all over with kisses while I whispered, 'You're so beautiful and caring and smart and fast in the pool.'

She laughed and I continued, still kissing her between every few words, 'And brave and strong and I love your accent and I love your skin and I love your hair and I love your eyes and I love your mouth and I love your breasts and I love your bum …'

She pressed both her palms against my chest to hold me back. 'But you have not even seen my breasts or my bum!'

'I've seen enough to know I love them.' I tugged on her bottom lip with my front teeth.

'How is it possible that we love each other already?'

'Don't know, don't care. I just know it's true.'

'Will it last, though? Will you tire of me? Especially if I am slow to sleep with you.'

'Never.'

She fixed her eyes on mine as I moved my hands over her breasts taking in the firmness of her bra. I slid them further down along her waist and then lifted her by her hips, bringing her up onto my lap.

'I'll wait as long as you need me to wait.' I breathed into her neck. 'I'm not going anywhere, I promise.'

'Nick, right now I do not want to keep you waiting for another second.' She let out a long soft moan while I sucked under her ear. 'I can feel you under my thigh. You feel hard.'

'Mmm, do I just? Do you like how it feels?' I explored the hollow of her neck with my tongue. 'Do you like what you do to me?'

'Yes,' she whispered. 'I do, I love it. But ...'

'But you're not ready to love it yet?'

She chuckled. 'Precisely. That's enough for one night, yes?'

I pulled away and smiled at the look on her face. She wanted it as much as I did.

'Yes, Anna. That's enough for one night.'

At midnight, we kissed goodbye in the car park at the back of the restaurant. It was pitch black out there now that the restaurant had closed for the night. The kissing developed into her climbing onto my lap and both of us panting as she rocked fast and hard against my erection. But again she put an end to it after only a minute.

'Am I frustrating you?' Her eyes were questioning when we'd both settled down.

I looked down at my crotch. 'Down there, at this exact minute, yes. Aren't you a little frustrated right now too?'

'Yes, of course I am. But for me it is different. I can control it.'

I laughed. 'Hey, just because I'm a man doesn't mean I'm an animal with no self-control, you know. I'm the king of self-control! I'm perfectly capable of going along with whatever you want. Nothing but kissing? That's okay. A bit more than just kissing? Also okay. Full-blown sex every day and every night? *Totally* okay.'

'Very funny, Nicholas Harding.'

'But seriously, listen,' I continued. 'Being intimate is just one part of what I want to have with you. You mean way more to me than just sex.'

'But what if in three, four, six months I still do not feel ready? Sex is a big thing for me, Nick. My culture – it influences me. Of course, five minutes ago, all I wanted was for you to take my virginity in this car park.' She let out a laugh. 'But I do not want it to happen this way, in the rush of a heated moment. I want my heart, soul, mind to all be ready and then I can give myself to you, without reservation or regret. I do not know how long this will take.'

I cupped her neck. 'I already told you, I'm not going anywhere. Take as long as you need. I'll wait for you. You have my word.'

'You won't be tempted by other girls between now and then?' She smiled but it was clear by her shaky voice that the concern was real.

My mind did an instant flashback to the girl from the beach. 'I swear to you, Anna, I won't cheat on you. You can trust me.'

Her face relaxed and she smiled. 'I trust you.'

* * *

My text message alert sounded a minute after I got back home from dropping her off:

I love you Nicholas Harding x

I stared at the screen and thought I might just be the happiest I'd ever been.

But then I opened Twitter and that fleeting moment of happiness vanished.

#annaisgoodvirgin was trending with meme after meme of her aunt waving her arms about at a reporter.

I sat down and went through my phone. Jesus Christ, Anna and I were all over social media.

There was an Instagram photo of Anna getting into my car at the restaurant tonight, taken from an angle that looked right up her red dress with the caption, '*Not your regular Muslim girl. Nick Harding's latest love leaves religion behind for the bad boy of football.*'

The Daily News had a close-up of Anna and me at the pool the other night, alongside a photo of her swimming at the last World Swimming Championships, as well as a whole slideshow of photos of Leila during her political career. The story read:

> *In a dramatic twist of events, it's been revealed that Nick Harding's 'mystery girlfriend' is none other than former world champion swimmer, Anwar Hayati, daughter of exiled Egyptian politician, Leila Hayati. Click below to see video of the terror attack that shocked the world after Anwar refused to wear a burkini.*

In four hours it had been shared over a thousand times.

Bluey barked for attention but I ignored him. I clicked back on the photos that showed Anna's knickers as she climbed into my car and panicked about how much danger I'd just put her in.

My phone rang at half past midnight. It was Craig.

'What the fuck's going on, Nick?' His voice was hoarse. 'I've just had Max on the phone ranting about you becoming a Muslim or something. He wants a meeting with you and me at seventy-thirty sharp in the morning.'

Max Dawson was the club CEO.

'What? Oh come on, Craig, you know that's not true!'

'Whatever. Just be ready for the meeting in the morning.'

When I put the phone down and checked Facebook again, another video of the bombing which tagged the Rangers was at the top of my newsfeed.

This wasn't just about me and Anna anymore, the Rangers had been dragged into it now. And there was nothing good in that.

NICK – FRIDAY

After convincing Max that I wasn't changing my name to Muhammad, I had to convince Aaron to take a look at the MRI scan again.

Nobody, including Aaron, had picked up the avulsion fracture before, but now that he was looking for it specifically, he could see it. 'Sorry we missed that,' he said. 'Tell your sister once she graduates to come and ask me for a job. That's a sharp eye she has there.'

He booked me in for surgery to have a plate and screws drilled into my foot in the morning.

'So it will be six weeks out of the pool now. It's not ideal, but we'll get there in the end. Your return to match play will be delayed further now, obviously. Again, I'm really sorry, mate. My bad.'

Fucking excellent.

PART TWO

THE FIRST WEEK
OF JUNE

LILY – THURSDAY

It had gone 11 pm. I sat bleary-eyed in bed, wrapped in a blanket, while Arielle flipped open to a random page in the heavy oncology textbook.

'All right, try again. HPV-related head and neck carcinoma is more likely to arise from which area?'

'The brain?' I crossed my fingers.

'No. Oral cavity.'

'Shit. Ask me something else.'

She flipped more pages. 'Okay, here's one. When Sorafenib is used for the treatment of patients with advanced hepatocellular carcinoma, the improvement in overall survival is approximately how long?'

I had zero clue. None. 'I don't know, six months?'

She sighed and shook her head. 'It's been shown to be ineffective, it doesn't increase survival at all.'

I groaned. 'One more, ask me one more.'

Arielle sighed and flipped to the back of the book. 'Okay. Concentrate on this one, all right? Which type of cancer is most likely to produce ectopic hormones?'

'Oh, oh, I know this one! Pancreatic cancer!'

Maybe I'd be okay in the exam after all. Thank God.

'Nope. Renal cancer.'

Or maybe I wouldn't be.

'What? Show me.' I snatched the textbook from her, checked the answer myself and buried my head in my hands. 'What am I going to do?'

She shrugged. 'Have you not studied at all? Like *literally* not at all?'

'Of course I've studied! There's just too much to know. It's impossible.'

She shot me a look. 'You're Lily-genius-girl-Harding. I've been testing you on stuff for the last ten years, there's never been anything that's too much for you. You obviously didn't study. Too busy shagging that Paul Walker doppelganger you're obsessed with.'

The hot volcanic ash rose in the pit of my stomach. 'I'm not obsessed. I *did* study. I studied every single weekend when he was at the football, and every Wednesday night when he went to Jenny's parents' house for dinner, and every Friday night when he went to his mum's for dinner. So don't tell me I haven't studied, okay?'

Arielle laughed. She actually laughed! I wanted to kick her.

'Can you even hear yourself? You study when Toby's doing this or when Toby's doing that. Why can't you study unless Toby's occupied? Doesn't he let you study? Do you have to spend every waking second together screwing?'

'Of course not!' I raised my voice. She was really pissing me off now. 'As if he *wouldn't let me* study. It's just that he hasn't done a degree in medicine, he has no idea how hard I need to work. He didn't even know I had an exam until I mentioned that you were coming over to test me.'

'Oh, please!' She snorted. 'Every idiot knows how hard

you have to work to become a doctor. Plus he's got a degree himself. I think we can give Toby some credit that he isn't a moron and that he realises study is a part of going to university.'

'Well, what's he supposed to do while I study?' I argued. 'It was easier with Ben – he was studying too. Toby's already graduated so it's heaps harder.'

She let out a long sigh. 'I don't know. Maybe he could watch TV? Read? To be honest, I don't care what Toby does to entertain himself while you study. But,' she yawned 'it's getting really late and I'm stuffed so I need to go home and sleep. I had an all-nighter with Stu last night. Mmm, he was so yummy.' She smiled dreamily.

'Who the hell's Stu?'

'He delivered my pizza last night.'

'That has got to be the worst cliché ever. You shagged the pizza delivery boy? Are you serious?'

She didn't look the least bit embarrassed. 'Dead serious. And because of all the shagging, my darling, I now desperately need to sleep. Goodbye and good luck.'

'I'm totally failing this exam.' I picked up a pillow and buried my face in it.

'Just try and study as much as you can now, okay?' She reached for her denim jacket. 'You're super smart. You could learn a fair chunk of this shit just by skim reading, if you put your mind to it. Will I still see you tomorrow after the exam?'

'Yeah I'll see you then. Hey, thanks for helping me.'

She bent down to kiss the top of my head. 'Night.'

'Why do you have it in for Toby?' I asked when she was in the doorway.

She took a moment before she turned to face me. 'I don't. Just study, okay?'

'Why am I even doing this to myself?' I moaned. 'I don't even want to be a doctor.'

She sighed. 'You keep saying that and not doing anything about it. The night before your exam isn't the time to think about it, though. *Just study*, all right? You're a night owl. You've got a good three hours left in you at the very least and I bet that's enough for you to scrape through. Work hard, babe. Make me proud.'

She left and I started reading about blastoma.

Six minutes later I texted Toby:

I want you Toby.

How much?

More than anything.

Give me fifteen minutes.

Helium Man caught me on my way out of the exam. 'Miss Harding, you've left three parts of your exam paper empty. What in the world happened?'

'I didn't know how to answer those questions. I'm sorry, Dr Leslie.' I couldn't meet his eye.

'Even with the good marks that I've given you on ward rounds, it's an automatic fail if you fail the end–of–topic exam. Which you have just done. You've failed. Over fifty per cent of the exam is unanswered.' He looked like his dog had just died. 'I'm having trouble understanding why you didn't even attempt these questions.'

I gulped.

He cleared his throat but it did nothing for his squeak. 'You could have at least had a go. I'm not sure why you sabotaged yourself this way, Miss Harding, but I'm terribly disappointed. Terribly disappointed.'

He scooped up the rest of the papers in his arms and stormed out.

I left the hospital shaking like a leaf in a storm. Wasn't this what I wanted? I wanted out and now I had an out. So why did I feel like vomiting?

The gravity of what I'd done hit me as I stood at Arielle's kitchen bench while she plugged in the coffee machine. I couldn't go through to my sixth year of medicine until I passed every unit in fifth year. So because of my performance today I'd have to re-sit this whole unit next year and graduate a year later. Just like that, I'd lost an entire year of my life. Plus, I'd just gifted myself an extra year's debt, on top of the fifty thousand I'd already accumulated. I'd be at least twenty-five years old by the time I could call myself a doctor. To become an anaesthetist was another five years on top of that. Eight more years of study.

For the second time in five minutes I needed to pee. As I flushed the loo, I looked at the water swirl in the bowl and said goodbye to my twenties as they went down the drain too.

Arielle rested her hand on my back when I joined her in the kitchen again.

'What are you thinking about?' she asked after a while. 'I've never known you to be this quiet.'

I leaned on the counter and sighed. 'I was just thinking about how nice it is to be here, at your place. It feels like I haven't been here for ages.'

'You haven't been here since you met Toby.'

'No way! I met Toby three months ago. It hasn't been that long.' That couldn't be right. Could it?

'It has.'

'I'm sorry.'

'It's okay. I'm just grateful that Toby has a full-time job and can't meet you during the day or I'd never see you.'

'I've been the shittiest friend. I really am sorry.'

'And it really is okay.' She handed me my coffee. 'I forgive you. But, Lilz, it's not okay to throw away a year of your degree on him.'

'It's not because of Toby.' I sighed. 'I think deep down I had already made the subconscious decision to fail. As a way out.'

'Why now, though? You were so close to the finish line. One more year and you would've had a degree behind you.'

'For a job I'm not interested in.'

'Who says you have to be a doctor, though? There's loads of careers you could choose with your degree. And anyway, what is it that you want to do with your life so badly instead?'

'I honestly don't know … There's nothing that inspires me, nothing I'm passionate about, nothing I want to do. Literally, nothing.' The tears began to build. 'Except for Toby. I know I want Toby but apart from him there's nothing else I want.'

As I said it, I heard it. I had nothing going for me except for my boyfriend. I sounded pathetic. I was pathetic.

She didn't say anything.

I sank down onto a bar stool and hid my face in my hands. I cried hot tears of self-loathing. 'When did I become such a loser? I've got no career goals, no ambitions, no hobbies, I don't go anywhere, I don't do anything. Why does Toby even love me? What have I got to offer?'

'Hey, come on. Don't say that.' She put her arm around my

shoulder. 'You have so much to offer it's insane. But hearing you say that all you need is Toby is kind of freaking me out.'

I sniffed. 'Toby's the same though. He hates his job. I think we're just as obsessed with each other.'

'No, you're obsessed with him, for sure. But that man's obsessed with his dead wife.'

It felt like she'd just punched me – hard. 'Excuse me?' I choked. 'What the hell do you mean by that?'

She took a deep breath and looked me in the eyes. 'I've been wanting to say something for a while. I chickened out before because I didn't want to hurt your feelings. And last night didn't seem like the right time to say anything because I just wanted you to focus on studying. But hearing you speak like this, saying he's all you've got . . . *I can't keep quiet about it anymore. He doesn't deserve this* kind of blind devotion from you.'

'What?'

'For three months he's been coming to your house every night and you've never gone to his unless his brother's out because he won't let his brother see you.'

'But I already told you about that. He's protecting me from John because he knows how humiliated I was after he saw me naked,' I argued.

'Bullshit.' Her tone was low. 'He wants you hidden. Have you met his mum, his dad, any of his friends? Have they all seen you naked too?'

I was silent.

She continued, 'For three months he's been running off and leaving you alone every week to see his psychotic mother-in-law. And every week you tell me how much he hates going and how he's never going back but, boom, as soon as the next week comes around, off he runs to her again.'

I stared at her.

'What's his relationship with you, apart from the woman he visits to get his nightly shag? What else do you guys actually do except shag? Think about it. You don't go out together like other couples. Have you been to see a single movie together? Gone out for dinner? Lunch? I don't think I've even heard you say you've gone for a walk on the beach with him, and you both live on the bloody coast. You stay home and you have sex. And you know why you haven't met his family and why he keeps you hidden from the world? Because he's still in love with Jenny. Now you think you're someone with nothing to offer and that all you have is him. And that really pisses me off because it's not true.' She took a swig of coffee and looked to me for a response.

Her words, once spoken, couldn't be unheard. And because I couldn't unhear the truth, rather than choose to face it I chose to lash out. '*I'm the one* who does nothing but have sex? Me?' I raised my voice. 'Not *you*? How many guys have you screwed since I met Toby? How many, Arielle? Eight, ten, twenty?' I wiped the froth at the corners of my lips with the back of my hand. 'I can't believe you've taken the things I've confided in you about Toby and thrown them all back in my face. Why don't we talk about you?' I said through tears. 'You're judging *me* for having sex with my boyfriend who I'm in a loving relationship with while you go around having meaningless sex with any random off the street.'

The anxiety formed a tight fist around my heart. My shallow breaths hurt.

Her face turned white. 'I wasn't judging you. I was only pointing out that you're not being treated the way you deserve to be treated. But hey, thanks for judging me.' She blinked hard.

'Let me tell you something. I know what I want from my life. I want to be a good lawyer, first and foremost. That's my dream, see – because I actually have one. One day, if I ever meet the right person, I want to be a good and loyal partner too. In the meantime I want to have fun, and to me that involves sex and lots of it. I don't *need* a different man every week. I *want* to enjoy myself with different people and try new things because I *like* it. But I'm smart about it and I'm safe and I'm not hurting anyone. I stand on my own two feet and I feel good about myself. But it's good to finally know what the person I considered my best friend actually thinks of me.' She took a shaky breath. 'Sort yourself out. Stop hiding behind Toby as a reason not to go out and live your life. Stop being his dirty little secret. Step out from that dead woman's shadow and find out who you are and what you want. If you don't want to be a doctor, fine. But at least be *something*. I'm done here.' She walked away, and a few seconds later her bedroom door slammed shut.

The air left my body and I sagged like a deflated tire. When I managed to finally unclench that fist of anxiety after some deep-breathing exercises, I picked up my bag and left. I sent her a text when I got in my car:

I'm so sorry I said what I said. I love you and I didn't mean it.
Xx

* * *

On the drive home, I couldn't stop thinking about Arielle's words. I'd had this romantic notion that the love between Toby and me was so intense that all we both wanted was to be holed up together all the time, that having each other was all that mattered and nothing or nobody else did. When we lay in bed together on weekends, watching movies, eating pizza, I felt content that this was all we needed to be happy. But Toby *didn't* just need me to be happy. He had a full and active life outside of our relationship.

He had photography and he had football. Every week he took time out to indulge his passions and I was never invited.

I'd barely seen Nick these last few months. But Toby had stayed connected to his family – and not just his family, but Jen's too. And why was he still tied to Jen's mother's apron strings anyway – a woman he couldn't stand? Arielle's words crashed in on me and broke down the wall of denial I'd built around myself.

She was right, he wasn't over Jen. He'd kept me away from his family – not to protect me because they'd see me as the other woman, but because *he* still saw me as the other woman. I really was his dirty little secret.

I'd put myself in a position where I had no life outside of him. And the thing was, that wasn't Toby's fault, it was my own doing. Here I was, twenty-two, almost twenty-three years old, with four and half years of a degree down the tube, no real friends apart from the one whose heart I broke today, no interests, and barely even speaking to my family, whose messages I didn't get around to replying to because my mind was saturated with Toby, Toby, Toby. And during those times he was out living his life and being with others, I couldn't go out and live mine and be with the people I loved because I needed to use the bursts of time away from him to study and make up for the rest of the time when it was just Toby, Toby, Toby.

I had to do something. It was not okay for this to be my life.

I arrived home and booked a late flight to Broome and a bus from there to Derby. Then I sent Toby a message. If I rang him I knew he'd come over. It had to be a text:

> I failed the exam. I need some time out to think about things.
> Going to Mum's.

Twenty seconds later he rang me. I hit decline and turned my phone off.

It was time to get my shit together and work out what I wanted from life. What that was I had no idea. But I knew one thing, I was sure as hell going to find out.

NICK – FRIDAY

I lay side-on, watching her sleep. She was peaceful now, purring softly through her nose. I woke earlier to the sound of her coughing and gasping and spluttering. The first time it happened, I thought she was having an asthma attack. But this was the third time that she'd fallen asleep here after a night off from the restaurant and I'd come to realise that it was normal for her.

The first time I woke her up, she reassured me that she wasn't the least bit bothered by it, that it comforted her instead to feel her sister close. I'd heard the stories about the surreal, almost spooky, connection between twins, especially identical twins, but I was still creeped out that she relived her sister's death night after night.

I raked my fingers through the hair that fell across her face and lifted it back. The covers were pulled up to her waist, leaving her bare breasts exposed. I'd never been with a woman long enough to become familiar with her body but I'd just about committed to memory every curve and contour of hers in the last few weeks.

I'd never known sex like this. It had always been rushed and mostly drunken and instantly forgettable. Not with Anna.

I loved that she kept her eyes open. I loved that she didn't hide her body from me by asking for the lights to be switched off. I loved that she talked dirty and that it turned her on when I did too. It had all been so unexpected and so great. She was a paradox – good girl out there and bad girl in here – and that just fuelled my addiction to her.

It was a Friday morning early in May when we first slept together.

We'd been fooling around before then, but I still hadn't even seen her fully naked. The furthest she'd got was down to her knickers twice.

'What are you so afraid of?' I'd thrown my head back in frustration one day when she'd unzipped my jeans and reached her hand inside my underwear before withdrawing it just as I was on the verge of an orgasm from her fast and frantic stroking.

'I don't know,' she replied tearfully. 'I'm sorry. You must hate me for this.'

'Of course I don't hate you,' I sighed. 'I just wish you could relax and have fun without worrying so much.'

'Sex isn't about fun for me. It's about love and commitment and respect and trust, and not having regrets.'

I was surprised at how much that hurt me. 'Are you saying you'd regret having sex with me?'

'Can I be very truthful?'

'Sure.' I held my breath.

'I am afraid that I might catch a disease from you.'

I was glad she was looking down when she said that so she didn't see my mortified reaction.

'Anna, I'm clean. I give blood every three months. Would you feel better if I went and got tested for chlamydia and herpes as well? I mean, obviously I can tell I haven't got them, but I'm happy to get a doctor's say-so if that would help you feel more relaxed.'

'Yes.' She nodded, unsmiling. 'Yes, it would help me. And the other diseases too please.'

'But I just told you, I give – okay, consider it done. I'll get tested for everything. That's easy. What worries me is what you said about love and commitment and respect and trust. What do I have to do to prove all of that to you? I thought I was already ticking those things off.' It was hard to keep the pain out of my voice.

'You are ticking them off.' She touched my cheek. 'When I give myself to you, I want it to be wholly and without any fear. Knowing I won't catch a disease helps very much with that. Thank you.'

'All right then, I'm glad,' I said. 'But I need to get up, get busy. Because I'm ready to give of myself wholly and without any fear this minute after your bit of handiwork there.' I nodded at my still unzipped jeans. 'And I think I'll go insane if you keep straddling me like that much longer.' I gave her butt a light tap. '*Yalla*, up you get. Let a man get some air! Coffee?'

'Turkish?' She raised her eyebrows hopefully.

'Never.'

* * *

I got checked out by a GP and I emailed her the report. But the next time we were alone sex still didn't happen, so I started to fret. I worried that the pressure she was facing from the press, the public, her aunty, her conservative Egyptian community, may all have been enough to stop her. I was too nervous about her answer to bring it up again and she didn't bring it up either. We kept going the way we had been, like fearful Catholic school kids – bending but never breaking the rules.

So four weeks ago on that fateful Friday morning, bang on 7 am, when I heard the front door being unlocked, I assumed she'd turned up, like she did every morning, to walk Bluey. The back door rattled as Bluey whined and threw himself against it to be let in. His love for Anna rivalled mine.

I grabbed the crutches but she called out, 'Stay exactly where you are, Nicholas Harding!'

She left Bluey outside rather than opening the door to him as usual, and at the sound of clicking heels on the wooden floor instead of her soft-soled runners, I smiled to myself.

And then there she was, standing in my bedroom doorway – wearing one of my white business shirts with the Rangers logo embroidered on the pocket, which I hadn't even noticed was missing. She had the sleeves rolled up and only the middle button done up. She'd paired it with black heels. She unbuttoned the shirt and let it slide off her shoulders to reveal a black bra that her breasts were practically falling out of and tiny matching knickers that sat deliciously low on her olive-skinned hips and showed off her toned abdominal muscles. Her hair had grown out since I first met her, and with half of it falling over her face she couldn't have looked any hotter.

I sat bolt upright. 'Jesus Christ, Anna.' My voice came out strangled. 'You're so beautiful.'

'Thank you.' She smiled, lingering in the doorway. 'I've been thinking that you have still not tried Turkish coffee. Every time I've offered you one, you have found an excuse, Nicholas Harding, isn't that right?'

I chuckled.

She continued, 'So I said to myself, this man is terrified of trying Turkish coffee. Let me do a little test. If he loves me enough to overcome this strange phobia and he agrees to drink it, then it must be real love indeed. And if the love he feels for me is strong enough that he is prepared to overcome this phobia, then this is a man I want to make love with. So, what do you think, Nicholas Harding? Do you agree to my little test?' She cocked an eyebrow.

It was only then that I noticed the takeaway cup on my bedroom dresser. She must have put it there when she arrived.

'Bring it here, I'll skol that in one gulp.'

She laughed and walked over, holding the cup. I couldn't take my eyes off the outline of her breasts as they bounced teasingly with each step. She placed the coffee cup down on the bedside table but quickly took a couple of steps back so that I couldn't reach her.

'Do you know what day it is today, Nick?' she asked as I peeled the lid off the coffee. There was only two fingers' worth at the bottom of the cup. It looked like soot and smelled even worse.

'The best day of my life, I'm guessing.'

She grinned. 'Yes, exactly. Today is the day you discover what real coffee tastes like. That is enough to be the best day of anyone's life, the day they first bring Turkish coffee to their lips.'

I had one last look at the tar at the bottom of the cup, tilted my head back and chugged it back in one long disgusting gulp. It was like drinking an oil leak. The sediment stuck to the top of my mouth and the back of my throat.

I smacked my tongue against my lips. 'Okay. There you go. I drank it,' I croaked, wiping my mouth with the back of my hand and reaching for the glass of water nearby. 'I've proven how true my love is. Now get over here, Hayati.'

Smiling, she reached her arms behind her and unclipped her bra. It fell to the floor and her breasts tumbled out.

'Oh, Anna,' I moaned. 'Oh, God.'

Keeping her eyes locked on mine, she hooked her thumbs into the sides of her knickers and wriggled out of them. And then she stood there, all of her in front of me, and she was even more beautiful in the flesh than she was in my imaginings.

The sight of her body, toned, tanned, nearly sent me over the edge. 'I swear I could come just looking at you.'

She stepped out of her shoes. I gently pulled her down onto my bed, climbing on top of her. She smiled but her eyes told a different story.

'Don't be scared. I'll be gentle, promise.'

'I might not be any good at it.' She bit her lip.

I brought my lips close to her ear and whispered, 'You're already the best I ever had, no contest.'

'Mmm,' she moaned while I sucked on her earlobe.

'Tell me to stop whenever it hurts, even if it only hurts a tiny bit,' I said in between kisses. 'We'll go real slow. You're the boss, okay?'

I teased her with her my mouth and my fingers until she was begging out loud for it. Then I reached into the drawer next to the bed but she pulled my hand back to her.

'You're clean, Nick. You don't need that. I took care of it.'

Slowly, slowly, I entered her. After a few tense minutes, I was fully inside. I let out a deep moan of pure contentment. 'That's it, beautiful, I'm all the way in now. We're completely connected now you and me.'

She had deep frown lines in her forehead.

I moved as gently as I could inside her. 'There's literally nothing separating us now. That's so special to me, thank you for this.'

She opened her eyes and when they met with mine, she had a look of complete surrender. 'I am yours now, Nick. I am yours and you are mine.'

I knew in that moment, with absolute certainty, that I would love this woman for the rest of my life.

And since then, despite all the dramas surrounding us, we've at least had that. We've had the bedroom – the one place where nobody could get to us.

I savoured moments like this one, right now, where it was just me and her, and the rest of the world was safely locked outside the front door. It was a testament to how much she really did love me that she was still here, still with me – the man who'd brought bigotry and ridicule to her world.

The press was obsessed with us, with her. Everywhere she went, she was followed. She'd been offered twenty thousand dollars to speak to *60 Minutes*. Fifty thousand to get topless for *Maxim*. From the first week we were together, the media couldn't get enough of our story. One of Australia's highest paid footballers with a notorious reputation, and the innocent young refugee, the daughter of a famous politician with a tragic past linked to terrorism. It was paparazzi gold, the kind of stuff that set social media on fire. I doubted there was anyone between the ages of sixteen and sixty who hadn't seen or at least heard about the footage of Anna's family being blown up.

There was an Instagram page called @warningsforanna set up by a girl I was with years ago, where girls uploaded photos and memes of me that didn't exactly paint me in the best light. And every comment had the same hashtag: #nickisnotagoodboy.

That page alone had over thirty thousand followers. Like driving past a car crash, I couldn't look away and found myself checking it daily. Each day I felt further removed and more disgusted by the person I used to be. I honestly couldn't remember three-quarters of the shit that was on there.

Anna had seen it, of course. How could she not? It was talked about everywhere. It was just bloody lucky for me that she believed that wasn't who I was anymore.

Last week, when I drove her back to the restaurant from the pool, I turned on the radio to the sports station I followed.

The DJ was in hysterics. 'Okay, the next caller is Aiden. What have you got for us, mate?'

I recognised the DJ's voice, an ex-footballer, James Round, who I never liked because he was dirty on the field.

'G'day, Roundy,' the caller's voice came through. 'All right, my title would be *You had me at Halal.*'

Anna and I looked across at each other as more laughter erupted from the car's speakers.

'That's a classic! Love it!' James sounded like he was crying with laughter. 'Stay on the line, Aiden. That might just be the winning entry. Okay, folks, after the ad break we'll be taking the last lot of calls and if you can come up with the best title for a movie about Nick Harding and Anwar – or should I say *Anna* – Hayati, you could win yourself a Gold Class cinema double pass.'

Anna and I both reached for the off switch at the same time and neither of us said a thing for the rest of the drive. It was getting harder and harder to ignore it all, though. We never went out, we were trapped in my house whenever we wanted to see each other, and even then, they wouldn't leave us alone.

We were on the front cover of a trashy magazine after they got photos of us deep in conversation and unsmiling standing

by my car in my driveway. The headline screamed, 'Refugee
Anna gives Nick Harding ultimatum "Convert to Islam or it's
over."' There was another magazine cover of Anna leaving
hospital with Ricky after a routine check-up accompanied by
the headline: 'Nick Harding's teen girlfriend has pregnancy
confirmed, shaming her devout Muslim family.' Leaving a
specialist cancer hospital!

'It's so convenient for them to forget my mother is Christian,'
she despaired. 'It doesn't suit their agenda.'

We turned on the TV one night to see a raging debate about
Australia's asylum seeker regulations. The talk show flashed
Anna's face up on screen with the banner: 'Special favours for
politician's daughter – how Nick Harding's girlfriend jumped
the queue.'

The media, the internet trolls, and the public – they'd had
three months to get used to the idea that Anna and I were
together. But they just couldn't seem to wrap their heads
around it.

At my initial meeting with Craig and the Rangers' CEO,
Max Dawson, when Anna and I first got together, I convinced
them that all that had happened was that my new girlfriend was
a refugee. The club then made a statement condemning the
inaccurate, racist headlines and the intrusion into our privacy.
But now even they were sick of me and this situation that
seemed like it would never go away. The players and managers
had lost their sense of humour weeks ago with the media that
hounded them daily for information about us.

And as I felt my teammates and coaches become resentful,
I distanced myself from them further. I felt like more of an
outsider now than I did when I wasn't training. And it was bad
enough then.

In the eleven weeks I was doing rehab, I wasn't just separated from the team at training but I didn't fly interstate with them every second week either. Players were together from the minute they arrived at the club to catch the bus to the airport, to when they got off the bus back in Perth. They ate all their meals together and did every activity in each other's company – without families, girlfriends, or any other distractions. I missed out on all of that.

Maybe the lines were blurred about how much of my isolation was brought on by the injury and missing stuff like the interstate trips and how much of it by my relationship with Anna. What I did know was that I was an outsider these days in the team I used to consider my family, and it was only getting worse.

Since I was cleared to weight-bear, I hadn't trained anywhere near as hard as I should have to get back into top shape. I wasn't even close to match-ready, even though there was a countdown on for my return to the midfield next weekend playing in the reserves.

Craig called a meeting with me on Monday. He waved me to sit down when I walked into his office, without looking up from his paperwork. He finally made eye contact after I'd been sitting in silence. I rolled up my sleeves and tugged at the collar of my shirt.

'Do you mind turning down the heater, please, mate?' I asked.

'It's not on,' he snapped. 'Nick, I'm going to get straight to the point. I've given you twelve weeks' leeway. For twelve long miserable weeks, I've put up with you going through the motions; let it go because I thought to myself, he's frustrated that the fractures came back, he's fed up, we screwed him over by saying he didn't need surgery when he did.' He paused. 'I thought that the second those crutches came off you'd get stuck right into training to make up for lost time, the way you did last time. But you've hardly worked up a sweat. You look bored out there, mate, and I'm seriously doubting your commitment to the club. I think all this fuss in the media with that young lady is messing with your head. We need you to have a clear head, Nick. You can't afford this distraction. *The club* can't afford this distraction. Am I being clear enough?'

'Yeah, mate, crystal clear. You're right, I know,' I said. 'I'm sorry. I'll fix it. I promise.'

And I wanted to fix it. I did. The very last thing I wanted was to let Craig or the team down. But the fire in my belly was gone. It was just gone, and I couldn't seem to get it back. I used to be the first one at training and the last to leave. Not anymore.

Even Bruce and Joel had turned cold on me and they had been the last two to stick by me. I'd still met them for a coffee or lunch regularly, we'd hung out for a bit after the match on game days. Plus, once they got to know her, they both liked Anna. Almost every time they saw her, they thanked her for being the one to finally keep me off the grog and out of trouble.

But as of this week, Bruce and Joel weren't returning my texts and they ignored me at training. And I knew why.

It was because of the march that was taking place in the city tomorrow that Anna helped organise with Asylum Assist. I was going to march with them. Because after hearing what it was like for the kids on Bluff Island, well, those kids might as well have been in prison. When I imagined that Ricky could have still been stuck there if not for his cancer, it made me sick.

The thing was, the company that provided security services to Bluff Island, SafeXone Security, was also the number one sponsor of the Rangers Football Club. And Bluff Island was one of its biggest contracts, bringing in almost two million dollars a year. The purpose of the Asylum Assist march was to demand the closure of the detention centre altogether.

When word got out that Anna was one of the head honchos behind the march and would be a speaker at the event, I found myself on the receiving end of a phone call from Max Dawson for the first time in my life.

He had already shown his distaste for my relationship with Anna months ago when the news broke out. Although the club had issued a statement that they were right behind me, he'd let me know in that private meeting with Craig that if I became an advocate for Islam there would be hell to pay.

On the phone this time he snapped, 'It's a conflict of interest for your partner to be involved in this protest. She needs to call the march off, or, at the very least, boycott it herself. The club isn't at all happy with her involvement.'

I pulled the phone away from my ear and stared at it with an open mouth. Who the fuck did he think he was?

'Anna's actually not associated with the club, Max. She's my girlfriend, that's it. She has nothing to do with the Rangers. So her involvement with Asylum Assist isn't a conflict of interest at all.'

'Nick, *you* won't be associated with the club if you're not careful. There's no place for politics in football,' he growled. 'You need to explain to your little girlfriend that the Rangers' sponsorship deal with SafeXone is worth millions upon millions of dollars, and that the future of the club, especially *your* future, is in serious jeopardy without SafeXone's support. Sponsors like SafeXone don't grow on trees.'

'What exactly are you trying to say, Max?'

'I think I've already said it pretty clearly, but I'll say it again. There's no Nick Harding if there are no Rangers, and there are no Rangers if there's no SafeXone. And there's no SafeXone if there's no Bluff Island, which is exactly what Asylum Assist are trying to make happen. Explain that to her. And make sure you understand it yourself.'

You're better than this. Deep breaths. Focus on one of the senses. You're better than this.

I zoned in on a print that Lily had given me on the opposite wall and made myself count how many waves were in the ocean in it. 'Max, I'm going to get off the phone now and I'm going to forget this conversation ever happened because I think a club CEO blackmailing a player wouldn't be looked upon favourably by the AFL. See you later, all right?' I hung up and realised I'd been clenching my fist so hard that my nails had left deep dents in my palm.

The rumour that I'd had a fight with Max Dawson got back to the team nice and fast. God only knew how, but it did. And the result of that rumour was that, even though nobody had ever actually liked Max, none of the team were now talking to me, including my best friends.

I understood why. I would've been the same. There was nothing more important to these guys than the Rangers. They would never do anything to go against the club. That used to be me.

As much as I loved my club, there was no way I was letting Anna do the march without me beside her. When it came down to a choice between standing by her and her fight for what was right or supporting the club, which wanted to ignore the desperate situation on Bluff Island so they could keep making money off it, that choice wasn't very hard.

I'd finally become the person I thought I would never be – a person with values, a person Dad would have been proud to have for a son. The missing link though was footy. I had to get my passion back somehow, I just had to.

Craig was right – my half-arsed efforts at training were just not good enough considering the amount of money I was on and the expectations that carried with it. Football was my livelihood, my future, and I'd been pissing it up a wall. I made a promise to myself to train harder starting Monday. I'd do everything Craig wanted of me and then some.

If they let me train, that was. What if they weren't empty threats from Max and I did end up getting sacked because of the march? No, surely it would never come to that.

Bluey barked twice in response to a dog across the road and Anna stirred. She gave a little shiver and pulled the doona up higher over her, sadly covering up her breasts. I grabbed the remote and flicked on the heater so it would be warm when she got out of bed.

It was getting late, and if I didn't have her home by eleven she'd panic. Every night she had to check in on her mother. It was a rule she'd made for herself that she wouldn't break no matter how much I begged her to spend an entire night in my bed.

Truth be known, these days Leila had no fucking idea whether it was day or night. So I doubted she would even notice whether Anna checked up on her or not.

Anna described her the other day as being like an autumn leaf. 'Mama is clinging onto her life the way the leaf clings on to its spindly branch, knowing that at any moment, the wind might pick her up and she'll be blown away. Or she'll drop straight down and be crushed. I'm terrified for her, Nick,' she said with a sigh. 'My mother is in big trouble, she is lost. She even has to be reminded to brush her teeth. This is no way to live.'

And it was no way for Anna to live, with the constant worry about her mum and the growing responsibility she had for Ricky the worse Leila got. Last night Leila was more with it than she had been for a while, according to Anna, who said she was completely aware of time and place.

'Maybe there is still hope for my mama, Nick,' she'd said hopefully.

Somehow I doubted it. Leila seemed too far gone to me. I wanted to shield Anna from Leila, from the press, from the trolls, from the Rangers' committee – from everything and everyone.

The whir as the heater kicked in woke her up.

'Hey there, dozy,' I whispered and kissed the tip of her nose.

'Mmmm, that's a nice word – dozy. It's a cross between dreamy and cosy. I like this word, d-oh-zee.' She rolled over and I was reunited with her breasts again. 'I might write you a dozy poem one day soon, Nick.'

I forgot about Leila and the stress of the upcoming march and its possible effect on my career and the hundred and one other things that had been worrying me.

'Yes please, I love your poems.'

I took a hold of her hips and slid inside her, moaning when I felt her wet warmth.

She giggled. 'Well, that was certainly very quick, Nicholas Harding. How do you even know I want to do this now? It's polite to ask and say please before just inviting yourself into my body.'

I could tell from her breathlessness that she was already turned on.

I started moving inside her. In my safe haven. 'Forgive me, I forgot my manners. Anna Hayati, may I please have sex with you?'

'You may.' Anna leaned her head closer so our noses were touching. 'I like dozy sex. It's nice.'

'It's not dozy and it's not fucking nice either when it's sex with Nick Harding, sweetheart. It's a good and proper fuck when it's with me,' I whispered.

'Show me then.'

'Show you what? Be clear now.'

God, she felt so good.

'Show me what a good and proper fuck is. So far it's very dozy.'

'Is this what you want? You want me to fuck you like I mean it?'

'Yes,' she breathed, as I thrust a little harder.

'Ask me then. It's polite to ask and say please, remember?'

'Please fuck me, good and proper,' said poor little innocent Anna. 'Please fuck me like you mean it.'

I rolled on top of her and gave her everything I had until she cried out and squeezed hard around me. The sound and feel of her coming made me come every single time.

'I love you.' She arched her neck right back and sucked in big gulps of air. 'I love you so much.'

'*Ana bahebek, ya habibti,*' I said back.

When she sat up, digging around for her clothes, she found *The Prisoner of Azkaban* on the bedside table. 'Your reading, Nick, is so *slow*. It's making me crazy. In three months, you've only read three books.'

'I lost interest after the first one.' I yawned. 'I've been reading other stuff. There's not enough intrigue in Harry Potter.'

'Blasphemer!' She flicked her bra at me. 'May you be forgiven for speaking such untruths.'

'Hey, speaking of Harry Potter, I have something for you – a good luck charm for tomorrow.' I pulled open the top chest drawer and handed her a tiny purple gift bag.

'Another present? You promised no more presents.'

I smiled at the memory of turning up to the restaurant in the bright blue Mini I bought her a month ago. I couldn't stand the thought of her still catching public transport when she was followed everywhere she went.

'This one doesn't count as a gift though. It's a good luck charm.'

She unwrapped the tissue paper and squealed, 'Hermione's time turner necklace! Nick!'

'Do I get another shag for that?' I kissed the back of her hand and then dotted kisses up along the length of her forearm.

'Dream on.' She laughed and slipped the pendant over her head.

She'd learned many new sayings in the last few months. Even her accent was getting fainter by the day. It made me happy that she was more comfortable with English, but I was also nostalgic for the girl I first met at Black Salt.

'Are you sure you still want to come tomorrow?' She pulled on a bright green fleecy jumper that had a freaky owl's head knitted on it in white yarn. 'I'm still not convinced it's the right thing to do. What if you get into trouble with the club?'

I hadn't told her about the phone call with Max Dawson or any of the tension at the club.

'For the millionth time, yes, I still want to come.' I had a big drink of water. 'You've spent hours and hours researching for your speech. I wouldn't miss it for the world.'

'But you have heard me give the speech. I've practised the whole thing in front of you three times.'

'Doesn't count.'

'Hokay.' She indulged my love of the word. 'I hope that the club doesn't find out you were there though. It probably won't get covered by the media anyway.'

'And the forecast is for rain, so if any reporters were planning to come they'll wuss out now and stay in their warm houses instead. So don't worry about the club, just focus on being brilliant.'

'Wuss out.' Anna laughed. 'I like this. Wuss out.'

After she left, Bluey jumped onto the couch that he wasn't allowed on, resting his head on my legs.

'It's going to be a big day tomorrow, Blue.' I sighed, and he sighed back.

TOBY – FRIDAY

'What's this?' I looked at the envelope that John slapped onto the dining table, where I was sorting through a mountain of invoices.

'Read it.'

'Can't.' I didn't look up. 'Busy.'

'Bad day?' he called over his shoulder as he walked into the kitchen.

'You could say that.'

He came back holding a Corona and took a long swig. 'What happened?'

'The council still hasn't approved the extension on the new job in Wembley,' I replied.

'And?'

I leaned back in my chair and looked up at him. 'Ten weeks I've been nagging them for it while the client's been breathing down my neck. I was promised approval would come in by last Friday. We've got contractors lined up to start Monday and I'm going to have to call them all and cancel, and they're all depending on the work. There's hardly anything around for them at the moment and they might have knocked other jobs back after I booked them. So I feel like shit, these guys have families to feed. Plus I spent most of the day painting ceilings with Dad because the painter on our current job didn't turn up for the third day in a row, so now my neck's stiff and my shoulders ache and I can't find the painter's fucking invoice to get our fucking deposit back.'

John passed me his beer. 'You need this more than I do, mate.'

But beer was the last thing I wanted. I rubbed my eyes. The painter's invoice was nowhere to be seen.

John tapped his fingers on the envelope. 'Read the letter.'

'Ugh, all right. What's it about anyway?' I tore open the envelope, addressed to me, and pulled out the single sheet of paper. I began to read. And for a moment, I stopped breathing. 'What the hell is this?'

'It's in English, isn't it? Can't you read?'

A tsunami was rising in my chest. 'It says I've won a national photography competition for a six-month mentorship with Keith Rayner in Far North Queensland.'

'Well, how about that, hey?' he smirked. 'Congrats, bro.'

I took a deep breath. And then another. 'I never entered this competition.'

John lit a cigarette, took a slow drag and said, 'Yeah, actually you did. I forged your signature and sent in a USB drive with five of your best photos on it.'

It took me a minute to register his words. Then I roared, '*What?*'

'Someone had to do something!' He stood up, his voice matching mine in volume. 'You've been rotting away at Watts Building, year after fucking year. I can't watch you martyr yourself anymore. Life's short, mate. If Jen hasn't shown you that, I don't know what will.'

'This has got nothing to do with Jen,' I growled. 'This is about you sneaking around and breaking the law to get me a mentorship I don't want and can't even take.'

'*A mentorship you don't want?* Didn't you read what it said? It's a fully paid residency in nature photography with one of the most famous photographers in the country. Six months' living allowance on top of that. There were over six thousand entrants and they chose you. You're going to have your own feature in *National Geographic*. Having your work in *National Geographic*'s been your dream for the last seventeen years. You don't want that? You'd rather stay here in a job that you hate?'

'How long has this been going on?' I asked, rereading the letter. 'It says here I was longlisted then shortlisted. How long have you been hiding this from me?'

'About seven months. I saw it in *The West*. Jen was really bad by then. I thought if you won it could get you away from here, once she'd, you know …' He trailed off.

I spread my hands on the table and hung my head. 'Mate, I'm sorry I shouted, I was shocked. I know you did this for me, but it's just impossible.' I picked up the letter. 'It says here "to commence July 1st". That's three weeks away. I'm in the middle of a job, with more jobs lined up. I can't just up and leave. What do I tell Dad? And what—'

He interrupted. 'There's never going to be a good time to leave. There'll always be jobs lined up. It's not like you're irreplaceable. There's a hundred others out there just as qualified as you who'd take over tomorrow given half the chance.'

'I'm in a committed relationship. I can't leave just like that, without even having a conversation with Lily about it.'

'Committed relationship?' He guffawed. 'You didn't even know her three months ago! None of us have even met her. Don't pull that bullshit on me – she's just your fuck buddy. Don't use your fuck buddy as an excuse to let an opportunity like this slip through your fingers.'

I felt my face burning. 'It's not like that at all. I love her and I'm not leaving her. Thanks for trying, but you're going to have to reply and say I decline.'

He put out the cigarette in the ashtray with a lot more force than needed. 'You want to reject it, you reply.' He pointed at me. 'And if you really do love this chick, stop sneaking around with her like she's a hooker. Show her some respect and bring her over for a meal or something.'

'You can talk!' I shouted. 'How much respect does poor Renee get?'

'At least I don't make out to be in love with her.' He glared at me, his voice low and even. 'I'm not the one who's lying to myself. Go ahead and decline the offer. I don't give a shit. It's your life.'

The front door slammed seconds later.

I sat there, numb, for a long while before I picked up the letter and read it again, properly this time. I'd won a national photography competition. Me. Out of 6,479 entrants. And Keith Rayner, my idol, had picked *me* to go on assignment with him for a *National Geographic* special over six months featuring coastal and inland Far North Queensland. A slow smile spread across my face.

But then I thought about Lily and the smile faded. I had no idea what I'd done to upset her so much that she'd ignored my calls all day and texted me with sudden news about going up north to see her mum.

I sighed and folded up the letter and slid it back inside the envelope. Then I flipped open my laptop to try to locate the painter's invoice.

ANNA – FRIDAY

Sometimes I wondered: what was it all for? Would it actually change anything? When we marched outside parliament, would it be no more than a mild disturbance to the traffic? All these weeks of planning, what would they amount to?

I wished I could know for sure that the hours spent gathering research, interviewing lawyers, social workers, counsellors and teachers who'd been to Bluff Island, listening to the recordings and interpreting from Arabic to English, and the weeks and weeks of planning the logistics of the march, would bring us the result we hoped and prayed for.

But in truth, I did wonder if it would all be for nothing. That although we would be loud and passionate and do our best, the children would still live stranded on a remote island indefinitely with no real hope for a future, and for the orphans, no real hope of a family.

I spent some time talking with Mama just now. I had told Nick how I hoped she would be awake when I returned from his house and she was! It was rare that Mama was alert this late at night. With the increase in her medication that came about last month after yet another one of her terrifying episodes, she slept more than she was awake and when she was awake, such was her drowsiness that she may as well have been asleep.

But this week she was different, becoming more and more like the old Mama from Egypt. And for the first time, I was sure that it wasn't because she was not taking her medicine, which was usually the reason for her being her old self again. I knew this wasn't the case because I had been giving the tablets to her myself and watching her swallow them every day. Maybe our prayers had been answered and she was beginning to show some signs of healing!

She sat in the corner chair near the lamp, which shone on her skin and gave her a beautiful glow as she sipped her tea. She didn't hear me come in, she must have been far away in her thoughts. Her legs were tucked beneath her and her long dark lashes cast a shadow over her high cheekbones – 'Those cheekbones could only belong to the descendant of a pharaoh. They are proof that I married a queen,' Baba used to say. And for that briefest of moments she even looked like the old Mama, the one who would sit like that with her legs curled up and read until the early hours. She used to finish a book every few nights. She couldn't sleep unless she escaped into a story first. She never read anymore.

She must have sensed my presence because she looked up. And although she may have seemed like the old Mama for that short moment, her eyes were not the eyes that belonged to the old Mama. When she looked at me tonight, her face had no light in it. The reality hit me that she was a still a long way from truly healing.

'*Ahlan, ya habibti*,' Mama yawned as she spoke. 'Would you like a tea? The pot is still warm.'

'Oh yes, please, *ya* Mama! It makes me so happy to see you like this, still awake and making tea. I think you might be starting to become healthier. Do you feel any different this week? Because I see a real difference in you.'

Mama gave me a long look, a look that frightened me terribly because I had absolutely no clue what she was thinking. Then she blinked and stood up to make the tea.

While Mama fixed my tea, I tiptoed into Ahmo Fariz's room to check on Ricky.

'Goodnight, my love,' I whispered as I bent to kiss the top of his warm head. He finally had a full head of hair, our dear little one. His slow breathing pattern did not change, he was dreaming deeply.

Ahmo Fariz stirred but stayed asleep.

When I returned to our room, Mama had made my tea and brought me a piece of baklava to eat with it. I wished more than anything that Nick could have seen Mama like this.

'I thought it was your mum who was supposed to be his primary carer,' Nick said last Tuesday night when I had gone to see him after a parent information evening at Ricky's school. 'I thought that was the whole point – he needed a mother, she was grieving a child. But it's you who makes his school lunches, who helps with his homework, who goes out to buy all his clothes, who organises his play days, who takes him everywhere.' He stroked my hair. 'It's too much for you. Your mum does nothing, she barely looks at him.'

'Nick, she is unwell. Do you not think if she could she would be doing everything for Ricky? What she needs is our understanding, not our judgement.'

'Well, what's going to happen next month when you start university as well? How will you manage? I'll keep helping as much as I can, but now that I'm back playing, my commitments to the club will be more full on. With both of us working, and you studying too, she'll have to step up. She'll have no choice, Anna, she'll just have to.' His tone was gentle but he had a steely look in his eyes when he spoke about Mama.

'How, Nick? How can someone who is this ill just *step up*? It is up to me to be the one to step up. It is me who has no choice, not her.'

If only he could have seen Mama making me tea and bringing me baklava to eat. Perhaps then he would judge her less harshly.

'I'm worried the march will achieve nothing, Mama,' I confided over our mugs of tea.

'The march? What march, *habibti*?'

The sadness pushed down on my shoulders and made them heavy. 'The same march we discussed for a long time last night, Mama. The one for Asylum Assist.'

'Ah, of course, yes.' Mama stared at her tea. 'That march, yes, yes, I knew that. I thought you said something else.'

'Mama, what if nothing changes even though we protest? There's a big chance that the government will ignore us. I desperately want things to change.'

'*Habibti*, change happens if you strike a chord in the heart of even just one person. Think of yourself like the whisper of wind in a meadow of dandelions – even if you blow only one dandelion away then you have created a permanent change in that meadow and the seeds from that one dandelion may end up creating many more in a new meadow away from all of the old dandelions. You must not give up hope, just keep being the whisper of gentle wind, forever blowing and changing one dandelion at a time.' She shut her eyes and rested her head back against the armchair.

'That is a wonderful way to look at it, Mama. Thank you.' I stood up and kissed the top of her head.

She kept her eyes closed for a minute then looked up at me and squinted. 'Noor, *habibti*. Go and check on Anwar and make sure she's stopped reading. She needs to be up for training before five, and you know your sister. She will read all night if we don't stop her, that girl.'

I turned my head so that Mama could not see my cry. 'Yes, Mama. I'll check on her. Come, *ya Mama, yalla*. It's time for you to go to sleep. Let me help you to bed.'

Sometime after one in the morning, Mama fell asleep. After she had cried many tears for Noor and for Baba, who she remembered were dead when she laid down. And then, just like she did unexpectedly a few nights ago, she began to laugh hysterically and was unable to stop. Over what, I didn't know, but her laughing chilled me. I had deluded myself that she was healing. This was the opposite of healing. After the march I would need to call the doctor and ask her to come to the house and review Mama's medication again.

It was now three-thirty in the morning and I could not have been more awake. I couldn't read, I was far too anxious for that. And these days I never wanted to check my phone or computer because I knew I would only be reminded of the terrible things that had been said about me – that I was responsible for the deaths of my family, or that I was a slut who had disgraced the name of Islam, or that I was a frigid religious freak who was ruining Nick Harding's career, that I was obsessed with fame, that I was part of an organisation that wanted no screening for asylum seekers so that Australia's sovereignty would be put at risk by allowing all the terrorists in.

When I first began my relationship with Nick, I knew I was giving up my privacy for him, but I didn't expect so much hate. The very worst thing was how it had affected my family.

Tante Rosa may have been full of theatrics, but she was also genuinely distressed by my relationship with Nick. She had lost too much weight and when I begged her to eat something she told me she was too scared for my soul and the punishment that awaited me after death to be able to eat.

And of course she worried about the restaurant.

In the end, it was she who was right and Ahmo Fariz who was wrong. Our community did turn against us, just as she predicted. Many of Ahmo Fariz's long-term patrons stopped coming to Masri's. They saw pictures of me on TV or in magazines and it was enough to keep them away. When Ahmo Fariz asked his friends why they had stopped coming, they told him that they could not be with a family who had no morals.

When I apologised to Ahmo Fariz, he replied, 'But we have our new patrons, *habibti*. Nick has brought with him to Masri's a new crowd, and unlike our old friends and their friends, and the friends of their friends, the new crowd are happy to pay us instead of expecting food for nothing. You may see the restaurant is emptier, but in fact it is making us more money now than it ever did and it is for less work!'

I sighed, remembering this conversation, and took out my journal in the hope that my writing would put me to sleep.

My darling Noor,

I feel tonight that I deserve nothing.

I don't deserve Ahmo Fariz to stand by me and pretend he doesn't care about the patrons who have deserted him. He tells me fibs about new customers paying him well, to protect me. Even at full price, how could twelve tables bring in the same amount of money as forty?

I see Mama, a broken, confused shell because my swimming career ruined her life; I see Tante Rosa gaunt and nervous because she believes my behaviour reflects poorly on our family.

I don't deserve to be happy – in fact it is an injustice that I am happy. And Allah promises that injustice will not go unpunished.

I'm scared as I wait for the punishment that is sure to come. I'm scared, Noor.

And something else – I am not well. I vomited again half an hour ago, just as I did as soon as I woke up in the morning and then again after lunch. The nausea eased while I was at Nick's this evening, but it's back again – it's a deep sick feeling in my stomach. I wonder if it's a reaction from my body to the knowledge that something terrible is about to happen. Punishment feels close.

Come and visit me in my dreams, dear one. Please come to me and tell me that I'm wrong. Tell me that no injustice has been done through my happiness and that no punishment awaits me. I have been punished enough. Tell me and I'll believe you.

All my love forever,

A x

That night, for the first time, Noor didn't come to me in my dreams.

NICK – SATURDAY

The march was over, but I still had Ricky up on my shoulders so he could see Anna take the microphone on the steps of Parliament House in front of what was estimated to be around four thousand protestors in the biggest demonstration in Perth for years, according to the speaker who just addressed us.

Listening to Anna, I understood why she gave up a swimming career to pursue a law degree. She was born to do this, to have a voice, to move people. It gave me a glimpse into what Leila must have been like. This was so clearly in Anna's DNA.

Last night she was worried that they wouldn't pull enough of a crowd. Not only had the masses turned up, but so had the media, and in force. The four major TV stations were filming her right now, and there was a row of press waiting at the sidelines. She got her wish – the plight of asylum seeker children was being heard today, through her. She was giving a voice to the voiceless.

Seeing her shine like this made all the bad press of the last three months feel like it had happened only to lead up to this moment. The media's obsession with her had been turned to her advantage. They were all here and they were listening.

I looked at the passion in her eyes and listened to the passion in her voice and I was hit with a new wave of passion myself. If Anna could overcome everything she'd gone through to follow her dreams, I could sure as hell overcome a few fractured bones to chase mine.

I *loved* football, I'd loved it since I first held that leather ball in my baby hands. And if Anna could use her hardships to spur her on to be this tough, then I could use my injuries to emerge tougher and stronger than before.

I clapped till my palms stung when Anna stepped away from the microphone and the president of Asylum Assist took over.

'She was good!' Ricky shouted in my ear.

'She was great, mate, the best.'

I hugged Ricky's skinny little legs tight. I couldn't imagine my life without this kid now. I'd kitted out my house for him – there was a trampoline in the back yard and a Wii U in the lounge that he and I spent hours on playing Mario Kart, often with Bluey (his new best friend) lying over both of us. I even did the school pick up a few days a week to help Anna.

Whenever I dropped Ricky back home after school, though, that pain in the arse Rosa ran out to the car park and put her arms around him, hurrying him inside and throwing me a dirty look over her shoulder, like I was a threat to his safety.

I didn't know how Anna put up with her, or how she put up with her drugged-out, depressed mother for that matter. But she had a way of taking everything in her stride, of being able to stand all that pressure, all that heartache, and still be quick with a laugh.

Anna looked visibly relieved that her speech was over and I felt so sure of myself, of our love, of our future together, and of my career that it was laughable that less than fifteen minutes later all of it collapsed and I was left with nothing.

Because what neither Anna nor I realised was that the media and press that turned up couldn't care less about the cause Anna was fighting for. In fact, none of the Asylum Assist speeches would ever be broadcast, or even referenced in the commercial news reports that followed. The reporters and camera crews were only there to witness the biggest football scandal of the year – the day that Nick Harding marched against his own club's sponsors. The media were only there to record the moment that I became the most hated man in Australia.

As soon as the protest was officially brought to an end and I met Anna at the foot of the stairs, there was a stampede of press towards us. The refugee who gave a speech before Anna and the president of Asylum Assist were left standing alone.

The reporters jostled with each other to get closer to us. I scooped Ricky down off my shoulders as the throng surrounded us, and Anna pulled him in close to her. We didn't get a chance to say a word to each other before the microphones were thrust in our faces.

And none of the questions had anything to do with the children being held in detention.

'Nick, the Western Rangers' sponsor SafeXone is the security company on Bluff Island, but you're here demanding the detention centre be shut down, which would cost hundreds of SafeXone employees their jobs. Is there anything you'd like to say to your sponsors about your appearance here today?'

'My appearance here has nothing to do with SafeXone and everything to do with the government leaving kids, including orphans, to rot for years on end in offshore detention,' I replied as dozens of flashes went off.

'Nick, there are rumours that you'll be sacked for your attendance at this march. Do you wish to address those rumours?'

'No.'

'Nick, is it true that you're planning to convert to Islam?'

'What? No.'

'Nick, Nick, can you tell us why your Muslim girlfriend doesn't uphold the code of dress expected of her religion? Muslim clerics have been quoted naming Anna and her mother, former Egyptian politician, Leila Hayati, as infidels.'

I rolled my eyes and crossed my arms. 'What's any of this got to do with the Asylum Assist demonstration that we're here for?'

They turned on Anna. 'Anwar, do you follow the Koran? Doesn't the Koran say a hijab is law? And doesn't the Koran also state that Muslims are banned from having relationships with non-Muslims? Can you explain how you call yourself a Muslim and yet you go against the teachings of the prophet Mohammed?'

I raised my voice. 'Hey! Stop it. That's not what today is about.'

Anna slipped her hand into mine and gave it a squeeze before she answered calmly. 'Firstly, it is well known that my father was Muslim but my mother is Christian. I proudly subscribe to philosophies from both religions. But let me clarify Islam for you. Islam teaches peace, tolerance and love, all of which I practise. I don't follow every verse of the Koran word for word, just as I don't follow the Holy Bible word for word. Are you a Christian, sir?'

The reporter hesitated then nodded.

Anna continued. 'Take for example, Leviticus 19:19 – "Do not wear clothing woven of two kinds of material." Do you believe, sir, that because today you are wearing those leather shoes with a cotton shirt, that this would mean you are going against the teachings of Jesus Christ who condoned the Old Testament of the Holy Bible and quoted from it himself?'

When the reporter didn't respond, she took a breath and continued, commanding their attention with her quiet tone, making them fall silent so that they could hear her. They were leaning in as she spoke, 'I don't consider myself to be sinning when I wear clothing made of different materials together just as I don't consider myself to be sinning when I am without a hijab.'

A stunned silence followed.

And that should have been it. The spontaneous press conference that had been forced on us should have been over. But it wasn't.

'Nick, do you have plans to marry Anna, and if so, would you raise your children as Australians or as Muslims?'

'Can you even hear how ignorant you sound right now?' Putting my arm around Anna, I turned my back on them. We started walking away. Her shoulders trembled under my arm.

'Anna, do you feel responsible that your protest has put Nick's career at stake?' someone shouted at her back.

We ignored the question and kept walking.

'Nick, do you think Australia would be proud of you going against the club that has nurtured you since the start of your career?'

Again we ignored the question. But even though we were walking away from the reporters, we weren't putting any more distance between us. They were hot on our heels.

'Nick? Nick! Do you think by supporting illegal boat people who could be terrorists, instead of supporting the football club that has supported you has made the people of Australia ashamed of you?'

I froze.

'Keep walking, Nick, please just keep walking,' Anna pleaded in a low voice.

I spun around so I was face to face with the middle-aged male reporter who had asked the question. His microphone was still held up to his mouth. I took another step so that I was close enough to feel his hot breath on my face. His eyes widened behind his glasses and I kept my curled fist by my side.

I looked him right in the eyes. 'I sure hope not. I hope that instead of being ashamed of me, Australians are ashamed of our government that allows children to spend years in detention without their most basic needs being met. I hope they're ashamed of the media and the biased, bigoted bullshit you guys put out there that destroys the reputations of the majority of innocent Muslims who live here.'

'So you don't think any Australians will be ashamed of your actions today, Nick?'

I pressed my lips together and blew out hard through my nose. 'Today it's me who should be ashamed of Australia, not the other way around.'

A hush descended on the gathered crowd. The reporters knew I had just dug my own grave. They knew they had just found the gold they came looking for. I'd delivered.

Once I dropped Anna and Ricky off at the restaurant and came home and fed Bluey, I flicked on the TV to a news channel.

Out of the entire march and speeches and Anna's and my interview afterwards, the only part that was televised was the reporter saying – 'So you don't think any Australians will be ashamed of your actions today, Nick?' and me replying, 'Today it's me who should be ashamed of Australia, not the other way around.'

And that's all that everyone who watched the news, listened to the radio, saw it online or read it in the papers, thought I said. Nothing else, just that I was ashamed of Australia.

Craig rang to warn me that Max Dawson had called an extraordinary disciplinary hearing coming up on Monday morning to discuss the action the club would take against me. Max also planned to announce the disciplinary hearing on Channel Seven news tonight.

'Craig, they edited the footage. It was taken out of context!' I argued.

'Max was already fuming that you marched – your words at the press conference were just the excuse he needed to call the meeting so he could teach you a lesson for going against him. Why couldn't you just keep your mouth shut?'

'Craig, please tell me that you believe me that the footage of the press conference was cut to make me look bad.'

'I believe you.'

'You're not just saying that, are you? I need to know that you *really* believe me.'

There was an extended silence.

'I believe you,' he finally said.

'Thank God,' I exhaled.

'Look, try not to stress about it too much. There's not a lot you can do for the time being. I'll be at the hearing, and I'll try and dig up the rest of the footage between now and then so we can all see the whole interview and put your statement in context. But even if I don't manage to get my hands on the footage, the people attending the hearing know you, Nick.

They know that if you say that's not how the conversation went, then it's not how the conversation went. Max is just one vote, remember. The rest of us are your friends. So it'll all work out, I'm sure. But the best thing you can do for now is to keep your mouth shut and stay out of sight.'

'Okay. Thanks.' I rubbed my forehead with my fingers. My head was splitting.

'You know what I wish?' Craig said after a long silence.

'What?'

'I wish you'd shown more dedication to the club recently. It would've made defending you come Monday and convincing the others to defend you a whole lot easier. As it stands, I'm going to go head to head with my boss. And what I say is guaranteed to piss him off, so it might be my job on the line next. And for what? For the benefit of a player I'm not even sure wants to be with the club anymore.'

'Craig, I'm so sorry, mate. I know I've let you down. But I really do love this club.'

He sniffed. 'Words, Nick. They're just words. I need action.'

'You'll get action,' I vowed, my voice trembling. 'Help me come out the other side of this hearing with my job still intact and I swear on my life I'll give it everything I've got.'

'You better follow through with that promise, Harding,' he said before hanging up.

I flicked the TV back on to watch Max deliver the statement. He was practically frothing at the mouth in excitement. 'It's with deep regret that I announce on behalf of the Western Rangers Football Club that midfielder Nick Harding is facing disciplinary action following his association with Asylum Assist and the march that took place in Perth today, particularly the comments made by Mr Harding at the post-march press conference, which do not in any way reflect the values of our football club. The future of Mr Harding at the Western Rangers for the rest of this season and beyond will be decided at an extraordinary disciplinary hearing to be held at 10 am on Monday morning. There will be no further statement from the club or any of its members until the outcome of the meeting is decided.'

I turned off the television and rang Anna. She didn't answer. I tried again an hour later, same thing. Where was she? She always carried her phone in her apron pocket when she worked so she could call or text me when she had a free minute.

Fifteen minutes later, my phone rang. It was Anna's number but it was Fariz on the phone.

'Nick!' he cried. 'Leila is dead.'

TOBY – SUNDAY

Lily had just posted an update on Facebook.

> *Tried to visit my brother this evening and had to park two
> blocks away from his house thanks to all the scumbag reporters
> lining the street. FFS people, leave him alone!*

Hang on, what? She was home and she hadn't contacted me?
What the hell was going on here? I grabbed the keys and
stormed out to the car.

With just a shirt on over my jeans when it was twelve
degrees out, I started to shiver. I drove along the coast, my
stomach churning until I reached her house. The lights were
on. I took a deep breath and knocked on the door.

Just when I thought she wasn't going to answer, the wooden
door swung open and it took me a few seconds to register that
the woman in front of me was actually Lily. Her waist-length
blonde ringlets were gone. She now had a mop of chin-length,
dead-straight bright red hair. I composed myself and creaked
out a hello.

She barely smiled. 'Hi. Come in.' She unlocked the screen
door and then turned her back to me and walked deeper into
the house without so much as a hug.

Who was this woman? What happened to my girlfriend?

I followed her into the kitchen, where she leaned back against the stove top. She was wearing flannel pyjamas. With that short hair and no makeup, she looked like a twelve-year-old. A sad vulnerable twelve-year-old. I stood on the other side of the room and neither of us spoke.

Her washing machine rattled away in the background.

On the bench was a wrapper from a block of chocolate and a half empty bottle of wine. Lily rarely drank. Was that dinner?

I finally found my voice. 'Lil, I'm so confused. What's going on? One minute everything's good between us and then the next thing, you won't return my calls, you take off to Derby out of the blue, you chop off all your hair, you don't even tell me you're home again. What have I done? What's happening?'

She gave me a long look. 'I failed my exam because of our relationship. I've barely studied since I met you. It's fifth-year medicine for God's sake. I should be studying my arse off every night. That fail was a wake-up call. I can't keep going the way I was. Things have to change.'

'What are you saying? Don't you love me anymore?'

'Of course I love you.' She sighed. 'That's the problem. I love you so much that every day for the last three months I haven't had a life outside of us.'

I gulped. 'I'm sorry.'

'Don't be sorry.' She sniffed. 'It's my fault for allowing it to happen. But it's not good for me, Toby. It's not healthy.'

I didn't know what to say.

'Everything needs to change now. Everything.' She ran her fingers through her hair.

'Even your hair,' I remarked.

'I hate this hair. It's horrible, look at it!' She pulled at a clump of it. 'But for my whole life I kept my hair long for my dad. He'd always tell me how much he loved my long hair so I never cut it. And then Ben was like, "Don't ever cut your beautiful hair." And then I met you and you called me Rapunzel. So I kept it long, even though it was a nightmare to look after, and weighed a tonne and made me overheat, just so I could please you all. Then on the bus to Derby it hit me. I've spent my whole life pleasing the men I love. But what about me? What about doing what pleases *me*?'

'I'm sorry,' I repeated.

'And you know what else?' Her voice caught. 'It's not even about my hair. I mean, honestly, could you get a more boring job than spending your days putting people to sleep? I'm studying a course that I hate, planning an extra five years *more* study to be an anaesthetist, just to please my dad, *and he's not even alive*! I want to do something that makes me happy – not my dad, not you, not anyone. Just me.'

'What would make you happy?'

'I don't know!' The tears welled up and she covered her face with her hands. 'I have no fucking clue! I just know I don't want to keep going like this!'

I walked over to where she stood and took her into my arms.

'I don't even know who I am,' she sobbed.

Instinctively I bent my head to kiss her once, twice. She tasted like Lily. I tilted her chin up so we were face to face.

'It's all right, we'll sort it out.'

We stared at each other for a moment.

I kissed her mouth and she held my face and kissed me back. We kissed with increasing urgency. I pulled her in closer and slid my hands inside her pyjama top, moaning when my fingers found her nipples.

But a moment later she pushed me away.

'No.' She took a step back from me. 'I'm not going to sort anything out if we just shag again. Arielle's right. All we ever do is have sex.'

'What? Arielle? What's she got to do with anything?' I edged closer to her again and touched her wet cheek with my thumb. 'We don't just have sex. We're so much more than that. Arielle's not right at all. What would she know? Just tell me how to fix this and I will. What can I do to make you feel better?'

'Haven't you heard me at all?' She shook her head. 'I'm not yours to fix. I need to learn to make myself better for once. I'm a complete disaster of a human being – my life consists of me bumbling along from one mess to the next. And it's because I have no idea how to take care of myself. I've always had someone there to do it for me. I need to learn to be independent. I need to be alone. I'm sorry, I can't have a boyfriend right now.'

The panic set in. 'Please don't talk like this. Don't say you don't want me.'

'Toby, it isn't just me who needs to find myself.' She sighed. 'You're as lost as I am. Look at your job. You hate building and you've made it your career. I mean, what the hell is with that? You're living for your dad as much as I'm living for mine. You've got this unbelievable gift with your photography and you don't have the guts to do anything about it.'

'It's not that I don't have the guts. It's that being loyal to my dad is more important to me than chasing a pipe dream.'

She shrugged. 'See, to me that's bullshit. Being loyal to your dad is the excuse you give yourself so you can stay in

your comfort zone and be the good son. You're so scared of
upsetting people that you let it rule your life. I mean, you're still
going around to Jenny's mum's every week when you say you
can't stand her! Jenny's been dead for three months, you were
separated for years before that, and she's still got a stranglehold
on you.'

'That's not true.' I crossed my arms tight.

'Well, tell me then, why aren't I allowed to meet your
family? Why? Why do we sneak around as if you're still married
and we're having an affair? What are you so scared of?'

'I'm not scared. I'm just being nice to someone I've known
since I was three years old who lost her only daughter.' How
dare she accuse me of being scared! 'I haven't introduced you
to my family yet because they were really close to Jen too. So
I'm giving them time to get over it.'

'Are you serious? Giving your parents time to get over
what?' she cried. 'The woman you separated from years ago?
Why on earth would they have a problem with you having a
girlfriend now? Wake up to yourself, Toby! The only person
who needs to get over her is you. Jenny set us up, it was the last
thing she did when she was alive. Why can't you let her go?
She's gone. She's never coming back. Maybe when you realise
that, you'll be ready for a relationship.' Her expression turned
hard. 'You need to sort your shit out and I need to sort out
mine. Just leave. I want you to leave.'

'So just like that, you decide what we both need?' My voice
broke. I squeezed my eyes shut tight but still the tears escaped.
'I don't even get a say?'

'No, you don't.' The resolution was clear in her eyes. 'For
the first time in my whole life – it's *my* say that goes. And my
say is that I want to be alone.'

She made no attempt to stop me as I walked out.

In the car, my hands shook so violently that it took three attempts to get the key in the ignition. There was a roar in my head as the blood rushed between my ears, drowning out the radio as I drove away from the house where my world just crumbled.

She didn't want me. All I wanted was her and she didn't want me. It hurt to swallow.

Before I knew it, I was home. But I couldn't face John so I stayed in the car, leaned my head back against the seat and shut my eyes. I didn't know how long I stayed like that for, but the roar inside my head gradually died down, my heart stopped racing, and then when all was quiet again, my mind cleared.

And that's when I realised that everything Lily said was right. Everything.

I found myself driving to the cemetery. It was eerily quiet apart from the sound of my footsteps crunching on the gravel. Spotlights along the paths led me to Jen's grave. I shivered hard, it was absolutely freezing. I lit a cigarette and the warmth spread into my cheeks and neck as I took one long drag after another.

'I'm sorry, Jen,' I said out loud into the night air once the cigarette finished. 'I'm sorry I kissed you that first time. You were too nice to tell me to bugger off. I knew you had a crush on Dylan Burns but I was a selfish bastard and I wanted you for myself. I deluded myself that you wanted me too.' I lit a second cigarette between trembling fingers. 'I'm sorry I proposed. You should've married someone who rocked your world. I saw that look in your eyes when I asked you to marry me and I should have let you go then and there, but I didn't.' I stretched my neck from side to side and it cracked. 'Jen, I'm sorry that you were so desperate to fall in love with someone, anyone, that you ended up with Xavier, instead of someone who deserved you. And then when you got sick, I still couldn't let you go. I could have set up the spare bed for you instead of guilting you back into mine.' I stopped for a minute to let the words reach Jen in her far-away place. 'Jen, you need to be free of me and I need to be free of you. So I'm finally letting you go. I'm not going to visit your mum anymore, okay? And I'm not coming back here either. So,' I let out a shaky breath. 'See you round, hey?' I took a last look at where she rested. 'I hope you're happy and I hope you're free – wherever you are. I love you. I always will. Bye, Jen.'

I turned my back on her and the further away I walked from her grave, the more the heavy layers of her that I'd been wearing like a cloak began to shed. By the time I reached my car, I felt lighter than I had in years.

I drove to Mum and Dad's house and pulled the phone out of my front pocket and called the landline. With my windows down, I could hear it ringing inside.

'Hullo?' Mum's voice was croaky.

'Hi, Mum. Sorry, I know it's really late but I need to talk to you and Dad. I'm out the front, can I come in?'

'Of course darling, you didn't need to ring first. Is everything okay?'

'Yeah, yeah everything's fine. It's just that …' I faltered. 'It's just that I'm moving to Queensland, Mum.'

ANNA – MONDAY

I clasped my hands together and shut my eyes tight.

Allah, ya Rab. *Please help me. I know I've wronged you many times, but I pray for your mercy now. I'm lost and frightened. Please help me be the parent that Ricky needs. Keep me safe for him. I can't bear for him to lose anybody else.*

I ask you to grant me resilience when all I feel is weakness. Grant me courage when all I feel is fear.

I've lost so much, too much. My mother has passed away and Noor has left me as well. Help me understand, Allah, why my sister abandoned me when I needed her most. I miss her and I need her to come back in my dreams. Please give her back to me. And in return, I promise to pray every day.

I know that bargaining with you is a sin – forgive me.

I pray that you help me be strong enough to stay away from Nick. Please give me the strength to allow him to live a life free from the public scorn that I brought. Without me, he can dedicate himself once more to his career. He doesn't need the responsibility of a nineteen-year-old orphan and the secret she carries as well as the responsibility of a child with malignant cancer.

Allah, I need to ask you for one more thing …

My eyes opened at the sound of Tante Rosa's voice.

'Anwar! Anwar! *Enti fen*?'

'I'm here, in my bedroom, Tante Rosa.'

'What are you doing down there on the floor? Did you fall? Did you find money?'

'I'm praying.'

'Praying?' She put her hands on her hips. '*Praying*? Haven't you left that a little late? Everything is done! You did not listen to me. No, of course not, you knew better! And look at the revenge Allah took on you.'

'Tante Rosa, please. My mother was buried today. Please, I beg of you, not tonight.' I sighed as I got myself off the floor and sat on the edge of my bed.

'Very well. If you're praying, pray also that the few patrons we had left at this godforsaken restaurant return after that rock the size of a melon came crashing through the window on Saturday. It is only because Allah blessed us, because of all the praying I do, that it happened when nobody was in the restaurant. Allah protects those who are faithful to him, don't forget that.' She pushed me sideways. 'Move over, I need to sit. Aye, that's better. It's good that you want to pray. Allah will be pleased after all that you have done to displease Him. See, only two days away from the footballer and you're already improving. Don't roll your eyes, it's true.'

I played with the duvet, avoiding Tante Rosa's eyes. 'Tante Rosa, thank you for washing my mother and preparing her body for the burial.'

'Yes, well, after the police came and wasted a whole day, I knew it had to be done quickly, to keep with our faith. I didn't want you to slow me down with your inexperience. This way I could prepare her body in the right way,' she said in a gruff voice.

'I know that was not the reason you wouldn't let me help and I'm very grateful. I don't think I would have coped.'

'Aye, more crying?' she clicked her tongue. 'Come, come, child, no more crying. You must be stronger than this. Pray. Pray for strength. You're all Ricky has left now.' She put her arm out and drew me to her bosom.

'He has you too, and Ahmo Fariz.' I reached for a tissue and wiped my eyes.

'Why are you so quiet?' She said after a while 'This is a very long silence for someone who always has too much to say. If you're going to sit here silently much longer, I have chores to do.'

'I was quiet because I was thinking.'

'About the footballer?'

'No. I was thinking about how you said that I'm all Ricky has left. What about me? Who do I have left?' I'd twisted the tissue into a long thin rope.

'Well of course you also have me, silly girl. Aren't I here sitting with you now, after all?' She gave my shoulder a squeeze.

I was surprised by how much her touch comforted me, by how much I actually needed to feel close to her.

'Tante Rosa, why are you always so angry with me? I don't understand. What did I do to you?'

She didn't answer.

'Now it's you who's silent,' I muttered.

'I'm deciding whether to tell you something or not. Be quiet, let me think.' She put her hands in her lap, closed her eyes and dropped her head.

After a while I cleared my throat. 'Tante Rosa, it's been a long time that you've been sitting here with your eyes shut. If it's this hard to decide whether to tell me or not, perhaps you just shouldn't tell me.'

She opened her eyes and when she spoke, the tone of her voice changed. She sounded far away. 'Listen, I will tell you why I have been firm with you. I didn't want you to end up like me. Pregnant and alone.'

What had she just said? Did I hear her correctly?

'Close your mouth, Anwar, you look like a guppy fish with it hanging open.'

I closed my mouth, but my eyes stayed wide.

'What?' she demanded. 'You think you're the first person to ever fall in love with the wrong man? You think I always looked like this?' She waved her hand over her body. 'I was just as beautiful as you when I was young. Beautiful enough when I was eighteen years old, to catch the eye of the son of one of the wealthiest sheikhs in the whole of the Middle East when he was visiting Mamoura. But the mistake I made cost me dearly. He lost all interest in me as soon as he found out that I was pregnant. My dream of attending university with your mother was over, just like that. I was forced to leave our home. My parents banished me like a leper to a special home in Lebanon for women in my situation. But then only a week before she was due to be born, my child died.' She swallowed and took a few seconds to continue. 'The doctors could not find the cause of her death. But I knew why. It was because my baby knew that she and I would be separated as soon as she left my womb and she could bear it no more than I could. And so, I gave birth to her and I held her little body in my arms and nobody ever got to take her away from me ... Aye, Anwar! *Allaho'akbar*, crying again?'

The tears burned my eyes. 'Thank you for sharing your story with me, Tante Rosa.' I placed my hand over hers and gave it a squeeze. 'You've helped me make an important decision.'

'What decision?' She narrowed her eyes at me.

'Nothing.'

'Hmmph. Well, now at least you understand why I've been firm with you. Let us not speak of it again. Now look what I have here for you. If you need more reason to keep away from that worthless non-believer, Nick Harding, here he is on Saturday night, look at him!' From the pocket of her apron, she pulled out a folded page of the newspaper and spread it out over her lap.

My breath caught at the picture of Nick with Arielle. He had his arm around her, leaning in close. It looked like he was talking in her ear.

'After he was here banging on the door and begging for you to let him in. Look at where he went and what he did no more than a few hours later. Full of beer to his eyeballs, I'll bet, and no shame – look at how he is falling over that girl. And look at her with that pink hair!'

'Stop, stop, Tante Rosa,' I sobbed. 'I can't deal with this today.'

'Stop your crying,' she said sternly. 'This is a good thing for you to see and for you to remember. It will make you strong. If you are ever tempted to go back to him, look at these pictures.'

'It hurts more because I know her. She's the one girl he loved before me. Couldn't he have even waited one day before going to her?'

'The *one girl* he loved before you? Have you not seen all the magazines? There were *one hundred and one* girls he loved before you, my dear, not just one,' she snorted. 'This is what I have been telling you all along. He belongs to a loose culture that you do not belong to. It is lucky you told him to go before you ended up pregnant and alone.'

I froze at her words.

'What?' Tante Rosa said with narrowed eyes. 'What is that look on your face?'

'No, nothing.' I gulped.

'Don't lie to me. You think I can't tell when you're lying?'

'It's just … I'm not ready to share this piece of news yet.'

'Why?'

'Because I feel weak enough already with my mother gone and now seeing those photos of Nick, that I don't think I could cope with you yelling at me as well if I told you what it is.'

'Listen to me, Anwar. What could you tell me that is worse than me ending up pregnant and alone?'

I let out a small sad laugh.

'Anwar, listen to me, I promise not to be hard. Just tell me.' She looked me in the eye and I believed in that moment that she was being truthful and that indeed she wouldn't yell at me. I trusted her. Ha!

'Tante Rosa, I'm worried you will think that the only thing worse than you being pregnant and alone is me being pregnant and alone.' I looked her in the eye.

'*Ah ya Rab!*' she hollered, startling me. 'You foolish, *foolish* girl. All the pain I tried to save you from, all the advice I gave you is wasted. You did not listen to me and now you are paying the price. Anwar, what have you done? *What have you done?*' she wailed.

'I knew I shouldn't have told you!' I shouted back, tearfully.

'Don't be ridiculous, of course you had to tell me.' She waved her arms in the air. 'Who else will go with you to have the abortion? You cannot go alone.'

'What do you mean? I'm not having an abortion.' I placed my hands over my stomach.

She shook her head at me. 'You are even more stupid than I thought. With what money will you raise a child? How will you go to university? Have you thought about any of this?'

'No. I've only known that I'm pregnant for two days and since then my mother died. I have thought of none of these things. All I have thought is that Allah has blessed me in the middle of all the heartache with a baby to love.'

'Forget this foolish talk of love and blessings. For once in your life, think.' She tapped her temple with her index finger. 'Perhaps it's for the best that your mother passed away. She was spared this shame. You're going to send me to the grave along with her, with all this scandal you continue to bring. It follows you like a shadow, Anwar.'

'You just told me the same thing happened to you! How can you judge me so harshly when you did the same thing?' I cried. Why had I confided in her? I should have known this was how she would respond. She was Tante Rosa after all.

'Help me up, Anwar.'

I stood and held out both of my arms that Tante Rosa gripped as she heaved herself off the bed.

'Aye,' she moaned. 'I need to see a doctor about this back of mine. I'm going to pray that you make a wise decision and stop being so foolish. And do not say I did the same thing. I never sinned with a non-believer.'

When Tante Rosa closed the bedroom door behind her, I counted my blessings that I still had Ahmo Fariz and his enormous good heart. On Saturday his kindness stretched even further than it had before. When he found my mother hanging, he locked the door and released her from the noose. I imagined how great his shock and distress must have been like to see her like that, but he did not make a sound to alert us until he had laid her on his bed, placed her tongue back in her mouth, closed her eyes, taken off and disposed of her underwear and pants, and found a hijab of Tante Rosa's which he used as a scarf to cover up the rope burns. He covered her bare legs with a rug before he unlocked the door and let us in.

I would be forever grateful to darling Ahmo Fariz for sparing me. To have seen my mother hanging, I think would have killed me. That she chose to set up the rope and stool in the bathroom that she knew only Ahmo Fariz used showed how much forethought Mama had placed in her death. And that horrified me even more.

I only found out about Ahmo Fariz's kindness and the incontinent, eye-bulging state he found Mama in, when I overheard him telling Rosa in a distressed voice all about what he had endured while they sat together in the kitchen, unaware that I was eavesdropping from the hall.

Strangely, before I even knew my mother had died, I already thought it was a cursed day because I had made the heartbreaking decision to end my relationship with Nick.

I had arrived at this decision when I witnessed what the reporters did to Nick after the march and with the news that he might be suspended from the Rangers. Hearing the Rangers' president tell the assembled media at the club grounds that Nick did not reflect the values of the club crushed me.

But then it got worse. There was an enormous crash and we all rushed to the front of the restaurant where the noise came from to see the front window smashed and a large rock inside the restaurant. We also found the words 'Rangers not Refugees' spray-painted all the way across the front wall.

Were it during dinner service that the rock was hurled, someone could have been killed. And all because of my relationship with Nick.

I couldn't bear for Nick to continue to have his career

damaged, nor could I keep putting my family in this kind of danger. The only right thing to do for them all was to let Nick go. It would be better for everyone this way – everyone except me.

And so even though I thought my heart was already broken, the worst heartbreak of all was still waiting for me. My mother, gone.

In my bedroom that night, after all the awful events of the day, I found a note under the sheet. A note that I tore up in a violent rage but the words of which could never be erased from my tortured mind.

Anwar, I cannot live. I've tried and I've failed. It's too much for me. And I can't keep taking bigger and bigger doses of the medicine. It's no good, this life, for me or for you. For a long time I've wanted to stop taking the medicine, but you, ya habibti, you forced me to take it against my will.

You gave me no choice but to be deceptive. I stopped the medicine, instead I just hid the tablets under my tongue to spit out when you turned your back. This is the best thing I could have done because it gave me clarity and I have all the answers now. Allaho'akbar! At last a solution! Now I know that I must die. And then I will be freed, and you, my precious one, will also be freed to live your life without me burdening you. In death I will find paradise. Isn't this what Allah promises? I've been faithful to Allah – Heaven awaits me now. I dream that my paradise will be an eternity of blissful nothingness where there are no memories, where there is no guilt. How my heart leaps for joy while I think of this! See how I'm solving all our problems? I leave you with love, ya amri. Please don't be angry with me – instead rejoice that you don't have to worry over me

any longer. Worrying is for the old. You are young. Be young!
Ya habibti ana, Allah maaki.
Mama x

Nick came to the door, soon after I had found the note. Fariz had called him and told him the news. I wished he hadn't.

I explained to Nick all the reasons why we must break up but I don't remember which words I used or if they even made sense. I don't remember what he answered. But I do know that I was as brief as I could be. I spoke only the words that needed to be spoken, and then I returned to my bedroom and screamed and screamed into the pillow, so nobody could hear me.

And I screamed only one word again and again – Mama.

Nick refused to go home. He stayed outside and called out to me during the evening from outside my window. He sent me message after message on my phone until I discovered a way to block his number. And while he called my name from outside, I turned to Allah, and He gave me what I asked for. I found the strength to resist him.

Seeing these photos of Nick now, that Rosa had left for me, where he was clearly drunk and leaving the restaurant with his arms around Arielle, I wondered, were they proof of him forgetting me? Were they evidence of him punishing me for the pain I caused him? I didn't want to believe he was really with Arielle. I was so sure of Nick's loyalty to me – but then again I had rejected him so I'd given him reason to lash out. Part of me did believe he was innocent and that these photos were misleading. Perhaps he was just very drunk and unaware of cameras as he held onto an old friend for support. It seemed impossible that he could turn to another woman so quickly.

But anything was possible now. My mother was capable

of abandoning me after I had already lost my father and sister, when she was all I had left.

Even if these photos told a truthful story, then it might be for the best. Nick needed to return to his old world. And that world included other women. And I needed to retreat into my new world – one where I was a responsible parent, not the girlfriend of a celebrity footballer.

I dropped to my knees again and clasped my hands together with my elbows resting on my bed. No sooner had I silently prayed the words, *ya Rab* than Ricky tapped me on the shoulder.

'Ricky! You gave me a fright. I didn't hear you come in.'

'Anna, why are you kneeling on the floor?' He tilted his head and frowned. 'And why are you crying?'

'Why don't you tell me what you have been up to first?'

'I was counting money with Ahmo Fariz. I counted fifty-cent pieces all the way up to ten dollars.' He spread his arms out wide. 'And Ahmo Fariz said I am a genius and geniuses deserve to be rich so he gave me another ten dollars and, look,' he pulled out two crumpled ten dollar notes from his trackpants pocket, 'it makes twenty dollars now to put with the other money in my money box. Why are you kneeling, Anna?'

'Come *habibi*, come and kneel with me. I'm saying a prayer. I'm very proud of your clever money counting. Let's pray together. Who would you like to pray for?'

He took his place on the carpet beside me and imitated my clasped hands. 'Henry.'

'Henry? Why?'

'Because he lost his tooth in the playground at recess and everyone looked but we couldn't find it, and he was crying because now he doesn't know if the tooth fairy will come or not because usually she has to have the tooth as proof, doesn't she, that you actually lost one and aren't just pretending because you want money? So I want to pray that the tooth fairy will believe that Henry really lost his tooth and that she'll come to visit him tonight.' His innocent eyes were wide with concern and my heart swelled for him.

'Okay, yes, that's a lovely thing to pray for. Shut your eyes tight and pray for Henry.'

'And Leila,' he added solemnly. 'I want to pray that Leila makes it all the way to heaven and that she isn't sad anymore.'

'Yes, that too.' I looked away from him.

'Are you crying again?'

'Yes, my darling.' My voice broke. 'I'm very sad because of what happened to my mother. I loved her very much.'

'I'm sad too. My mum died too, remember? And my dad.'

'I remember.' I reached for his clasped hands and put mine over them. 'It's very, very sad that your mum and dad died.'

We were silent and eventually I wiped away my tears.

'Anna,' Ricky tapped my shoulder again. 'I just had an idea! Maybe my mum is looking after your mum now.'

'That's a lovely thought.'

'I want my mum and your mum not to be dead anymore. Especially my mum.'

'Come here, sweetheart.' I sat up on the bed and pulled him up onto my lap. '*Opa*, there we go.'

He rested his head in the crook of my neck and although he was silent, I soon felt his hot wet tears spill onto my chest.

'It's okay, Ricky. Oh *habibi*, it's okay, it's good to let out all the tears when you need to. You'll feel better after this little cry. It's all going to be okay. We still have each other.'

'But what if you die too?' he sobbed. 'What if your heart stops, just like Leila's? Or what if you drown like my mum?'

'Oh no, my heart won't stop for a long, long time. I'll be an old, old lady before my heart stops. What you must understand is that my mother was very sick for a long time, and I'm very healthy. And I was the champion of the whole world in swimming. Remember when I showed you that video on YouTube of me winning the world championship? I could never drown! So I'm not going to die. I promise you I won't.'

He wrapped both of his arms around my neck and I held him even closer to me. 'Listen, I have an idea. Here's a tissue for you. Big blow. Why don't we think of something else to pray for, shall we? What should it be, hmm?'

He sniffed two or three times and then replied, 'I want to pray that Ahmo Fariz lets me count money every day because I like counting money and being a genius.'

'Perfect. Let's shut our eyes and pray for that.'

While he squeezed his eyes shut, I kept mine open and on his innocent face. Once again I begged Allah to keep me safe and well until he was all grown up. 'Okay, I think that's enough praying for tonight, Ricky. Now run off and brush your teeth. Then find Tante Rosa and Ahmo Fariz and say goodnight and I'll tuck you into bed. It's way past your bedtime and you have school in the morning.'

'Why weren't we allowed to go to Leila's burial? Why did we have to leave after the church?'

'Well, she had written in her will that after her Christian funeral, she wanted a Muslim burial. And there's a rule in the Koran that says that Muslim women can't go. Only non-Muslim women can go. I'm part Muslim so I couldn't be there. And young boys like you aren't allowed to attend either.'

He sighed loudly. 'That's a dumb rule. I didn't like it when we had to leave.'

'Well, it isn't my favourite rule.'

'So why didn't we just go anyway?'

'I think it's best we didn't go. There's lots of crying that goes on at burials. I think you were much better off at school. So that's why we left Ahmo Fariz to lay my mother's body to rest, but we know the important part of her is bound for Heaven.'

'I would have liked to see Leila go to Heaven. I'm sad I missed that part.'

'Oh no, you didn't miss that part at all. You can never see someone going to heaven, you can only feel it in your heart.'

He looked unconvinced. 'When will I feel it in my heart? I haven't felt it yet.'

'Possibly tonight in your dreams, you'll feel it. Okay, go brush your teeth like a good boy.'

He walked towards the doorway but then hesitated and turned around. 'Anna?'

'Yes, Ricky.'

'Is Nick coming back?'

He watched my eyes closely.

'No, he's not going to come back. Nick isn't my boyfriend anymore.'

His face fell. 'But I want him to be.'

'I know, I'm sorry. Okay, off you go, brush your teeth.' I used a firmer tone now.

He didn't move. 'But I *really* want him to come back. And I want Bluey!'

I sighed. 'I know, I'm sorry, Ricky. We might see Nick and Bluey later on, but for now it will just be us and Ahmo Fariz and Tante Rosa.'

His stamped his foot. 'It's not fair! I want to go to Nick's!' he whined.

I couldn't deal with this today. I knew that I should explain things better to him but I didn't have the energy to. 'I know it's not fair,' I said sharply, standing up and walking over to him. I passed him a tissue, and with my hand on his shoulder I guided him out of my room. 'Here you go, here's another tissue. Go straight to the bathroom now, please.'

'Anna?' He asked when he was no more than two feet down the hall.

'*Ah ya Rab*,' I threw my head back. 'Are you *ever* going to brush your teeth?'

'Is Nick still going to pick me up from school?'

'No. From now on I'll always be able pick you up myself.'

He grumbled, 'But that's boring,' and walked away.

*** * ***

'Anna, *habibti*, are you all right?' Ahmo Fariz found me leaning against my open bedroom door.

'*Ahlan*, Ahmo Fariz.'

'I wanted to check if you need anything before I go to bed.'

'No, thank you. There's nothing I need.'

He frowned. 'What is troubling you, *habibti*? I can see it all over your face. I know you're grieving but you look anxious. Is something else worrying you?'

I burst into fresh tears. Ahmo Fariz pulled me into a hug and I let myself cry as hard as I wanted to in the safety of his protective arms.

'Shhh, shhh, don't cry, my girl. Ahmo Fariz is right here and I won't let anything happen to you.' He cooed.

His warmth made me cry even harder.

'What is it, *habibti*? Tell me. You can trust me.'

'I can't tell you,' I sobbed. 'You'll think differently of me.'

'I leave the judging to God, Anna. Tell me your problem. Problems can weigh you down. They are much better shared.'

Sharing my secret with him was very tempting, but I hesitated. I had shared it with Tante Rosa and all that happened was that she yelled at me. But this was Ahmo Fariz, not Tante Rosa. Ahmo Fariz would never treat me that way.

'Ahmo Fariz, I'm pregnant.'

His strong arms around me went flaccid and dropped to his sides. I lifted my head to meet his eyes, but he was staring off into the distance.

'Ahmo Fariz, did you hear me?'

His nostrils flared and his entire face turned a deep red. 'How could he let this happen?' he growled in a low voice. 'Why wasn't he more careful? I will kill him with my bare hands. Wait until I find him, that, that ... piece of shit. I'll make him wish he was never born.' He sucked the air in and out through curled lips and gritted teeth.

I'd never seen him like this before and I feared for Nick. It was clear to me that Ahmo Fariz meant every word he said.

'Ahmo Fariz, it's not his fault!' I pleaded in a panic as he stormed off towards the back door of the restaurant to the car park. 'Please, stop. *Stop!* Listen to me, please.'

He stopped but kept his back to me.

'Ahmo Fariz, I told him I would take care of it and then I forgot to take my pill – twice.' My heart was thudding so hard and fast it hurt.

He spun on his heels to face me with hard eyes. 'How could you? You barely knew him! It must have been only a month or two at the most before you went to his bed like a whore. Have you forgotten all of our morals? Have you forgotten who you are?'

'You said you would leave the judging to God.' I looked him in the eyes and he returned my stare.

His eyes watered. If it was only anger that he felt, it would have been easier for me to deal with.

'*Oof.* I have to go. I cannot talk to you while I'm this upset. We'll talk about this tomorrow. In the meantime, I'm going to drive to that animal Nick Harding's cursed house and give him a piece of my mind and a piece of my fist. That filthy, disgusting ...'

'Ahmo Fariz,' I grabbed his arm as he turned to go. 'I beg you not to go! He doesn't even know about the baby.'

'What? You haven't told him?'

'No, I couldn't. And anyway, Tante Rosa found photos of him in the paper with another woman. He has already moved on.'

'*Ebn el kalb.* I'll slice off his testicles and then feed them to him,' Ahmo Fariz's mouth frothed. '*Ebn el kalb,*' he repeated.

'Please, Ahmo, please,' I begged. 'Stop talking like that. His father was no dog. I'm terrified that you really will do something to physically hurt Nick. You're scaring me.' I wiped at the tears that were yet again falling on my face.

With that one line, his demeanour changed. 'Scaring you? No, no, don't ever be scared of me.' His shoulders sagged. 'Aye, Anna. I need to sit. I'm tired all of a sudden.' He brushed past me and let himself into my bedroom, taking a seat on the bed. He looked up at me with a more gentle expression. 'So this pregnancy, what will you do?'

'I'll give birth to my baby when the time comes, that's what I'll do.' I followed him into the bedroom and closed the door in case Tante Rosa overheard us and came back.

'You're too young to be a mother.' He put his head in his hands.

'I'm already a mother, Uncle Fariz. I have Ricky.'

He nodded. 'This is true. And you still want to have Nick's child? After all that has happened? After seeing him already with another woman in the paper? I curse the home his father—'

'Yes!' I interrupted before he got angry again. 'Yes – it's my child too, not just his child.'

'Your pregnancy will be the final straw with our community. They will completely shun us now. Already my brothers at the mosque questioned me and my morals when I allowed you to date him. And you saw how they reacted each time photos of you were in the news. They ask me why I have not insisted you wear a hijab like your Tante Rosa, but I tell them that I would never be so stupid to think that I can ever get any woman to do as I say. Of course I would prefer you in a hijab but ...' he dropped his gaze to his knees. 'I understand you are not fully Muslim like I would like you to be. If you were fully Muslim, this would not have happened.'

'It happened to Tante Rosa, nobody is more Muslim than her,' I answered.

His eyebrows shot up. 'You know this story?'

I nodded.

'Rosa made a mistake, indeed, but it was not in the public eye like this mistake of yours. Ever since you began your relationship with this man, we've had fewer customers every week. Now, with your pregnancy, that will take care of the remaining few we haven't offended yet. What am I to do?'

'I could move away, move out.' I suggested, the guilt heavy on my shoulders.

'You think I can turn you out? And then, tell me – what

would I live for, if not for you and Ricky? My life would be too lonely without you.'

'I'm so sorry. I've caused nothing but heartache and trouble to everyone I love, including you. I really do need to leave, though, so you can rebuild Masri's without my bad name destroying it for you any longer. I know how much you love this restaurant. I'll look for somewhere to rent. And I promise I'll stay close by so you can still see Ricky and me every day.'

'Over my dead body will you go and pay rent. Listen to me,' his eyes met mine, 'this place is your home as much as it is mine. Don't forget that. And even though I am upset and angry and very disappointed with you for your bad choices and for disregarding our morals, it is important that you know that you can still lean on me. I am a large man, I can take your weight. Do you hear me, Anna? You can lean on me, now and always.'

He looked old for the first time. I could not have loved him anymore as he sat at the foot of my bed with his hunched shoulders, examining his hands.

'I hear you, Ahmo Fariz. And I love you. And I thank Allah for you. You really are a father to me, not just an uncle.'

'Child, listen to me.' There was an urgency in his tone. 'You *must* tell Nick. He must know and he must stand up to his responsibilities like a real man.'

'I will, Ahmo Fariz, in time I will tell him. But I can't face him just yet.'

'*Tayeb, ya habibti.*' He let out a groan as he stood up. 'Sleep well. The worst is over. You have survived the first two days of losing your mother. You can survive anything now.' He kissed both my cheeks on his way out. 'Goodnight.'

'Goodnight, Ahmo Fariz.'

LILY – TUESDAY

I looked like Ed fucking Sheeran. I knew that hairdresser in Derby was dodgy when she licked her fingers to pat down a clump of hair that was sticking out on the kid whose hair she butchered before mine. Why didn't I run out then? Or if not then, why didn't I make up some excuse to leave when she sat me in the chair and then sneezed onto my head, twice?

Instead I was all, 'Oh thank you, it's lovely,' after she gave me a fire-engine-red shaggy hairstyle when I specifically asked for a dark auburn pixie cut.

That was the old Lily, though, the Yes Lily, and I left her in Derby on the weekend.

By great planet alignment, Mum and Ross had booked a weekend away for themselves at Cable Beach on some Scoopon deal so I had their place to myself and, with no Toby around and my phone switched off, I had the space I needed. I went for three or four walks a day and when I wasn't walking I alternated between sitting in the garden swing on the back porch and the papasan chair on the front porch. With the exception of the spontaneous haircut, I was in solitary thought from sunrise to sunset and well into the night.

And I sorted my shit out.

What I came up with was that I wouldn't leave medicine altogether, but that I'd defer the next semester instead and see if I missed it. Having to repeat oncology next year anyway meant that deferring a semester didn't add any extra time to the course. For the rest of this year, I would take the pressure off myself, look for a casual job and rest my tired, overworked brain.

Dad died just before I started Year Twelve. I dealt with his death by throwing myself into my studies and burying my grief. And I hadn't stopped throwing myself into my studies for the next four years after that.

My slack attitude this year, culminating in my accidentally-on-purpose failing an exam was a signal to stop. To rest. To re-examine.

If in six months' time I still didn't feel that medicine was the right path for me, then I'd have to consider my options. But for now I'd stop thinking about the future, I would rest my head. And I would rest my heart.

The only way for me to have peace was to end it with Toby. He and I were never meant to be. Sleeping with a man the day he buried his wife was never going to end well. How deluded I was to believe it would. He needed time and space to grieve Jenny. His brother was right that fateful day when he caught me naked in the toilet. Toby was trying to fuck the grief away. I couldn't be his crutch anymore.

At the end of the weekend up north, when I hopped on that plane home to Perth, my resolve was that from now on the number one person to please was me.

I squeezed another handful of mousse into my hands in an attempt to give the red mop on my head some kind of structure, but it was no use. I plopped down on the closed toilet lid, defeated. It was going to have to grow itself out. One good thing was that at least every time I looked in a mirror it would serve to remind me not be a doormat anymore.

I shut my eyes and rubbed my temples, sick of the headache I'd had since the realisation that my entire life was a mess had truly hit me. What annoyed me was that my new-found self-awareness had done nothing to improve things so far. Nothing. Unless an awful hairdo, dropping out of university and losing my boyfriend were supposed to make me feel great about myself, then self-awareness was a lying bitch.

The decision to be on my own and to live just for me sounded perfect yesterday, but here I was, only one day later, and all I felt was lonely and lost. I missed Toby. As much as I knew how wrong he was for me, God, I missed him.

I took ten deep breaths while I waited for the urge to call him to pass just like I'd done dozens of times over the weekend. At the end of the ten breaths I called Nick.

'Hey.' His voice was heavy.

'Hey. Any word from Anna today?' I hadn't told him about Toby and me breaking up. He had enough on his plate already.

'No. But her uncle drove the Mini around here earlier tonight and gave me the keys back. Called me a few choice words. Waved his Swiss Army knife in my face and threatened to slice off my dick with it. You know, the usual.'

'What? That's awful! He's got no right to do that to you. Are you okay?'

'Well, his business has gone down the gurgler because of Anna and me, so I can't really blame him. Especially after the vandals attacked it on Saturday.' He sighed. 'I don't know what to do.'

'Anna adores you. She's in shock. She'll come around, be patient.'

'I have this feeling that she won't. If you could've seen her on Saturday night, she was a completely different person to the girl I was with earlier that day. She literally changed personality in those few hours.'

'But that might just be the shock. I mean, what do you think we were like the day Dad died? We probably changed personality in those first few hours too.'

'Nah, this was different. It was like she didn't know me. She sounded like a robot, with this cold look in her eyes. She didn't want to hear a word I had to say. She wouldn't even let me in the house. She talked to me through the screen door.'

'Give her time. Try to call her again next week, maybe?'

'I can't, she's blocked my number. And now she's even returned the Mini. It's over.' His voice cracked. 'Plus, those photos in *The West* made it look like I was actually *with* Arielle. She'll be thinking I was out scoring the night her mother died.'

'It didn't look like you were with Arielle in the photos. It just looked like you were leaning on a friend after a rough night out,' I lied. Those photos completely implicated him. 'Anna's had enough experience herself to know not to believe everything she sees in the paper. And she knows you, Nick. She knows how much you love her.' I hoped that was true. It would take a whole truckload of trust and understanding from her to believe in Nick's innocence after the photographic evidence, that was for sure.

But thank God Arielle was out at the same pub as Nick and his mates on Saturday night, photos or not. After Anna dumped him, Nick rang Bruce and told him everything. Bruce told Joel and they put their fight with Nick behind them. A couple of hours later they were at the pub where Arielle happened to be. She saw some guys heckling Nick and she could tell he was wasted. She got him out of there just in time. Only minutes after they left, there was a massive brawl between Joel and one of the men who'd been hassling Nick. Joel was now up for a disciplinary hearing himself, and that kind of extra trouble was the very last thing Nick needed.

He only just got to keep his job after his own disciplinary hearing yesterday.

'Nick, I know you don't want to hear it but you need to stop obsessing about Anna. You came out on top of Max Dawson. Nobody ever comes out on top of him. Why don't you think about that instead? Celebrate how bloody lucky you are that you still have a job!'

'Yeah, you're right. What will I do about the Mini though? She really needs a car.'

I was glad he couldn't see me roll my eyes. 'Why don't you drive the Mini back to their car park and leave the keys along with a letter in the mailbox saying you want her to keep the Mini but with no strings attached. But don't go in there looking for her. She needs her space.'

'That's not such a terrible idea, Red.'

'Shut up. I'm wearing a beanie until it grows out.'

'So, have you thought more about what to do now that you've deferred the rest of the year?'

'A bit, but I haven't come up with much. I've applied for a job at Cold Rock. That's about it.'

'The ice cream place?' He laughed. 'Shoot for the stars, Lil.'

'It's only temporary and, anyway, have you got any better ideas?' I snapped.

He chuckled. 'Well, if I had to pick a job for you I reckon you'd make a pretty good doctor.'

'Get lost.' I was secretly happy that I just heard him laugh for the first time in days. 'Hey, I have to go, there's someone at the door.'

'See ya, Red.'

It was nearly nine-thirty. Who would be knocking unannounced on my door now apart from Toby? Or a murderer? No, a murderer wouldn't knock. It had to be Toby. Things had been so heated the other night, maybe he'd come to talk more calmly.

'Do not have sex with him,' I told my reflection. 'Under *no* circumstance are you to have sex with him, Lily Harding.'

I rummaged in a drawer for a beanie, scooped up most of my Ed hair and tucked it in. Tufts of red fringe stuck out no matter how much I tried to hide them.

'Do not have sex with him,' I repeated in a whisper several times over as I fussed with the beanie, put on clear lip gloss and sprayed perfume on my wrists. I made myself walk as slowly as I could to the front door. 'You're toxic for each other. He still loves his wife. More than he loves you.'

My sad lonely heart didn't agree – 'Go on, have sex with him. It will make you feel so good, so loved.'

The debate raged back and forth until I opened the door and saw that it wasn't Toby who was waiting outside.

And it wasn't a murderer.

Standing on my porch, clutching a bouquet of red roses and with a heart-melting smile, was Ben.

NICK – TUESDAY

I screwed up another piece of paper and threw it across the dining room. Bluey bounded after it, galloped back to me, dropped it at my feet and gave me a dopey grin.

Despite the way I was feeling, I laughed. 'We're not playing fetch, you big boofhead.'

I picked up a fresh piece of paper. He whined and curled up on the floor next to me when he realised I meant what I said.

I hadn't written a letter since I could remember. Had I *ever* written a personal letter? Maybe not. I knew what I would say to her if she was standing in front of me, but I just couldn't articulate it in writing. So I pretended that Anna *was* standing in front of me and I started talking out loud. I felt like an idiot but it worked. When I was done I'd filled two pages, front and back. I read over it once and then, without giving myself time to change my mind, I shoved it in an envelope and walked out to her car.

It smelt like her inside the Mini. Her perfume penetrated the upholstery. If she didn't take me back, I honestly didn't know how I'd ever get over her.

It was cold and dark when I pulled up outside Masri's. The lights were on in her bedroom and there was movement behind the curtains. It took all my self-control to stay away from her window and walk up the drive to the front of the restaurant, stuff the car keys inside the envelope marked *'Anna – please read'* and push it into the letterbox.

I sent Joel a text. He pulled up a few minutes later.

'What are you doing here too?' I tapped the top of Bruce's head as I squeezed myself into the back of Joel's Porsche.

'Intervention!' Bruce shouted.

'Intervention!' Joel laughed as he spun the wheels and the car took off like a bullet up South Terrace.

'What intervention? What the hell are you talking about?' I scrambled for my seatbelt. 'Slow down, mate, you'll kill someone!'

Joel looked over his shoulder, grinning at me. 'It's about time you chilled out, Harding. Remember the days when you used to just fucking chill out? Before you turned into a complicated miserable prick?'

'You're telling me to chill out and you've just been done for punching someone at a pub.' I laughed. 'Where are we going anyway?'

'Back to mine,' Bruce said. 'The missus would crack the shits if I'm out again tonight after Saturday.'

Joel made the whipping sound and action he always made when Bruce talked about his wife.

Ten minutes later, we were sprawled on Bruce's lounge, a repeat of a weekend game between Brisbane and the Swans on mute on his cinema-sized screen, and a bottle of water each in our hands.

'We know how to party, don't we?' Joel shook his head in disgust as he unscrewed the lid of his water.

Bruce tilted the neck of his bottle towards me with a nod. 'Cheers, Harding. Welcome back. I put my balls on the line for you yesterday so don't fuck up again, all right?' He winked but it was obvious he was dead serious.

'Hey, I just want to say thanks to you two for having my back,' I said. 'I know you guys were pissed off about me supporting Anna at the march.'

Bruce shook his head. 'It wasn't about you supporting Anna, it was about you not giving a shit about the team. All that mattered to you was the march.' He had a gulp of water. 'It felt like "Harding versus the rest of the Rangers" ever since you screwed your foot up at the start of the year. And then you pretty much told Max Dawson to bugger off and went and marched without worrying about how that could affect the rest of us. You didn't care about what happened to the Rangers. *That's* what pissed me off.'

'I'm sorry.' I couldn't look at either of them. 'I've had my head up my own arse for a long time.'

'Yeah, you big nob. You have, but then you finally did pull your head out yesterday.'

I looked up. 'Huh? What did I do yesterday?'

'What? Are you serious? How can you not know?' Bruce screwed his face up at me. 'When we walked out together from the disciplinary hearing – what you said at the press conference.'

'What about it?'

He laughed. 'It was bloody inspiring, mate. Thought I was going to break down and cry like a baby standing next to you!'

'Really? I can't even remember what I said. I was just so relieved I still had a job.' I reached across and slapped his shoulder. 'Thanks for batting for me in there. I owe you big.'

'You should watch the footage of your press conference yesterday – you'll be that inspired, you'll cheer for yourself!' Joel said.

'Is it on the Facebook page?' I already had the Facebook app open on my phone and was entering a search for the Rangers.

'Don't look at it on your phone. Wait, watch it on this.' Bruce brought YouTube up on his television and found the clip. 'It's worthy of the big screen, mate.'

I watched myself emerge from the hearing room flanked by Craig and Bruce. The Head of Media ushered us to the press conference desk and we took our seats.

'Do I look nervous or what?' I was surprised by how wide my eyes were, like a deer caught in headlights.

'Shh. It's starting,' Joel hushed.

My cheeks were flushed on the video and I loosened my tie while Craig read off a sheet of paper that I was found to have done no wrongdoing and that the club president wouldn't be taking the matter any further.

Then he told the gathered press that we'd be taking only three questions. Almost every journalist shouted my name at the same time. Craig pointed at one of them.

'Nick, certain sections of the press have pointed out that you marched with Asylum Assist knowing that you were jeopardising the relationship between the team sponsor, SafeXone, and the Western Rangers. What's your response to the accusation that you marched knowing it could harm the future of the team?'

'The Rangers are in my bloodstream. The fact that anyone would think I'd ever wilfully hurt the Rangers is a joke. I marched against a human rights violation. That was all. It had absolutely nothing to do with SafeXone.'

And then: 'Nick, will it be awkward for you to wear the SafeXone jersey the next time you play?'

'I just said that I have no issue with SafeXone. So why would it be awkward to wear my jersey? I'm sure SafeXone are doing a great job with security on the island and I'm proud to wear their logo on my shirt. What I have an issue with is offshore detention for asylum-seeker children.'

'The best bit is coming up now,' Joel leaned forward towards the TV.

We listened to the third and final question from the press.

'Nick, do you feel like you have to prove your commitment to the club and to the Rangers' fans after this morning's disciplinary hearing?'

'Finding out about the disciplinary hearing from my coach on Saturday was the worst news I've had in my whole life, bar finding out my dad had passed away. Because what matters most to me in life are the people I love and this football club. If anyone thinks I'm not committed to the Rangers, the only way I can show you how much this club means to me is by making every Rangers member and fan a promise right here, right now, that I'll train harder than I've ever trained before and that at every single game, I'll play four quarters of football like my life depended on it.' And then I tipped my head forwards a little and looked right into the camera and pointed, saying, 'Don't edit the press conference this time.'

The next clip started to play on YouTube.

Bruce slow clapped and Joel joined in.

I blew out hard, lifting the hair off my forehead. 'I can't believe I said that.'

'Neither can I.' Joel laughed. 'You usually give one word answers and do your wanky double thumbs up shit.'

'It's okay, mate, don't be jealous that you don't have a trademark.' I grinned.

'Yeah, Harding, you totally invented the thumbs up sign,' Joel guffawed. 'And here I was thinking you'd gone all mature and stuff after that press conference. Good to know you're still the same douchebag you always were.'

It was after one in the morning when Bruce asked me about Anna. 'So you're pretty serious about her, yeah?'

I played with the sticker label on the water bottle, peeling it from one corner. 'I am. But she won't have a bar of me.'

'Is that since her mum topped herself?' he asked.

I nodded.

'She's probably just messed up over it, mate, and needs some time to come around.' Bruce patted my shoulder. 'Don't stress.'

'Yeah, losing your mum is massive,' Joel added. 'Especially one like hers. They put this photo online of Leila Hayati with Princess Diana at the pyramids in 1995. Leila was a human rights lawyer, not even a politician then, but she was already famous. It said 'The women who are changing the world.' Freaky, hey?'

'Hmm, it is.' I thought about the woman who wanted to change the world and ended up hanging herself in the bathroom out the back of a restaurant on a cold Saturday morning in Fremantle.

'Have you seen Ricky?' Bruce asked.

'No, she won't let me anywhere near him.'

'Why?'

I sighed a deep sigh. 'Because she's convinced herself that she's bad for my career and that she's burdening me with a child – she's Ricky's guardian now.'

'But she knows how much you love that kid. *Everyone* knows how much you love that kid. You turned your house into a virtual play centre for him.'

'I know,' I groaned. 'I wish she could see that she's hurting me more by staying away from me than she ever could by being with me.'

'She'll come around,' Bruce said confidently.

'I think she will too.' Joel nodded.

I stared at my feet. 'Who knows.'

Joel threw a plastic bottle top in my direction and it hit me right between the eyes. 'Mate, tonight's about you chilling the fuck out and having fun, not being the miserable prick you've been all year. That was the whole point of the intervention!'

I threw it back at him. 'It's hard to be chilled when Anna's doing my head in.'

'Anna, Anna, Anna,' Joel moaned. 'First him,' he pointed at Bruce, 'and now you. It sucks being friends with you losers when all you talk about are your bloody women.'

'She's not my woman,' I said under my breath.

'You'll get her back, Nick,' Bruce tapped my leg with his foot. 'You've got the power of television. Make yourself irresistible to her on TV. You keep doing shit like that press conference yesterday and she'll be putty in your hands, guaranteed.'

'Hell, *I* would've fucked you after that!' Joel laughed.

'Like I'd let you within ten feet of my privates.'

He pointed at me. 'Hey, I could have had you if I wanted you. I think we both know that, Harding. I've seen the way you look at me when you think nobody's watching.'

I laughed a real laugh for the first time since last Friday.

'Don't stalk her.' Bruce warned. 'Play smart, mate. Win her over by being Nick Harding – the man no woman can resist. See out the season being your charming self whenever cameras are on you, and then try approaching her again after she's had enough time to actually miss you. And for God's sake, don't get caught hooking up with other girls in the meantime!'

'Do you really think she'll be watching me on TV?' I asked.

'Oh, hundred per cent.' Bruce nodded decisively. 'She'll be glued to the TV, mate.'

I nodded slowly as a plan began to hatch in my head.

TOBY – TUESDAY

I lifted the hard hat off and wiped the sweat away with my shirt sleeve. The dust was in my eyes, up my nose, down my throat, under my fingernails. But it didn't matter because today was my last day on this site, my last day of work and my last day being Toby Watts, building supervisor. As of tomorrow, whenever I filled in a form with my job title, it would be Toby Watts, photographer.

A smile formed on my face.

I'd almost finished loading up the ute with my stuff and in the morning I'd be filling it up with fuel and driving across the country to Mission Beach, Far North Queensland. I was giving myself time to settle in before my first project shooting with Keith Rayner in the Daintree Forest. It was too good to be true, but it *was* true. It was!

In the end, it was so easy to leave. I didn't even have to tell Dad I wanted to leave the building business – he was the one who told me I had to leave.

'So six months, Toby, and then what?' He tilted his head down and gave me a questioning look over his glasses.

I took a deep breath. 'I guess it depends on how successful the six months are.'

He nodded slowly. 'Well, I'm passing down a business to you. It's completely up to you what kind of business that is. If this photography gig works out for you, I'll sell Watts Building and set you up a studio.'

I choked on my coffee. 'Dad! You can't do that!'

'Of course I can,' he said with conviction. 'It's my money, I'll do what I damn well like with it.'

'But, Dad, you've always said you wanted to pass the business down to us.'

He leaned back in his chair and crossed his legs. 'Yes I did, and I never should have. That wasn't fair to you boys. Life's short, you need to do what makes you happy. Give the photography a go, God knows you've got the talent, and then decide what you want to do when the mentorship's up. I'll put that kid Damien on as supervisor for the next six months. If you decide photography isn't your thing after all, I'll sign the building business over to you. But if you reckon you can make a go of it, I'll cash in Watts Building and set up Watts Photography.'

I found it hard to speak and just nodded my thanks instead.

'So it starts in three weeks, you said?' Dad asked.

'Yes, three weeks. It's not very long notice I know. I'm sorry. I only just found out about it myself.'

'Forget the notice, Toby, just tie up as many loose ends as you can in the next day or two. Then you can get yourself over to Queensland and be good and settled by the time the new job begins. It'll take you the best part of a week to drive there.'

'Dad, are you really sure about this? I know it's a shock to you.'

He leaned forward and rested his hand on my knee. 'Don't you worry about me. I'll be all right. Just worry about yourself and go make the most of this opportunity.'

After leaving Mum and Dad's, I walked next door to Marcia and Pete's to let them know I was going away. I stayed there for all of five minutes before bolting out again.

Marcia, who looked as frail as a little old lady, was hysterical. 'So cruel, Toby! You're so cruel to leave after I've lost one child already. I can't lose you too!'

'Marcia, I'm sorry, but it's a once-in-a-lifetime opportunity. And I'm not your child, remember? Luke is and he'll still be here with you.'

'Don't you patronise me, Toby Watts. Don't you abandon me and then patronise me,' she hissed.

'Not your mess. She's not your mess,' I said out loud to myself as I walked to the car.

I stopped at the bottle shop to buy some beers and handed them over to John when I got home. 'Here's a belated thanks for entering me in the competition and giving me the kick up the arse that I needed.'

There was just one thing left to sort out before I left. Lily. I hadn't spoken to her since our fight. I couldn't leave and not see her for six months on these bad terms.

I had a lot to tell her – I had to admit to her all the things she was right about. I should've stopped visiting Marcia a long time ago, and more importantly, I should've let Jen go a long time ago too. I should've been proud to introduce Lily to my family because, Christ, I *was* proud of her. There was nothing I wished for in a partner that I didn't have in Lily. And I had to tell her that she was right about me being too scared to quit my job and chase my dream but that I'd finally found the guts to do it.

I understood that she needed space, which she'd be getting with me living on the opposite corner of the country for the next six months. But I wanted her to know that when that time was up, if she'd only give me another chance, I'd do it better. I'd treat her the way she deserved to be treated.

In the end it took me longer to pack than I thought it would. It had gone ten-thirty by the time I was ready to go to Lily's. But it didn't matter because she'd still be up watching Netflix for sure.

John was sprawled in front of a replay of the Rangers game. I put out my hand to help him up and gave him a hug goodbye. He'd be asleep by the time I got home and I'd be leaving at sunrise.

'I'll see you in four weeks, hey? Try and line me up a hot Queensland chick to hammer when I'm there, all right?' he drawled.

'Um, what about a small detail called Renee?'

'She's too needy for me, mate.' He waved his arm dismissively. 'It's totally over with her. I'm as free as a bird.'

'Oh. Right then.' What kind of person broke up with his girlfriend and didn't tell the brother he lived with? 'How did she take it?'

'Oh, haven't got around to telling her yet. She'll just cry and shit.' He pulled a face. 'I need to psych myself up for that. In the meantime though, I'm having a bloody good time being single! It's awesome, eh?'

That was the kind of person who didn't tell his brother.

I drove the loaded-down ute to Lily's. When I pulled up to her house, there was a car I didn't recognise in the driveway. I swore under my breath at the unexpected company and rang the doorbell. There was no answer so I rang it again – same thing. I knocked but she still didn't come to the door, so I let myself in with my key.

All the living areas were lit up but empty. Then I heard Lily talking from somewhere deeper in the house so I headed up the corridor following the sound of her voice to the TV room. I was about to call out 'Hello' but stopped dead in my tracks when I heard a man's voice.

My hands and feet went numb and I couldn't move. Which guy would be here this late at night?

'What was that?' Lily stage-whispered.

'It's only me,' I tried to call out but the words got stuck in my throat and a weird muffled moan came out instead.

Lily screamed. '*Oh my God! Someone's in here!*'

'Hey!' A guy came charging towards me. 'What do you think you're doing? Get out!'

As he lunged at me, Lily shrieked, '*Ben! No, stop!* That's Toby!'

My eyes met Lily's and the look on her face was one of pure horror. Somewhere in my brain fog I noticed she was in her pyjamas. The sexy ones.

'Ben?' I asked in a strangled voice, not looking at him, but straight at her. 'This was what you meant by needing space? You meant Ben was back?' I couldn't swallow. I turned and headed for the door as fast as I could go on my jelly legs.

She yelled after me, 'Toby! No, wait!'

I broke into a run, smashing the screen door against the brick wall as I burst through it onto the front porch.

'Toby, stop! Just listen! Let me explain,' Lily cried out behind me but I managed to get in the car and slam the door shut just as she caught up to me. The woman who had just trampled my heart to a pulp frantically banged on my window with open palms, mouthing words I couldn't hear. I looked away from her, slid the car into reverse and screamed out of her driveway and up the road.

I'd be getting to Queensland earlier than planned. The trip started now.

ANNA – WEDNESDAY

My dear Noor,

I ache for you. It's been four nights since I lost my mother. Time stands still. Every day is an eternity I must endure, and every night my dreams are lonely with you gone.

All I can do to comfort myself is think that my mother must have needed you more than I do. She must have needed you desperately.

The only way for me to survive each day is to be too busy to have any time to think. Thank goodness for Asylum Assist, where there is always twice the amount of work than the number of volunteers. It not only spares me from myself, it is also the only thing that doesn't bring me guilt.

I can't swim – I can't be alone with my thoughts in the water. I can't read – I tried and found myself reading the same page again and again. The guilt! The guilt engulfs me unless I am working.

This evening at Masri's we had only one table to serve and two takeaways the whole time. The patrons are scared. Everyone is scared. I have brought fear to a place where there used to be only good food, laughter and music.

Ahmo Fariz called on his insurance company who organised

for the windows to be replaced yesterday and the wall repainted today. But already, less than two hours later, the wall was vandalised again. This time the words to hurt us were 'Go home Muslim freaks'.

The vandals were out of luck though, because a police car happened to be driving by and they were arrested. I don't think they'll be back again.

I see the toll all of this is taking on Ahmo Fariz – his frown lines have deepened this week. And Tante Rosa, well, she is praying aloud day and night for Allah to lift his curse on our family.

This can't go on. Ahmo Fariz will lose everything, and then what will we do?

He met today with a man from the local paper to arrange an advertisement offering a discount voucher for one person to eat free with every group order. The cost of the ad alone is more than he can afford, but he believes this is the only way to bring in new patrons and tempt back the old ones. He's even organised a three-piece band to come and play on Saturday night to accompany Shamia, who usually belly dances to music from a CD. The newspaper man who came to meet Ahmo Fariz took photos of him and Ricky holding up bowls of Roz Bel Laban to go along with the ad.

Ricky cries every night when he comes into bed with me and falls asleep with wet cheeks. My mother's death has ignited something in him and he grieves for his own mother and father like they drowned yesterday. I spend most of the night with him in my arms. Now that you're gone, he does not need to be afraid of my coughing and choking in my sleep.

His warm body in the bed where my mother's used to be is a great comfort to me.

Thankfully it is only at night when all is quiet and still that Ricky's sadness hits him. In the daytime he's mostly settled, if a little subdued. He is young and easily distracted. He still has a good appetite and plays his usual games. He still asks for stories to be read to him and follows Ahmo Fariz like a little shadow when he isn't at school. And he cries for Nick too. This has added to my guilt tenfold.

But I must not weaken and succumb to my desire to go back to Nick.

Nick left the Mini he bought for me here again last night after I had begged Ahmo Fariz to return it to him. We found the keys to it this morning in the letterbox along with a letter. When Ricky saw it parked outside he jumped up and down and cheered. So I've decided to keep it. Having the Mini back was one small consolation I could give Ricky for taking Nick away from him.

But I can't read Nick's letter. I will most definitely fall if I see words written from him to me. So I have tucked the letter here inside this diary where it will be safe for the day my heart is strong enough that I can read it and not succumb. Until that day comes, I must work at becoming stronger and braver for Ricky and for this precious baby who's already creating havoc inside me.

I've calculated that I must be five or six weeks along. I begin every morning by racing to the toilet and the nausea stays with me for most of the day. I'm ill after most meals, no matter how small or bland they seem. I don't think I'll ever be able to have Cornflakes and milk again after today – the list of foods I cannot stomach is growing. And the smell of cumin this afternoon, ugh, I could have been ill again just from that spice!

I'm not going to tell Nick about our baby until his football season is over. He doesn't need this big distraction when he's already suffered such a hard season, especially now that he has a chance to redeem himself. Yes, best to wait and it will also give me more time to build a thick wall around my heart in these months so that he can no longer penetrate it.

Even knowing how difficult the road ahead will be by having a child without a partner by my side, I cannot bring myself to regret it.

I find it astounding that I discovered I was a mother the same day that I lost mine. Was it a consolation from Allah? I believe so. Allah is good and loving.

And I want to be good and loving too. Which is why I'm banishing my mother from my mind. As soon as I start thinking about her, I am consumed by such hot anger I can feel my insides burn. This hatred is harmful for my soul and especially harmful for my baby. So I will keep my mother away from my thoughts and my heart to protect this little one who is relying on me to look after her as best I can.

I'll give our mother what she asked for. She wanted to be dead? Well, she is dead to me. Noor, believe me when I tell you, I will never forgive her what she did, and for the darkness she has brought.

And she took you. She even took you with her.

Please come back, I need you. I am not ashamed to beg for you to return to me.

A x

LILY – THURSDAY

I walked up to Toby's front door with my heart in my throat. *Please be home, please be home.* His car wasn't in the drive but he did park it in the garage sometimes.

I lifted the door knocker and gave three sharp taps. And I waited. This was my one shot to convince him that he had got it all wrong about Ben and me.

Ben showing up out of the blue like that was nothing but one huge disaster from start to finish. His timing was uncanny – he turned up on the night when I needed a hug the most. And hug me he did while I bawled my eyes out about Toby and the fact that I had no idea what I wanted to do with my life.

Except Ben thought I was crying because I'd missed him and because I was so happy to have him home.

'It's all right, Lil, I'm home now. Everything's going to be okay.'

He cupped my face with one hand and leaned in to kiss me.

'Ben!' I jerked my head back and peeled myself off him. 'What are you doing?'

'What do you mean?' He frowned. 'Isn't this what you want?'

'*No*! What would make you think this is what I want?'

'Huh? In your last letter you said how much you still loved me and how jealous you were of Karan.'

Oh God, the letter!

'Lil,' he continued. 'That letter made me realise how much I missed you. Plus, I'd kind of had a gutful of the mud-brick-school building. So I came home. For you. Can I please kiss you now?' He took a step closer to me and I took two steps back.

'But ... but ... what about Karan?' I stammered.

'God you make me laugh. Karan's fifty-one years old. She was my group leader.'

'But what about when you kept telling me how inspiring and amazing she was ...'

'What about it?'

'You actually meant she was inspiring and amazing? You weren't shagging her?'

'What?' he guffawed. 'Ah, no, definitely not. And even if I was into old ladies, Karan's a lesbian.' He leaned in again. 'Come here, I've missed you. Don't make me beg.'

'Oh shit, Ben. You'd better come in.'

On account of my job seeking, I had bits of the paper spread all over the lounge-room and it was uninhabitable so Ben followed me to the TV room.

He sat there bewildered while I cried and told him all about Toby.

Then he sat there even more bewildered at my hysteria after Toby let himself into the house and caught us together and immediately jumped to the wrong conclusion.

'I don't get why you're so distressed. You were just telling me how you didn't want to be with him anymore. How you wanted to be alone.' Always cheerful, Ben was significantly less than cheerful when I walked back in sobbing, after Toby had sped away without giving me a chance to explain myself.

'Yes that's right, I don't want him!' I wailed.

'So who cares what he assumed when he saw me here? You've broken up with him anyway.'

'I care, Ben. I love him!'

'I'm so glad you made that clear to me before I caught a flight home to be with you.' He glared at me. 'I was planning to ask you to marry me, you know,' he said under his breath.

Then he did what Toby had done a few minutes before him and he jogged out to his car.

I didn't chase Ben down the driveway the way I'd chased Toby.

Now here I was at Toby's front door, hoping to resolve the misunderstanding and the bitterness between us and maybe even stand a chance of being friends. And who knew, maybe when we'd both had enough time away from each other to sort ourselves out properly, we could get back together. I certainly loved him enough for that to be a possibility in the future.

My stomach twisted as Toby's front door lock turned and I fixed a smile on my face.

Except it wasn't Toby who opened the door. It was his brother, John. Ugh, great.

'Hello?' he said with his eyebrows up.

'Er ... uh ... um.' *Think, Lily, think, for the love of God!* 'Hi ... yes ... I'm looking for Toby, please?'

'He's not here.' His voice was impassive.

'Um, any idea when he'll be back?'

'He reckons he'll be back at Christmas.'

'*What?*' It came out in a shriek. '*Christmas?*' Even shriekier. '*What are you talking about?*'

He laughed and looked me up and down. 'Who are you?'

I gulped. 'I'm Lily.'

'You're Lily?' He tilted his head. 'I thought you had long blonde hair. Was that like a wig or something you had going on? Nice one.' He grinned at me. 'I'm right into that shit.'

I rolled my eyes. 'I just had a cut and colour.'

'You looked way better blonde, babe.'

I shut my eyes and took a breath. 'What do you mean about Toby not coming home until Christmas? Was that a joke?'

'Nope. Spoke to him last night and he had just hit the border of the Northern Territory.'

'*What?*' I screeched again. 'Why? Why is he in the Northern Territory?'

'Hey, how come you don't know this? Didn't he go around to yours to tell you everything?'

'Um, he ended up leaving straight away. He misread a situation at my house.'

'Is that right?' He narrowed his eyes. 'Mmm, well … anyway he's taken up a six-month photography mentorship in Queensland. He wasn't going to take it. He said he couldn't leave you. I'm glad he changed his mind.'

I swallowed. 'Oh. Can you please tell him I said congratulations and that I'm really happy for him?' It hurt to breathe.

'Sure.'

I walked towards the car but then I turned around, remembering something else. John was leaning against the open door, watching me.

'John, how's Anna doing? My brother's worried about her.'

'What's your brother got to do with Anna?'

'He's her boyfriend.'

'No shit? Your brother's Harding? Tobes never said. Yeah, I can see it actually, if I think of you as a blonde again. You're pretty tall, come to think of it, aren't you?'

'Anna. How's Anna?'

'Oh yeah, she's completely fucked. Total mess. Can't get a word's sense out of her since her mum necked herself.'

How could this vile person be Toby's brother?

'Will you tell her that Nick really wants to hear from her? Please?'

'I can send her a text, but she won't do it.' He smacked his lips together. 'I don't know how well you know Anna, but if that chick makes a decision she sticks to it, and she's decided no more Nick.'

'Oh.'

'You Hardings aren't having much luck this week, hey?'

No. No we weren't.

PART THREE

THE FIRST WEEK
OF OCTOBER

NICK – SATURDAY

We had this in the bag, I was sure of it. There was no way they could come back and get us now, but I wasn't slowing down anyway. My legs screamed in pain as I sprinted up the wing looking for Joel. He was right where I wanted him, directly in front of goal – he could always predict my play better than anyone. My kick went long, really long, and landed smack bang in the middle of his chest.

The twenty thousand or so Rangers fans who'd made the trek across the Nullarbor to be here at the MCG were on their feet, roaring. I turned to the cheer squad when the umpire waved through Joel's goal, sealing the Grand Final for us. Raising both arms straight up in the air, I gave them a double thumbs up.

Almost every person in that stand responded by mirroring me with their own thumbs up.

Then the ball was back in the centre and it was time to shut the crowd out again, and to shut out the blinding pain in my calves and thighs as I ran back to position.

'Finish it, boys! Man up! Let's do this!' I yelled above the crowd to my teammates.

The final siren sounded.

I fell onto my hands and knees and kissed the turf.

Before I knew it, Bruce was on top of me, shouting in my ear, 'You fucking beauty, Harding!' and within a couple of minutes, the entire team, the coaching staff and the ground crew were in a pack surrounding us – cheering, back-slapping, hugging, crying.

I looked up into the stand where Mum, Lily and Ross were seated. All three of them were jumping up and down with their arms around each other. They saw me wave and they waved back manically.

As one, the team ran over to the cheer squad and we clapped for them while they clapped for us. Then we sat with our legs stretched out in front of us, leaning back on our hands while the runners-up sat a bit further away with sombre faces and hunched shoulders – a feeling I remembered well from this time two years ago. We all waited for the formalities to begin.

There were a couple of speeches that I was way too buzzed to listen to and then the MC said it was time to announce the Norm Smith Medallist. It was Joel – for sure. It had to be Joel. Nobody came close to the amount of touches he'd had out there today.

The person giving the Norm Smith Medal speech was a player I grew up worshipping – Brendan Chesson. I assumed he was talking about Joel until I heard the words, 'missed half the season with stress fractures'. My breath caught as he continued, 'But since his return in June, he's blown the nation away with his courage and determination, both on and off the field. He's shown himself to be a true leader and he brings his A-game to every match, including today where he singlehandedly turned the game around in the third quarter. Ladies and gentleman, please show your appreciation for this very deserving Norm Smith Medallist, number 4 for the Western Rangers, Nicholas Harding!'

I was pushed from side to side by my teammates as I stood up, astonished.

The world moved in slow motion as I walked towards the stage and the noise drowned out until all I heard was the blood rushing between my ears. It sounded like the sea and I was taken back to a hot summer morning sitting out past the break on my surf board with Dad next to me on his as the sun beat down on our faces, thinking how peaceful it was to hear nothing but the sound of the lapping waves.

The clouds over the MCG parted to reveal the sun that had been hiding for the entire game. I lifted my face up to the sun, just like I did that morning out in the ocean with Dad and the rays from heaven shone right onto me. A deep warmth spread through me from my face, to my chest, to the tips of my fingers and toes. And I felt Dad – not figuratively, but actually here with me. He was here to see me play in the Rangers Premiership squad.

And just like that the sun disappeared behind the clouds again as did the sound of the sea between my ears.

The world shifted back into focus and my eyes adjusted after the bright glare of light. The cheer squad chanted my name as I jogged up the stairs to shake Brendan's hand.

'Um, well, I'm in shock really,' I said into the microphone that echoed my words out to the ninety-thousand-plus people in the stadium. 'Firstly, commiserations to Collingwood. They gave us a run for our money and made us work hard for this Premiership, so well done, guys, and good luck next year.' I paused to let the crowd applaud. 'Next up, to my teammates, we played some beautiful footy out there today, boys, and it was an honour playing with you all. To the coaching staff, Craig, in particular, thanks for the monumental effort you put in, week in, week out, to get us here. And to the Rangers fans, especially all of you who made the trip over from Perth to support us today.' I turned my head to look at them. 'The Rangers have the best football fans in the country. We'd be nothing without you. So cheers!' A thunderous cheer erupted from the stands. 'I'm lucky enough to have my family here in the crowd today, I want to thank them for all their support and I know my dad, who was my biggest supporter, is here watching over me too. And finally, to a special person who's back home in Perth and I hope she's watching.' I found the camera and stared straight down the barrel. 'Anna Hayati, thank you for showing me what it is to be brave and to believe in something.' I held up the medal. 'I love you and this is for you.' My voice broke and I dropped my head.

When I sat back down, Joel leaned over. 'Another perfect Nick Harding moment, mate, well done.' He slapped my back.

But it wasn't a perfect moment. It couldn't be perfect unless I could share it with her.

I'd done everything she wanted these last four months. For a whole month I gave her the distance she asked for. But then I couldn't take it anymore so I went to the restaurant.

Fariz was coming out through the back door just as I was about to walk in.

'Nick!' He eyed me warily. 'What are you doing here?'

'Um, hello, Fariz, I … ah … I came to see Anna.' I wondered if he was about to pull a knife out on me again. He certainly looked like he wanted to.

'Well, she doesn't want to see you,' he growled. 'And she is not even here. She goes to Asylum Assist on Tuesdays. If she was here, I would forbid you to see her anyway.'

'Is she okay, Fariz? I just need to know that she's all right. I've stopped myself from going to Black Salt or the pool to see her, but—'

'Well, you would not have found her at Black Salt or at the pool. She left her job there and she stopped swimming.'

'What? She stopped swimming? She used to get anxious if more than a day went past and she couldn't get to the pool. Swimming's like breathing to her.'

'I know.' The wind picked up his combed-over hair and it spun about like a mini tornado on his head. 'But, yes, it is exactly like she isn't breathing these days.'

I flicked my own hair out of my eyes. 'What do you mean?'

He leaned against his van and crossed his arms. 'What is troubling Anna is no small matter. It hurts me here to see her like this.' He gave his chest two big thumps with his chunky hand. 'She has never once spoken of Leila since we buried her. Never once. And as if that was not enough you took advantage of her and now you have left her with a broken heart!'

'What? I never took advantage of her in any way. What are you talking about Fariz? *She's* the one who broke *my* heart!' I said with feeling.

He didn't answer. But he looked unconvinced.

'Fariz, I love Anna. I'd do anything for her. Tell me what I can do to help.'

He sighed. 'I think the pain is too deep for her to be helped. The mention of Leila makes her eyes blacken.'

'It's understandable that she's angry. Leila abandoned her.'

He clicked his tongue. 'No, no, she is not angry. I know my niece like I know my own heart.' He looked me in the eyes. 'She is only protecting herself from grieving by closing her heart off to her mother. It is easier to live without the mother you hate than without the mother you adore.' He raised his eyebrows. 'But closing off her heart like this is not who she is, so it is affecting her badly and she has lost her spirit – she is just surviving now for Ricky and the—' He coughed. 'For Ricky. She has become the same shell her mother was before her. History is repeating itself, like it always does.'

'Oh no.' I couldn't bear to think of Anna as the lifeless person her mother was.

We stood in silence in the wind.

'Fariz, please don't get angry but I need to know. Does she ever ask about me?' I ventured.

'No, but she appears from wherever she is if you are on the television. She reads every piece in the paper about you and every day I see her on her phone checking the internet for news of you. Do not be fooled by her silence. I myself was wishing she could forget you because you brought so much misery with you.' He gave me a filthy look and I squirmed under his stare. 'But as the time passes, I am seeing that she is even more miserable without you than she was with you.' He sighed.

'Well, I know how miserable I am without her, and without Ricky too. Is he okay?'

'Yes, he is well. He watches every Rangers match.'

My heart thumped. 'How's he coping without Leila?'

He shrugged. 'Leila was dead long before she left her body. Ricky's life is not much different to when she was alive. It was Anna who took care of him.'

I nodded.

'And Anna is wonderful with him.' There was real pride in his voice. 'For Ricky, she smiles and laughs and plays. But as soon as he turns his head the other way, she stops acting, and as soon as she stops acting, I see how broken she is.'

'Is she eating, Fariz?'

'Enough to stay alive. She eats, she sleeps, and she cares for Ricky. This is all she does.'

'But she goes to uni too, right?'

'She has deferred her university degree.'

This was too much. 'Are you kidding me? She deferred uni?'

Studying law was her one big dream. Anna had fought so hard for months to get her Baccalaureate recognised. She even had a countdown going on her phone for the number of sleeps left before she started her degree.

What was her dream now? Anything?

'I don't understand, why did she defer uni?' I asked him.

'I am ashamed to admit to you, that it is my fault she made this decision. I was unable to keep paying two of my staff because of the debt I am in. These days, Anna, Rosa and I must work longer hours. She cannot go to university while she is working this much. Since the vandalism and attacks on the restaurant we have had almost no business. And the conservative members of our community disapprove of Anna so they do not want to eat here anymore, and they were the ones who filled our tables every night. Even though Anna is only in the kitchen now and does not waitress anymore to keep hidden from their view, they still do not come and I am sinking quickly. I am more in debt every week.' He stared into the distance. 'I have tried different things, costly things, to bring our patrons back or to encourage new patrons to come, but I am afraid none of them have worked. We are lucky if two small groups come on any one night and if we get one or two takeaways.'

I thought back to the Masri's I first went to that was packed to the rafters, with Fariz in his element as the host. I remembered his smiling eyes, his passion for the place, and I compared it to the beaten man who stood here now, his face wracked with worry for both his niece and his business.

'I'm so sorry that's happened to your business. I'm really sorry, Fariz. I feel responsible.'

He didn't argue.

I knew what I had to do to rectify what had happened to his business because of Anna's involvement with me, but it meant enlisting Rosa's help, and she was quite possibly the person I liked least in the entire universe.

'Listen, I have to get to the club.' I extended my hand and was relieved when Fariz shook it. 'But is it okay if I come back another time to see Anna?'

A panicked look came over him. 'Why would you want to come back and upset her? No, I forbid it. She does not want to see you and I will not let you, do you hear?'

I was taken aback by how aggressively he spoke after he'd just been open with me.

'Okay, okay,' I put my hands up in surrender. 'I'll leave her alone. But could I at least come to see you next Tuesday to check in on how she's going? She'll be at Asylum Assist then won't she? So the coast will be clear, right?' I gave him a pleading look.

He sighed a long sigh. 'I will not have anything new to tell you, but you can come back.' He gave me a sideways look. 'But do not think I am your friend after you betrayed Anna with that pink-haired lady.' He curled his lip at the word lady.

I threw my head back. 'Oh God, you saw the photos. Do you know if Anna saw them?'

He scoffed. 'Pfft, of course she saw! Everyone saw! You broke her heart.'

'No, no, no,' I moaned. 'Fariz, I wrote her a letter explaining those photos. That girl, Arielle, she's a friend of my sister's who was helping me get home when I'd had too much drink. There was nothing between her and me, I swear to you. I honestly swear, I—'

'I believe you, Nick. Okay, okay, I believe you,' he said with a dismissive wave as he climbed into his van. 'Go home now, let me go to the market and see who will rob me the most today, the butcher or the fishmonger.' He slouched forwards over the steering wheel, his face full of worry lines.

Once he drove away, I knocked on the back door before walking in with gritted teeth to face Rosa.

Her face registered the shock of seeing me for the briefest of seconds before she gave me the stony stare I was used to as she pulled her hijab further down her forehead. 'Why you here? What you want?' she barked. 'Anna, she no here. You goes please away.'

She shooed at me with her meaty hands.

'Rosa, I have money.' I rubbed my thumb against my index and middle fingers, the universal signal for cash, and her eyebrows shot up.

It was easy from there. She might've thought me destined for eternal damnation up until that moment but as soon as I explained my plan to her in a mix of English and charades, she put her arms out and slammed my head into her bosom.

'*Ya habibi! Ya habibi, enta!*' she repeated over and over while I gasped for air with my nose and mouth buried in her massive bust.

When she released me she walked to an antique wooden wall unit and opened the second drawer, producing the newspaper with the photo of me and Arielle. 'Zis, no more zis?'

I shook my head. 'Not. My. Girlfriend.' I enunciated each word separately and loudly so she could really get it.

She didn't get it. Her expression stayed the same.

I sighed and pointed at the photo of Arielle, then shook my head and said 'No!' several times over.

'No choppy-choppy?' Her eyes searched mine with suspicion.

'No choppy-choppy,' I confirmed, whatever the hell that meant. I tapped my heart. 'I love Anna.'

She looked me up and down. 'You pray to Allah!'

I chuckled. 'Yes. Okay.'

She patted both my cheeks at once. It hurt. *'Allah maak, ya* Nick.'

This was one of the many Arabic sayings Anna had taught me. I knew that Rosa's words meant, 'God be with you', and I remembered how to say it back to her, using the correct feminine version when addressing a woman. *'Allah maaki, ya* Rosa.'

She grabbed my head and rammed it back between her breasts.

***

It took ten days for the paperwork to go through and on the Friday of the following week, the mortgage on the restaurant and the house was paid off. Fariz was debt-free.

I drove straight from the bank into town and offered up my services to the young woman behind the desk at Asylum Assist. Her name tag said Kathryn, and her jaw hung wide open as I introduced myself.

'I want to help out, doing whatever I can. How can I use my media presence to help?'

'Um, what about the Rangers? And SafeXone?' Kathryn's eyes darted from side to side, as if SafeXone had hidden cameras on her.

'Nothing to worry about there,' I assured her. 'I sorted it all out with the club before coming here.'

Kathryn chewed her lip. 'I'm sorry but after what happened last time you were involved, I think your media presence might actually hurt us rather than help us. We received a solicitor's letter from SafeXone, threatening to have us shut down after the march. And our individual donations have decreased by thirty per cent since then too. We also lost two corporate sponsors.'

I leaned my forearms on the desk. 'Kathryn, I've got here a formal letter of apology from SafeXone that also says they're behind Asylum Assist one hundred per cent. And what about if I can convince some of *my* corporate sponsors to sponsor you guys? I've got billion-dollar companies behind me, Kathryn. Sports shoe companies, breakfast cereal companies – the big guns. They're always looking for causes to lower their taxes.'

She looked doubtful.

'The Rangers haven't lost a game since my comeback. I don't want to sound full of myself, but I'm in demand right now. I get interview requests every week. I could use that time in front of the camera to share some asylum-seeker stories. What do you say? Want to use me to get some more attention and some more action for this place?'

She looked tortured. 'It sounds great but I just don't know if it's a good idea.'

I looked her in the eyes, giving her *the* look. And I gave her *the* smile to go with it while I flexed both arms, making it look like I was just innocently raking my fingers through my hair. It was the never-fail combination I used to rely on to get what I wanted in the days before Anna. 'You sure you don't want me, Kathryn?'

And so I became an ambassador for Asylum Assist.

It felt good to be actively involved in something where there was no reward except the knowledge that I was doing good. Sure I'd done loads of charity work with the club, but that was because it was in my contract. It wasn't through choice. Asylum Assist – that was all me.

I was given a mountain of material to read through so that I wouldn't sound like an ignorant idiot, and once I'd got my head around the facts and figures, as well as committing to memory some personal stories, and with everything I already knew about Ricky's situation, I went on a national morning talk show and spoke about what Asylum Assist stood for. The donations from that day alone doubled what had come in over the previous month.

I was anxious to see what the reaction would be at the club when I went to training later that morning, but all that happened was that a few of my close mates laughed at the pink shirt I wore on TV.

'It wasn't pink, it was salmon,' I defended myself.

Craig cornered me after training. 'Careful, mate.' He spoke in a voice low enough that nobody else could hear him. 'It's one thing to be supportive of asylum seekers, it's another thing to go on TV taking on the government. You're a footy player, not a social commentator. Don't get in above your head. They'll make mincemeat of you.'

I blew air out hard. 'All I want is to use my name to give those orphaned kids a voice.'

'Are you prepared for a backlash from media, from fans? There *will* be one.'

'Yes.'

He gave me a long look. 'It's your life, Harding. You have to do what's right for you.'

As I walked towards the lockers he called out. 'Nick?'

'Yeah?'

'Proud of you, mate.'

The next day Kathryn called me with a shaky voice. First she told me about the donations that had come flooding in. Then she said, 'Thank you very much, Nick, you were amazing. You really were, but Asylum Assist won't be requiring your help again. So if you could please stop speaking on behalf of Asylum Assist to the media from now on that would be greatly appreciated.'

'Why? I don't get it.'

'I'm not at liberty to say,' she replied.

'Kathryn, I spent a whole week memorising facts about asylum seekers and the Australian policies and procedures. I deserve an answer.'

'It's Anna,' she blurted. 'She's worried you'll lose fans or get yourself in trouble again. I'm sorry.'

She hung up.

* * *

I was waiting for Fariz again in Masri's car park. It was our third Tuesday meeting. He had been much less hostile last week than he had been the first week.

This time when we said hello he crushed me in a bear hug and thanked me a hundred times over for clearing his debts.

'Please don't tell Anna that I paid off the mortgage,' I said.

'Why?'

'I don't want her to feel manipulated.'

He didn't answer.

'I hope the restaurant starts to pick up for you again now, Fariz.'

'Nick, I must work out a way to bring our patrons back.' He stroked his chin. 'Our community has abandoned us and whatever I have tried to bring in new customers has failed.'

'I've got an idea.' I pulled out my phone and messaged Joel.

> Reckon you could pull a few people together and turn up for
> dinner at Masri's tonight? Anna's uncle needs the business
> really badly.

His reply was immediate.

> Course I can.

So I sent out a tweet to my forty thousand followers.

> Best food in Freo – Masri's, South Terrace. Authentic
> Egyptian. Get on it! @therealjoelcoombs you'll be there
> tonight right?

> @nickharding you bet your sweet falafels I will be.

A minute later Fariz's phone started ringing. And it didn't stop
ringing.

'You won't need the old patrons anymore.' I slapped his
shoulder as I left. 'Once these new people taste your delicious
food, you'll be turning people away.'

***

Fariz and I fell into the comfortable habit of catching up every
Tuesday morning before I reported to the club for the day and
before he drove to the farmers' markets. He took to fixing me
Turkish coffee, and he would walk out from the kitchen with
one freshly brewed when he heard the sound of my car pull up.

Not wanting to offend him, I chugged it down each time. But I would never get used to that sludge.

Every week, I wondered if he would tell me that Anna had spoken about me or said she was ready to see me. But he never did.

At least I got to see Ricky once.

I squatted down when I saw him waiting for me in the car park and he ran into my arms.

'Look at your hair, it's curly!' I smiled. 'And look how much taller you are. Are you eating ten meals a day or something, mate?'

He beamed.

'He says he is "sick",' Fariz made quotation marks with his fingers. 'He overheard me talking to Rosa about you coming this morning.'

Ricky smirked. 'I have a sore tummy.'

'You do not!' I laughed, scooping him up onto my shoulders. 'Would Anna be okay with me seeing Ricky?' I asked Fariz.

'No, I am certain that she would skin me alive.' He chuckled. 'As we say though, *Tajannub ma yatatallab aetdharaan* – Avoid that which requires an apology.'

I gave him a sideways look. 'But you're doing the opposite of that saying. You're sneaking Ricky out here to see me, knowing she'd demand an apology.'

'What I mean by this saying is that Ricky and I will avoid telling her about this rendezvous. Then we will not need to apologise.'

I pursed my lips together. 'Hmm, I don't feel good about making you to lie to Anna, mate.'

'Not lying. Avoiding apologies.' Fariz tapped his nose.

'Please, Nick, I'll keep it a secret. Please, please,' Ricky begged. 'Can you watch the replay of last Saturday with me?'

He clasped his hands around my neck in a hug that nearly choked me.

I reluctantly agreed. As much as I felt guilty being in Anna's home against her wishes, I couldn't let down Ricky.

We sat and watched the Rangers and I hung onto every second of him curled up on my lap, his little hands on top of mine, and his head resting on my chest, just like he used to do before. Three hours went too quickly.

After the match finished, I patted his leg. 'I missed training this morning, buddy, so I could hang out with you but I really have to go now. I've got a school to visit today. But it was really good to see you, hey?'

His face crumpled so I quickly added, 'I'll see you again, for sure. I'll check with Anna if you can come over to my place one weekend when the season's over. Maybe you could have a sleepover? That would be cool!'

Ricky shook his head. 'Anna will say no. She doesn't care.'

'She does care, Ricky. You're the most important thing in the world to her.'

He shrugged. 'Anna told me how your dad died.'

The wind got knocked out of me. 'Did she?'

'Mmm-hmm.' He fiddled with my Apple watch. 'She told me your dad drowned just like my dad drowned.'

'Yeah, he did.' I didn't know what to say next so we sat in silence. 'I miss my dad.' I said more to myself than to him.

'I miss my dad too.' He pressed a button on my watch that turned the backlight on. 'I saw him drown.'

As far as Anna had told me, Ricky couldn't remember anything about the sinking boat or the journey at all. She'd said it was all gone from his memory.

'Did you? I didn't see my dad drown.' I wished Fariz would walk in. He'd know the right thing to say. I felt completely out of my depth.

'Mmm-hmm. I didn't see my mum drown, but my dad was holding me, then the big wave came and we both went under it and he didn't come back up. And I called him but he didn't hear me. Because he drowned. I think your dad went under a big wave too.'

'Maybe.' I could barely speak.

'I don't like the ocean. I like swimming in the pool but I don't like the beach. Anna said I should go to the beach this summer and just put my feet in the water but I said no.'

'I don't blame you.' I stroked his hair.

'It's not fair that Anna doesn't want me to see you because when we watch football I feel better.'

I swallowed hard. 'I'll make sure she lets it happen soon, Ricky. I absolutely promise. Watching football with you makes me feel better too.'

I left a note for Anna, letting her know that I'd been there and asking if I could please spend a few hours with Ricky once a week or so. The next Tuesday Fariz gave me her answer: 'No.'

* * *

As more weeks passed, my panic rose that maybe Anna was lost to me for good. But two weeks before the Grand Final my heart soared when Fariz announced with dramatic flair, 'Yesterday Anna went swimming at Challenge! She told Rosa that she plans to go back to swimming again every day from now on! She is smiling again, Nick. Something has changed inside her.'

'Do you think she'll go back to university too?' I asked hopefully.

'Perhaps one day she will.' He placed his hand firmly on my shoulder, bringing his head in close and lowering his voice as if we were exchanging details for a drug deal out there in the car park. 'When she is less burdened.' He gave me a long look that I couldn't read.

'Has she brought up Leila's name at all yet?' I asked.

'Not a word.' He sighed.

'And me? Has she talked about me?'

'Sorry, Nick. No.'

When it was time to go, I asked him for the first time in weeks if it would be okay to visit Anna. 'I want her back, Fariz. I want her back and I want Ricky back. I want us to be a family. Please allow me to see her.'

'Yes, yes, I think it is time now that you see Anna.'

I told him that I'd go around and see her the day after the Grand Final when I got back to Perth. 'I've waited this long, I think it's best I wait until the season's done and I can put all my energy into it. What do you think?'

'I agree, and I will make sure she is home the Sunday after the Grand Final, Nick. I hope you return from Melbourne with a Premiership medal to show us.'

* * *

And tomorrow was the day I'd finally get to see her. I hoped she would at least hear me out and not refuse to let me in like the last time I saw her, that awful day of the protest march.

But first was the celebration of the Premiership with my teammates. None of us had won a Grand Final with another team so it made this first win special for us all. I hadn't touched a drink since the night that Anna dumped me. But tonight, everyone would be drinking, including me.

My phone buzzed. It was a text from Mum saying they'd made it through the crowds and were waiting outside the club rooms. When I went out there to meet them, Lily did a running jump into my arms.

Ross slapped my back. 'We're so bloody proud of you, mate.' His voice was choked up.

I looked at his face, so full of pride in me when all I'd done was be cold towards him. It was about time I let him in. I gave him a hug and he hugged me back hard.

'You won a Premiership, honey!' Mum threw her arms around my neck. 'All those sacrifices you made, over all those years – you got there. You did it, Nick! Your dad's smiling on you, sweetheart. I know he is.' Her eyes were wet.

I pulled her in close. 'I know, Mum. I felt him out there with me today. I swear I did. There was this moment, Mum.'

'I saw.'

'Had nothing to do with you, though.' Lily joined in the hug, just as teary herself. 'As if Dad would ever miss a Rangers' Premiership no matter who was playing.'

That made me laugh.

'Premiership, Nick!' Lily pulled out of the hug and jumped up and down like she was on a springboard. 'You won a bloody Premiership!'

As I walked back into the MCG club rooms, with my arms draped over Mum on one side, and Lily on the other, and with Ross out in front, walking backwards so he could take photos of the three of us, again, I thought about how Anna should have been here for this. Anna would have completed the picture.

TOBY – SATURDAY

'*Yes!*' John and I hollered along with the rest of the crowd at the pub as Joel Coombs put through the goal that guaranteed the Rangers were the new Premiers.

My cheeks were burning and my head spun – how much of that was from alcohol and how much was from passion was hard to tell. Seconds later, the final siren blew and John and I leapt into each other's arms.

Nick Harding played an absolute blinder, staying true to the form that had taken the Rangers all the way to the Grand Final. Throughout the game, the cameramen kept cutting across to his mum and Lily in the crowd, so I found myself confronted by her smiling face whenever Nick did something spectacular, which seemed to be every few minutes. John poked his elbow into my ribs every time just to drive the point home further.

She still had such a hold on me, Rapunzel from the café. She'd never looked more beautiful than she did there in the crowd, and it created such chaos in my head that when the minute I'd been waiting for my whole life happened and my team finally won a Grand Final, my overriding thought wasn't that the Rangers were Premiers but how much I missed Lily.

It had been four months since we last saw each other, when

I walked in on her with her ex-boyfriend. I analysed and re-analysed that night a hundred times over. Had anything actually happened between her and Ben or could I have jumped to the wrong conclusions? But the way she broke up with me completely out of left field was just too coincidental. And she was in her pyjamas that night when she was with him. The sexy ones.

I wasted a stupid amount of time obsessing about it – my entire drive to Queensland, and the first weeks afterwards. I spent hour after hour making myself crazy imagining them having sex.

But then when July rolled around, my mentorship with Keith Rayner began and the new job saturated every brain cell I had and it cured my fixation with Lily and Ben.

Keith and I started most days out on location at no later than five in the morning and we stayed out until the sun was at its highest. Then it was back to the studio to play around with editing software before packing the equipment back into the truck to catch the afternoon and evening light.

Even after fifteen years of dabbling in photography, I discovered on my first day – no, in my first hour – with Keith, that everything I knew actually amounted to fuck all.

The man was a genius. A patient genius, who was prepared to wake up at 3 am, drive for hours and then spend the next seven hours lying on his stomach in long prickly grass, letting the mosquitoes and bull ants eat him alive and the sun dehydrate him, while he waited for the rare Richmond Birdwing butterfly to fly down to the patch of daisies where it had been spotted by a ranger the day before.

And when the butterfly didn't come, he did the exact same thing the next morning. And when that day yielded nothing, he set his alarm for two-thirty in the morning, went back for a third day and waited until the magnificent insect fluttered down onto a flower close enough to photograph. When it picked at the pollen, its striated, almost fluorescent wings opened fully, and all twenty centimetres of those magnificent wings lit up with the morning sun's rays shooting through them. And it was all caught on camera.

The pair of us took close to three hundred photos of that butterfly and we spent the rest of the day and night running filters through forty of the best then blowing them up to poster size to check them for clarity.

After getting my opinion, which he disagreed with, Keith chose the best five to send to *National Geographic*.

All five were photos that I took and would be credited for.

I sent John a text:

My photos will be in National Geographic next month!

He replied:

Cool. How much are they coughing up?

I rolled my eyes.

Doesn't work that way. I'm on $200 a day, it's not commission based.

His reply came back quickly:

Bahaha $200 a day!

I sent the same message to Dad about my photos being chosen. At least he would be happy for me.

'You've got to be joking!' I said out loud in my empty bedroom when Dad's reply came.

Excellent news Toby! How much did they cough up for those?

I let that text go unanswered.

There was nobody else to tell really, I hadn't made any friends in Mission Beach. And I didn't have any real friends back home either. I had done here what I did there, made loads of acquaintances – like the dude who operated the canoe- and blo-kart-hire place on the beach, the lady who owned the bakery, my retired neighbours. But no real friends.

It didn't bother me, I'd never needed people. My family and a girl to love were all I ever needed. I had neither of those here in Queensland but I wasn't unhappy. The job was enough. I was satisfied at the end of a day's work for the first time I could ever remember, and what I learned during the week I practised on the weekends.

I took day trips to different parts of the Far North every Saturday, and in each place I found more magic than the one before. The dense tropical foliage, the white sandy beaches that were every bit as stunning as the ones in Western Australia, the mountains, the gorges. Any wonder Keith chose to base himself here, you could never run out of inspiration.

One Sunday morning as dawn broke, at a watering hole southeast of Cairns called Alligators Nest, I took a shot of a lavender orchid, with water droplets clinging to its silver-rimmed petals.

When I showed it to Keith he said, 'We're going to sell that one, Wattsy.'

And he did, three days later to a Japanese art collector.

Then Keith refused to take a cent for it. 'Just remember me when you're rich and famous.' He smiled.

I sent John another message.

$6k for a flower with a raindrop on it.

He replied:

Bullshit.

So I sent him a screenshot of the payment and then had a laugh at his reply:

Go fuck yourself Toby.

It was the middle of August when I realised I wasn't pining for Lily. It was around then that I also started thinking seriously about making the move more permanent. The rent on the apartment I lived in was astronomical and eating up the funding I'd been given, because it was a short-term lease one block from the beach. I was so busy with work that I barely saw the beach anyway. I was after a cheaper place further inland I could get long-term. So I went to see a real estate agent.

And her name was Carly.

***

'Same again?' John interrupted my thoughts.

'Yeah, yeah, that'd be good.'

He returned a few minutes later. 'She's fucked you around this arvo, hasn't she, that Harding chick?' He clinked his glass against mine.

'What do you mean?' I played dumb.

'Barely had a word out of you all night, mate, and the Rangers just won the Premiership. That's not the Tobes I know. You're sitting there spewing that you're stuck with that ball and chain real-estate agent waiting for you in Queensland, when all you want to do is screw Harding's baby sister, right? I don't blame you, mate. I'd tap that for sure.'

I shook my head at him. 'She's not a *that*.'

He snorted. 'Good deflection, Tobes. Truth hurts, huh?'

I ignored him and pulled out my phone to text Carly. I had to do something to quash the guilt. Because John was spot on. I did want Lily. I wanted her a lot.

Miss you Carls. At pub with John xx

Missing you too, hun. Go Rangers! Tell John to piss off from me ☺. I'm sure he's said something by now to deserve it ...

Carly. Gorgeous Carly. She unlocked a vacant apartment for me one particularly humid Saturday afternoon, and I was so aroused by the way she'd been coming onto me during the drive there that when she announced with a sexy smile, 'So, want to see if the shower works?' I answered with, 'Fuck yes.'

Seconds later we were ripping off each other's clothes. After some of the hottest sex I'd ever had in three separate rooms of the apartment over the next few hours, I felt it was only right to rent the place from her.

By the start of September, I was settled in with a two-year lease and I gave Dad the go-ahead to sell the building business.

I never planned for it to be anything more than a bit of fun with Carly, but it developed into more than either of us had intended and we were happy. Really happy. Lily had slipped further and further from my mind.

Which was all well and good until today. Until I found myself staring at her on a giant flat screen and realising that I'd been kidding myself. I still loved this woman as much as I ever did.

**

'Marcia was telling me how lovely it was to see you last night, Toby,' Mum said.

John and I were drinking coffees on our parents' back deck, a few hours after the Grand Final was over.

'Has she had any counselling or anything, Mum?' I shuddered at the memory of Marcia draping herself over me the night before at Mum and Dad's anniversary party. Her hot breath that reeked of rum had hit me in the eye.

'No, she's refused to see a counsellor. It hasn't been easy on poor Pete or Luke.'

'Pete was telling me he's found a good rehab place for her,' Dad added. 'He can get her in there on her doctor's say-so, whether she wants to be admitted or not. But he's not sure if he can make the call. Poor bugger.'

'Toby,' Mum touched my knee. 'Go around there and say hello again, love. Just for a few minutes. It would be so appreciated. What do you think?'

'No, Mum.'

As sorry as I felt for them, I had no sense of obligation to go next door and no guilt at saying no. And I felt no pull towards Jen's grave either. None whatsoever. I'd finally done it. I'd let her go.

'Do you really have to leave on Monday, love? Can't you stay for just one more week? You only just got back,' Mum pleaded.

Dad looked just as hopeful.

'Sorry, Mum. I'm on assignment this week. There are shoots already lined up for me in Kalgoorlie and Esperance before I drive back home. Promise I'll stay longer next time,' I said. 'You guys should come visit me. I really want you to meet Carly. We can't leave it that the only family member she's met is him,' I nodded at John.

I really did want them to come and visit me next because no way was I coming back to Perth any time soon. Perth was where Lily was and Lily still messed with my head. Perth was a place I needed to keep away from, for as long as it took me to get over her.

ANNA – SATURDAY AND SUNDAY

'Anwar! *Yalla!*' Tante Rosa called out to me from the lounge room. '*Yalla!*'

'*Tayeb*, Tante Rosa, in a minute.'

I was putting the last of Ahmo Fariz's chef's coats away, when Tante Rosa shouted again, '*Yalla, ya* Anwar!'

Joined by Ahmo Fariz this time, 'Anna! *Yalla!*'

And Ricky, 'Anna! *Hurry!*'

It was like the house was on fire, such was their urgency!

'I'm coming, I'm coming. Calm down all of you,' I groaned.

I threw the chef's coat over the back of the chair and walked as quickly as I could through the house to where they were seated on the couch with their eyes on the television.

Nick's face filled the screen. The sight of him took my breath away. I was sure it always would.

I'd failed miserably in my attempt to harden my heart to him, to get over him even slightly. How did I stand a chance at forgetting him when he was everywhere I looked?

Next time, stay away from famous people, I berated myself whenever I turned on the television and he appeared on the screen, or I walked through a shopping centre and saw a life-size cut-out at the front of a sporting goods store, or whenever his smile teased me from the pages of newspapers and magazines.

Yet each time I was tempted to call him, I remembered how he nearly lost his career and how the restaurant almost closed down because of my relationship with him. No matter how much I missed Nick, I simply could not take the risk.

Nearly every day, Ahmo Fariz nagged me about Nick. 'He has a good heart and he gives without expecting in return, this is a rare trait. He doesn't know that we told you how he paid off our debts and that he got people to come to Masri's again. And now look, even our old patrons have come back again. They have come back to us once more. Egyptians are quick to forgive, *habibti*. Why is it so hard then for you to forgive?' he questioned me. 'My fears about him were unfounded, he is a decent man. You are carrying his child. Do not deprive him any longer. It is becoming harder and harder for me to keep this secret of yours from him.'

'Ahmo Fariz, don't you see? It's not that I don't forgive Nick. I've seen what he has done, not just for us, but for Asylum Assist. Nobody knows how kind he is and how good his heart is more than me. This is why I've stayed away from him deliberately. If he knew about our baby then he would put the baby and me first, and look what happened the last time he put me first? I have to wait until his football season is over to tell him. Please keep my secret for only a few more weeks. Let me tell him in my own time.'

'And when his season is over, will you accept him back into your life? Will you let him commit to you the way I know he is desperate to?'

'Ahmo Fariz, I wish you understood.' I sighed. 'I can't take him back. I'm bad for his image and his career. If he can't see that, then I need to be the one who does. I won't risk his career a second time.'

'You realise how greatly you disrespect him with this stubbornness of yours?' Ahmo Fariz frowned.

'Disrespect him? How?' I raised my voice, insulted. 'It's only out of care for him that I'm protecting him.'

'Hmmph,' he muttered. 'I cannot listen to any more of your nonsense. What makes you so wise that you know what a man needs more than he himself knows, *ya* Anna? Hmmm? The father of your baby wants nothing more than to be a family with you and Ricky. These are the exact words he spoke to me himself. Instead you will make him suffer in not allowing him to be with you and his child, you will suffer alone as a mother without a partner and your poor child will suffer – wake up to yourself, girl. I used to think you were wise beyond your years. Now I think you rival my feeble-minded sister Rosa in your stupidity!'

Ahmo Fariz stormed out of the kitchen in a huff but his words bothered me for the rest of the day. And I began to wonder if he was right.

But it was only when Tante Rosa called me Leila in passing that his words sank in.

'Tante Rosa, did you just call me Leila?' I gasped.

She raised her eyebrows. 'I did? Yes, I think I did. It must be because you remind me so much of her these days. You are like her in so many ways, it's as if she is still here sometimes when I look at you.'

I wondered how she could possibly confuse me with my mother. The thought plagued me. And slowly over the course of the day, I came to understand.

In my mission to cast my mother from my mind, in my quest not to repeat her mistakes, I had in fact become her. *I* was now the martyr giving up on life and drowning in guilt, *I* was the one whose laughter no longer echoed through the house, because I had forgotten how to be happy … What had happened to me? How did I get so lost? What kind of example was I setting for Ricky and for the daughter growing inside me?

I even performed my work for Asylum Assist with no passion, just a sense of obligation – a kind of penance that every spare minute I had should be devoted to helping others.

Well, I refused to be this person for one second longer. I wouldn't let myself shrivel and die like my mother did. I had to find Anna again, and bring her back to life.

'Tante Rosa,' I called out later that day. 'Please keep your eye on Ricky. I will come back and finish peeling these garlic cloves soon. But right now I need to go to the pool and swim.'

And from that moment, I tried my very best to rise up from my mother's ashes – the ashes that had left my spirit covered in her dust.

Every morning, instead of praying for strength to survive another day without the people I love, I woke up and thanked Allah for allowing me to feel the sun and see the moon once more.

I vowed to myself that I would show my child and Ricky how important it was to have dreams to chase. As soon as I could after my daughter's birth, I would begin university and chase my old dream of a law degree. I would make everything good again.

I would not be my mother.

And Nick. I had to accept his love. I had to let Nick love me. I had to believe I was worthy.

When I made this discovery, I wanted to call Nick straight away. But he was in Melbourne with the Rangers and it was the eve of the Grand Final, the most crucial and special day of his career. The very last thing he needed was an emotional call from me, announcing a pregnancy, to unsettle him.

I would wait those two extra days until he was back home and then I would go to him and beg for his forgiveness for the way I had shunned him so undeservedly. And I would tell him about our baby. Well, I would let my new shape tell him, because the moment he saw me, he would know! I knew with my whole heart that Nick would welcome and love our baby without a second of questioning.

And today the Grand Final day had arrived. I joined Ahmo Fariz, Tante Rosa, and Ricky in the lounge room as the Rangers ran through the banner onto the ground at the MCG. The others were able to simply sit there and watch. I was not. First I peeled four kilograms of potatoes, then I folded all the washing, then I finished two baskets of ironing and I chewed off every nail and bit my lip until it bled while Nick played for his first Premiership.

I was hanging up the ironing when Tante Rosa and Ahmo Fariz began to holler like maniacs for me to come back into the lounge room. And when I returned to where they were seated, there was Nick's dear face frozen on the television.

'Rewind, Rosa, rewind!' Ahmo Fariz yelled. 'No, you old buffalo, that is record, not rewind! Here, here give it to me.'

Ahmo Fariz pressed rewind on the remote control and I saw that Nick was being given a special medal for being the best and fairest player.

Oh, how my heart burst with joy! I clapped my hands together and my eyes filled with happy tears for him. But although I assumed this was what they had all been shouting at me to come and see – it was not. The reason for all the yelling they did was because of what Nick said afterwards in his speech.

He thanked the opposition, his coach, his teammates and then he thanked his fans and his family, but it was the way he spoke of his father watching over him that made me cry the most. As soon as he started his speech, our baby, who had been peacefully asleep all day, began to kick furiously inside me as if she recognised her father's voice.

At the end of his speech he looked into the camera and said, 'And finally, to a special person who's back home in Perth and I hope she's watching. Anna Hayati, thank you for showing me what it is to be brave and to believe in something. I love you and this is for you.'

'I need to sit down,' I whispered.

'Come sit.' Tante Rosa patted the sofa next to her and I sat with a thud.

She placed her hands on my rounded stomach. The baby whose existence she had once cursed had miraculously become the one whose birth she eagerly awaited.

'Can you feel her kicking? She's kicking like mad at her father's voice. How is this possible?' I said to her.

Tante Rosa snorted. 'I do not know why you are sitting here asking me this stupid question instead of telling the father of this poor child that he has one.'

I shook my head in wonder at Tante Rosa. 'You've changed so much. Why?'

Tante Rosa took a deep breath. 'Anwar, when the man I loved disappointed me, *that's* when I changed.' She sighed. 'But the father of this child …' She patted my stomach. 'The father of this child, has restored my faith in men. So I haven't changed, Anwar. All I've done is change *back* to who I was before.'

I smiled. 'Tante Rosa, I always wondered how you and Mama could have become such close friends at school when you were so different. But now I can see why.'

'You just said "Mama",' she exclaimed. *'Allaho'akbar.* This means your heart is healing, Anwar. It makes me glad. Say her name, Anwar, say it often. Remember her and remember how much she adored you.'

Ahmo Fariz joined in. 'Leila loved you, Anna. Her death was no reflection of her love for you.'

'I think I'm just starting to understand that now,' I replied.

***

It was yet another busy evening in the restaurant, and when everyone had gone to bed, I looked for my journal which I had not written in for a long time. It wasn't in its usual place in the top drawer in the bedside table. Disturbed, I searched all the drawers.

Ricky stirred when I closed the last drawer a little too harshly.

'Shhh, Ricky, back to sleep, *habibi.'*

Where could it have gone? When did I last write in it? I could not remember. Then I remembered the rage in which I had packed away all of Mama's things and anything at all that reminded me of our life in Egypt and how I had thrown everything into large black bin liners at the very back of the wardrobe.

I sat in the wardrobe and pulled one of the bags close to me. It was heavy but that did not deter me. I would go through them one by one until I found the journal. I needed to write to Noor. I *had* to write to Noor. When I tore the bin liner open, the scent of Mama floated out of it. I pulled out the top item. Her bathrobe. I held it to my nose and inhaled her and I cried like I had never cried before. One by one, I pulled out Mama's clothes, her toothbrush, her wallet. Each item brought back more of her to me. Then I found her phone. I tried to turn it on but it had no charge.

I scrambled through the bag, looking for a phone charger. Once the phone was plugged in I watched it light up. I had forgotten that her screen saver was a picture of me posing for her in the kitchen at Masri's with enormous zucchinis, one in each hand. I looked through her list of contacts. There were hundreds. Some made me laugh and some reminded me just how amazing my Mama was – under P was Patrick Doha (Noor's Boy From Downstairs) along with Prince Charles (UK), under M was Moustache Waxer (Kharoufa) and Michelle Obama. For the first time in my life I read text messages between my parents going back to 2014 when she must have bought the phone.

I had nagged Mama several times to upgrade her iPhone to the latest model but she was firm in her refusal. I thought she was being stubborn, but now as I read through the hundreds of text messages between my parents, I understood why she could never part with the object that was such a tangible link to her husband and her marriage. The messages ranged from the mundane (*Six lemons please* habibi *and a bag of rice*), to the funny (a photo of our puppy Lucky sitting next to emptied bin contents), to the romantic (*I miss you* ya habibti, *come home soon, the nights are too long with you gone and the bed is cold*), to the alarming (*They're here again. The same two. Send Hamdy quickly. I will go back into the office until he arrives. Make sure the girls stay indoors. Do not let them take their studies out onto the balcony*).

But the biggest surprise awaited me when I clicked on the calendar app in the phone. Every day (with the exception of a few dates that I identified as times when she was ill and hospitalised after skipping doses of her medication) Mama had kept a kind of journal. But unlike my long journal to Noor, hers was always one sentence only and always followed by the words '*Shoofi? Aho*'. 'You see? There you go.' And every sentence for every day, starting from the week after the fire and ending the week before she died, was about me – *Anwar's pink face and wet hair when she returned from the pool.* Shoofi? Aho. or *The sound of Anwar's laughter today when she found a vibrator inside Rosa's apron pocket in the washing basket.* Shoofi? Aho. or *Anwar wasn't able to sleep until her feet were tucked between my shins.* Shoofi? Aho.

My mama was giving herself a reason to keeping living and every day that reason was me.

I sat on the floor going through all of Mama's things until Ricky woke up the next morning.

'What are you doing, Anna?'

'Remembering, *ya* Ricky. I'm remembering.'

I finally found my journal in there too and I took it to the kitchen to write in it while Ricky ate his breakfast and watched SpongeBob on the television.

My precious Noor,

I know it has been months since I wrote to you. I found it impossible, you see, when I thought you had abandoned me. I associated your absence with Mama's death and I didn't open myself up to there being any other possibilities to explain your leaving me. Even though you let me know very clearly where you were and that you were in fact closer to me than ever before – I was so buried in grief that I didn't hear you calling to me.

It wasn't until I had my ultrasound two days ago when my baby was confirmed to be a girl that I finally understood where you were. I didn't need an ultrasound to tell me I was having a girl, you see, because I already knew with an absolute certainty from the first day that I was.

You didn't leave me for Mama, Noor, you simply moved from my dreams to my womb to keep watch over my baby. This is why I've felt so connected to my child, as if I've known her intimately from the day I discovered she was there.

Whenever my baby moves I feel you. When I look down at my stomach I see you. And then when my baby is born, I will see your spirit shine through her every day. I don't need you in my dreams anymore because now you're with me when I'm awake too.

So, my darling, this is the last time I will write to you. Today I start my life anew. Nick arrives home from Melbourne today. I will go to him and we will start over together. And just as my life is starting over, your life, Noor, ya habibti, is starting over too.

Goodbye my precious sister. Allah maaki.

A x

NICK – SUNDAY

The day after the Grand Final – after a flight alongside a plane full of my pissed teammates and jubilant fans, with the added bonus of my family on board – we landed back in Perth. The fans turned out in force and the Arrivals area went off when we came down the escalators. It was like we were rock stars – even the team trainers were mobbed.

Mum, Ross and Lily waved goodbye and made a quick exit. I got out over an hour later, after taking selfies with every kid who asked, signing every jersey shoved at me and speaking to every journalist who approached me. I was the last player to exit, but Craig waited for me and together we got on the team bus, which took us straight to Subiaco. At the oval another fifteen thousand people filled the stadium to celebrate with us. I held up my Premiership and Norm Smith medals to the crowd and they went mental. Then we all got drenched in a shower of champagne.

'Holidays,' Craig yawned when we reached our cars.

'Holidays,' I yawned back.

He pulled his sunglasses over his eyes and cleared his throat. 'You did good, Harding.'

I got a somewhat quieter, but just as enthusiastic welcome from Bluey when the neighbour who'd been minding him dropped him back home as soon as she saw me pull into the driveway.

'Well, that's this year's job done, Blue.' I scratched him between the ears. 'You reckon it's about time I go beg Anna to take us back?'

He spun in frantic circles, sliding all over the tiles. I took that as a yes.

I showered, shaved, put product through my hair, sprayed on some aftershave and threw on a clean shirt over my jeans. Then I changed the sheets, put on a load of washing, fed Bluey, checked emails, got up to date with social media, paid two bills, hung out the load of washing and emptied the dishwasher.

After finding there really was nothing left to do and realising if I didn't leave now I'd never make it to Anna's, I picked up my car keys.

'Wish me luck, Blue,' I called out to him.

I was out on my porch, locking the front door, when a police car pulled up and two cops stepped out. They walked towards me and flashed their ID badges.

They obviously had the wrong place.

'Nicholas Harding?' asked the taller of the two men.

A bowling ball dropped in my stomach.

'Yes. How can I help?' My mouth was dry.

He drew a long breath. 'Nicholas, I'm very sorry, but there's been a head-on collision involving the vehicle your mother was travelling in on the Great Northern Highway.'

'Oh, Jesus! Is she alive?'

'Yes. Yes, she is. The collision was fatal but your mother survived it.'

I breathed again. 'Oh my God. Thank God.' I slumped against the door.

She was alive. Mum was alive.

'Nicholas,' the second policeman brought me back to earth. 'Your mother was airlifted to Royal Perth Hospital, and during that time she had to be revived twice. She's in a critical condition. We're here to escort you there as fast as possible. We should leave right now, if you can?'

'What about my sister?' I asked as we took off at high speed, sirens blaring.

'A police escort's already picked her up.'

I reached for the phone to call her and slammed my head back against the seat when I realised it was still sitting on my bedside table, charging.

We were on the freeway before my thoughts moved past Mum.

'And Ross? What about Ross?'

Silence.

'What about Ross?' I repeated, louder this time, the panic rising fast.

The policeman in the passenger seat turned to face me. 'Ross wasn't as lucky as your mother, I'm afraid, Nicholas.'

LILY – SUNDAY AND MONDAY

It was hard to breathe. My chest was closing in, tighter and tighter. Through pursed lips, I sucked on the Ventolin puffer.

Breathe, Lily, breathe. Keep it together. Be strong for Mum. One breath at a time.

I looked down at my hands. They were shaking uncontrollably. *Stop it!* But they didn't stop it and my teeth chattered too, just as my legs began trembling. I reached for a plastic chair opposite the nurses' station in the intensive care unit. I sat and I prayed. I prayed hard. I made all kinds of deals with God.

'Oh sweetheart, you're as white as a ghost. Here, let's get you warmed up.' An older nurse wrapped a space blanket around me. 'Can I get you a cup of tea?'

I tried to say, 'No, thanks,' but all that came out was a strangled cry.

'It'll be all right, love.' She patted my shoulder. 'There, there. Have you got anyone to call to sit with you?'

'My bro-ther. N-Nick. He's c-coming. They told m-me.'

'Who's they, love?'

'P-police.'

She nodded sagely. 'I'm sure he won't be long, then.' Her pager beeped and she excused herself and rushed off.

I shut my eyes and rocked myself, begging my body to cooperate and stop the trembling that was becoming really annoying.

Every time the door swung open and doctors or nurses bustled out, I got my hopes up for an update on Mum, but none of them so much as looked my way.

Nick arrived after what felt like hours but was probably only about twenty minutes. I flew out of the chair and we clung to each other. He didn't let go until my shaking stopped.

I filled him in on what I knew about Mum's condition.

'They had to revive her for a third time soon after they brought her here. Since then she's responded to pain stimuli and to light, but only from her right eye. She's got a fractured skull with swelling underneath, so they've induced her into a coma to drain the fluid and ease the pressure on her brain, which should stabilise her faster. Once she's stable, we'll know more.'

'Right. Okay.' Nick slumped down onto a chair, dropped his head into his hands and sobbed.

I wrapped my arms tightly around his heaving body till he finally settled down.

'I've been a prick to her for years,' he said quietly. 'I hardly ever call her. I've never once been up to Derby. And now we might lose her, Lil. She might die. And then what? What do we do then?'

'She won't die, Nick. She just won't. Mum's a survivor.'

'And Ross.' His eyes filled with fresh tears. 'Poor Ross. Do you know what happened?'

'Apparently he was gone on impact.' I choked down my sob. 'Never stood a chance.'

'Oh, Jesus.' His face was a mix of panic and confusion.

I must have looked like that too. If only Mum could see how terrified we both were right now, she would make sure she got better. She wouldn't let us go through losing her.

'Do you know how the accident happened? Did they tell you?' Nick asked.

'Apparently a car crossed over to the wrong side of the road, straight into them.'

He shut his eyes and blew out through pursed lips.

Evening turned to night and they still wouldn't let us see Mum.

Every now and then a different doctor gave us a vague, unhelpful update, like 'All's going as is expected' or 'No new changes', until finally at eleven-thirty they came and got us. We washed our hands, put on surgical caps, gowns and shoe covers, and followed the nurse into where Mum slept in the ICU.

It wasn't my mum. It was a bloated, bruised stranger with a breathing tube inserted between her cut and swollen lips. They'd shaved off a chunk of hair on the left, revealing her bald scalp where the drain was inserted. Attached to her were two monitors, three separate drips and a tube leading to a catheter bag.

'Ten minutes only,' the nurse monitoring the screens whispered to us. 'And stay at least three feet away from all the drips.'

'Nick.' I squeezed his hand. 'Pray with me?'

'Yeah.' He squeezed mine back and we prayed.

Once we were back out, a nurse spoke to us in a gentle voice. 'She's stable now and has been for the last six hours,' she said. 'I suggest you head home now and try and get some sleep. We've got your numbers and we'll call you at the first sign of any change.'

'I'm not going anywhere.'

'Me neither.' I added.

Go home? As if!

***

'I wish these stupid seats had arms you could lift up,' I moaned to Nick in the early hours of the morning, pulling one of the thin cotton blankets higher around my shoulders. 'My back's killing me, I need to lie down so badly.'

He replied in a hoarse voice. 'What if I sit on the floor over there against that wall and you can use my thighs as a pillow?'

'But what about you? Don't you want to lie down too?'

'Lil, I'd take up the whole visitor's lounge if I did. Come on, come and lie down.' He got up and took a hold of my hand, pulling me up too. 'One of us may as well get some sleep.'

As soon as I lay down with my head on Nick's legs, I fell asleep.

When the sunlight woke me up, I opened my eyes to see Nick's jaw wide open and his head tilted back. He was snoring deeply. Nobody had come to wake us up, which meant that Mum survived the night. And if I'd learnt anything in my four and a bit years of medicine it was that if a trauma patient survived the first night, their odds of survival improved significantly.

'Wake up, boofhead.' I tapped Nick's chest. 'Mum's going to be okay – I know it.'

We were allowed to be with Mum today. We sat in chairs a few feet away from where she slept. I got more information out of one of the registrars when I told her I was in my fifth year of medicine, conveniently leaving out the parts about deferring this semester and failing the last one.

'Ah, a future doctor! Good for you.' The registrar, called Orla, smiled warmly. 'I'll leave permission for you to access any of her records so you can keep track of her yourself.'

By midmorning, mum's blood pressure was close to normal and her heart rate was almost regular. The neurosurgeon said they'd do another scan to check the brain swelling and that she might be brought out of the coma earlier than planned.

On a toilet trip later in the morning, I spotted an elderly lady sitting in the same chair I had sat in yesterday outside the ICU. She was crying into her hands. She cut such a lonely figure that I couldn't just walk past.

I crouched down in front of her. 'Hey, hello. Are you okay there? Can I get you a glass of water?'

'Thanks dear, but I'm okay,' she sniffed.

'Have you had some bad news?' I asked.

'They're intubating my husband. He was having trouble breathing so I called an ambulance. But I wasn't expecting all of this.' She let out a sob. 'They've put him in a coma and they're putting an artificial breathing tube in. I think I made a terrible mistake and he was better off at home. At least he was conscious then. What if they kill him?' She put her hand over her mouth.

'They're really good doctors here, he's in the best hands, I promise.' I placed my hands on her trembling knees. 'They would never intubate him unless they were absolutely positive there was no other choice. They're doing it to save his life. So you didn't make a mistake. Far from it.'

'Thanks, dear.' She managed a weak smile. 'Do you work here?' She eyed my ripped jeans and Nick's hoodie, which I'd thrown on.

'I'm a student doctor.' For some bizarre reason, it felt good to say that.

'And what's your name dear?'

'I'm Lily.'

'Would you sit with me please, Lily? I'm frightened.'

I took a wistful look at Mum's room. 'Sure.'

'I'm Nola.'

I sat with Nola until a nurse came and took over.

On my way back to Mum's room, Orla the registrar walked up behind me and hooked her arm through mine. 'Nola just informed me that a lovely student doctor named Lily took great care of her. Thank you, you're a real gem. You'll make a great doctor.'

Her words made me feel warm inside.

'If you want to follow me around on my rounds later, I'd be happy to have you,' she continued.

I swallowed. 'Um, Orla, I feel really bad about this, but I'm um, well, I dropped out of medicine a few months ago. I was in my fifth year but I deferred second semester. I only said I was studying to get more information about my mum.'

'I know,' she replied, without breaking stride. 'We all know. Bill had me check up on you.'

Bill was the neurosurgeon in charge.

I stopped walking. 'You knew? So why are you treating me like I'm a student and inviting me to join ward rounds?'

'Technically you're still enrolled. You haven't dropped out, you've simply deferred a semester. I don't like seeing talent go to waste. So whatever brain-lapse you had that made you defer, perhaps I might be able to motivate you back.' She gave me a knowing grin.

I took a big breath. 'That's so nice of you, Orla, thank you. But I don't belong here at all. I mean, the whole reason I deferred was because I didn't belong in the course. I'm so emotional and the things I was confronted with tore me apart. I wasn't strong enough to handle it. Plus I hated the study, and every new ward round I did depressed me more than the last.'

She spread her arms out. 'Lily, who doesn't hate the study? We all fecking hate it!'

I laughed.

'And I call bullshit on you being too emotional. I cry me eyes out at least once a day!'

'Do you really cry or are you just saying that?'

She pulled out a handful of used tissues all scrunched up in a ball out of her lab coat pocket. 'I don't have a runny nose, Lily, look.' She breathed in an exaggerated way through her nose. 'See? Clean as a whistle in there.' She glanced at her pile of sodden tissues. 'All tears, I tell you. Cried myself a river over the young man up the hall there who came off his motorbike. His poor mother broke my heart. It would be a shame for a doctor not to have a heart, don't you think, Lily?'

I had to agree with her.

'And as far as you saying it's all so horribly depressing.' She rolled her eyes. 'Have you done an ICU round?'

I shook my head.

'Well don't generalise then because I've never met a doctor who thinks it's depressing here. When we lose a patient, yes for sure, it gets everyone down. But the majority of the time, we're *saving lives* – it's uplifting, life-affirming, wonderful stuff.' Her eyes sparkled.

'Mmm.' I stared straight ahead. 'Perhaps ICU would be better than burns or oncology.'

'Burns and oncology?' She threw her hands in the air. 'Well, *of course* you want to quit after those! Why don't you come on my round today and I'll show you?'

'I would have loved to, but I don't want to leave Mum.'

She nodded. 'I get it. But just think, Lily, in only two years, the study will be behind you and you could be working on our team. Now I might be wrong, but I have a good feeling about you—' She was interrupted by her beeping pager. 'Oh no, I have to go. I'll catch up with you later.' She blurted, not looking at me as she ran off.

Another doctor and two nurses morphed out of thin air and ran alongside her, charging through the doors of another room on the ward as a woman's voice calmly and softly announced 'code team, ward 11' just once over the PA system in contrast to the urgency unfolding before my eyes.

Something stirred inside me as I watched them race off with purpose and intensity – responding to a life-or-death situation, and knowing that their actions would be the difference. I felt a kind of hunger, an intense visceral pull that I had never experienced before.

I crept back in to Mum's room. Nick wriggled in his seat and opened his eyes, squinting at me.

'You okay?' He yawned.

'Yep. I'm okay.'

For once I really was okay. What I had waited my whole life for had happened at last. I had finally been called to be a doctor.

* * *

Early in the afternoon, orderlies came and took Mum away for more scans. Nick used my phone to call Craig and let him know what happened.

He walked back into the room a few minutes later with a frown. 'Craig already knew. It's all over the news.'

He passed the phone back to me. I ignored the messages and scrolled through my Facebook feed, bored until I saw something that made me freeze.

'Nick. Nick!'

'What? What's wrong?'

'There's a video here of the paramedics cutting Mum from the car. Oh my God, there's Ross. They've got Ross on film and you can see that he's died … Over half a million views already – what the hell? Why are people watching this?' I quickly closed the video, feeling ill. 'Don't watch it,' I warned him.

'No, no way, I can't see that.' He looked away. 'Craig said there's a shitload of media camped outside the hospital too. He told me to go out there and tell them the truth because he reckons they're reporting things like she's brain dead, that she's a quadriplegic. They've even quoted someone saying I've been admitted after having a mental breakdown.'

'You've got to be kidding me. Well if you're going out there, do you want me to come out with you?'

'Okay, yeah, if you want.' He paused. 'Lil, I'm sorry. It's all because of me.'

'You haven't done anything wrong. You don't need to be sorry. Let's just get it over with.'

'Yep.' He held his hand out to help me out of the chair.

We covered our eyes with sunglasses and stepped outside to dozens of camera flashes. Nick gave the forty or fifty paparazzi huddled outside a one-sentence statement about Mum, then he said in a no-nonsense tone, 'You can all leave now. There's been a tragic accident and we need privacy. That's my mother in there, guys. I mean, come on.'

I was so proud of my big brother in that moment that I thought I might actually burst.

* * *

Some hours later, Mum was wheeled back in, minus the tube that had been draining the swelling in her brain. She was breathing on her own now. I cried tears of joy this time.

'She'll start to rouse soon,' the specialist said, looking at us over his glasses. 'From what we can see there's minimal scarring on the brain but of course there's no way to be sure without testing her when she's fully conscious. At this stage we're cautiously optimistic, but it's best to prepare yourselves for some physical or cognitive impairment.' He coughed and continued. 'And she may have trouble speaking at first because the tube might have irritated her trachea. The good news is that her skull, cheek and wrist fractures are all stable so it's looking like your mother won't be needing any surgery, which is rather miraculous, to be honest.'

Nick and I exhaled together.

* * *

Nick took a back exit to catch a cab home and get his phone while I kept vigil over Mum. When he returned, he was in fresh clothes and in his hands was a book.

'*Harry Potter and The Deathly Hallows*?' I raised my eyebrows. 'You do know that's the last book in a series right?'

'Yes, Captain Obvious, of course I know.'

'Since when do you read anything except crime books?'

'Since I discovered the magical world of Hogwarts.' He smirked. He pulled out a book that was hiding behind the Harry Potter one. 'Here, I got you this.' He held the book out in front of my face. The price tag from the hospital gift shop was on the front. 'It's got a dress on the cover, it's even called *The Dress*. And you like dresses so ...'

'Aw, thanks, Nick. It looks great.' I tucked it inside my bag.

'You're not going to read it, are you?' He gave me a dirty look.

'Not here, no. How could I concentrate? I'll read it at home when Mum's better.'

'When Mum's better, things are going to be different,' he said quietly. 'I won't treat her badly from now on.'

'What are you talking about? You already treat her fine.'

'Nah. I never really forgave her for what she did to Dad. I was still punishing her. No more, though.'

'When she cheated on him, you mean?' I whispered in case Mum could hear us.

'Mmm-hmm.'

'Remember how they used to think we were asleep but we were actually sitting at the top of the stairs, listening to them fight about that mysterious Matt?'

'Yeah, and how they would say to each other, "As long as we protect the kids, that's the most important thing".' Nick snorted. 'They were pretty dumb for smart people, weren't they? Thinking we didn't know.'

'Not dumb, delusional,' I corrected him. 'I wonder what he was like though, that Matt.'

'I never want to find out,' Nick replied. 'But if she does come through this, I'm moving on. It's time.' He gulped. 'I regret not getting to know Ross more.'

'Count yourself lucky. It's less pain for you now.' My tears came back.

'Hey, hey. Come here.'

'I loved him, Nick.' I leant on his arm. 'Poor Mum, first Dad and now Ross.'

'Poor Mum,' he agreed.

Time seemed to stand still, and the minutes took forever to creep by, while Mum slept and we waited.

'Nick?'

'Mmm?'

'I think I want to be an ICU doctor.'

'Yeah?'

'This is what it's about, you know,' I went on. 'If I knew I could work here, it would make going back to uni for two years worth it. I like the buzz in ICU. It's intense, but it's hopeful – not like oncology or burns. I can see myself working here, I know I'd be good. I mean, these doctors, they *save lives* – like, every single day. How cool would it be to do that as your job?'

He stifled a laugh.

'What? What's so funny? I'm being serious.'

He looked at me with an exasperated expression. 'You've just realised for the first time now that doctors save lives? You really are the biggest idiot I've ever met.'

I flipped him the bird. 'Well, I'm going back to uni next year and the year after that will be my final one. Then I'll get a job in ICU and I'll be saving lives every single day. And you? You're just an overgrown dork who kicks a ball around.'

'Are you sure you can give up your job at Cold Rock to go back to medicine? I mean you're probably only three or four years from making manager there.'

'*Fuuuuck!*' I slapped my forehead. 'I was supposed to work today. Oh no! Pass me my bag, quick.'

I checked my phone. Sure enough, there was a missed call from my boss.

I held the phone to my ear and listened to the message as he fired me. 'Hmm, well, that makes leaving that job easy.'

Nick shook his head. 'And to think people's lives are going to be in your capable hands.'

***

'Excuse me, Lily, there's someone called Arielle asking to see you. Would you like to come out and see her?' A nurse popped her head around the door to ask.

I raced out into Arielle's arms.

'Oh my God, Lilz! Are you okay? How's your mum? I've been stuck out in the front foyer for hours and my stupid phone was out of charge.'

She took both my hands and I held onto hers, nice and tight.

Arielle wasn't allowed into Mum's room, so I left Nick there and sat with Arielle out in the corridor. I told her everything and half an hour passed by before I knew it.

'I suppose I should get back in there in case Mum wakes up,' I said reluctantly.

'Oh, okay. I'll just tell Toby to go home then.'

She giggled when she saw the look on my face.

'What?' I gasped. 'Toby? As in *my* Toby? He's here?'

'Uh-huh. He was already here when I got here. He's been here all day. Hey, his brother is *shit hot!*'

'I can't believe you didn't tell me until now!'

'He was the one who made me promise not to until I was ready to leave,' she replied, unapologetically. 'He's actually not the pig I thought he was. He really does care about you.'

My sleep-deprived, traumatised brain was overwhelmed. Toby was here!

All I wanted was to see him, to hold him, to kiss him.

'Lil,' Nick came out of Mum's room in a rush. 'Mum's stirring. I think she's about to wake up. Hurry!'

'Tell Toby not to leave!' I ordered Arielle.

'Sweetheart, I *promise* you he's not going anywhere.' She kissed my cheek and pulled me close. 'Good luck with your mum. I hope she's okay when she wakes up.'

* * *

I ended up seeing Toby at close to midnight. Because that was when Mum finally settled down after waking up.

When she opened her eyes, her first word in a deep scratchy voice as she clutched her throat was 'Ross?'

'Mum!' I cried jumping out of the chair to stand at her bedside. Nick had beaten me to it.

Nick stood there wordless but I exclaimed, 'Oh, Mum! I love you so much. Thank God you're awake.'

She shut her eyes briefly and smiled slightly in recognition.

The nurse was out from behind her desk in a flash. She buzzed the doctor and before I knew it, Nick and I were forcibly moved aside while staff swarmed around the bed.

'Hello,' said a doctor I hadn't seen before. 'Relax, everything's all right. You're going to be just fine. Take some nice deep breaths and have a cough ... Great, well done. Can you tell me your name? Do you know where you are?'

'Ross?' Mum croaked.

'Do you know what year it is?' The doctor ignored her question.

Mum thrashed her head around. 'Ross? Ross?' She had a desperate look on her face. Our eyes met when she located me standing behind the doctor. 'Ross?' she begged of me.

The idiot doctor continued, 'Can you just tell me your name and date of birth first, please?'

I pushed in and nudged myself between him and Mum. I leaned my forehead in close to hers. 'You and Ross were in a car accident yesterday.' I said it slowly and clearly. 'Do you remember that, Mum?'

She nodded, looking me right in the eyes.

I bit my lip. 'Ross died in the accident. It was instant, he didn't suffer one tiny bit.'

She frowned at me like she didn't get it.

'I'm so sorry, Mum.'

Nick and I had been so fixated on Mum surviving that we forgot that would be the easy part for her. Waking up to discover Ross was dead – that was the hard part.

She shut her eyes. 'No,' she whispered through quivering lips. 'No. Not again.'

* * *

The rest of the day was a blur as poor Mum underwent a slew of assessments and observations while dealing with Ross's death.

And there was nothing Nick or I could do for her except wipe her tears, trying not to hurt her broken cheek as we did so.

She cried for so long that she was literally out of tears and then she dry sobbed after that. In the end she was given a sedative and fell asleep, peaceful at last.

Once she was sleeping, I checked my phone and found a text sent to me at nine-thirty. An hour and a half ago:

> Hey Lily, the café downstairs is shut now so I'm out in the car
> park in my car. No rush, I'll be here all night. Toby x

'Toby's come to see me,' I whispered to Nick. 'He's been waiting downstairs for hours. Will you be okay here on your own with Mum if I go down and see him?'

He gave me a long look. 'I'll be fine. The question is will *you* be okay if you go down and see him?'

My tummy did major tumble turns when I stepped out into the cool night, looking for his car. I saw it parked right under the lights. I remembered all at once how thoughtful and considerate and kind Toby was. Of course he parked his car where it was easily seen so that I wouldn't have to go looking for it.

As I got closer I felt suddenly self-conscious. I hadn't showered since Saturday morning in Melbourne – my hair was limp and greasy. I hadn't even brushed my teeth or put on any deodorant for two days. Jesus, I must stink! And I was about to come face to face with him for the first time in four months. Excellent.

When I looked through his driver's side window, he was leaning back against the headrest, asleep. Those leapfrogs in my heart, which had been hibernating all winter, woke up full of beans. I put my hand on my chest in a futile attempt to settle them down.

He was here! And he'd stayed all day and he hadn't gone home even when it got late and he still hadn't heard a peep from me. He loved me and I loved him, and we'd had enough time to sort ourselves out so everything would be okay now.

I gave the window a gentle tap. He didn't move. I tapped a little louder and he startled. He looked around disorientated. The 'where am I?' look on his face made me giggle.

Then he saw me and he broke into a huge Toby smile and my heart almost bounced out of my chest.

He got out of the car and enveloped me in a hug that took all the bad stuff away.

'Toby.' I inhaled his smell, familiar and foreign all at once.

'You all right?' he murmured.

'I am now,' I said into his chest, tightening my grip on him.

'Your mum? How's she?'

'She's lost her sight in one eye which is the worst thing. She had a lot of swelling on the brain but that's settling down, thank God. They took her out of an induced coma. I think she'll be okay now.'

'That's great.'

'But Ross— '

'I heard,' he interrupted. 'I'm so sorry.'

'Yeah. My poor mum.' I shook the image of Mum's devastated face out of my mind to stop myself crying and took in the sight of him again. 'I didn't know you were back.'

'It was just supposed to be for the weekend. I just finished a shoot along the Nullarbor so drove the extra day to get home. I was already three hours into the drive back when news of the accident came on the radio this morning so I did a U-turn and here I am. I was worried Ben would be here with you or that you'd refuse to see me but I couldn't not come just in case you needed me.'

'No, no Ben. And I do need you.' I slid my arms down to his waist. 'Thank you for making that U-turn.'

'Nothing mattered except being here for you. Nothing from the past mattered anymore,' he murmured into my hair.

'I need you to know that there was nothing going on between me and Ben when you saw us together. I didn't even know he was home from Africa, he just rocked up unannounced. When he knocked on my front door, I thought he was you. Nothing happened, I swear to you, it didn't. All I did was talk about you to him.'

He nodded. 'I should have trusted you. I'm really sorry.'

'It's okay. I'm sorry about turning on you so suddenly. That was mean of me.'

'You don't need to be sorry about that. I came over that night to tell you that you were right about me needing to get over Jen and being too scared to chase my dreams. You were right about everything really. I came to tell you I'd quit my job and about the photography mentorship over east. And I wanted you to meet my family the next time I was home. I came over that night to see if we could start over again. But then I saw Ben there and well ...' He trailed off.

We stared at each other for a long time. I stood on my tiptoes and found his lips. As soon as my mouth touched his, it all rushed back to me, every buried feeling at once, and I kissed him harder, devouring him. He kissed me back with just as much hunger but then he pulled his head away sharply and looked off to the side.

'Lil,' he breathed. 'This isn't a good idea.'

I was having none of that. 'God help me, Toby, if you don't get in the backseat of your car with me and make love to me right now—'

'No.' He shook his head. 'I can't.'

'No,' I countered. '*I* can't. I can't not be with you. I can't not have you. Just get in the car, Toby … please … please,' I whispered in his ear. 'Remember that night after Jen died when you were grieving? Remember how much it helped you to be with me? That's what *I* need now. I need you to help me.'

'I want to … believe me, I want to,' he panted. 'I want to give you everything you need. But you don't understand. Back in Queensland, there's a g—'

'No! Stop!' I pressed my index finger over his mouth.

Whatever was about to come out of his mouth next, I didn't want to hear it. I'd had more than enough pain in the last two days, I couldn't take anymore.

I put my lips back up to his ear and whispered the words I knew full well would hit Toby Watts' weak spot. The one thing I knew he could never, ever say no to. I whispered what I wanted to do to him, not skipping a single graphic detail.

'Shit,' he exhaled. 'Why are you doing this to me? Why?'

'Say you don't want it, Toby.' I let my breath fall inside the collar of his shirt, down his chest, and he shivered.

'Don't. You know how much I want it.' He dropped his head backwards and shut his eyes while I licked the hollow of his neck.

'How much?' I unzipped his fly.

'More than anything,' he moaned.

'Get in the car, Toby.'

He opened the door and fell into the back seat, kicking off

his boots. I helped him out of his jeans in a frantic rush, then I climbed in and positioned myself between his bent legs.

As soon as I slammed the door shut behind me, I did what he loved in the way he loved it, until he cried my name out loud and his entire body shuddered as his orgasm exploded into my mouth.

When his breathing finally slowed down, he sat up on his forearms. 'That was just … oh my God … you're unbelievable … that was … the best thing I have ever known.'

He pulled me down onto my back. 'Your turn now, beautiful.'

And with that first wet stroke of his tongue, I got exactly what it was that I needed from him – I forgot all about the horror of the last day and my whole world dazzled as I immersed myself in nothing but Toby.

Later, when I was snuggled against his chest, our clothes draped over us as makeshift blankets, he kissed the top of my head and cleared his throat. 'Lily, I've got a girlfriend in Queensland. We were planning to move in together.'

I didn't answer. Hot tears rolled off my cheek and onto his chest.

'I'm sorry,' he murmured.

'What's her name?' I asked, like it even mattered.

He paused. 'Carly.'

'Oh.'

He kissed my forehead.

'Do you love her?' I tried to keep my voice neutral but failed dismally.

'I thought I did, until now.'

'So what will you do?'

'Well, I'll tell her that this happened for a start.'

'Do you think she'll forgive you?' I wiped the tears that refused to stop falling.

'No. Nope. She'll tell me to fuck off,' he sighed. 'And rightly so. I'm actually not even that upset about breaking up with her, which says a lot I guess.'

'I'm sorry I pushed you into having sex with me,' I said.

'No you're not,' he chuckled. 'You're not sorry at all.'

And I couldn't help but laugh too, regardless of how huge our mess was.

'Toby?'

'Yeah?'

'Even if you break up with her, you're not coming back, are you?' I held my breath.

He was silent. Then, 'No. My life's over there now, Lily. I don't think I could ever live here again. I feel free there. I feel like myself for the first time.'

We fell into silence again before he asked. 'Would you consider moving there with me?'

I sighed. 'It's your life that's over there, not mine.' I expected to feel more broken-hearted than I did. I wasn't sure why I wasn't more devastated because I still adored him. Perhaps I'd fall apart later. But for now I felt nothing but calm.

'So what do we do now?' he asked while he played with my hair. 'What happens next?'

'You go back there and you live your life how you were meant to live it, that's what.'

'What about you? What happens to Lily?'

'Me? I look after Mum, and then next semester I go back to uni and in a couple of years, I become a doctor. I meet an incredibly hot guy, way hotter than you, whose life I save after he smashes his Harley. Oh, and he's loaded too. And really nice and smart. Basically he's perfect. We get married, have three perfect, impeccably behaved children, buy a big house in the suburbs and a vacation home in the south of France and we live happily ever after. That's what happens to Lily.'

He chuckled. 'I hate that rich fucker.' He lifted his head up to make eye contact with me. 'Are you really going back to study medicine, though? I thought you hated it.'

'I thought I did. Turns out I want to be a doctor, after all.'

'That's a gutsy call to go back and repeat a year. I'm proud of you.'

I pushed myself up on my hands and stared into his eyes. 'Thank you for making a U-turn. I'm really glad you did.'

The look he gave me melted my insides. I kissed along his jawline, down to his neck and chest and I brought his nipples to life with my tongue.

He moaned a deep throaty moan and I felt him stiffen against my groin.

'Do you have anything on you?' I murmured between long kisses, hoping against hope he did.

'I was a boy scout, you know.' He grinned. 'I'm always prepared.'

The car steamed up from our heat.

* * *

I found my way back up to Nick at four in the morning.

'You guys get back together?' he asked sleepily.

'Nope.'

'Glad to hear it.'

'Shut-up, douche,' I slurred and fell asleep, leaning on his shoulder.

I woke up to a long goodbye text message from Toby, and a few minutes later Mum opened her eyes and cried out for Ross again, starting another day of physical and emotional anguish for her.

Later in the morning, she was transferred from ICU to the lesser dependent – but still not out of the woods – critical care ward.

'I wish there was more I could do.' Nick stood over her bed wringing his hands. 'I feel bloody useless!'

'Nick – you, Lil, you're what's keeping me going. You haven't left my side. You're the opposite of useless, you're everything I need.'

'Excuse me, Nick, there's a visitor for you.' A nurse stuck her head into the room.

'Who would that be?' I asked him.

He shrugged.

Joel and Bruce had already been in and Nick wasn't that close to anyone else. 'Maybe it's Craig?' I wondered out loud.

'Maybe,' he replied. 'Back soon, Mum. I'll get rid of whoever it is quickly.'

NICK – TUESDAY

I stretched and yawned and walked out of Mum's room.

I was pretty sure I actually stopped breathing when I saw her standing there, hands on her belly near the nurses' desk. She took a few steps forward and stopped before she reached me.

'*Habibi*.' She smiled.

I swallowed hard and looked at her rounded belly.

'I came as soon as I heard yesterday, but they told me that it was too late to visit and sent me home.'

I nodded.

Her voice shook. 'I'm so sorry about the accident. And I'm so very sorry about how I treated you when Mama died.'

'S'okay,' I tried to say but it came out in a whisper.

'No it's not okay. I have so much to be sorry for. Nick? Are you all right?'

I stood there, trying my best to take it all in. Her, the pregnancy, what she was saying.

'Nick? Are you all right?' she repeated. I'd forgotten how she nodded with every question she asked.

I tried to reply. No words came out. So I just held my arms out and when she came in close enough, I wrapped them around her and I let myself go.

She showered me with her Arabic terms of affection that I'd so desperately missed hearing, and she kissed my tears while she cried too. 'I'm sorry I abandoned you. Forgive me.'

'Don't ever leave me again,' I said when I was finally able to speak.

'Never, I swear to you. Never.'

I rested my palm on her rounded stomach. Even though I was sure of the answer, I still had to ask. 'Mine?'

She chuckled through her tears. 'Who else could she belong to? Of course she's yours.'

'She? It's a girl?' My voice was raspy. 'We're having a baby girl?'

She nodded and I broke down all over again.

'You're so young to be pregnant, Anna,' I said when I was composed. 'Are you okay about this?'

'Very okay.' She smiled. 'I've never been young, anyway. You know that.'

'But your studies? Your career?'

'I plan to have it all.' She held my face in her hands. 'Don't worry about me. But what about you? This is a big shock for you.'

'It's the best thing that's ever happened to me in my life,' I answered, meaning every word.

'Even after I shunned you? How can you ever forgive me for what I did to you?'

I shook my head. 'Shhh.' I didn't need any apologies. 'Shhh, Anna, it's okay.'

She was here. She came back. She was having my baby. Nothing else mattered.

But she insisted, 'I owe you a long explanation. I thought I was doing the best for you, protecting you by staying away. I wanted you to have—'

'Another time,' I interrupted her, my eyes fixated on her mouth. That gorgeous sexy mouth that I'd pined for so many nights on end. 'Save it for later. There are more important matters to attend to now.'

I actually moaned with relief, the pure relief of having her lips on mine once more when our mouths touched. I had no idea how long we stood there kissing, but neither of us pulled away until one of the nurses at the desk behind us called out, 'Get a room, Nick Harding!'

'Let's go sit.' I motioned towards the visitor's lounge.

Time stood still in that lounge, where it was just the two of us pouring out our hearts to one another, listening to each other's grief at what had happened to our mothers, rejoicing in our baby, planning a new life together.

'Will you move in with me?' I held my breath.

'Of course. But I have Ricky now. Is that okay?'

'Do you even have to ask?'

'He's missed you dearly. But not as much as I have. I ached for you every day.'

'Same here.' A thought came to me. 'Should we get married before the baby arrives? Would that make things easier with your family?'

She patted my thigh. 'Are you afraid Tante Rosa will chase you up the street with her rolling pin unless you marry me?'

I laughed. 'I tell you what, your uncle Fariz is no bloody picnic when he's angry either. I just want to do the right thing by you. I don't want you to feel embarrassed or ashamed or anything like that. Isn't it expected in your culture that you're married before you have kids?'

'Generally yes, that's the way it is.'

'Well, let's do it, then. I'd marry you today if you want to.'

'Thank you, Nicholas Harding. And a fine husband you would make too. But I don't want a rushed marriage. Let's make our marriage an important decision we come to agree on in our own time, the way it should be.'

I rested my hand on her belly. To my amusement, our baby wriggled and squirmed under my touch. 'You and me and Ricky and Noor,' I named our baby girl and looked to Anna for approval.

She gave me a double thumbs up and a smile as fresh tears surfaced in her eyes.

'Always together,' I continued. 'This is it, all right? Promise me, that this is it, Anna. The four of us always together, no matter how hard it gets.'

'The four of us always together, no matter how hard it gets,' she promised.

'Even if the media give us hell?'

'Even if the media give us hell,' she repeated.

'Even if Ricky gets sick again and it affects my career? You won't pull away to try and "save" me?'

'Nick,' she looked into my eyes. 'This is it. I promise.'

And when she said that, my heart was rested.

CHRISTMAS DAY, TWO YEARS LATER

ANWAR

'Mewy Kwismas, Gwamma.' Noor toddled towards Mel, struggling to balance while she carried the gift that was almost her own size. Her wobbly walk, as though she had just stepped off a horse, wasn't helped by her chunky nappy.

'Thank you, precious.' Mel took the box from her and Noor hoisted herself up onto her grandmother's lap, using Bluey, who was lying at Mel's feet, as a stool.

My daughter really did live up to her beautiful name. She truly was the 'light' of all of our lives. I looked on proudly at our little 'tsunami', the name Ahmo Fariz had given her as soon as she was mobile, as she babbled happily to Mel.

And now that she had a year's more personality, our second Christmas with Noor was more magical than the first. But I was disturbed at how Mel and Lily had spoilt her with gifts between them. And then there was the shopping that Nick had done for her behind my back. A motorised Barbie car, almost the size of a ride-on mower, *ya Rab*. For a child who was not quite two years old. Outrageous! But he was completely unapologetic.

From where I sat on the floor leaning against him, I was in the best position to hand out the presents from under the Christmas tree for the children to distribute.

I loved Christmas. And I loved that our children were lucky enough to celebrate both Christmas and Eid – what a blessed life they had!

'And here's my present, Mel.' Ricky clambered up onto Mel's lap, joining Noor. At eight years old, he was still as affectionate as ever.

'It's a Rubik's cube to help make your bad hand better,' he announced before Mel had a chance to unwrap the gift. 'Anwar bought me one and I said you should have one too. I can do it in forty-seven minutes. But you probably won't be able to do it,' he said earnestly.

My heart surged with love for him. The fact that he was still here with us this Christmas was something to be celebrated. The cancer that surfaced in his liver earlier in the year had terrified us. He had suffered greatly with it, more than ever before. But once again he was undefeated and his hair was just starting to grow back, now that the last dose of chemotherapy was finished and he was cancer free again.

How long Ricky would stay healthy was anyone's guess. Every time the cancer came back the doctors almost seemed to give up on him. But so far he had proven them all wrong. I prayed he continued to do so. I still prayed for a miracle. When I thought about it too much, my stomach twisted in knots and my brain became cloudy. So I had trained myself to think about Ricky's future as if the cancer did not exist, which was what he managed to do so wonderfully himself.

'A cock! A cock of meeee!' Noor interrupted my thoughts, clapping her hands in delight when Mel unwrapped her gift of a round wall clock that had a backdrop image of Noor in Mel's arms.

'C-l-ock,' I corrected, laughing along with everyone else. 'You say *clock*, Noor.'

'Oh, it's perfect. Thank you!' Mel blew kisses at Nick and me. 'Now you'll be with me all the time, Noor, every second of the day with this special clock.'

'She already *is* with you every second of every day!' Nick laughed.

It was just about true. Since I began full-time studies eighteen months ago, Mel had been minding Noor every weekday except for Wednesdays when Tante Rosa took over to give her a break.

I was forever grateful for the help. Studying law full time with a family to look after and keeping up my commitments to Asylum Assist wasn't easy. But Mel repeatedly told me how important it was to her to feel needed. Because of the blindness in her left eye and a tremor in her right hand that began a few weeks after her accident, she had had to give up her work.

It gave me great joy to witness Nick become so close to his mother, after he had confided in me about his resentment towards her before her accident. The accident tragically cost Mel her partner, her health, her career – such unimaginable losses – but moving back to Perth at least brought her a deeper connection to her children and of course it also brought her Ricky and Noor who kept her busy and smiling most of the time.

'Ooh, is it my turn now? How exciting!' Lily hugged Ricky when he took the next present over to her. 'Thank you, matey!' She gave him a high-five and stifled a yawn while she waited for Noor to carry a present to her as well.

I was thankful for Noor having someone like her Aunt Lily in her life. Lily's passion and dedication to her studies and career set a brilliant example and young girls certainly needed those. Lily had chosen to forgo her summer holidays, instead starting her practical training year as a Registered Medical Officer early in the very same ICU department where Mel had been a patient. She entertained us with her many war stories from the hospital where she had worked till two in the morning today.

She had a few boyfriends come and go in the last two years, but none of them lasted. Being in a relationship didn't seem to be on her mind until recently. I did wonder about Dan, the cardiothoracic surgeon she'd mentioned of late. She was wearing a chain he had bought her for Christmas and she seemed particularly interested in her phone this morning, smiling at the screen often and blushing more than once when she read her messages.

I had been convinced that Lily and Toby were destined to be together. I still refused to let the idea completely go, even though she didn't even contact him when Gianni informed her recently that Toby was back in town for a holiday.

Toby seemed happily settled in Queensland and had opened his own studio that was apparently overrun with tourists. Gianni and Arielle showed us photos of it when they came back from visiting him. Lily examined their photos with much more interest than Nick or me, and it was little things like that which made me hang onto the hope that there might one day be a reunion between them. Although, even I had to admit it was looking less likely as time went on.

But unlikelier things had most certainly happened in the last two years. None more surprising than Gianni and Arielle's abiding love, and a marriage between them occurring next month. Now *that* I would never have expected of my womanising ex-boss who was now astonishingly devoted to his fiancée. Perhaps that's how people who knew Nick before I came along would have felt about him too. Gianni was as regretful about his old ways as Nick had ever been, and it filled my heart to see the boss who I always knew had goodness in him finally let it shine. I still thought of him as Gianni and would never think of him as John. Just like Arielle would always be Arielle to me, even though I found out a long time ago that her real name was Amy and she called herself Arielle after falling in love with the movie *The Little Mermaid* as a child and giving the name a French twist.

I was in no place to judge their change of names. For years I had been foolish enough to insist that everyone call me Anna when my real name, chosen by my precious mama, represented the light I brought to her life, just like Noor brought to mine.

There was a knock at the door. 'I'll get it!' Lily chirped. 'I'll open these pressies in a sec you guys,' she told Ricky and Noor.

She opened the door and hugged Tante Rosa who walked in with her fiancé.

'Merry Christmas, everybody,' Tante Rosa said in perfect English.

I had never seen Tante Rosa as happy as she'd been since she became engaged a month ago. She took every opportunity to brag about what a handsome catch her fiancé was and how envious the other ladies in her swing dancing class were of their engagement.

He may not have been handsome, but Allah bless him, Omar was one patient man. At seventy-nine years old, he could barely put one foot in front of the other without the help of his cane, let alone master the swing dancing classes he was dragged to every week. When the lonely widower dropped in at Asylum Assist to donate a large portion of his oil-inherited money, I had the genius idea of match-making him with Rosa.

'He's Lebanese, he's a devout Muslim and he's filthy rich,' was all it took to convince Rosa to have her makeup professionally done, get a manicure, buy a beautiful new hijab and matching outfit and finally, *finally*, wax that dark bushy moustache of hers before she stepped out for her first date since her heart was broken over forty years before.

Two minutes later Ahmo Fariz, who had driven Tante Rosa and Omar to Mel and Lily's home, walked in, weighed down by gifts. I groaned inwardly at more presents for the children, who I feared would never learn to be humble with this ludicrous amount of spoiling by their overzealous relatives.

Ahmo Fariz was still a bachelor and I suspected he would die as one, to my endless frustration. Being over sixty years old, of course he was set in his ways, but I still hoped that he would one day come to his senses and confess his feelings to his perfect match who was right under his nose six evenings a week. I'd seen the way he looked at Victor, the waiter who was a similar age to him and who he employed to replace me, and I wished with all my heart that both of these stubborn men would just admit to each other how they felt. It was not my business to intervene, but whenever we ate at Masri's, which was often, I saw their stolen glances and tragic sighs and bit my tongue.

Fariz's exuberance every time he described Shamia, the belly dancer, and her large breasts to the restaurant patrons may have fooled them but it didn't fool me one little bit.

Once Ahmo Fariz and Tante Rosa and Omar were settled on the couch, I looked around the room and realised that everyone I loved was right there in the same room. Nick had his hand on my head, playing with my hair. Noor, exhausted from the day's excitement, sucked her thumb, cradled in my arms. Ricky was engrossed in showing Mel how to solve the Rubik's cube puzzle.

In that perfect moment I sent a prayer of thanks to Allah and a thank-you to Jesus Christ whose birthday had brought us all together.

I looked forward to my future, even though it would inevitably bring more pain (for how could life not bring pain with it?) because I knew more boundless joy and more beautiful love awaited me.

The love I had for the people who surrounded me and the way I loved those I had lost was messy – it was complicated, difficult and sometimes unbearably painful. But that didn't make it any less beautiful.

ACKNOWLEDGEMENTS

To the powerhouse team at HarperCollins Australia, thank you, you collective group of absolute legends! Thank you to my miracle worker, my magician, my editor Dianne Blacklock. And massive thanks to my rock, my guardian angel, my backbone, Jacinta di Mase. Smartest thing I ever did was put a poster on my bathroom wall and manifest you.

Big thanks to the AFL big guns and all round good guys who answered all my footy-related questions – Adrian Hickmott and Rohan Smith.

To my formidable support network of author friends, my inner circle of trust – Engy Neville, Renee Conoulty, Jennifer Ammoscato, KJ Farnham, Natasha Lester, Lisa Ireland, Sara Foster, Gen Gannon, Alli Sinclair, Lily Malone, Steph Pegler, Jennie Jones, Louisa Loder, Lana Pecherczyk, Melissa Sargent, Jenn J McLeod, Deborah Disney, Mae Wood, Sunni Overend, Louise Allan, Vanessa Carnevale, Spiri Tsintziras, Nic Moriarty, Rebecca Sparrow, Karen McDermott and Rachael Johns - you girls are my spirit animals. Having you on this roller-coaster makes the ride much more fun and much less lonely, thank you.

Special thanks and extra love to my solid seven – my husband, Paul, my children, Tommy and Lara, my mum, Marianne

Massarany, and my three best friends, Sarah Lamb, Daniella Hassett and Emma Cockman. Thank you for everything, I love you so much. And Dan, thank you also for being the best editor-before-the-editor anyone ever had.

To the world's asylum seekers, may you find the shelter, the welcome and the acceptance you deserve. Know that there are millions of us who stand with you and who will not be silenced. The day will come when your voices will be heard, and until that day, know that we will continue to make our voices loud enough to drown out the others.

Finally, to you, my readers – when the words all sound the same and I become crippled by doubt, I remember that you're out there, that you're waiting and I keep typing. You'll never know how much your messages and emails, your presence at my events, your support of me on social media and your championing of my books to your friends means to me. I'm only an author because of you and I hope I keep making you proud. Thank you xx

AUTHOR'S NOTE

I was born in Alexandria, Egypt, and grew up in a large, loud and passionate extended family of Catholic, Orthodox, Coptic and Muslim relatives. The Egyptian women in *Beautiful Messy Love* are inspired by the women who made up the loving village of grandmothers, aunties and older cousins that helped raise me. From my ultra-conservative paternal grandmother, who centred her life in her faith, to my maternal aunt who's a passionately vocal advocate for marriage equality and my cousin who's a champion for feminism in her role as a prominent African human rights lawyer, my family is full of strong, bold, opinionated Arabic women. I hope the characters of Anna, Leila and Rosa convey the true depth, breadth, strength and humanity of Middle Eastern women, regardless of their religious affiliation.

 Tess Woods is a physiotherapist who lives in Perth, Australia, with one husband, two children, one dog and one cat who rules over them all. Her debut novel, *Love at First Flight*, received acclaim from readers around the world and won Book of the Year in the 2015 AusRom Today Reader's Choice Award. You can also contact her at

www.tesswoods.com.au
www.facebook.com/Tesswoods.harpercollins
Twitter: @TessWoodsAuthor
Instagram: TessWoods_Author